CHARITY JOE;

OR,

FROM STREET BOY TO LORD MAYOR.

By GEORGE EMMETT, Author of "TOM WILDRAKE'S SCHOOLDAYS."

"IT WAS A STRANGE SIGHT THAT MET THE EYES OF MR. SIVINS."

CHAPTER I.

MR. JAMES SIVINS, AGENT—CHARITY JOE AND HIS
DOG TOBY.

IT was an oft-repeated assertion of our great moralist that "No book was ever written but something, however small, may be learned from it."

With all the respect such an humble individual as I am must feel towards the doctor whose words I have used, I must differ with his opinion; feeling assured that many books are now written from which it would be utterly impossible to glean the most infinitesimal spark of information.

In the days when the doctor was wont to make this assertion, perhaps authors wrote and printed their experience or thoughts, but now-a-days, when literary bookmakers spring up like mushrooms, and to carry the simile yet a point farther, with as much experience of the work before them as one of the by-no-means-to-be-despised fungi, I think my opinion weighed in the scale against the great moralist's, will cause my side of the weighing machine to go down with a plump, and I declared the winner.

Here's a flourish of trumpets, says the reader, mentally. Not at all, my friend. Wait, and if you do not learn something from the ups and downs that fell to the portion of Charity Joe, I pray you set me down as one unworthy of the favours you have so liberally bestowed upon the labours of my pen.

In one of those narrow streets leading from St. George's-road, and near the Elephant and Castle, a street not yet widened at the parish expense, lived Mr. James Sivins, and the street door of the dingy, two-story house was ornamented with a square brass plate, which bore the words:

"J. SIVINS,
"General Agent, &c."

On one side of the lower window hung an illuminated prospectus of the "Moon Fire and Life Assurance Company;" at the bottom of this were a few words, stating that James Sivins was an agent to the company.

On the other side of the window was an oblong board, stating the lowest price for coals of the various kinds, from best Wallsend to Nuts; likewise at the bottom of this was to be found the name of James Sivins, agent to the Anti-Mutual Coal-Consumers' Association.

Against the centre window pane, and suspended by a piece of dirty (once) red tape, was a card, which announced to the not over-moneyed denizens of the locality that the easiest way to obtain money was to borrow of the loan society of which Mr. James Sivins was the secretary, proprietor, auditor, and chairman.

The card did not make known these facts; it went no further than to tell those in want of the circulating medium that all inquiries were to be addressed to the secretary, Mr. J. Sivins.

With the multitude of business Mr. J. Sivins had to perform it would be but natural to suppose that he had but little spare time upon his hands; the supposition would not be correct, for Mr. J. S. took the chair nightly in a dingy parlour at a dingy house near the corner of the narrow street in which he resided.

True, he left a representative to collect the small sums due from the borrowers, to take orders for unlimited tons of coals; also to take the preliminary fee for the fire and life assurance company.

True, there were not many orders for the Anti-Mutual, nor many fees for the Moon Fire and Life, but scarcely an evening passed without an ill-clad, thin-faced borrower, or a pale mechanic coming to Mr. Sivins's to repay a portion of the advances they obtained when baby died or father was out of work.

The representative left by Mr. James Sivins was a bold, handsome-looking lad, nearly sixteen years of age. The boy was kept by Mr. Sivins, as he stated, out of charity, but as the shrewd, long-headed villain had never been known to do a charitable action in his life, people who knew him best, said there was something "under it," whatever this may have implied.

If Mr. Sivins kept Joe out of charity, certainly the Samaritan feeling did not extend to clothing the lad, for he was ill-dressed and ragged even for the locality wherein he existed.

Yet in spite of his rags, dirt, and evident ill-feeding, Joe looked a cut above the boys of the neighbourhood — there was the difference of porcelain to common earthenware.

Joe did not pride himself upon this—far from it. His was a most fraternising disposition; he was a good-natured lad, too, for he would give the scanty pittance Mr. Sivins allowed him "out of charity" to a boy who needed it, and he would fight while he had a leg to stand upon with any lad, even a head taller than himself, if he saw the tall one taking advantage of a lad who was not able to take his own part.

Joe, as may be expected, was not without a certain amount of evil in his nature; but it was more the result of those with whom he had been put to associate with than a natural depravity, and many of the scrapes he fell into were caused by his buoyant spirits, for Joe was the very embodiment of fun and mischief.

Joe had not been many months under the charitable care of Mr. Sivins when our story opens. In the anterior period, Joe had gone through enough to make him old before his time, and to poison his mind and heart against the world, had not those useful portions of his corporeal existence been of the truest and soundest kind.

He had a dim recollection of being happy, and of a lady whom he called mother, but the memory of this was like the flickering of an expiring candle, and Joe was compelled to believe he had but remembered a very pleasant dream.

He had a strong remembrance of the time which succeeded the dream up to the period when Mr. Sivins took him out of charity. A portion of this related to the interior of a workhouse, wherein he was taken care of and baptized, for Joe had no name until the parish officials gave him one.

The board, like embryo authors, were fond of romantic names, so they had Joe baptised Joseph Chudleigh Cholmondeley. The last name, in consequence of its formation, soon degenerated into Chummy, and as long as Joe remained in the "house," he was known as Joe Chummy. Truly, there is but one step from the sublime, &c.

Joe was taken from the "house" by an elderly, unpleasant, military-looking gentleman, who generously repaid the parish for Joe's keep; and, much to the lad's delight, took him in a real carriage which stood outside the "house."

It was a brougham, and very nice and comfortable Joe felt when he was being driven through the streets, and, childlike, clapped his hands with glee.

"Be quiet," said the elderly gentleman, sternly, and Joe subsided into the furthest corner; "be quiet, sir."

There was something in his companion's tone that had more effect upon the lad than even the harshest of the officials at the "house" had produced.

"Now, sir," the old gentleman continued, looking savagely at the boy; "I have taken you from the workhouse to do something for you, therefore I hope you will behave yourself, and remember with lasting gratitude what I have done."

"Yes, sir."

Joe felt ready to cry, not with joy, for the harshly-spoken words had fallen heavily upon his heart.

The old gentleman did not speak again until the brougham drew up at the corner of a street, near St. George's Market in the Borough.

The footman promptly opened the door, and Joe's companion, telling him to alight, turned to the servant and said briefly:

"Wait."

The boy walked beside his conductor until they reached a small bootmaker's shop; here they turned in, as Joe thought for the purpose of buying him a pair of boots, for those he had brought from the "house" were not of the best fit or the most elegant make.

Alas, for Joe's hopes! a dirty-looking red-faced man came from behind the curtain and looked like a Chinese mandarin, when the elderly gentleman said:

"Here is your charge; take him, keep the boy well, and a similar amount will be forwarded to you every quarter; but remember what I told you before, seek not to find out from whence it comes, or you will lose a good income.

The bootmaker promised never to make the least inquiry, and Joe was left in the shop; his conductor, beyond favouring him with a scowl of hate, paid no attention to the childish voice crying out:

"Oh take me away, I don't want to stop here."

Perhaps he read in the man's besotted and bloated face the cruel life that was before him, for the perception evinced by children of the characteristics of those with whom they are brought in contact, is sometimes marvellous—it is an instinct which seldom errs.

The bootmaker drank more than ever after Joe fell to his charge, and although he kept his shop open as of yore, he never solicited or cared about customers either to purchase or for repairs.

The man's days being spent in a tap-room and his nights in sleep, Joe was left to run wild among the children of those who lived by being in "the coster line," and the offspring of bricklayers' labourers, sweeps, and many whose parents had no visible profession.

So far the change was for the better, but when the drunken brute was tired of beating his wife, he refreshed himself by belabouring Joe with the thick strap he kept for the purpose; here the change was for the worse.

Five years' hard drinking had ended in a parish funeral for the shoemaker, and a few days after the drunkard was buried Joe was fetched away by Mr. James Sivins; he had been a friend of the shoemaker's, who took especial care to inform Joe on their way from St. George's Market that he was to consider himself lucky at having a friend who could take care of him for the future out of "pure charity."

Joe took to his new abode an attached friend, it was Toby, the dog that had belonged to the shoemaker, and Mr. James Sivins was grimly pleased to allow this addition to his household.

Toby was not a handsome dog, rude boys were wont to call him mongrel, until Joe stopped their gibes by bringing his clenched fist against the scoffer's nose. Toby's breed was perhaps hard to name, for he in size and appearance was not unlike a shepherd's dog, but in place of having a long sharp head, Toby's was rather flat, and not unlike a mastiff's.

The dog had taken a fancy to Joe when he first came to the drunken shoemaker's and that fancy soon ripened into a sincere attachment.

Whatever love he had felt for his old master, Toby transferred it with interest to Joe, and had not the animal been securely fastened when Joe was being beaten, he would have torn the drunken brute limb from limb.

The boy soon came to love the faithful creature, and soon Toby could perform sundry tricks which would have gained him rounds of applause from any audience.

Docile and obedient as Toby was to Joe, a word or gesture from the boy, and he became a dangerous assailant.

Joe, as he grew in years and intelligence, taught Toby, among other accomplishments, to run after any boy he pointed out, and take his cap off, and Joe levied a species of black mail in consequence of this feat; for he would not surrender the cap until he received a penny if the loser was rich; a few buttons if coin was not forthcoming; or marbles, or tops, according to the season.

Joe and Toby soon became a terror to the juvenile population around St. George's Market; and many who longed to pay Joe off for old scores, taunted him by saying—

"Meet me when you ain't got your dog, and I'll punch your nose for you."

"Look here, my pippin," Joe would reply, "you can have all you want in that line now. Here, Toby, mind my jacket and cap."

He would fling off these somewhat ruined articles of attire, and the big dog would place his paws upon them, and watch his master give his adversary all and more than he wanted in that line.

One evening the stout and pursy Mr. James Sivins, after the labours of the day, called Joe from the back-yard to his august presence.

"Look here, Joe," he said, "you know I cannot afford altogether to keep you out of charity, therefore I shall expect you to do something towards your keep."

"What am I to do?"

"Well, there's Cheeseman opposite wants a boy, I've spoken to him about you and he's willing to try you, so mind what you are about."

"Should say I will, too—when am I to go?"

"To-morrow morning at eight."

Joe went at eight next morning, but his time of probation was very short, for Joe could not resist stopping on his errands to have a "go in" at any boy who insulted him, and the consequence was that other juveniles less combative helped themselves to the butter, eggs, and cheese which were in the basket he had set down until the "go in" was decided.

If a mischance of this description did not befall him, he was sure to make all sorts of mistakes in the delivery of the goods entrusted to him, and those who wanted butter would have cheese left at their doors, and the reverse.

Joe left before his week had expired, but Mr. James Sivins soon found him employment at an oilman's in the London-road.

Here Joe tried some experiment with the matches, and nearly set fire to the premises, and was expelled; his master's boot-toe accompanying him to the door.

Joe's next situation was at a green-grocer's, and his occupation mainly consisted in standing at the door and keeping watch over the goods outside.

Joe found the time very long on his hands; so, to while it away, he amused himself by cracking nuts and throwing the shells at the boys who who passed the shop.

This led to several fights, and finally to the appearance of the irate green-grocer, armed with a whip; and Joe, at the sight, forsook his post and decamped.

Mr. James Sivins was very wroth, but in spite of all his faults, he could not help liking the mischievous lad, and after reading him a long lecture, he wound up by saying—

"Well, as you seem to have no taste to make your fortune, I suppose I must do it for you."

Joe felt grateful, and Mr. Sivins, as a preliminary step towards the good result, taught the boy sufficient of writing to enable him to enter in a book the payments tendered by the thin, ill-clad women, and the pale mechanics, when they came to repay the loans.

All went on well for upwards of a week after Joe was installed as clerk; and Toby, evidently surprised at the cessation of the evening gambols, would stick himself at the lad's feet, and look wistfully towards the door.

One evening Mr. Sivins dressed himself preparatory to going to the public-house near the corner, and pausing on the doorstep, he said—

"Now mind, Joe, you do not leave the house, and if Mrs. Harris comes, do not take her money, unless she pays the fines; she has been two weeks in arrears since Monday last. Let me see, this is the third, if she doesn't pay up, we must go to her securities."

"All right, I'll tell her."

"And, Joe," said Mr. Sivins, "if that man

Brown calls, and instead of paying what he owes, begins one of his crying stories about his wife being ill, and himself being out of work, tell him we shall do the same as I have told you about Mrs. Harris."

" All right, I shan't forget."

" And, Joe, mind you do not leave the house; if you do, and I find it out, I'll thrash you within an inch of your life."

With this promise, Mr. Sivins left, and Joe for the first hour was kept pretty busy jotting down the sixpences and shillings he received; the invitation from a party of boys who had congregated outside, had no effect upon him.

After this, business became slack, and, as neither Mrs. Harris nor the man Brown made their appearance, Joe began to look longingly over the blind at the group who were playing about the road.

He would liked to have joined them, but Mr. James Sivins's injunctions on that point were not to be mistaken, so he sat swinging his legs to and fro as he sat on the high stool and sucked the pen-holder he had been using.

As he sat thus a well-known voice shouted outside the window—

" Chick-or-um! coming out to-night, Charity?"

" That's Bob Martin," thought Joe; " I'll just go to the door and tell him I can't come."

He went to the door and told Bob Martin; but Master Bob only laughed and called the attention of those who were in the road by saying—

" Look here, Charity's afraid to come out, because old Siv has promised him a licking."

" Yah! yah!" yelled a youngster, turning head over heels; " you must be a funker; why don't you come and have a game at duck in front of the door? old Siv can't be home,—it's free-and-easy night, I heard 'em squalling like tom-cat's in a fit when I came past just now."

Free-and-easy nights were generally late nights with Mr. Sivins; Joe liked a game of duck, besides, he could be in front of the door, so there could be no harm; yes, he should go, and go he did, and being the best player he had to be duck.

During the time he was watching for an opportunity to catch one of the players a running fire of conversation was kept up among the group.

" I say, Charity," said one, " what did you have for dinner to-day?"

" A lump of bread," Joe answered; " what did you have?"

" Some cold scran mother brought home last night, and it was fine too; didn't you have anything but dry toke, Charity?"

" Yes," said Joe, " I dipped the corner in the salt for a relish."

" I say, Joe," said another, " who krissened you Charity?"

" Don't know," Joe answered; " I suppose it's because old Siv calls me Charity, he says he keeps me out of charity."

" He's a bad 'un, is old Siv, anyhow," said Bob Martin, " he sold a poor old woman up last week and then——"

Crash went a stone through one of the windows opposite, and the sash was thrown up immediately afterwards and a voice in excitement shrieked.

" Police! Police!—Murder! Murder!"

A member of the force came rapidly down the street, and the boys fled, except Joe, who for a moment did not know what had occurred.

" Seize him," shrieked the voice, " seize him, he's been and broken my window; hold him, the young thief."

The constable seized Joe's collar and gave the lad a shake as he said—

" I've been waiting to catch one of you, now I've got you at last."

" I have not done anything," said Joe, " so you let me go or it will be the worse for you."

The reply Joe received for this bold speech was an open-handed slap on the side of his face which made his ears tingle and burn, and aroused the lad's anger so much that he forgot the majesty of the law and began to kick the policeman's shins.

The boy was no mean antagonist, for his naturally strong frame had been hardened by his life in the streets, and the almost daily encounters he had engaged in had brought out his muscles to a degree of perfection seldom seen out of the prize ring.

The policeman enraged at the resistance he had met with thrust his knuckles down the lad's neck, and would have well nigh suffocated him had not an unexpected ally made his appearance.

It was Toby, who had been lying at full length on the doorstep, until he saw his young master so roughly handled, then with a sudden bound and an angry bark he sprang upon the policeman, and seized him by the calf of the leg.

The man fairly trembled with pain, and releasing Joe he drew his truncheon to beat off the dog.

Joe saw the danger his favourite was in, and catching the staff in its descent he said fiercely:

" You sha'n't hurt my dog, you may kill me first."

It was a strange scene that met the eyes of Mr. James Sivins as he turned the corner of the street upon that bright summer evening; Joe wrestling with the policeman, the large dog with his fangs embedded in the calf of the policeman's leg, and at every window in the dingy street one or more head thrust out watching the fray.

Mr. Sivins called off the dog, and Joe released his hold upon the truncheon, then the three went to Mr. Sivins's opposite to see if the matter could not be arranged.

The constable would not listen to any arrangement, he was determined to take out a summons against Joe, and departed limping up the street.

"Joe," said Mr. Sivins, "you must be out of the way to-morrow, pack up your traps, it's time I placed you at school—I told you not to leave the house—had you obeyed me this would not have happened."

Joe made no reply, he felt crestfallen and rebuked, and whilst he went to his little room over the kitchen Mr. Sivins soliloquised:

"I must get him out of the way, not for his sake but for the allowance—let me see, Dothem offers to take him for sixteen pounds a year and no extras, that will do—I shall make——"

He was interrupted by Joe entering the room, ten minutes after, with Toby at his heels, they left the house and went towards the Waterloo-station.

CHAPTER II.

BAREAM-IN-THE-WILLOWS.

BAREAM-IN-THE-WILLOWS is situated about nine miles from London, and one mile and a half from a small station on the South-Western line.

In the Parliamentary returns Bareain-in-the-Willows is returned as consisting of eight houses, a population of sixty-five souls, exclusive of the boarders at Bareain Hall, who, not being natives of the soil are not returned as inhabitants.

The return also states that the rates for the hamlet of Bareain-in-the-Willows were commuted in 1840—a wise measure, no doubt, to keep the sixty-five inhabitants in the skeleton of a village which, in the sunniest of sunny days, wore a damp, melancholy aspect, from the oldest inhabitant down to the newest arrival.

The peculiar situation of the place, coupled with the long walk necessary to reach it, prevented even the sturdiest tramp from visiting Bareain-in-the-Willows; so the sixty-five more or less were left at liberty to study each other's faces from year's end to year's end.

The study did not seem conducive to jollity; for a more dismal-looking lot it would have been impossible to find than the villagers of Bareain-in-the-Willows.

The straggling village and the Hall stood in the midst of what had once been a large forest of willow-trees, but bad times and want of fuel had caused a sad devastation among the weeping trees—would that hard times had made an alter-ation in the soil wherein the trees grew; far from this being the case, the damp marshy ground became damper and slimier as the years rolled on, and every year saw an increase in the clouds of black gnats that danced up and down in the pestilential vapour.

They seemed to thrive better in Bareain than any part of England; for they were larger and more numerous, and their sting was more poisonous than elsewhere—a fact one day's residence at the uncongenial spot would fully illustrate.

True, they had it all their own way, and could float over the green and slimy ground in perfect security from the birds: for not a feathered songster ever made the willows, in which stood Bareain, their resting-place.

If one by chance perched himself upon a tree and began to warble it would suddenly cease, and fly away as though the lonely place had struck the little creature with dread.

Land was cheap at Bareain, and the villagers by untiring toil, drained sufficient of it for the growth of enough esculent vegetables to supply their own tables and the market of Bareain Township—a bustling little place some three miles across country from village.

One year was very much like another for the sixty-five, more or less, and the gnats, and the sixty-five went their way dismal and resigned; and the gnats grew bigger and became fiercer as the time went on.

But a change suddenly came over the dismal community—a change as sudden as it was unexpected—a change that caused the very oldest inhabitant—he was not very old, for the pernicious atmosphere was not conducive to longevity—to convert his dismal face into a dismal smile, and declare the better times were coming. He might not live to see it, he said, but his children would.

The cause of this change was rather astounding to the sixty-five, for some time they refused to believe it.

A tall, thin gentleman dressed in black, and wearing a white neckcloth and an eye-glass (double), was seen to enter the mildewy gates of Bareain Hall.

A boy brought the news, but he was not believed until he said the gentleman was dressed in black; he was believed then, for the sixty-five in their exceeding simplicity had long been prone to the belief that the Hall was tenanted by *the* Gentleman in Black.

A week passed, and the stranger appeared again, but he was accompanied by the well-known person of the carpenter from Bareain Township.

The oldest inhabitant gave the dismal smile

I have referred to, and deliberately gave his opinion that the Hall was to be inhabited; the news spread, and the whole population of Baream-in-the-Willows were kept in a state of ferment for nearly a fortnight.

They were not sure whether the new comer was a lord, a duke, or a prince; but he was something, they were sure of that, for during the fortnight—barring a few days—a country waggon came from the Township to the Hall laden with deal planks at first, then trusses of straw, then small iron bedsteads, and lastly part of the load was about one hundred and fifty coarse canvass bed ticks about 2½ by 5.

At the end of the fortnight the inhabitants were thrown into a further state of excitement by the tall gentleman making his appearance amongst them, and desiring all who required work to at once go to the Hall.

Nearly the whole of the sixty-five went, for the stranger told them, men, women, and children could do all the work he required.

In the courtyard they found a large pile of straw, and besides this the hundred and fifty ticks; these the tall gentleman told them to fill, then the canvass bags, and be sure not to put too much in each, for he wanted his dear boys to sleep well at night.

The mystery was over now; the Hall was to be a school, and the hamlet of Baream-in-the-Willows would yet reap riches from the young gentlemen from London.

Baream Hall, although gradually giving way to the blue, insidious mildew which clung to the roof and walls, and on the ricketty and decaying stables and outhouses, yet bore some traces of its former state.

There was a high and still solid wall around the spacious building and grounds; the only opening a pair of massive gates that opened in front of a flight of wide steps covered with dark slimy moss; these steps led to a pair of huge heavy doors, then a cold-looking marble hall had to be traversed before the interior of the gloomy mansion was reached.

The windows, and they were many and small in size, were guarded outside with rusty iron bars placed transversely, and added not a little to the prison-like appearance of Baream Hall.

It must have been a place of importance before the district by which it was surrounded became a pestiferous marsh, but now it bore the appearance of a place accursed.

Outwardly there was no change made by the new occupant, but inside the transformation was great, and most comfortable for those who were doomed to pass their young days in the out-of-the-way and gloomy old Hall.

The large chambers were divided by unplaned boards, and the great fire-places were closed up save a small slit left for the grates, which would not hold above a couple of pounds of coal.

The small beds stood side by side in the rooms, and with scarcely sufficient space for the smallest boy to pass between.

The bedding consisted of a couple of coarse thin blankets, the texture so open that sand could easily have been sifted through them, a rough brown sheet, one degree removed from sacking in texture, and a rug, also of the commonest material, completed the covering for the straw palliases.

The great hall, where in days of yore high revelry and wassail had gladdened those who dwelt in the Hall, was fitted as a dining-room, such fittings being long deal forms and tables, supported by iron trussels—tin plates and mugs formed a fitting accompaniment to this furniture.

Although there were many chambers fitted up for the reception of the hapless pupils, there were yet more than two-thirds of the Hall untouched—true the new proprietor looked forward to the day when every chamber should be occupied, but of that anon.

These events happened about twelve-months before the opening of this story, so having given these details it may be as well to introduce the proprietor and his family as they appeared on the evening when everything was pronounced ready to receive the pupils of the new academy, and allow them to explain to the reader the purposes for which Baream Hall Academy was called into existence.

CHAPTER III.

MR. SAMUEL DOTHEM, SEN., SAMUEL DOTHEM, JUN., SYLVIA DOTHEM, DEBORAH DOTHEM, AND MRS. DOTHEM.

MR. SAMUEL DOTHEM was a man of about fifty. His head was bald on the crown; below this was a fringe of iron-grey hair; his whiskers were of the same hue, and of the pattern called "dogs," for they grew in little tufts just below the cheekbone.

His face was the colour of a dirty wash-leather; his eye-brows long and ragged; his nose hooked a little; and as his mouth was large and his lips always kept closed, unless in speaking, the general configuration of his face was not unlike that of a kite.

He was very tall, very thin, and had a slight stoop, and to carry off any short-comings in face and form, he invariably dressed in deep black, save his shirt, tie, collar, and wristbands: these were always faultlessly white.

In introducing so important a personage as

Mr. Samuel Dothem, it may be as well to state that previous to his being the possessor of Bearam, he had been employed in London as a collector of taxes, and while in that capacity he had been in the habit of lending the money belonging to the parish out at the moderate rate of 75 per cent.

A sudden collapse brought the affair to light, but before the authorities could bring Mr. Dothem to a sense of his misdeeds, he collected a quarter's taxes, and, with his amiable family, left London.

Chance brought him to the township of Bearam, chance also brought him in contact with the party who had the selling—on most advantageous terms—of Bearam-Hall-in-the-Willows. The party suggested a school. Mr. Dothem was not asleep, so he closed with the advantageous offer.

Samuel, his son, was a "little snip" of a fellow, between one-and-two-and-twenty; vain, arrogant, and conceited by nature, and having nothing in face or form to carry out his absurd pretentions, he was the laughing stock of all who knew him.

The amiable Samuel believed he was destined to become a poet, and as his family fostered this belief, the poor, empty-headed creature became more insufferable every day.

Sylvia Dothem was a young lady of about thirty, and was a feminine likeness of her papa. She was romantic, fond of reading milk-and-water novels, where there was plenty of love and mystery and high-flown language to be found. She liked to read about lovers whose glowing passion oozed out of their finger's ends, and particularly dwelt upon such passages as these—

" 'Then you love me, Claudio?' "

" 'And she gazed spoonily up at his noble face, and her liquid eyes bespoke any amount of unutterable tenderness, while the soft tinge of maidenly modesty irradiated her lovely and pensive countenance, &c.' "

She liked this sort of thing, and could take any amount, and she received large doses week by week when the amiable family were in London. For week by week she read the *Family Trumpeter* and the *London Towler*.

Her sister Deborah was a somewhat stout maiden of twenty-seven summers and winters. She was also romantic, but the disease was in a stronger form. She contributed to the weekly serials, but her choice was the *London Roarer* and the *Bow Chimes*.

She liked a little sensation mixed with her romance; such as an amiable daughter having poisoned her mother, and then bolted with the cash box, and some one else being taken up for the murder, etc.

Deborah was the best-looking of the family, for although of a stumpy, squat figure, she had a plump good-natured looking round face, and her bright little grey eyes when she was listening to her brother's pompous nonsense, were the very embodiment of good temper and fun.

Mrs. Dothem's portrait may be drawn in a few words. She was about five years older than her husband, and when going about her domestic duties, a stranger who had been to the play and had seen the witch scene in Macbeth would have taken the respected lady for one of the repulsive trio.

Truly, a pleasant family was this to be sitting in the most comfortable room in Bearam Hall, on the evening when everything was found ready for the coming of the pupils.

They were all gathered around the table. Mr. D. was writing; Mrs. D. was darning stockings; Samuel was standing near the fireplace in an "attitude" he thought becoming to a future great poet.

Sylvia was deeply buried in a love story, and Deborah—or Deb—was laughing over the comic column in her favourite periodical. Suddenly Mr. Dothem raised his head, placed the pen he had been using upon the table, rubbed his hands and said—

"There, I think that will do; now listen all of you."

EDUCATION.

To the relatives and guardians of young gentlemen. A gentleman offers a home where the pupils will receive parental care and maternal watchfulness; the house is spacious and airy, the grounds extensive and varied, and being situated in a most delightful valley, pupils of the most delicate constitution will not feel the keen winds of winter. Terms, inclusive, sixteen guineas. No extras. A good plain table, and separate beds. Address—Preceptor, Post-office, Bearam.

"Beautifully expressive." sighed the tender Sylvia; "oh, papa, how clever you are."

"I should think that would do very nicely," said Deb, "it sounds well."

"Especially," said Samuel, "about the plain table—I believe it has been planed."

The family laughed; plain and planed sounded to them like wit; and the poor fool who had shown his weakness by this wretched attempt at something he scarcely understood, passed his fingers through his hair, and looked pensively at the fire-grate.

Mrs. Dothem nodded her head in approval of the advertisement, and Deborah said—

"How lucky you were, papa, to think of forming a school upon the plan you have laid out."

INTERIOR OF BAREAM HALL SCHOOL.

"Your mother Deb—your talented mother's brain—created the shadowy outlines of my bold plan, which, if it succeeds—and it will, for there's six boys coming to morrow—we shall make our fortunes."

"If we succed as you remark, Samuel," said Mrs. Dothem, "and we shall do so if we get the pupils."

"And get them we shall," said Mr. Dothem. "An establishment like this is wanted—very much wanted—by relatives and guardians, and those who have particular reasons for placing boys out of the way."

"Well, we shall see," said the witch-like lady. "If you get the boys I'll wager we make it pay."

"Let mother alone for that," said Deborah; "she has planned it all out so nicely: the biggest boys are to dig up the garden and look after the vegetables."

"Ah!" said Mr. Dothem, suddenly, "that reminds me. Now, as vegetables, occasionally varied with oatmeal, will be the principal diet in the dining-hall, the management of that must department must be left to you, mother."

Mrs. Dothem nodded approvingly.

"The boys' linen, Sylvia, you must superintend; and as Samuel is not of a coarse, vulgar growth it must be your care to see the dear boy does not want for those essential changes of clothing which the bags and boxes of the pupils, as they arrive must supply."

"I'll take care of that," said Sylvia the romantic; "they shall all pay toll."

"Now, Deborah," said the elder gentleman, "your share of the great work will be to assist your mother, for we shall not be able to hire any servants for a year at least."

"What am I to do?" said the magnificent, striking a fresh attitude.

"You will assist me, Samuel," said his father; "in fact the whole discipline of the school will be placed in your hands, the educational department will be mine."

"I'll thrash the young whelps, and no mistake," said Samuel, "so let 'em look out."

"I will leave the matter in your hands, Samuel; now we have come to another and a most important part of the business, namely that of punishment.

The future Byron, Shakespeare, and Milton, struck another attitude, and prepared to listen.

"Now," said Mr. Dothem, "the less we have to give the boys to eat the greater the profit will be to us, therefore our system of punishment will be stopping a meal, or two meals, as the case may be—in some cases confinement in a dark room will be added. Oh, I forgot to state in the advertisement for the London papers that there was no corporal punishment, I must add that."

"But," said the lady Dothem, "do you think you can play that game safely?"

"Why not? Mrs. Dothem."

"Some of the boys may write to their friends, ex——"

"There, my dear, you seem to quite forget the object of this establishment. The boys who come here will not have friends who take such an interest as to receive letters from them. No, Mrs. Dothem, there will be no letters written from here, and whenever a boy passes these gates, he will never go beyond them unless I turn him out, because the money I have received has been worked out, and no likelihood of another remittance. Mine shall be a model academy, devoted to the interests of the guardians and relatives of such as may be wanted out of the way; and," he mentally added, "a safe place for those whom the guardians and relatives may wish to keep out of the way for ever if they like. Capital atmosphere for settling a half-starved lad.

Must give in to it. That is why we must be careful to live well."

"There is another thing, Sam," the father said to the poet, "I shall require you to do. You must, of course I mean when the school gets strong, have two or three boys in your favour whose duty it will be to report to you anything they may overhear from their schoolfellows."

"A good idea," said the Attitude, glancing down at his feet. "Of course they will lose a part of their grub for speaking against the rules of the school."

"Quite so, Sam; and now I think of it, my dear," he said to his wife, "when our numbers increase it will be as well to have a good heap of raw carrots near the place I shall allot for a play-ground, so that the boys—they are all fond of raw carrots—may eat their fill when they leave the school-room. It will save many a dinner."

Mrs. Dothem nodded approvingly, then said, "That sort of living will incur the extra expense of medicine for the boys."

"I have thought of that," said Mr. Dothem, "and ordered a pound of bitter aloes for those who may be ill. One dose will cure them, I know."

"If it does not," said Mrs. Dothem, "I will find something that will."

The grin upon her hag-like face was not promising for the bodily welfare of the future pupils of Baream Hall.

Such were the principles upon which the school was started, and Mr. Samuel Dothem did not err when he anticipated a success.

He knew there were hundreds, nay thousands, of parentless children under the care of unfeeling relatives and friends. He knew, also, there were many who for various reasons, would be glad to place a boy out of the way; especially upon the terms Mr. Dothem offered to take them at per annum.

Before six months had passed Baream Hall had fifty borders. Fifty unpitied, uncared for, unloved lads, passed through the mildewed gates; many never to leave them again until they were carried out.

Let us hope that those who passed away from their troubles, were richly rewarded by Him who suffers not the smallest bird to fall to the ear unheeded.

Such was Baream Hall, the place toward which Charity Joe, Mr. Sivins, and Toby, who had crept into the carriage unperceived, were journeying.

Should the readers have any doubt respecting the revelations I am about to make, I would advise him to procure a copy of the Inspectors of Schools' Reports to Government, therein he will find that truth far exceeds the wildest fiction.

CHAPTER IV.

A FURTHER ACCOUNT OF BAREAM HALL, AND THE RETRENCHMENT DECIDED UPON BY MR. AND MRS. DOTHEM.—ALSO HOW SYLVIA AND DEBORAH DOTHEM WERE BROUGHT FROM THE LAND OF ROMANCE BY THE ARRIVAL OF MR. SIVINS, CHARITY JOE AND HIS DOG TOBY.

MR. DOTHEM, SEN., was well aware that self-preservation was the first law of nature—a knowledge that had no doubt been impressed upon his mind in early youth, and time, instead of obliterating the imprint, caused it to sink deeper into the tablet.

In conducting the affairs of the school he kept the primary law full in sight. Possibly to the force of this juvenile impression we may attribute the great change perceptible every day between the master and pupils of Baream Hall.

For the former began to grow sleek and respectable, and the latter, in a corresponding ratio became thinner and more ragged as the time "rolled on," according to the app ro ed mode adopted by great novelists when speaking of the flight of the old gentleman with the scythe and hour-glass.

Yes; the time rolled on and these changes took place.

By the end of the first year after the establishment of the Baream Academy, Mr. Dothem had under his charge nearly one hundred pupils, their ages varying from nine to eighteen.

His words had been prophetic; there were many persons to whom a school of the description he had founded was a great boom; and had many more been acquainted with the delightful place there would not have been many empty rooms in the great mildewy, desolate mansion.

There was a great difference in the appearance of these lads compared to the pupils of an academy where every boy had a father, mother, or relative to love them, write letters, and send "tips," baskets and presents, so acceptable to the schoolboy mind.

There was no joy in perspective for the poor hopeless lads at Baream—no jolly holidays to look forward to; no visiting friends; to be brief they were consigned to the care of Mr. Dothem and his amiable family, and beyond the regular transmission of the quarterly sum (in advance) no one cared whether they lived or died; had it been otherwise, Mr. Dothem would not have taken them under his paternal wing.

But a small proportion of the lads could look back with pleasure to the joyless life they had passed. Many were orphans—many had either a mother or father living who could or would not acknowledge their children; others had been brought up by relatives in whose way they stood; for while they lived their greedy relatives could not finger the money left by the boys' parents.

It was impossible to look upon some of the little fellows without feeling that the cheerless life they had been doomed to had already made them vicious and cruel beyond their years.

These lads had an expression of sullen savage despair upon their faces, and the low, receding foreheads and deep-set eyes added se'fishness and precocious cunning to the unpleasant appearance of their pale, pinched faces.

Others were meek, penitent boys, whose tearful eyes looked as though they were always on the watch for some one to protect and love them.

This class of the boarders were the youngest —so young that their faces had not lost that childish expression of openness and innocence in which the mind feelings are depicted upon the countenance.

There were some lads—about a dozen—who gave Mr. Dothem and his sallow-visaged son an infinity of trouble. These were the high-spirited lads that no starving or punishment could subdue.

Sturdy, broad-chested fellows, whose animal spirit rose triumphant over the hapless life they led; boys whose frames seemed to gather strength from the meagre diet of Baream Hall, and who arose as refreshed from their night's slumbers upon a straw pallet as though their limbs had reposed upon a bed of eider down, and their covering a quilt of the ermine's beautiful skin.

Whatever fun and mischief took place in the dismal school these lads were the projectors, and Samuels, junior, the superlative, was an especial object of their plotting; and, although the sucking poet had more than once boasted of terrific combats he had gone through when in London—and with men who, from Samuel's description, could have doubled him up like a wisp of hay—he received from more than one of the said lads more than his slender form could bear.

They were too careful to repay his tyranny in the daytime; they chose the hour when the poetic Samuel was wont to creep about the passages, and with his ear to the keyhole, listen to the boys' conversation when they were in bed.

In one instance he had been caught, and severely pommelled in the dark, and in spite of Mr. Dothem's liberal offers of reward for the discovery of the offenders, none of those in the secret would split.

The business of the day was over, and most of the boys were out among the wild, rank weeds which grew to perfection in that portion of the ground allotted for their use.

The strongest of them were debarred the pleasure of the rank playground until they had finished attending to the vegetable garden, and as the weather was warm and dry, there was much labour required to pump water from the well to water the cabbages and other beds.

Mrs. Dothem had charge of this department, and being a woman of tact, she soon found a system of getting the work well done, and with but little trouble to herself.

One of the lads (and such is the weakness of human nature that plenty were always to be had to carry out her wishes) was ordered to stand over the pump and keep an account of the number of buckets filled by each of the young gardeners.

The principal and his family were seated at the open window of a comfortably-furnished sitting room, the senior Dothem in the enjoyment of a cigar and a glass of cold gin and water, his amiable son was in the background studying a book; Sylvia was reading the *Jowler*; Deb ditto the *Roarer*; and Mrs. D. sat winking and blinking at the fading sun, and mentally resolved to effect a saving in the expense of the establishment by a substitution of mangel wurzels for the more expensive carrots and turnips used in the soup for the boarders. (Soup days were twice a week at Baream.)

Doses of grated ginger and chalk usually followed soup days; and something of the sort was necessary, or there would have been work for the doctors at Baream township.

"Well, so far," said Mr. Dothem, "I think we may safely say our school has been a success."

"A great success," said Mrs. D., "but I think, my dear, there is room yet for improvement."

"In the school, Mrs. Dothem?"

"No, Mr. D., in the provision department."

"But, my dear, the boys look well—we have had but ten deaths since we began."

"Quite true, Mr. D., therefore, as I said before, there is room for improvement—perhaps I should say retrenchment—in our expenditure."

"Let me see," said the principal, "Mondays, meat, vegetables, and pudding—pudding without suet; Tuesday's dinner, oatmeal and salt to prevent grossness from Monday's rich food."

"Wednesdays," said Mrs. Dothem, when her husband paused, "soup, good soup—the meat we have for dinner is boiled in the water, which is thickened with rice and vegetables."

"Quite true, my dear, and well the boys look upon the German diet."

"Thursdays, meat pudding and vegetables.

By-the-way, Mr. D., you forgot to put a barrow-load of carrots outside the schoolroom door last Thursday, and the consequence was, the edge not being taken off the boys' appetites, there was nothing but grumbling after dinner."

"I must see to that in future, Mrs. D. Well, Fridays, oatmeal porridge and salt."

"Saturdays," said Mrs. D., "bread and cheese and beer; Sundays, meat, soup, and vegetables."

"Yet, after such a generous bill of fare, some of the biggest boys grumble about the beer, Mrs. Dothem. I find the last eighteen gallon cask is nearly empty; of course you have not given them beer more than once during the week?"

"Only on Saturdays, Mr. D.; then the usual quantity, four boys to a pint."

"Strange; perhaps the barrel was not full. Now eighteen gallons cost nine and six——"

"Ten shillings on the bill, Mr. Dothem."

"Yes; but the brewer makes a reduction in consequence of that gawky nephew of his having been admitted to Bareham Hall."

"The young viper," said Mrs. D.; "he told the boys in his room, dear Samuel overheard him, that you put water to the 'swankey,' that was the term he used, so that it should not cost more than a halfpenny a quart."

"Did he?" said Mr. Dothem; and the "did he," meant a great deal. "Now, my dear Mrs. D., about the retrenchment you spoke of."

"I have been thinking," said the amiable lady, "that in place of giving the young whelps doses of chalk and grated ginger when they are unwell, it would be much more economical to send a few of them out to cut stinging-nettles—nettles boiled, and the liquor taken before breakfast, is a good purifier of the blood."

"Perhaps you are right, Mrs. D., but I think it would be less expensive to buy a little chalk and ginger than to risk any of the boys running away, which might happen if they got beyond the gates."

"No fear of that," said the lady, "the system of making the big boys punish the younger ones answers so well that I should not feel the least fear respecting the result you mentioned."

"Well, Mrs D., I will be guided by your judgment in this; to-morrow six boys of the fourth class, with one of the first in charge, shall go and cut the nettles you require."

"Now," said Mrs. Dothem, "there is a great many carrots and turnips used in the soup on Wednesdays and Saturdays, so I've been thinking of trying mangel wurzels chopped up. What is your opinion of the matter?"

"Well, my dear, we can but try the experiment. At any rate I will purchase sufficient to last until the carrots and turnips we have growing are fit for use."

"SEIZE 'EM, TOBY! SEIZE 'EM!"

"That will be in about three weeks' time," said Mrs. D., "therefore, we shall have an opportunity of trying the new vegetable. I saw you at your books yesterday, Mr. D., may I ask how much clear profit you make out of each boy's allowance?"

"In the year, Mrs. D.?"

"No, each week, Mr. D."

"I will soon tell you. Now, let me see, the terms are sixteen guineas, but I always have to strike off the extra shillings, that brings it to sixteen pounds."

"Sixteen pounds a year, Mr. D., is——"

"Four pounds per quarter, Mrs. D.; one pound six and eightpence per month, six and twopence per week, tenpence halfpenny per day."

"I daresay it's right. Well, how much do you reckon the cost for each board, by the week?"

"The charge is a trifle over four shillings."

"That leaves two and twopence profit."

"Quite so, Mrs. D., and I hope under your careful management to increase it to two and six."

"It shall be done, Mr. D."

"Samuel," said the principal, turning to his sallow-faced son, "I wish to speak to you upon a little matter that occurred to-day."

The slim one looked up from his book with an affected air of abstraction.

"Now, my boy," said the father, "I must give you every credit for the manner in which you have kept up the discipline of the school, but at the same time I think it would be as well to desist for a time from the practice of holding the youngest boys up by the hair of their heads."

"I only adopt that mode of punishment, father," said the spider-waisted youth, "when they caricature me upon their slates, and pencil underneath, 'Young Nipguts' portrait.'"

"Do they? 'Young Nipguts!'—well, I will alter this—let me know next time, Samuel, and the dark cellar and starvation for forty-eight hours will teach them to respect you if nothing else will. By the way, Samuel, there is a boy in the cellar now whose time of punishment must have expired—here's the key, go and release him."

Samuel ran his fingers through his hair, struck an attitude, then walked slowly from the room.

There was a long silence after this, Mrs. Dothem fell asleep, Mr. D. refilled his tumbler and lit another cigar, but long before he had consumed a quarter of the weed his head fell back, and he dozed in peace.

The silence was conducive to the better understanding of the stories which at the moment engrossed the minds of the romantic Sylvia, for she became so interested that she read aloud.

"'Is it cruel to love, oh, my soul's sweetest idol?'

"'Love makes us cruel and selfish, for the passion is so engrossing, so purely a matter of self, that I feel jealous of the very fly that has settled upon your nose.'"

"The sweet, low, musical laughter of the beautiful girl thrilled his frame, and as he raised his face and gazed into hers, a feeling of inexpressible bliss stole over him, and clasping her hand he pressed it to his lips and murmured—'"

"'Ha, ha, villain! sayest thou so!'" said Deborah, also reading aloud; "sayest thou my maternal parent fell by thy ruby-stained hand? oh, thou double-faced wretch to tell me this to my face!'

"But she would not listen; her white fingers worked convulsively, then she threw back her long golden hair and shrieked aloud as the golden shower swept her swan-like neck.

"'False, black-hearted wretch! was it for this I gave up the youth whose pale, pensive face, and dark, mournful eyes still warm up my soul, and the metallic sound of his voice still rings in my ears, as he——"

Clang! clang! clang! sounded the rusty bell that hung inside the gates, and caused the two sisters to return from the land of poetry and romance and place themselves near the window to see who it was demanded admission to Baream Hall.

Mr. Dothem awoke with a start, and drawing his silken handkerchief from his head, he exclaimed—

"What is it? eh! oh! the bell; who can it be?"

He ran to the window and saw the boy whose duty it was to open the gate admit a stout, fussy-looking man, a rather seedily-dressed boy, and a large dog.

CHAPTER V.

CHARITY JOE BECOMES AN INMATE OF BAREAM HALL, AND TOBY IS PROVIDED WITH A LODGING UPON CERTAIN CONDITIONS.

"AH!" said Mr. Dothem, sen., when he saw the strangers; "Mr. Sivens and boy; Sylvia, dear, wake your respected mother, and you, Deborah, find Samuel—he is no doubt perfecting some good idea for his poem in a lonely portion of the yard, and Sylvia, this boy will require a bed, his luggage, I am afraid, will not require much arranging——"

"Not if it is all contained in that spotted cotton handkerchief," said the romantic Sylvia. "I'm sure it's shameful the way some of the young whelps are sent here, quite a disgrace to the establishment."

"An indisputable fact, my dear, yet we cannot help it; let's see; No. 3 room has a spare bed, I don't think No. 38 has been occupied since he died."

"It has not, papa."

"This boy's number will be 97, my dear; now leave me me to see this gentleman alone."

"Come, my sister," said Sylvia, the romantic, "let us away before the rude eyes of the stranger falleth upon our charms."

The doses of the *Jowler* and *Trumpeter* were taking effect upon the gentle maiden of about thirty springs and autumns.

"I follow," said Deborah; "come, my mother, let us away from the haunts of men and bury ourselves in the seclusion of our chambers, where no mortal eye, unless one looks through the keyhole, can perceive us."

Mrs. Dothem followed her daughters, and possibly owing to the sudden manner in which she had been aroused from her nap, she was a little confused, and in her confusion she caught up Mr. Dothem's glass of cold gin and water, and carried it away in her hand.

Mr. Dothem went to the door and met his visitor; they shook hands, and by the manner in which their eyes met, " they perfectly understood each other."

" Glad to see you," said Mr. Dothem to Mr. Sivins; " very glad to see you. Is this the young gentleman you wrote about?"

" Yes," answered Mr. Sivins, " this is the hopeful youth. What a beastly, out-of-the-way place this is, Mr. Dothem. Why, there is not a decent road between here and the station.".

" Sit down; and you, my little man, find a seat. We are not ceremonious here. Beastly roads, Mr. Sivins? Just like you London gentlemen to make that remark. You forget we are quite Arcadian down here. No roads, no bustle, no hurrying to and fro of eager crowds—no Mr. Sivins, our lives are passed after the manner depicted in the old pastoral poems."

" Give me, then," said the innocent Mr. Sivins, " the region of the ' Elephant and Castle,' and an adjacent pub."

" Every one to his taste, Mr. Sivins. Now I prefer to dwell among the beauties of nature, surrounded by my family and my dear boys. I could not now be happy in any other sphere. What is your name, my man?"

The gentleman with the taste for Arcadian life addressed the query to Joe, who promptly answered—

" Joseph Chudleigh Cholmondeley."

" A beautiful name. So you have come to stay amongst us here? Yon will—I hope you will—do your friend Mr. Sivins, and the school of which I have the honour to be the principal every credit."

" I'll try," said Joe; " no cove can do more than that."

" Cove," said Mr. Dothem, " is a slang word. But never mind, we shall soon make you forget such expressions here, for we have young gentlemen of the highest families in the land, and by following their conduct you will leave Bareani Hall—the seat of learning and eloquence—a perfect gentleman."

" Shall I?" said Joe. " Well, that will be something to be a perfect gentleman, 'cos they don't have not nothing to do."

" We must all work," said the benign Dothem, " but of that hereafter. Whose dog is that?"

" Mine," said Joe, " and a rare good 'un he is, too. Get up, Toby, and chuck your bats about. See him! doesn't he do it fine?"

Toby, in obedience to his master's command, stood upon his hind legs, and " chucked his bats about " by moving his forepaws quickly to and fro.

Mr. Dothem looked at Mr. Sivins, and Mr. Sivins looked at Mr. Dothem; then the former said—

" A very obedient, but not one of the handsomest of his kind. I suppose you intend to take him back with you?"

This was to Mr. Sivins, but before the agent could reply Joe struck in with—

" No fear of that. Toby stays here or I don't, that's the way to settle this matter. Where Toby is there's Joe, and where Joe is there's Toby, for one don't stop without the other."

This was very plain—too plain for Mr. Dothem, who began to see countless punishments in store for the young gentleman so free of speech.

" Really," he said, " although I admire the affection which caused that speech, I must inform you, Mr. Cholmondeley, that I do not include dogs in my charge for pupils."

" You don't get a dog," said Joe, " like that in this part of the country. Why he can and will kill anything from a fly to a cat, and, as for a watch dog, there ain't his likes in all England, no mistake about it. Isn't it right, what I say?"

" Very likely," said Mr. Dothem; " but you must be aware, I cannot afford to keep a large dog like that and you for the small sum I charge for boarding, washing, lodging, and educating you."

" Nobody asked you to," said Joe. " Toby don't want any keeping, he'll forage for himself, if there ain't anything to be found, I'll tell you what I'll do, I'll clean all the knives, and brush up the things, or do anything you like, if you let him stop, if not——"

" If not, my man, what then?"

" Why I won't stop here. I don't like the look of the crib much, so you know what to do."

Mr. Sivins had taken no part in the foregoing " passage" between the principal of Bareani Hall and Joe, but when he saw a red spot make its appearance upon each of the principal's cheeks, he thought it time to interfere; so with a gesture he called Mr. Dothem to the window, and while Joe stroked and patted Toby's head, Mr. Sivins said—

" A pennyworth of poison will settle the dog, therefore, the matter is easily managed, and as the boy is as headstrong as he is spirited, it may be as well to take him upon the conditions he proposes. I have no doubt the excellent discipline of this establishment will soon bring him to reason."

" Very soon," said Mr. Dothem; " therefore, I will follow your advice."

They left the window, and Mr. Dothem, addressing Joe said—

"Your guardian, Mr. Sivins, tells me you are very fond of dogs, and as I like to encourage feelings of humanity in the hearts of my pupils, your dog can stay with you upon the conditions you have yourself named."

"What, if I clean the knives, eh? Is that to pay for his lodging?"

"Exactly so, my little man."

"But," said Joe, "what about his keep?"

"That," Mr. Dothem answered, "will be an easy matter here. We keep a good table."

"Many people," Joe said, "keep good tables, but they don't put much on them.'

"You——"

Mr. Dothem's exclamation was stopped by the entrance of the romantic Sylvia, who said—

"The young gentleman's room is quite ready, sir." Then to Joe, "Will you please to follow me?"

"Like a bird," said Joe. "Come on, Toby; good-bye, Mr. Sivins. I'm much obliged to you for all you've done for me out of charity, but as soon as I get on my own hook I mean to have a look out for that old gent who brought me from the workus, and if I find him I shall ask if you have kept me out of charity, for that ain't one of your failings."

"Good-bye, Joe," said Mr. Sivins, biting his lips with vexation, "I hope you may find the old gentleman, then, perhaps, you will be convinced of the disinterested manner in which I have behaved to you."

"P'raps I shall. Good-bye."

Joe took up his bundle, and as Miss Sylvia led the way with the air of a tragedy queen at a country booth, he left the room, followed by Toby.

"Who is the old gentleman referred to by this boy?" Mr. Dothem asked; "judging by the name he gave me I should think he belonged to a good family."

"The name was given him in the workhouse," the agent answered; "as for the old gentleman I know no more about him than you do."

"Yet he pays you for the boy's keep."

"He does; but he is a cunning old dog. I have tried all I know to find out his name and address, but artful as I have been, so far he has been too cunning for me."

"It was strange," Mr. Dothem said, "that you should have met him just after the drunken cobbler in the Borough died."

"It was."

"I had not time when I last saw you, to listen to the account. You may perhaps remember the cause of my haste."

"Perfectly well," said Mr. Sivins, "but since you are curious upon the point, I will tell you how it occurred."

"Have a cigar?"

"Thank you; of course, you are aware that I was a particular friend of poor Lasts, who drank himself to death?"

"Quite aware of it."

"I was coming to see him at the time this boy was brought to the borough, and as I never forget faces, I knew the old fellow when I met him on the steps of the Duke of York's column."

"This was after Lasts died."

"Yes, a few days. I told him the bootmaker was dead, and at once offered to take charge of the boy, an offer he accepted, and gave me the same terms as Lasts had been in the habit of receiving."

"These terms are——"

"Only known to myself and the old gentleman."

"Quite right to keep the knowledge from going further," said Mr. Dothem. "Well, how go affairs in a certain quarter?"

"Much the same; the fellow you employed at times to collect the rates has got your berth."

"Well, he deserves it, for the fellow is honest as far as the world goes. How does your loan office answer?"

"Pretty well; but I have to sell up a few of them now and then."

"Ah!" disagreeable necessity; still it must be done."

"Yes."—A pause—then Mr. Sivins carelessly asked, "How do you find this answer?"

"The school?"

"Yes."

"Pretty well; better, I daresay, when I have perfected my arrangements."

"It requires time. Of its ultimate great success I should think there is not the least doubt, Dothem."

"Not the least. You see it is just the sort of thing that is wanted."

"How about the lads when they get too old for your establishment?"

"Well," said Mr. Dothem, "I have scarcely thought of that. Of course I must be guided by those who send the boys here."

"Undoubtedly; but most of them, I should imagine, would be ready and willing to recompense you if you can get them comfortably off their hands."

"I have been thinking so," said Mr. Dothem, "and wish now that I had selected a place nearer the sea."

"Why?"

"Because boys, when they imagine themselves

oppressed, immediately rush off to sea, and as shipwrecks are not unusual things, they would, 'n many cases, be as much out of their guardians' and relatives' way as though the black oblong box held their carcases."

"Still, there would be the chance of some of them returning and uttering unpleasant things about your excellent establishment."

"Our walls are high," said Mr. Dothem, and the gate is always fastened; therefore those who escaped would do so when the gate was left open on purpose, and it would be my care that nothing unpleasant should arise hereafter."

"I can see as far through a brick wall as most people," said Mr. James Sivins, agent, "but hang me if I can see this very clear."

"It is a suggestion of my wife's—a clever woman she is, Mr. Sivins, and has been a fine woman in her time."

Mr. Sivins merely said "Indeed!" perhaps he doubted the lady had ever had any pretensions to the praise her worthy spouse bestowed upon her form.

"I should not be able to get on without her," Mr. Dothem continued; "she is such a wonderful manager—very wonderful."

"She must be so to manage such a number of unruly boys; but the suggestion, Dothem, what was it?"

"Well, a very simple one, and one I have no doubt I should have thought of afterwards; we'll suppose it became necessary to let one of the overgrown whelps escape—he goes—I watch him sneak through the gate, and then my excellent wife goes at once to his box and places some of our property inside. Samuel brings the box down and places it under the wall; I go at once for the constable at Baream township. He comes and bears witness to the narrow escape I had of being robbed."

"A capital idea—if he is caught, what then?"

"He must not be caught," said Mr. Dothem; "I shall be aware of the route he has taken; I will send the constable the contrary way."

"Still I do not understand the purpose of the supposed attempt at robbery."

"Don't you? It is simple enough. If he opens his mouth about the regulations of my establishment I can at once prove him to be a thief, and as a matter of course his word will not be taken."

"Not a bad idea, upon my word," said Mr. Sivins. "Now you were regretting your distance from a seaport town, I think I have a plan that will answer quite as well, if not better."

"I am open to suggestions."

"Mine will be worth hundreds of pounds to you in time, so if you accept it I shall expect a reduction in the payment for Joe's education."

"You shall have it if I find it feasible to my mind."

Mr. Sivins did not place much reliance upon the pledge thus held out, but as he had nothing particular to do at the moment he shook hands with the principal of Baream Hall, justly arguing that if it served no other purpose it would keep the muscles of his arm and shoulders in exercise.

"Now," said Mr. Sivins, thrusting his thumb into the armholes of his waistcoat, lifting his chair back and crossing his right leg over the left, "my suggestion, which I flatter myself is an improvement upon the seaport you just now wished to have named, is that when you have any lads to turn out upon the world, providing they are strong healthy lads—mind you, it's no use sending any narrow-chested sickly fellows——"

"I shall bear that in mind."

"Do, unless you wish your trouble to be for no purpose. Now such a lad as Joe when he is a few years older, would be about the clip. Now to put them effectually out of sight and mind suppose at the time you had worked them into a fit state of mind to escape when the gate was left conveniently open, you went to the expense of paying the fare of one of the recruiting fellows belonging to a line regiment."

"Ah! Go on, pray."

"A regiment, bear in mind, that is stationed in the East Indies, China, or anywhere you may select as the most unhealthy spot possible to find; you can easily get all the information you require from the *Gazette*, and if you are able to obtain the attendance of a man from a regiment just embarking for an unhealthy station, I think you will do much better than being near a seaport, for, after all, it is not the better class of boys who prefer the dirt and discomfort of a ship to the pomp, glitter, and parade of military life."

"Perhaps not; at any rate, I can fire their minds for the military service by purchasing a few books upon the subject, and leave them in the way of those it may be necessary to see beyond the gates of Baream, but——"

"Well? but what is the doubt, Dothem?"

"Will the soldier come down here upon the chance of obtaining a few recruits?"

"Will ducks swim? Will a young wife married to an old man look out for a jointure? Will a—— ?"

"You need not go any further, I can see the plan will succeed, that is, if the red coat will not mind being in such a miserable place as Baream-in-the-Willows is."

"It's the fellow's interest to come, he gets a

pound for every recruit, less the shilling for enlistment."

"Ah, that alters the case. I see now it would be an inducement for a recruiting party to come down here when I sent for him."

"Yes; and I can tell you something else, friend D."

"What is it?"

"Why, the man who brings a recruit is entitled to a few shillings for bringing-money; that, of course, you would claim. Now what is my suggestion worth?"

"A half-year's money for the boy you have brought, which I will pay when I have tested the working of your admirable scheme."

So the pair of rascals talked until the bell rang for the boys to assemble for *prayers*, and the arch fiend must have been proud of two such worthy followers.

During this time Joe had deposited his little bundle on the bed, over which hung a ticket numbered ninety-eight, then with Toby he went to the exercise-ground—they did not use the term play-ground at Baream.

Joe's appearance was soon followed by a crowd of the biggest boys getting round him, and a volley of questions were put to the lad before he could answer one.

"Halloa," said a pale-faced youth, nicknamed, from his voluble tongue, Tommy Nimblejaws, "here's another guy—pull the string, boys."

"I say," said another, "how much for your tyke? he ain't up to much."

"Here's a go," remarked another hopeful youth, "here's a new boy brought a tyke to be boiled down for soup."

"Who's your tailor?" said another; "that jacket of yours is all a fit—strike me if it ain't."

"I say, new 'un," shouted another querist, "can you fight?"

"One at a time," said Joe; "now I don't wish to sell my dog, neither will he be boiled down for soup; as for my tailor, it strikes me he is as good as any of those who made your clothes; my name is Joseph Chudleigh Cholmondeley, but in case it should break any of your lantern jaws to call me by it, you may as well give me the name I have always been called, and that is Charity Joe; now about fighting, I can't do much in that line, but I'll swallow Toby here, tail and all, if I can't find any fellow's nose with my thumb and finger without having to use all the gas lamps on London Bridge to see my way to it."

Joe paused to gain his breath, then continued—

"I say, where's the cistern? Toby wants a drink,"

"Cistern!" said Tommy Nimblejaws, "we ain't up to a cistern here; there's a pump—but for fear the well should get dry, and old Nipguts have to pay for water, there's one of the bullies in charge of it, and he wouldn't let his own father have a drink."

"He'll let Toby have one," said Joe, "or I'll knock his two eyes into one—smash his nose, and if that ain't enough, Toby will eat him for supper, and he's awful hungry and no gammon."

The Baream boys yelled and capered with joy at the prospect of a "mill," and in a body they followed Joe and Toby to the pump.

Such was Joe's introduction to Baream, and if the remarks he had made were not remarkable for their choiceness, it is not my fault! I can only recount them as they were spoken, and in so doing let not the hypercritical reader blame me for not introducing him to more genteel company.

CHAPTER VI.

WHICH RECOUNTS JOE'S FIGHT WITH THE KEEPER OF THE PUMP, AND HOW TOBY MADE A LITTLE WORK FOR THE TAILOR.

THE boy in charge of the pump had all the characteristics of the youthful bully depicted upon his features, perhaps the indulgence shown to the bigger boys had much to do with this, for Mr. Dothem encouraged the strongest to punish and oppress the weak, and as there is always a love of power latent in the human breast, the older lads enjoyed the opportunities thus given to give their latent passions scope.

Joe measured the lad who was sitting upon an inverted bucket when he approached with Toby, and his mental comments proved he did not care much about coming to a bout of fisticuffs with the pump guard.

"He's half a head taller than I am," Joe thought, "and his arms are precious long, so if there's a row I shall have to look out for my face, but I hope there won't be a row."

"Hallo!" cried the youth on the bucket, when he saw Joe, Toby, and the crowd of youngsters approach, "what's your little game now—who's tyke is that?"

"It's mine," Joe said, civilly, "and I have come to get him a drink of water."

"Have you? well, you can go back without it; we can't afford to give water to a lot of mongrels, we're only allowed a pint a day, if we were to have more the well might get dry, and there'd be a pretty go."

"Toby's come a long way," Joe said, "and he's awfully thirsty; I'll pump him a little drop in the bottom of that pail—I don't want you to do it."

"Look here," the master of the pump said, "you're a new boy, ain't you?"

"I am," Joe said, "I only came to-night."

"I thought so. Now look here, my name's Boggins."

"And a very nice name too," Joe said, hoping, for Toby's sake, to propitiate the tyrant. "I hope, Boggins, you will give Toby some water."

"Not a drop," said Boggins, "so be off, the whole lot of you, or I'll give you something you won't like."

Joe saw the youngest of the crowd cower and fall back at this threat, and the anger which began to burn within him rose higher at the sight.

Three or four long, gawky youths of the Boggins class came up at this moment, and one of them brought matters to a climax by saying—

"Look out, Boggins, this chap said if you didn't give his lurcher some water he'd knock your two eyes into one, so look out."

"Ah," said Boggins, "he doesn't know who I am yet, does he, Faggy?"

"No," said Faggy, "but he soon will if he doesn't take his hook."

"Now look here, short jacket," said Boggins, "you've put your legs too far through your trousers this morning."

"That's nothing to do with you," said Joe.

"P'raps not, but I'll tell you what now, you've been talking about me, but I shall let you off as you are a new 'un; now be off, and when you get safe away out of my sight ask these youngsters who I am, and they will tell you that Ned Boggins can take any three in the school—two up and the other come on: now, my pine-apple, what do you think of that?"

"About as much as I do of you, and that's not much; and as I don't want to stand jawing here all night either give me a drink of water for Toby or I'll precious soon make you."

Two or three very faint bravoes came from the youngsters in rear of Joe, and Faggy and his companions cheered ironically.

"Going to stand that?" said Faggy, "if you do you'll soon have all the young whelps down upon you. Give him his dose, and have done with it, Boggins."

"Let him go on a little further," Boggins said; "it will be all the hotter when he does get it."

"Bounce is very good," Joe said; he had now lost his temper, and felt eager for the fray, "but it don't sell here. I can't do much in the punching line, but if I can't knock all the bounce out of such a pitiful, sneaking, bullet-headed, dirty-minded varmint as you are, may I be rammed, jammed, and pounded into little bits. Blow me, now, up you get, that's my way of doing it."

Joe's way of doing it was a sudden kick at the pail, which capsized and tumbled Boggins over on his face.

The cheers from the youngsters were a little louder this time, and they rubbed their hands and looked into each others faces, delighted beyond measure at the humiliation their tyrant had sustained.

Boggins arose, red and white by turns with rage, and his passion was further augmented by Faggy saying—

"Don't hit him, he's taken all the pluck out of you."

Boggins came straight up to Joe, and delivered a straight shoulder hit at Charity's chest.

This was all Joe required; he wanted to know the extent of the other's strength, and the blow, although delivered with all the force Boggins could muster, failed to shake the sturdy street boy.

"If that's all you can do," Joe said, "you had better fetch a basket for the pieces, for I shall have to pick you up in little bits, and carry you to the graveyard."

Joe stepped nimbly aside while he was speaking, to avoid a blow in the face.

"Wait a minute, Boggins the brave, or the king of the pump," Joe said, slowly taking off his jacket and folding it up. "I always pays my tailor's bills, so can't afford to spoil my clothes. Here, Toby, take care of this. Now, my pippin, I'm ready; come on, unless you want to make your will first. You had better do that—leave that speckled nose of yours to somebody. Je-ru-sa-lem—but wouldn't they give something for it at the British Museum!"

During the delivery of this speech Joe danced around his adversary, and exhibited such a knowledge of the noble art that Boggins contented himself with acting on the defensive until he found out Joe's weak points.

The disagreeable knowledge began to dawn upon Boggins that he had a far different adversary to deal with than the half-starved lads he had been wont to thrash at his pleasure.

This knowledge made him careful; but respecting the ultimate issue of the battle he had not the least doubt but it would result in a complete victory on his side.

"One," said Joe, as he gave Boggins a rattler on the face. "Don't grin so spitefully, my pumpkin (g)."

Joe showed a little bad taste in attempting a pun, but there is a consolation in the knowledge that he will know better when he gets older.

The rattler caused Boggins to lose all his caution, for he went in at it with both hands, and

Joe too, nothing lotn, struck and parried, parried and struck, until they were both tired.

The combatants were not without seconds. Faggy did the needful for Boggins, and Tommy Nimblejaws officiated for Joe.

The tussle had been a sharp one, so Joe was not at all sorry to rest for a few seconds on the angular knee held out by Nimblejaws.

"You're an out-and-outer at a slog," Tommy whispered to Joe; "but take my advice and use your feet a little more, keep him on the move and punch his long ears when you get a chance. I had a turn up with him about a month ago, and only lost it because I didn't do what I am now telling you."

"All right," said Joe; "I'll follow your advice, but I say while the next round is going on, get Toby a drink."

"Right, my Bendigo, go in and win."

"Time," one of the big ones called out, and the lads faced each other again.

There was a great deal of head punching in the round that followed, for Boggins was determined to polish Joe off at once, and Joe, in his eagerness to punish his adversary, forgot all about his friend's advice, for the upshot was that Boggins landed him one on the forehead, down Joe went at full length.

"Who want's the basket now?" said Boggins's supporters, derisively; "be careful of the bones, Tommy."

Nimblejaws took no notice, but helped his "man" to rise, and whispered—

"Hurt?"

"No," Joe said, "that served me right, but I'll nail him the next time he tries that dodge."

The youngsters who had hoped a champion had arrived at Baream who would protect them from Boggins's tyranny, were very quiet when they saw Joe's horizontal position, and many a little heart quaked at the prospect of the thrashings in store for them should Joe be defeated.

"Use your legs, Charity," whispered Nimblejaws, " and keep cool. Now, off you go."

The combatants came up to the scratch at the word time; but Joe kept his adversary at arm's length, and in so doing led him half way round the ring.

"Finish him off," said Faggy; "he's getting down in the mouth. Make room for him there, he wants to bolt."

Joe suddenly pauses, advances, and strikes out with his left. Boggins parries, and returns with his right, hoping it will be as effective as the last.

Charity took a step to the right, and evaded the blow, and before Boggins could recover his balance Joe sprang upon him, passed his left arm round the back of Boggin's neck, twisted that astonished youth half round, and placed his head in chancery.

Joe's grip was like a vice, and his right hand went to work upon Boggin's face with a will

At this sight the small boys, who had quaked but a moment before, yelled with delight, and Toby joined in with his bark, for he understood all about the noble art.

The Boggins faction take a different view of the case; they see their man getting awfully punished and unable to protect himself, so they raise a cry of—

"Foul, foul—no hugging—let him go!"

Joe only replies to their clamour by hammering away all the harder at Boggins's nose, and Tommy Nimblejaws yells and capers about with as much vivacity as a Red Indian when performing the war dance.

Faggy detects Nimblejaws at his demonstrations of joy, and stepping over to that hopeful youth gives him a blow in the side which stops his dancing and his crowing.

"Take that," says Faggy, "and learn to behave yourself."

Nimblejaws gave a gulp, regained his breath, and landed both hands on Faggy's face, and the latter nothing loth returned the blows, so a second contest went on in the rear of Charity and Boggins, a circumstance they were both ignorant of, the one too busy using his right hand, and the other wriggling about like an eel being skinned, to escape from the grip of Joe's arm.

Boggins's face was not pleasant to look upon at this stage of the proceedings, but Joe was remorseless, he felt much of his future comfort at Baream depended upon the issue of the fight, and he determined to compel his adversary to call out for quarter.

"Own you are licked," he said punching away at the head as he spoke, "give in or I'll knock your handsome nose as flat as a flounder—own you are licked, my nice Boggins."

Boggins punched away at Joe's back with his right, and tried all in his power to reach his adversary's face with his left, but Charity was too careful, he did not mind the drumming at his back, he could take any amount of that he said, and rather liked it.

"Let me go," said Boggins, "or it will be the worse for you when I do get away."

"Which," Joe said, "will not be until I have knocked you into the middle of the week after next."

Let him go," shouted Boggins's friends, "let him go."

"Pull his arm away," shouted Boggins, "he's choking me."

JOE HEADS THE REBELLION AT BAREAM HALL.

Three of the big lads responded to Boggins's cry, and came to Joe, one seized his left arm, and another caught him by the hair of the head, and the third squared up in front of him, and gave Joe three or four taps on the nose.

The small boys were afraid to interfere beyond calling out:

"Shame, shame! Fair play!"

The seconds were of course too busy with their own little affair to help their principals; so poor Joe, who did not desist from punching Boggins, had to endure his hair being pulled out by the roots, his arm pinched black and blue, and his nose not at all improved by the performance of the gentleman in front.

"Cowards!" Joe said. "What! four to one? Come and help, some of you young beggars."

The young beggars were too much afraid, so they thrust their hands deeper into their pockets, fearing the sight of a naked hand would be construed by the big tyrants as a challenge to fight.

"I can't stand any more of this," said Joe, writhing with pain ; "now look here, let me alone or I'll call somebody that will make you ; you won't, eh ? here dog—seize 'em, Toby—seize 'em !"

Toby had been watching the scramble evidently in some doubt whether the increase in the number of his master's antagonists was not a part of the programme, but when he heard his master's voice he quite understood the mistake he had made.

Toby did his best to rectify it; the first of Joe's extra assailants was the youth who seemed bent upon trying how long the human hair was capable of being tugged at without coming out at the roots.

This youth Toby seized by the collar and tore the back clean out of his jacket, waistcoat, and shirt.

The experimenter upon Joe's scalp gave a howl, picked up the remnants of his clothing, and fled, fully persuaded the dog was after him open-mouthed.

The gentleman who was pinching Joe's arm, in the attempt to compel him to release the head of Boggins, next felt Toby's wrath.

The dog fixed his teeth not only through the cloth that covered the pincher's legs, but in the flesh, and he soon had employment sufficient in rubbing the affected part and giving vent to his feelings in a prolonged note in altissimo.

The youth that was operating upon Joe's nose wisely desisted from his interesting occupation, and moved out of the way in the hope that Toby had not seen his purpose, but Toby was a cunning dog, he knew the whole of Joe's assailants, and was about to give chase to this one when a cry arose—

"Old Nipguts ; old Nipguts is coming !"

The old gentleman who bore this exceedingly vulgar epithet made his appearance, cane in hand, followed by Mr. Sivins.

Faggy and Nimblejaws desisted from their encounter, and slunk away in a manner they hoped would enable them to pass unnoticed.

Joe took no notice of Mr. Dothem, sen., while he kept up the punching, and said—

"Give in, or I'll smash you ; now you're licked off your perch."

"I give in," said Boggins, " don't choke me."

"He gives in !" shouted Joe, triumphantly, He—oh, what's up?"

His query was addressed to Mr. Dothem, who caught Joe by the arm and drew him from Boggins; who stood the picture of misery and grief.

"What's the meaning of this," said Mr. Dothem, " here at the very moment when the bell is ringing for evening prayers, I find two Christian lads with bloodstained hands and faces? Tell me, sir, what caused you to behave in that manner ?"

"Put that cane down, then," Joe said, " and I'll tell you all about it."

The principal had by mere force of habit held the heavy cane uplifted, he had no intention of using it before Mr. Sivins, so he lowered the instrument of punishment, and said—

"I shall not chastise you now, and your after punishment will depend upon the aspect of this very serious infringement of the rules of this establishment. Now, sir ?"

"Well," said Joe, " the long and short of it is, this fellow, this mouldy, mean-spirited wretch, wouldn't give Toby a drink of water, and because I asked him a second time, he talked about knocking me into the middle of next month, so I upset him, and we had a slog ; and there he is, ask him, and if he tells a lie, I'll give him worse than he's got now. I——"

"Hush ! hush ! I can't allow this sort of thing. We shall have to tame you, young gentleman. Now, Boggins, what have you to say ?"

"He wanted some water for his mongrel, sir, and because I wouldn't give it him he kicked me off the pail I was sitting on, and of course—of course—I—I"—

"You struck him. Is that it ?"

"Yes, sir."

"You were to blame, much to blame. Your proper course would have been to have made a report to me, and I would have explained the rules of this establishment to Master Joseph Chudleigh Cholmondeley."

"Crikey," whispered a small boy to his neighbour ; "there's a name."

"Yes, sir," Bogging said, " I thought to have done so ; but while I was gone he would have taken water from the pump."

"There's no mistake about that," said Joe. "I should have been all there at that fun."

Mr. Dothem reflected for a few moments, then he said—

"The bell has rung for prayers. Go to the dining-hall at once, and you who have lifted your hands against each other, ask for forgiveness.

The boys went towards the dining-hall, and as they filed through Toby would have followed Joe, but the poetic Samuel gave him a kick, and Toby, seeing he was not wanted, stayed outside.

Joe saw the action, and making straight towards the magnificent, said—

"Look here, don't you do that again, or there"l be a row."

"In your place, sir," Samuel said, imperatively: "and keep a civil tongue in your head."

"I'll do you a kindness," thought Joe, "before I've been long here. So make no error about that, my sallow-faced, ginger-waisted pup."

Mr. Dothem came in, and Samuel called out "Silence," and the elder hypocrite added another item in the black book by affecting a religious fervour as he snuffled out the prayers for the evening.

CHAPTER VII.

MR. SIVINS TAKES HIS DEPARTURE—SAMUEL THE POETIC RECITES THE FIRST VERSE OF HIS GREAT POEM—THE OPINION OF THE FAMILY RESPECTING THE POEM—CHARITY JOE AND HIS DOG TOBY.

AFTER prayers, the amiable Dothem family assembled in the best furnished room in the old mansion, with Mr. Sivins as their guest.

"I've just half an hour to stay," said Mr. Sivins, referring to his silver-gilt watch, for Mr. Sivins thought himself above wearing a plain silver timekeeper; he fondly imagined the gilding would pass for gold, and in this, as in many other things, he showed his snobbish taste. "Now, my friend Dothem, you ought to keep a trap for the service of taking the guardians and relatives to the railway station; it would look well."

"I have thought of so doing," said Mr. Dothem, "for it would be so useful, not only for business purposes, but for the girls."

"Ah!" sighed Sylvia the romantic. "How pleasant it would be to drive among the hedgerows lined with hawthorn blossoms, and mossy banks covered with violets and wild thyme."

"And," said Deborah the strongly romantic, "what joy it would be to go to the fields when the reapers are gathering the hay, and to romp among the haycocks. Oh, so delightful!"

"How useful," said Mrs. Dothem, "the horse and shay would be for me to go to market and buy from the country people, instead of being swindled as I am now."

"To the lovers of solitude, to the poetic mind," said Samuel, jun., "how delicious, how agreeable it would be to drive far away from the haunts of men, and seek a lonely spot to commune with nature in her loneliness and loveliness."

"It would be devilish useful just now," said the matter-of-fact Mr. Sivins, "to drive me to the station."

"All this may come to pass," said Mr. Dothem, "if you will have a little patience—that's all that is required. Come, Sivins, a glass before you go. What will you take?"

"A drop of whisky and water, as hot as flames; that's the stuff for me."

"Sylvia, my dear, will you join us?"

"Yes, papa, but my drink must be as cool as the zephyr's wing. Oh, would that in these degenerated days one could slake their thirst in the nectar such as the gods of Homer drank."

"A little lemonade and sherry," suggested Dothem, pére; it is about the coolest thing I can recommend."

"That will do," sighed Sylvia; "but I should prefer the dew gathered from the flowers——"

"Don't be silly, Syl," said Deb; "why don't you drink a good glass of beer? that's the stuff to do you good."

"Oh, Deborah, how can you say such things before this gentleman?"

"Mrs. Dothem," said Mr. D., "will, of course, take the usual?"

"The usual," said Mrs. Dothem; "but I will have it warm and a little lemon."

"Samuel, my dear boy, as this is the anniversary of the opening of our school, and to the success of which you have done so much, I must ask you to join us. I know the sacrifice will be great for your lofty mind to descend from Mount Parnassus to the mere enjoyment of the appetite. What shall I bring for you?"

Samuel ran his fingers through his hair, struck an attitude, glanced down at his broomstick leg, then drawled—

"I will take a glass of wine, but it must be good; bad wine is such an infliction.

Mr. Sivins had stood the peculiarities of the family without smiling, but when the silly fellow made this speech, the agent was compelled to turn his face towards the window and indulge in a quiet laugh.

Little wonder he did so, for he knew the antecedents of the Dothem family, and remembered the time when a glass of cold fourpenny would have been a treat to Samuel, junior.

"Well," thought Mr. Sivins, "the world is coming to something. Here's an empty-headed fool who a year or two since was an errand boy, and now he——I beg pardon."

The apology was addressed to Mr. Dothem, who from the interior of a large closet kept up the conversation by saying—

"I'm afraid, friend Sivins, I shall have a little difficulty with the lad you have brought here."

"He's a bold, high-spirited fellow," said Mr. Sivins; "but I have no doubt you will be able to tame him."

"I shall try," said Mr. Dotham, "and the success, I have not the least hesitation in saying, will be complete. We tame 'em here, eh, Samuel, my boy?"

"We do," said Samuel, twisting a very brassy-looking watchguard, "and we can do it."

Mr. Sivins gallantly drank to the ladies, and Mrs. Dothem, with the refinement of a well-bred lady, responded by raising her glass and saying—

"Here's to your very good health, sir."

"The school," said Mr. Dothem, rising, "the school, and success to it. I drink also to the worthy monitor, my talented son Samuel, to the lady superintendent, to the wardrobe keeper, my dear Sylvia, and the useful assistant, my youngest child, the gentle Deborah!"

Mr. Sivins and the family honoured the toast in a becoming manner, and Mrs. Dothem wound up by raising her glass and saying—

"Here's jolly good luck to the whole lot!"

"Now," said Mr. Sivins, "I must be off. Good bye, all of you. Ladies, your humble servant; Dothem, my friend, I hope to see you again soon. Possibly I may find a pupil or two; if so, shall receive the pleasure of a visit."

"'Come when you will,' as the song says," responded Mr. Dothem, "'and you'll find there's always a welcome for thee.'"

The whole family saw Mr. Dothem to the door, and wished him God speed and a safe return; and when he passed through the entrance gates, Sylvia the romantic said—

"What a shocking vulgar man, papa. I saw him turn away and laugh when you were proposing the health of the school."

"Certainly, said Mr. Dothem, "my friend Sivins is not the best-bred man in the world; but he is useful, my dear, and another thing, it would not do for me to quarrel with him."

The family went back to the sitting-room, and Mrs. D., mixing herself a glass of the usual, soon fell asleep, and slept the sleep of the good, until she was awakened by her son, the tape-waisted, —the vulgar boys in the school called him narrow-back Sam.

"Mother," he said, "I want you to keep wake for a few minutes."

"Mrs. Dothem opened her eyes, looked at the empty glass before her, then said a little snappishly—

"What do you want now?"

"'I am about to read a few lines of my poem," Samuel said, with an air of importance befitting the occasion; "and as I wish to get as many opinions as possible upon its merits, it is but natural that I should wish yours."

"Poem,—stuff," said Mrs. Dothem,—"rubbish. Can't earn your salt by it."

"Mrs. Dothem," said Mr. D. severely, "a few ds like that has often daunted many a bril-

liant genius. Pray be careful, Mrs. D., for Samuel is like all great geniuses, very sensitive."

"Mix me another glass, and don't be a fool, D."

The amiable principal of Baream Hall perfectly understood the mood his gentle partner was in—the usual mood, by the way, after a few glasses of the regular. Like a prudent general, he refrained from any attack while the lady had her artillery (tongue) ready, and too powerful for him.

"Come, Samuel," he said, "take another glass, it will steady your nerves after the long study you have had. You don't find it an infliction, I hope."

"Well, no, no—it's pretty good."

The tone, the attitude, and the play of the fingers as this answer was given must be imagined, for I cannot find words to convey the just impression upon the reader's mind.

Having pushed his dark hair back from his forehead, Samuel the poetic drew from his pocket the manuscript poem.

"The subject I have chosen for my first poem," said Samuel, spreading the paper out before him, "is an episode depicted by Harrison Ainsworth in his account of the madman who took a blazing cresset to the top of old St. Paul's, and waved it about until the flames devoured him."

"An historical subject," said Dothem senior, "your choice does you credit, my boy, for at present we are inundated with senseless stuff about love, and bright eyes, and all that sort of thing."

"So I thought when I chose the subject; another thing, father, I have placed it in the plainest possible language, so that the very poorest people will be able to understand the meaning of true poetry. Now this is how it begins:

"'Up the dome, higher and higher,
    He went,
    With his cresset of fire,
    And glared around with his eyes so fierce.'"

"What do you think of that for a beginning?"

"Very well, indeed," said Mr. Dothem; "but I think you might with advantage substitute another word for glare, for you see glare really means a clear dazzling light—to look with fierce piercing eyes. Now, I should certainly say a person looking at you with fierce piercing eyes would be different to another who glared around; the same as the madman in your poem; besides, the word is so common—besides, I am almost sure the word in its proper use would be applied to signify a blaze, a flare, a radiation, as the re-

"LOOKEE! THAT BE OLD HUNTER, THEY BE YOUNG 'UNS, AND THAT BE WOLF."

flection of a fire such as we often see in the sky when there is a fire."

"Perhaps it would be better," said Samuel, "I will think it over."

"I'm sure," Sylv'a said, "the words are beautifully placed, and so expressive—now what can be clearer than the opening, where it explains the man going up the dome—'higher and higher,'—there you have it all before you, as it were—don't you think so, Deb?"

There was a mischievous smile upon Deb's round face, as she answered—

"Yes, Sylvia, dear, I think it most beautiful, and it will look so much better in print. What do you mean to call it, Samuel?—it ought to have a taking title.

"It's merely, you know," said the tremendous, "one of the book of poems I mean to write. I was thinking of calling the volume "The People's Book of Poems."

"That will look lovely," said Sylvia; "all done in beautiful gold letters, upon a pretty blue cover."

"Very nice, indeed!" said Deborah; "of

course you intend to put a nice name on the inside for yourself?"

"Yes, yes, of course, I must do that, because all literary gentlemen nearly do it; or else we should see more Browns, Jones, and Robinsons as authors. Now, I was thinking Horatio Byron St. James de Montmorency would sound well."

"Very well, indeed," said Deborah; "but it would require a whole page of the book to put it on."

"Of course," said Samuel; "it will be easy enough to find a name when the book is ready for the press."

"Suppose," Deborah said, "you should not be able to get any one to publish your book after all the trouble you have taken."

"Samuel has nothing to fear upon that score," said Mr. Dothem; "publishers will only be too glad to take the manuscripts when they perceive the fire that is in the verses. Now, you girls, read a part. Deb can't you see the fire of genius that shows itself in every line?"

"It is beautiful," said Sylvia, "really beautiful."

"Yes," said Deborah, drily; "there is plenty of fire."

Samuel the sensitive did not fail to notice the way in which Deb uttered these words, and fearing a roasting from his sister, he folded the precious manuscript and put it in his coat pocket, at the same time changing the conversation by saying—

"By-the-bye, father, what boy is that brought here this evening?"

"He was brought by Mr. Sivins."

"Oh, he seems pretty free with his tongue, for he had the assurance to be impertinent to me when I kicked that brute he has brought with him."

"We will soon take that out of him, Samuel; very soon."

"Surely you will not allow that dog to remain here?"

"Decidedly not. I have already arranged that with Mr. Sivins. A dose of arsenic will do the needful for the mongrel."

"I wonder Mr. Sivins brought him here with the boy?"

"There was no choice left him," said Mr. Dothem; "the wilful young scamp would not come without the mongrel. Now the brute has already begun his mischief by tearing three or four of the boys' clothes."

"I heard something about it. There has been a fight, hasn't there, between this new boy and Boggins?"

"There has," said Mr. Dothem, "and I am not sorry, in one sense, that Boggins has received

a thrashing, for owing to the leniency with which we have been obliged for certain reasons to treat the gawky fellow, he began to presume upon it."

"Is this young whelp any relation to Mr. Sivins?"

"No, Samuel; if he were, I would not have taken him. Sivins is a very cunning fellow; now, I have no doubt he receives a very handsome allowance for keeping the lad, which allowance I mean to possess, if possible."

"But how will you find out the boy's friends?"

"I have not thought the matter over yet, but I have no doubt but I shall be able to manage it."

"No more, thank you, Mr. D.," muttered Mrs. Dothem in her sleep; "poetry—rubbish—I say —stuff."

Mr. Dothem quietly cleared the table of the bottles, and Samuel looked anything but pleased at the maternal criticism.

"Now," said Mr. Dothem, "it is time you went your rounds, Samuel. Mind you try and find out the young thief who has so long baffled us, for there were no less than four candle-ends stolen out of the lanthorn last night."

CHAPTER VIII.

JOE'S FIRST TURN AT SCOUTING—WHAT HE HEARD, AND WHAT HE RESOLVED UPON—A BOUNTEOUS SUPPER—CONSTERNATION OF THE DOTHEM FAMILY.

BEFORE Joe retired to the small bed, he made a snug corner for Toby in the disused stable. He bade his four-footed friend remain there until the morning; then, guided by Tommy Nimblejaws, he went to his chamber, and feeling a little strange respecting the manners and customs of the Bareamites, he sat on the side of his palliasse, and listened to the conversation that was going on when he entered.

"Who's turn is it to scout to-night?" a pale-faced little fellow asked. "Aint it yours, Nimblejaws?"

"No," Tommy promptly answered. "I scouted the night before last, and was nearly nailed by Sammy Narrowback."

"You're a good scout, you are, Tommy," said another lad approvingly. "We always gets more the night you scout. We got beer once, we did."

The little fellow smacked his lips at the recollection, and gazed at Tommy in silent admiration.

"Well, I ain't so bad as some," Nimblejaws modestly responded. "Some that I could name only turns up with a raw turnip or carrot—a thing as isn't good for suppers."

"It's as good as I could get," said a lad sitting up in bed, and drawing his knees up to his chin, "and if you'd been chased as I was by old Mother Skinflint, you would have been glad to have got away without even a raw turnip."

"All right, Jack Shaw," said Nimblejaws. "I didn't mean to throw off about you, for you are an out-and-out scout. It was you who first got up the dodge of finding the candle-ends before they were lost. But that ain't it. No, what we want to know is, who's for scout to-night?"

"It's the bed next to yours, Tommy," said young Shaw, "but it ain't hardly fair to set a new hand on the first night he comes."

"No," said Tommy Nimblejaws, "not by no means, but as I've taken a fancy to Joe, I'll do his turn so as to keep the scouting regular."

Joe had been swinging his legs to and fro during the conversation, but when he found it became personal he said—

"Look here, I don't exactly know what this scouting means, but if Tommy will explain it to me, I'll go like a bird."

"You'd better not," said Tommy; "you don't know your way about here yet."

"Leave me alone for that," said Joe, "I'll find my way back, no fear, so tell us what this scouting means."

"Well, it's just this," said Tommy, "we're regularly half starved here, and if we say anything about it, old Nipguts finds an excuse to send those who complain for twelve hours' punishment in a dark cellar, and no grub all the time. I had it once; it was awful, and no mistake."

"Should think it must be," said Joe; "if he tries it on with me, I'll jolly soon slope from this crib."

"That's what lots of us would do," said Nimblejaws, "but we don't get the chance without we climbed up the high wall, and then the sharp glass on the top!—my eyes! why it makes the water run down your back to look up at it, and fancy you are sitting there."

"I'd chance that," said Joe. "Never mind talking about it, let's hear all about the scouting."

"Well, you know," said Nimblejaws, "of course, as we are all pretty nigh starved, we gets awful hungry about this time, so, to get something to eat, we have planned it so that one of us shall go and look everywhere for what we can get."

"Do you always get something?"

"Always," said Tommy, with a grimace. Sometimes we gets more than we wants, but that's when Old Nip catches any of us out of our rooms after the candles have been put out——"

"But about the——"

"Wait a minute, and I'll tell you. Well, sometimes old Mother Skinflint has too much of the gin and water than is good for her, she leaves the cupboard door open where the grub is——"

"But that ain't often," remarked young Shaw, "I wish it was."

"Then," Tommy said, "the scout gets as much as he can carry, and though it's soon found out, we has it all demolished long before old Nip or his shadder of a son can get up to our room, even if they come up straight, which they don't, because, of course, there is other rooms besides this."

"Ah!" said young Shaw, "you should have seen old Nip and his cub the last time there was three loaves collared, they went down on their hands and knees to see if there was any crumbs on the floor; but there wasn't, was there, Nimblejaws?"

"Should say not," said Tommy. "We were too wide-a-wake for that, we broke up the loaves over one of our rugs, and when we heard 'em coming up, the rug was soon out of sight."

"I shall certainly learn something here," thought Joe; "this, I suppose, is an illustration of what old Siv used to call the learning that is begotten of cruelty (then aloud)—go on, Tommy, you did em fine that time,"

"Should say we did, too; there was one Bob Allen found the beer cellar door open, and didn't we have a guzzle, that's all; but it made us ill, it did. It's awful swankey, Joe, we only have it once a week."

"Enough, too, I should say," said Joe, "if it is anything like the stuff old Siv used to keep for his friends; if they had one taste they didn't want another. He was a bad 'un was old Siv; you should have seen him grin when anyone he asked to have a glass pulled a face like the head of an old fiddle when they tasted his swipes. But go on, Tommy."

"Right you are, my flower," answered Nimblejaws, "I ain't told you about the candles, have I, Joe?"

"Not yet."

"On dark nights, you know," Tommy said, "we has a little bit of candle to go to bed by; but bless you, Old Nip only allows us about two minutes, and sometimes we want a light, for it's awful dark here in the winter, I can tell you. So when we can't sleep, a light is a sort of company, you know."

"Of course," assented Joe.

"That's what we all thought, so we made it up when the shadder comes to take away the little bits of candle, which he does every night, and puts 'em in a tin box which he leaves outside the door, one of us was to hide in the passage, and while he takes the candle from one room the chap that's in hiding collars two pieces. So you see we gets a light after all."

"I see," said Joe. "But are all the rooms working upon the same system as this?"

"No," Nimblejaws answered, "ours is the biggest lot next to Boggins's room, and Old Nip allows them half a candle, and sometimes bread and cheese every night, because they spy upon all the young 'uns in the school. We calls 'em Nip's bullies."

"I understand," said Joe.

"And the little 'uns in the other rooms, you know," Nimblejaws said, "is afraid to go on the scout at night; besides I don't think they know anything about it. Of course we ain't going to tell them, for one secret is quite enough out here at once."

"So I should think. Well, what's the first thing to be done?" Joe asked; "I daresay I shall find the way there, although it is my first time."

"You're an out-and-outer," Tommy said, "a real plucky one, and no mistake, so there's no fear but you will bring something in, although it is your first time. But where's your tyke?"

"I put him in the stable."

"That's all right—he'll do there. Now, look here, the first thing you must do is to go quietly to old Nip's room, and listen quietly at the keyhole——"

"What for? I don't——"

"It's all right," said Nimblejaws; "'cos, if you don't do that, how are you to know whether they are all in the room where they sits of a evening?"

"I understand," said Joe; "if they are not all there, what then?"

"Why, you must come back and wait till they are, 'cos if they ain't there, they are most sure to be about the kitchen, or where the vegetables grow."

"Suppose they are all in the room?"

"Then," said Tommy, "go down to the kitchen; that's the window, just behind the pump, where you licked Boggins."

"All right," said Joe; I know my book now, and if there's anything to be lifted you'll soon see it here."

"Hope we shall; look here, Joe, before you go, don't forget to keep out of the way of the fellows in Boggins's room, for if they catch you they'll make you cry out pen and ink—make no mistake about it."

"I shan't forget," said Joe; "but at the same time I shall be there when they do it, and I shan't want a three dip to find my way to the chap's nose as first interferes with me."

"He's all there and no mistake," said Nimblejaws, when Joe left the room; "and old Nip will try and come the soft over him to get him on his side; but I don't think Charity will go, for he ain't got a bit of the sneak about him."

"No," assented young Shaw: "and can't he slog, that's all!"

"He can," said Bob Allen, "and the licking he gave that bully of a Boggins will bring all of 'em in Boggins's room down upon us."

"Yes," Nimblejaws said, "they're sure to be down upon us, but if all was of my mind, there would be a little alteration here, not only with the big fellows, but with Old Nip and his son."

"What would you do, Nimblejaws?"

"I've been thinking over lots of things since I came here, and that's nigh upon six months, and when I came I was a bigger chap than I am now."

"So was I," was the general response.

"And no wonder," said Tommy, "for although I had a brute of a mother-in-law, she used to give me plenty of grub, and she wasn't a brute neither until she got married after my father died, it was the man as used to set her on; for I've often heard him say—'The brat is not yours, why should you keep him here?' I suppose she thought so too after he'd said so lots of times, for she began to whop me, and tried to make me run away; but I couldn't do that, because I'd nowhere to go to. I stood all the whoppings; but they weren't half so bad as old Snip has given me; but he'd better drop it, and so had his shadder, the yellow-faced Samuel."

"But what could you do, Nimblejaws—you ain't a man yet?" said Bob Allen. "I feels it is precious hard to be starved and kicked as we are because we ain't got no fathers and mothers."

One of the boys burst into tears and sobbed—

"I had a mother once, and if she'd a lived I know I wouldn't have been here."

"Never mind, Charley," said Nimblejaws; "it ain't for life, unless we are starved to death, and that won't be till the scouting is found out."

"I'm so hungry now," said a little fellow, "old Nip's stopped my dinner and tea, because I said I was ill, and I was ill too this morning; I felt burning like, all over."

A glance at the speaker's face would have told the cause of that burning sensation, for the boy was in a consumption, and the disease was being accelerated by the meagre diet and cruel punishment in vogue at Baream Hall.

"I was ill once," said another boy, "and old

mother Nip gave me a cup full of bitter stuff, and old Nip said I had been over feeding myself, so he stopped my breakfast; I'd sooner die like poor Phil Carter did than say I was ill again."

So the conversation continued, as the poor boys one by one spoke of the cruel treatment they had endured since they came to Baream.

There was no noisy romping, no jolly stories told of the holidays, as in other schools, no pleasant anticipations of coming vacations, no prospects of hampers sent by loving parents, no anticipations of cricket or football, for Mr. Dothem would not allow any exercise likely to expand the frames of his victims; for he justly argued boisterous amusements would make them feel weak and hungry. Heaven knows they were both already.

As the conversation continued sharp eyes were turned towards the door, and the hope was strong within many a hungry frame that Joe would succeed in his mission.

There was a little difficulty experienced by Joe in finding his way among the wide corridors to the oaken stairs that led to the lower part of the old mansion.

When he reached the large hall he took his boots off, and went on tiptoe towards the room occupied by the Dothem family.

Luckily for Toby, Joe placed his ear to the keyhole at the time he was the subject of conversation, and when he heard the plans of Mr. Dothem respecting himself, he clasped his hands tightly, and with difficulty restrained himself from entering the room and giving Mr. Dothem a specimen of his powers of language.

"Poison Toby, will he?" Joe thought as he rose from his knees; "and find out the old gentleman as dubs up the coin for my keep; he won't do neither, I'll take my davey. This crib won't suit me; I shall have to give notice to quit; but I don't go before I've had a turn up with that yellow-faced pup; and if there's a large stone handy perhaps old Nipgut's head won't be any the better for it. As for the old woman—there's only one thing I should like to do for her, and that's to turpentine her clothes then set 'em on fire."

The conversation with the boys upstairs, and the further revelations he overheard when kneeling outside the door, fully enlightened Joe's mind respecting the advantages to be derived from a long sojourn at Baream.

"It's worse than the workus," he thought as he leaned over the kitchen stairs; "ten times worse, and as for that old Siv, he ought to be burked for bringing me here. I knew it all along that he didn't keep me out of charity; and as I ain't going to have two rascals—thieves—worse,

that they are, than the highwaymen as comes out in penny numbers every week. Old Siv is a rank bad 'un, but——"

Here Joe slipped down the three last stairs.

"I know what I'll do," he resumed, when he found his feet again; "I'll slope, and tramp all over London but I'll find the old fellow (and I should know him again, too), and I'll ask him to give me all the coin, and not let two such thieves as old Siv and this one have it between them; here's the kitchen, and as I don't care that"—Joe snapped his fingers—"for the whole lot of them here, if the cupboard door is not open I'll open it and give the poor little chaps in my room a good feed for once. Poison Toby, will he? and keep me until he finds out the old gent? but he won't though, or my name's not Joe."

The cupboard was locked, but the wood-work was old and worm-eaten, and Joe's clasp knife was strong and sharp.

"That beats the old locksmith," said Joe, as he cut the lock out, "who came to open old Siv's box; I know it aint right for me to do this, and I wouldn't do it to anyone else, but this gang here is worse than these, for they takes money for the boys' keep, and starves 'em—poison Toby, will you?—out you come."

Joe took the lock out and then the door opened. Luckily for the hungry boys it was the private store for the use of the Dothem family; had Joe opened the cupboard on the other side of the fireplace he would have found bags of oatmeal, a heap of potatoes, and a scraggy neck of mutton (uncooked).

"Poison Toby," muttered Joe, "will you?—well it won't be with any of this cold meat, I know, and none of you won't have too much supper to-night—let's see, a piece of cold beef, half a ham, part of a cold fowl, and a pie—currant pie, too—I like currant pie, so as they haven't asked me to have any supper I'll invite myself—two half quartern loaves and a jar of pickles—now how can I carry them—I wonder if they keep baskets here."

The bright harvest moon streamed through the quaint old windows and enabled Joe to see all the large kitchen contained, and under the table to his joy he found a half sieve.

"Just the ticket," said Joe, "this will carry the lot to rights."

The sieve was nearly full when Joe hoisted it upon his shoulder, for he had made a clean sweep, as he termed it, but before he left he closed the door and put the lock back in its place, and surveying it with a grin upon his features, he said:

"I should like to see old Mother Skinflint when she comes to the cupboard; talk about old

Mother Hubbard in the story book, she's nothing to the face old Skinflint will pull when she finds the grub gone."

Joe's appearance in the room was hailed with joy, and the hungry lads crowded round the basket.

"Pitch in," said Joe, "here's a knife; skin the bones, and I'll take 'em down to Toby."

"You're a prince, you are," said Nimblejaws—a regular out-and-outer—first-class, and no mistake. Here's a feed!"

Tears of joy trickled down more than one pale, pinched face, as the boys devoured the good things Joe had promised.

"Turn out the pie," said Joe, "and I will take the dish and the basket, and put them outside the bullies' door."

Joe did not forget himself during the operation of taking the meat from the bones and turning out the pie, for his jaws were at work as much as the hungriest there.

It did not occupy many minutes for twenty famished lads to consume the provisions, but before they had picked the last bone, the half-sieve was placed between the rooms occupied by the bullies and the youngest boys. This done, Joe took the bones to Toby; and as he patted the dog's shaggy head, he said:

"Watch 'em, Toby; watch 'em, boy. Don't let 'em take your bones away."

Toby wagged his tail, and Joe knew it would not be the best thing in the world for Mr. Dothem or his wasp-waisted son to come near the dog before he had finished crunching up the bones.

When Joe returned to his room, Nimblejaws was shaking one of the rugs out of the window.

"There were a few crumbs on it," he said to Joe, "but long before old Nip is up, the fowls will have eaten them."

"Does he keep fowls? Joe asked.

"Yes, a lot, and we have one sometimes, if one of 'em dies of anything, but the others he keeps for himself."

"Does he?"

Joe said something else not polite enough to be written in these pages, as he thought of Toby's prospective fate.

"If I don't poison every one of the blessed roosters," Joe thought, "I'm not here. Poison Toby will, he?"

"Look here," said Nimblejaws, "Narrowback will go his rounds directly, so keep your mouth shut, or else begin grumbling about being hungry."

"Does he come in?" Joe asked.

"No," answered Nimblejaws, "but we always know when he is listening outside, for the latch of the door sticks out a good way, and he's sure to knock his nose against it."

"But how does he collect the candles?"

"We don't have any yet, it's only the bullies that have a light allowed this time of—— Hush, there he is."

The latch clicked as Tommy spoke, and Joe drew out one of the straws from an opening in his bed-tick, and crept on all fours to the door.

His aim was good, for when he thrust the straw through the hole that allowed the latch to move up and down, a suppressed howl was heard, then a pair of slippered feet shuffling along the long corridor.

The boys executed a dance of joy at the success of Joe's dodge, and Nimblejaws said—

"That serves him right; he's always prying about and listening. I hope it went in his eye."

"So do I," said Joe. "Look here, if he comes to-morrow night, let's have a piece of wire; that's the thing for him."

"They have supper when the shadder goes back," said Bob Allen, "so let's get into bed, in case old Nip comes up."

The suggestion was acted upon, and soon the lads were listening, not without certain feelings of dread, for the sound of any footsteps.

"What's the matter with your eye, Samuel?" said Mr. Dothem, when his son entered the room, holding a pockethandkerchief to his right eye, "come to the light and I'll examine it."

"One of the whelps in No. 9 room," said Samuel, "thrust a piece of wire or a sharp pin through the door just as I was stooping down to——"

The door was thrust open at this moment, and Mrs. Dothem staggered in, and when she reached the table she clung to it for support, and gasped—

"We have been robbed, Mr. Dothem, plundered. There's every blessed thing gone from the larder, and the lock cut out of the door."

Mr. Dothem snatched the poker from the fender. Samuel struck an attitude, and Sylvia and Deborah clung to each other as they exclaimed—

"There must be robbers in the house. None of the boys dare do this."

"Follow me," said Mr. Dothem, flourishing the poker, "I will soon find them; come on, Samuel."

The amiable family went in a body to the scene of the diabolical outrage, Mrs. D. bringing up the rear, for she had stayed behind for a moment to fortify herself with a drop from the long-necked bottle that contained her usual stimulant.

CHAPTER IX.

MR. DOTHEM HOLDS OUT MANY INDUCEMENTS TO
JOE—SAMUEL TRIES HOW MUCH PULLING JOE'S
EAR WILL STAND, AND GETS SOMETHING FOR HIS
TROUBLE—JOE CARRIES THE POISONED DISH FOR
TOBY, BUT HALTS ON THE WAY.

BEFORE the summer sun could make much impression upon the damp soil around Baream Hall the boys in Joe's room were aroused by a thumping upon the door, and the dulcet voice of Mrs. Dothem calling out—

" Now, then, you Joseph Cholmondeley, get up, and look sharp about it, or I'll come and fetch you."

" All right," said Joe, jumping out of bed, " I'll be down in less than no time."

" What's up?" asked Nimblejaws." " Why it can't be four o'clock yet?"

" It's all right," Joe said ; " I'm to do the odd jobs for Toby's keep and lodging. If I don't do 'em before school-time, I shan't afterwards, I expect."

Joe found the lady at the end of the corridor, and by the expression of her face he mentally augured the light supper he had left them had not agreed with her constitution.

" You know what you have to do, I suppose?" she said. " It has all been arranged between Mr. Dothem and you, hasn't it?"

" Well, mum, not exactly," Joe said ; " I offered to make myself useful if Mr. Dothem would allow me to keep Toby here."

" Ugh ! quite enough to feed, I should think, without having a lot of mangy curs brought here."

" Toby ain't a cur," said Joe, bridling up, " neither is he mangy."

" I don't want any of your sauce," said the lady ; " and if you don't keep a civil tongue I'll wring your nose for you."

" You're a nice one," Joe thought, " you are ; wouldn't it have been a treat to have seen her when she found the cupboard empty—ha ! ha !"

" What are you laughing at, you young whelp?" the lady asked, turning round fiercely upon Joe ; " you'd better not laugh at me."

" I wasn't laughing, mum," said Joe ; " it's a bad cough I have always of a morning, mum."

" Cough ! I'll cure that for you," said the matron, gravely ; " you shall have some of my medicine for it."

" Medicine makes it worse," said Joe, quickly ; " besides, it's much better now than it has been."

They reached the kitchen by this time, and Joe saw the savage look Mrs. Dothem bestowed upon the cupboard, and his cough broke out again.

Fortunately the amiable female was too much occupied in the contemplation of her wrongs to notice Joe's cough, or he certainly would have been compelled to have swallowed a teacupful of aloes and water.

" Now," she said, facing round upon Joe, who had scarcely time to pull a long face, " the first thing you must do is to take that chopper, go to the back of the house and you will find some tree stumps, chop enough to make the fire, and don't be long about it."

" No, mum."

" After that clean all those boots, there's only six pairs, they won't take you long, and mind and don't waste the blacking."

" No, mum."

" When you've done that pump enough water to fill that boiler and the large butt in the washhouse."

" Yes, mum."

" After that sweep out the dining-hall and take up that pile of tin mugs. By that time the water will be hot, so you can scrub down this table with hot water and sand ; after you have done that sweep down the steps and take up all the weeds you can find in front of the door."

" Yes, mum, anything else."

" Clean the windows of our sitting-room, and if you have time when you have done, there's a few odd jobs before breakfast. Come to me and I'll find you something else to do."

" Yes, mum."

" Joe took the chopper, and the lady went upstairs to have a few hours' sleep.

" Well," said Joe, scratching his head, " get through this lot. I can't, that's impossible. Why it would take two days. Oh, Jemima Jane, not for Joe."

He came in view of the gnarled trunks of the trees Mr. Dothem had had dug up for fuel, and limited as Joe's knowledge of arboriculture was, he knew that it would take at least two hours to chop sufficient wood for the boiling process.

" It's no use beginning," said Joe, " so I'll step over and ask Toby what's best to be done under these very pleasant circumstances."

Toby welcomed his master, and in his eagerness to meet him knocked down an old plank.

" I knew Toby would manage the business," said Joe, hoisting the plank to his shoulder ; " this is a little softer than the tree stumps."

Joe fell to work with a will, and soon cut the worm-eaten wood to pieces, and as he began to collect them he was surprised to see Nimblejaws, followed by the whole of the boys belonging to his room.

" We would have come before," said Tommy,

"but we wasn't sure the old dame had gone back to bed. Now what's she given you to do?"

Joe told him.

"Just what we said," said Tommy; "she would give you more than you could do, so that she could find an excuse to stop your breakfast, or get you a good licking at school time."

"She's a nice old girl, I don't think," said Joe; "of course she knew I couldn't do a quarter of it in the time."

"'Tain't likely," said Nimblejaws; "but we'll do it for you. Now then, my pippins, go in, and if the old woman doesn't stare when she comes down I ain't here, that's all. Now, Bob, off you go, and clean the boots; young Shaw and two more pump the water. Off with you, Charley, Dick, George, and Jem to the big hall, and sweep it out, then bring the mugs up."

Nimblejaws soon arranged matters, and long before Samuel came down and rang the bell for the boys to leave their rooms, the work was all done, and Joe doing a little extra by dusting the sitting-room.

Mrs. Dothem opened her eyes as she inspected each of the tasks she had given Joe, and he could scarcely help laughing when she took up the boots and examined them, for Nimblejaws had dexterously cut all the stitches round the welts, remarking as he did so—

"Work for the snob; they'll not last above a day."

"You've worked very well," said Mrs. Dothem, examining Joe suspiciously: "have you done it all yourself?"

"Toby helped me, mum."

"Toby!"

"Yes, mum; he's a clever dog, mum. Bless you, he thinks nothing of taking a scrubbing brush in his mouth and cleaning a room. You should see him using the flannel, he does it with his paws, and can't he work the pump, too; you've only to fasten a bit of rope to the handle and tell him to pump, and he does it, and——"

"You can go," said Mrs. D., she had a suspicion that Joe was not sticking to facts; "that will do; the work is done; that's all I care about. To-morrow morning, I'll stay and see how you manage it."

Joe reflected over this as he went to the breakfast of oatmeal porridge flavoured with salt, and he began to feel a little puzzled how to manage affairs.

He talked the matter over with Nimblejaws as they went to the stable where Toby was fastened —for Joe saved his four-footed friend a portion of the oatmeal porridge—but they could not come to any satisfactory arrangement.

"There's only one thing to do," Nimblejaws

said, "I can come downstairs and set fire to something in the kitchen, and when you see the smoke you must shout out 'fire;' that may put the old woman off the scent."

"But," said Joe, "it will never do to set fire to the place."

"No; I shall only light some brown paper, and throw it in the fender, so as it will smoke."

"No good," said Joe, "as soon as it is put out she'll be at me again. No, Tom; we must think of something else; we've all day to do it in."

The school bell rang, and Joe and Nimblejaws sat on the same form, and during the time the elder Dothem was examining a class, one of the boys made a mistake, and the heavy ruler the principal held was brought down upon the lad's head.

The culprit dropped his book, and clapping both hands to his skull, danced and howled with pain.

"What a brute he is!" whispered Joe to his neighbour. "He ought to be kicked for doing that."

Samuel, the poetic, was passing close behind Joe at the time, and heard the words intended only for Nimblejaws.

Joe soon had evidence of the monitor's presence, for Samuel's thin cane twined around the boy's shoulders, and caused him to leap from his seat.

"Drop that," Joe said; "I've not done anything to be hit like that."

"Silence!" said Samuel; "keep your seat."

Joe returned to his seat, and as the junior Dothem was moving away, the boy whispered loud enough for the vain monitor to hear—

"I should like to have a turn up with that effigy of a man. Crikey! look at his shoulders; they ain't a bit wider than a mackerel's."

Little men, as a rule, are very vain. Samuel was no exception to this rule. The boy's jeering words cut him to the quick, and as his sallow visage became a fiery scarlet, he rushed at Joe and caught him by the ear.

"Come out," he said. "Come out, you impertinent beggar's brat, come out, or I'll wring your ear off."

There seemed every prospect of Joe being minus of one ear, for the vindictive Samuel not only twisted the organ, but imbedded his nails in the lobe.

"You'd better leave go," said Joe, writhing with pain, "or I'll mark you. Do you hear, you brute?"

"Come out," repeated Samuel, "and I'll cane you within an inch of your life."

"Will you? Take that, you effigy.

Joe, in muscular strength, was by far the su-

BILL ADLER RELATES HIS ADVENTURES.

perior, although the principal's son had the advantage of six years' seniority in age, so the well-delivered blow coming full upon the monitor's narrow chest, sent him sprawling upon his back.

Mr. Dothem looked up when he heard the fall, and rapping the boys on the head who stood in his way, he ran and raised Samuel.

"What is this?" he asked. "Who has dared to raise his hand against my son?"

"I have," Joe said, boldly, at the same time snatching up a large slate to defend himself in the event of another attack. "Look here, sir, my ear's bleeding, where he dug his nails into it."

Mr. Dothem looked at the boy's ear, then at his attitude, and being a cool, calculating man, he forbore to punish Joe then, for he saw at a glance there were many of the bigger lads who were quite ready to take the boy's part.

He was quite aware of the spirit of rebellion which was so rife among his scholars, and knowing how he would be likely to fare should the forty or fifty boys make an attack upon him, he placed the ruler under his arm, and with a calm visage, despite the boiling rage he felt within, he said—

"There seems to be something that needs explaining in this case, therefore I will hear it when the morning lessons are over."

A look of intelligence passed between the principal and his son as the former went back to his desk, and Joe resumed his book and paid as much attention as could be expected to his lesson in orthography.

"A diphthong," Joe read, "is the union of two vowels, pronounced by a single impulse of the voice. How my ear burns; I wish I had given him a nose-ender instead of that punch on the chest."

"I wouldn't be in your shoes, Joe," Nimblejaws whispered, "you'll get something hot; it's always worse when old Nip says he'll see you after morning lessons."

"If I· do," Joe answered, in the same tone, "I will give that mackerel-back something."

"Won't Charity get the dark cellar and no grub?" the small boys whispered to each other. "Crikey! I shouldn't like to be him!"

"He will, and no mistake; why, Harry Hogden got tied to the banisters and flogged because he threw a book at young Nip. What'll Charity get for knocking him down?"

They could not measure out a punishment proportionate to the crime, so gave it up and looked forward to the conclusion of the morning lessons for a solution of the grave matter.

Boggins and his clique were in high glee, and had Mr. Dothem asked any one of them to hold Joe down while being flogged they would have been only too glad to have obeyed.

Joe himself was perhaps the least concerned about the matter; he had made a resolution to quit the joys of Baream at the first opportunity, therefore he determined to resist to the best any punishment for his offence, justly arguing if he even used a poker to defend himself, it would make no difference, as he was about to leave.

When the school was dismissed at twelve, Mr. Dothem desired Joe to follow him to his private room, and when they reached the apartment, Charity's surprise was great at the mild address Mr. Dothem thought fit to favour him with.

"I'm very sorry," the angry old rascal said, "that such an unpleasant affair as this should have marred the harmony of the morning lessons, and as I believe you have erred through a little hastiness of temper, I am disposed to overlook the offence, if you will promise never to do so again."

"I won't," Joe answered, "if he lets me alone."

"Well, well, I will speak to Mr. Samuel Dothem about the affair, therefore I hope the friendly feelings that exist between all my pupils and my son will not be altered as regards yourself."

Joe was silent, he did not wish to feign the hypocrite, knowing as he did how cordially the junior Dothem, as well as his father, was hated by the whole of the boys.

That old Siv is a bad un," Joe thought, "but I don't think he's as bad as this one. Now I wonder what move he's up to with me? there must be something, or he would not let me off."

"There is a little matter I wish to speak to you about," Mr. Dothem blandly said. "I merely wish to know if you can remember the old gentleman who took you to the shoemaker in the Borough?"

"I remember him well enough."

"You do. I am glad of that. Now what sort of a looking man was he?"

"Well," Joe answered readily, "he was rather a short man, and he had red hair, and a squint, and when he walked he seemed to have a sort of limp."

Mr. Dothem committed this fancy portrait Joe had drawn to memory.

"There will not be much difficulty in finding him," he thought; "for the upper classes, like a swarm of bees, are always to be found in certain places."

"I think I have put it in pretty strong," Joe thought, "for the old gent was as straight as a lamp-post, and very tall, and grey hair and whiskers, and no more of a squint than I have."

"Thank you," said Mr. Dothem. "Now, Joe, as you are a sharp lad, and not like many of the numbskulls I have here, I think you can be useful to me."

"Can I?" Joe thought. "Here it comes. Oh, you old reptile!"

"And as I have been shamefully robbed by some of the boys, I will give you a new shilling if you will find out the thieves for me; you can easily do it, you know."

"Yes, sir; but there's such a lot of them. Haven't you any suspicion?"

"No," said Mr. Dothem; "we found a clue, but the things had evidently been placed where we found them by the thieves to throw suspicion upon a number of well-conducted lads."

"Very well, sir; I will do my best. What did you lose?"

"Well, our larder was ransacked, and the lock cut out of the door, and as the thieves are almost sure to boast of their exploits, you must keep your ears open."

"Yes, sir."

"Now you can go; but no, stay one moment." Mr. Dothem went to the cupboard. "Here's a plate of bones and potatoes for your dog; and as you are passing the yard where the fowls are you can give them these few pieces of stale bread. Break the bread up and throw it in their water, for I want them to get used to you, as you will have to feed them."

"Yes, sir."

Joe went upon his errand, the conviction being stronger that bad as old Siv was, Mr. Dothem was worse by far.

Joe halted when he reached the yard and looked for a few moments at the fowls, then at the plate of poisoned food.

"I don't know," the boy muttered, "whether it is wrong for me to poison these birds; perhaps it is. They can't help the old scamp's doings; so I won't poison them, although he would have killed poor Toby. Well, he's a bad 'un, he is. Here, chuk, chuk, chuk! here's half the bread; the other half is for Toby, as for this——"

Joe looked spitefully at the plate, then taking a spade that stood against the wall, he went to an unfrequented part of the desolate grounds, and carefully buried every particle of the poisoned food.

He trampled the earth over it, then beat it down with the flat of the spade.

"I feel better," he thought, "than if I had given it to the fowls, because I know it's not right to take away life—not even of an insect; so I'm glad I have not done it."

After this, Joe replaced the spade, and went to Toby, and as he caressed the faithful dog the tears came from his eyes, as he in fancy saw his canine friend stiffened out in death.

"I won't leave you here, Toby," he said; "there's the dinner bell; so come on, old fellow. You must sneak in after me and lie under my seat."

Toby frisked about with joy at being released from the cord which had fastened him to the old manger, and Joe, as he admired the shaggy animal, little thought the important part Toby would play in the great rebellion at Baream Hall.

CHAPTER X.

JOE BECOMES THE CHAMPION OF HIS SCHOOLFELLOWS' WRONGS, AND HEADS A REBELLION.—TOBY DOES GOOD SERVICE, BUT DAMAGES THE POETIC SAMUEL.—THE FOE RETREAT, BUT AT THE MOMENT OF VICTORY AN UNEXPECTED ALLY ARRIVES UPON THE SCENE OF BATTLE.

It was "meat" day at the Hall, but there was no reckless profusion of the flesh of animals. Three lean breasts of mutton graced the table, and at the head, where Mr. Dothem was seated, a leg from the same lean animal was placed.

Large bowls of half-grown potatoes and a few cabbages (the hearts, by the way, had been taken out by the lady superintendent before they came to the boys' table).

Joe took his seat and glanced at the double row of pale hungry faces, from thence his eyes rested upon twenty little fellows who were seated at a side table looking as wretched as boys could look, who were compelled to partake of a bowl of oatmeal porridge, while their companions were upon the point of feeding upon the lean breasts and the small leg.

The side table was the punishment table, and the boys who sat there had, for divers trivial causes, had their meat stopped for that day.

This batch of delinquents were, strange to say, always very strong upon meat days.

Tom Nimblejaws was uncharitable enough to say, that old Nip always took especial care to have, at the very least, one-fourth of his pupils debarred from the luxury of meat, and further, Nimblejaws averred that old Nip so managed this punishment, that the whole of the lads were subjected to it in turns.

The master was in the act of saying grace when Joe entered, and when he had concluded he pushed his spectacles up until they rested upon his forehead, and, looking sternly at Joe, said—

"You are late, Joseph Cholmondeley, mind it does not occur again, or I shall have to stop your allowance of meat; much as this punishment goes against me, the discipline of the school must be maintained."

"The bell has only just rung, "Joe said, "And I"——

"Silence!" said Samuel the poetic, from the lower end of the table. "Silence! or leave the hall."

"I'll drop you one yet," Joe thought: "you yellow-faced, herring-backed apology for man."

The carving continued until the three breasts were distributed in minute fragments; the leg was reserved for Mr. Dothem, Samuel, and a few of his favourites.

Joe's plate was passed to him by Nimblejaws, who took the opportunity to whisper—

"You'll find the meat underneath one of the taters; it won't choke you, if you swallow it all at once."

So Joe thought when he held the small piece of greasy mutton upon his fork, and mentally calculated its weight and measurement

"It don't weigh more than an ounce," thought Joe, "and it don't measure an inch from corner to corner. This won't do for me, I shall ask for some more, and if he don't give it me, there will be a row, and no mistake about it."

Mr. Dothem had kept his eyes upon Joe, and when he saw the lad eyeing the fragment of meat, his temper got the better of his prudence.

"Well, Sir," he demanded, "what do you mean by misbehaving yourself in that manner?"

"What manner?" said Joe saucily, "I'm only looking for my meat."

"Go on with your dinner, sir, or perhaps you will find something else."

"Shall I?" Joe said. "I should like to have a little more meat than this; I didn't come here to be starved."

"Samuel," said Mr. Dothem, "remove that ill-bred boy from the table."

Joe stood up, and Samuel, who had not forgotten the knock down, came behind Joe and rapped him over the head with the handle of the carving knife.

"That's it, is it?" the plucky street-boy said. "Take that, you spider—and that—and that."

He threw the potatoes at Samuel's poetic face, and the plate followed, and was broken upon the Byronic head.

Samuel retreated, and in passing the corner of the table snatched up another knife.

"Seize him! seize him!" shouted Mr. Dothem; "you Boggins, Black, and Reynolds, pounce on him!—Mutiny, mutiny—rebellion!"

"Yes!" shouted Joe, in reply, "mutiny and rebellion, you old thing. Who do you think is going to stand your starvation game? I won't; and if the other chaps had any pluck in them they wouldn't. Now then, boys, follow me, and we'll soon clear the table."

The three bullies paused before they attacked Joe, for Nimblejaws, Jack Shaw, and a few more had responded to Charity's war-cry, and the hungry lads from the punishment-table, taking advantage of the confusion, came to the long table and helped themselves to all that was within their reach.

"You first," Joe said, throwing off his jacket and moving towards the poet; "you white-looking, dirty sneak! that's my way of doing it."

Samuel tried to defend himself with his two knives, but Joe floored him, and Mr. Dothem, partly to defend himself, partly to save the leg of mutton, seized it by the shank, and climbing upon the table, exclaiming—

"Boggins, Black, Reynolds, all of you," he yelled, "will you see my son killed, my son, who has always been your friend?"

"Come on, lads," Nimblejaws shouted; "down with the bullies, and hurrah for Charity Joe!"

Nimblejaws and party attacked the three bullies, and while their combat was taking place at the end of the room Mr. Dothem belaboured Joe about the head and shoulders with the remains of the leg of mutton.

Joe took no notice of this attack; his attentions were solely for Samuel.

"Get up," he said; and as fast as Samuel attempted to rise the boy knocked him down again. "Get up, you pitiful sneak. I'll knock all the poetry out of your brains. That's it, give it him. Pitch into the grub, youngsters. Hurra! here's a lark!"

One blow delivered by Mr. Dothem was better aimed than Joe relished, for it caught him on the crown of his head, and caused him to stagger.

"A little of that goes a long way," Joe thought. Then raising his voice, he called out, "Toby, Toby, seize him, boy; seize him on the table."

Toby had been curled up under the table, until he heard his master's voice; then he made a jump from the floor to the form, and from the form to the table, and seized the benign Dothem by the skirts.

The scene became lively now; for the mischievous began to throw the breakable articles upon the floor, and the pieces at Mr. Dothem's head, and the hungry were busy demolishing all the eatables.

Those fond of fighting joined Tommy Nimblejaws' party, and helped to belabour the bullies, Joe still punching the poet, and Mr. Dothem was belabouring Toby with the leg of mutton.

"Run, run one of you, the old rascal cried, "run and fetch Mrs. Dothem and my daughters."

One of the boys made his escape from Nimblejaws' war party, and sped towards the door to bring Mrs. Dothem to her lord's assistance, but before he could place his hand upon the lock the door swung open, and he was met in the face by a dirty wet mop.

Down went Reynolds on his back as Mrs. Dothem, who had been alarmed by the uproar, ran past him to the scene of action.

In spite of the shower of missiles that greeted her appearance she went bravely on, and as she passed the fighting groups headed by Boggins and Nimblejaws, she dispersed the belligerents.

From this part of the battle-field she rushed to the table and began to belabour Toby, but the dog only tugged more fiercely at the preceptor's long dressing gown, and by a sudden wrench

THE WILD HUNTERS OF THE FROZEN MOUNTAINS.

caused Mr. Dothem to lose his balance, then Mr. D., Mrs. D., and Toby all rolled to the ground together.

Joe had by this time beaten Samuel until his arms ached; this done and the poet grovelling on the floor and blubbering like a great calf, the leader of the rebels turned to see how matters stood with his captain, Tommy Nimblejaws.

He found the bullies were getting the best of it, so calling upon the lads who had by this time finished everything eatable, he made for the point where the battle seemed to be going against him.

"Good dog," said Joe, as he saw that sapient animal making off with the fleshy weapon Mr. Dothem had been using.

Joe came to the rescue of Nimblejaws, who was being well punished by Boggins and Black; but before he could do more than settle Boggins. Mrs. Dothem, wielding her mop as a warrior of old wielded his two-handed falchion, came behind the redoubtable Charity, and with one sweep of the weapon knocked the rebel leader sprawling upon the floor.

She would have repeated the blow upon the fallen enemy, but as she swung it back to give Joe a demolisher, Toby left the mastification of the cold meat and hung on to the mop.

"Hold it tight," shouted Joe, struggling to escape from the grasp of Mr. Dothem; "stick to it, Toby. Here, Nimblejaws, pull this old reptile off or he'll choke me."

True to his colours, Tommy came to the rescue, and taking the elder Dothem by the back of his neckcloth, compelled him to release his grasp upon Joe's throat.

Joe jumped to his feet, and saw the day was lost, for the whole of his army had retreated, evidently afraid of what they had done, and to make matters worse, Boggins and his compeers were belabouring Toby to compel him to relieve his grip of Mrs. Dothem's weapon.

"Stick to me, Nimblejaws," whispered Joe, hurriedly; "let's make a dash at the bullies, then slope and go on our own hook."

"I'm with you," said Tommy. "Come on."

The pair of sturdy lads rushed at the boys who were playing upon Toby's ribs; there was a scuffle, then the sound of blows being given and received, and Toby was free, and Joe stooping, wrenched the mop from Mrs. Dothem, reversed it, and gave that lady such a lunge under the left ribs, that she went down, as Joe afterwards expressed it, all of a heap.

Retaining possession of the weapon, Joe snatched up his jacket, then with Nimblejaws and Toby ran from the hall, pursued by Mr. Dothem.

Sylvia the gushingly romantic, and Deborah the strong ditto, stood in the doorway as though to bar their path, but Joe flourishing the mop, and the sweet girls yelled murder and bolted.

"Now for the gate," said Joe. "Who's the fellow on it?"

"Brownling," said Tommy; "but we'll smash him, if he attempts to stop us."

Across the rank lawn, down the avenue of trees, sped the boys, and when they came in sight of the gate, the boy in charge was in the act of opening it to admit the baker's cart from Baream township.

"Shut the gate," yelled Mr. Dothem from the rear. "Shut the gate."

Too late; the baker's cart prevented the gate from closing, and as Joe and his companion ran out, Brownling went on a few steps after them, but Joe stopped the pursuit by hurling the mop at the gatekeeper's head, and the handle striking him across the nose, caused a dozen Joes and as many Nimblejaws, not reckoning the millions of stars, to dance before his eyes.

Mr. Dothem gave up the pursuit, and returned to the hall, and addressing his pupils in a crying speech, bade them be good boys for the future, and not be led away by such ne'er-do-wells as Charity Joe and Tommy Nimblejaws.

CHAPTER XI.

JOE STARTS UPON THE WORLD—ARRIVES AT BUD-DLETON-CUM-PETERS—MEETS AN OLD ACQUAINT-ANCE—ASTONISHING THE YOKELS.

THE fugitives ran for nearly a mile, then finding they were not pursued, sat upon a heap of stones by the road-side.

"We're on our own hook now," said Joe; "now which way shall we go?"

"It don't matter now, I expect," said Tommy. "There's one good thing: no matter which way we go, or where we go to, we shan't be robbed."

"No," said Joe; "I haven't a copper; how much have you?"

"Exactly the same amount, so it wont take long to spend."

"That's true," answered Joe; "but what's to be done?"

"I'm blowed if I know, Joe. Can't you think of something?"

"Well we must make for London; that's the first thing; but how we are to live till we get there I don't know yet; but I suppose we shall find plenty of fields as we go along."

"Plenty; but what's the good of fields?"

"Every good," Joe said; "'specially if they grows mangel wurzels, beet roots, and them sort of things."

"I see," Tommy said. "We must be content, I suppose. Now where does this road lead to?"

"To London perhaps," said Joe. "Anyhow, we must follow it, for the other leads to Baream town, and if we go there we shall be collared and taken back."

"They won't know us."

"P'raps not; but the baker will, and old Nip's sure to put him up to us. So along this road we goes. There's the mile-stone; let's see what it says."

They read the half-defaced inscription, but could make nothing of it, beyond the fact that they were six miles from somewhere.

Joe hoped it was six miles from London, for he felt sure he should meet the old gentleman who took him to the shoemaker's in the Borough, as soon as he reached the great city.

"Six miles ain't much," Tommy said, "so let's be jogging, for the sooner we have it over the better."

They started, Toby gambolling on before them, as though delighted at obtaining his liberty.

"I tell you what it is," said Tommy, as they trudged on side by side; "I wish these were the days of highwaymen, Joe."

"Do you? what for?"

" Why, we'd do the same as the young chap I used to read about in penny numbers."

" What did he do, Tommy ?"

" Why, he used to ride a beautiful horse, and was dressed in a red coat and gold lace, and used to fight the Bow-street officers, and go to all the noblemen's houses, and sometimes he was caught, then he used to draw his sword and fight ever so many of 'em, and always got away."

" What became of him ?" Joe asked. " He was hanged, of course ?"

" No, he wasn't ; he married a beautiful lady, and the king made him a knight or a duke, or something of the sort."

" Did he ?" Joe said. " Well, Tommy, I didn't think you were so soft as to spend your money upon such rubbish."

" Rubbish !" Tommy repeated; " why, it's all true."

" Not a word," Joe said: " I took a number or two of the ' Red-nosed Pirate, or, the Highwayman of the Bounding Ocean,' but old Siv, bad 'un as he was, wouldn't let me read such stuff."

" What for, Joe ?"

" Because he said it was no good, and only a pack of lies and rubbish ; and the highwaymen you used to read about were all sneaking cut-throats, and used to have to hide away in all sorts cf dirty holes and corners, and they were always caught and hanged by the neck at Tyburn; and I believe old Siv, too, for he had got an old book where it gives you the true life of all the highwaymen, but, bless you, Tommy, there wasn't a word about 'em like you read in the penny numbers."

" Wasn't there, though?" said Tommy, " Will I won't read any more ; there's plenty of good books to be had for a penny."

" Plenty," said Joe, " and books that wouldn't put such silly ideas into your head as turning highwayman—boy highwayman—what rubbish —why, do you suppose any man would let a boy rob him on the road ?"

Tommy began to see his cherished heroes melt away as he confessed it was not likely.

" You are not a bad sort, Joe," he said, " after all, for some chaps would have said, ' Yes, let's turn highwaymen,' and a pretty pair of fools we should have looked if a big countryman got hold of us and knocked our heads together."

" We should," said Joe, " perhaps I ain't a bad chap, if you mean that way, for I never stole anything in my life except the grub at old Nip's, and that was to punish him."

" Old Nip's a wretch," said Tommy ; " fancy, Joe, after the way we stuck up for those fellows for them to leave us in the lurch."

" Just what we might have expected," said Joe, " for you can never get many fellows of one mind unless it is to help themselves, the same as those fellows did who pitched into the grub and left us to do the fighting."

" They're a bad lot," Tommy cried, " and I hope old Nip will starve 'em ten times worse."

" So do I, Tommy."

The six miles were soon walked, for the lads talked the whole way, each reciting the most interesting events of their former lives, and Joe lengthening out his recital by various anecdotes of Toby's wonderful exploits.

They were a little disappointed when they reached Buddleton-cum-Peters in place of London, and, to increase their disappointment, they found they had come exactly six miles farther from London than when they started at the milestone.

" Had 'ee looked to this side o' mile-stone," said the rustic who gave the unwelcome information, " thee would ha' seen it was only ten miles to Lunnon ; now it be sixteen."

" Thank you," said Joe ; " I hope the next time you put milestones up you will put the London side in front. However, it does not matter ; our carriage is waiting for us, so we can see you back."

" Kerredge !" grinned the youth of the smock-frock, " 'ee be s pretty fellers to keep a kerredge. Why, thee clothes baint worth three brass far-dens."

" That's all you know about it," said Nimble-jaws, " and shows you've never seen noblemen in disguise before, Mr. Chawbaken. Now what is the name of this place ?"

The youth grinned until he must have had a pain in his face before he answered—

" This is Bud'ton-kom-Peters."

" Thank you," said Tommy ; " which way are you going ?"

" Over to Farmer Lee's farm, to be zure, where do 'ee think ?"

" Didn't know, but thought if you were going down the road we came, you might tell our coachman to bring the carriage on to us."

" Haw, haw, haw !" laughed the rustic, " ker-ridge ! Bet a bran-new shilling to a brass farden you both be nought but tramps. Haw, haw, haw ! Kerredge ! Haw, haw, haw !"

" Leave us, sweet youth," said Joe ; " your noise is offensive."

The youth left them, his haw-hawing continuing until he was out of earshot of the pair.

" Well," Joe said, " that fellow's mouth would do for a horse collar, much less than to grin through one. I'll wager Toby against a dead cat that he has often won a prize that way."

"Looks like it," Tommy said; "but what's to be done, now, Joe?" We can't do the sixteen miles back?"

"No," Joe answered; "let's have a look at this place, and by the time it is dark, we can go to that haystack and have a sleep. I like sleeping in hay, do you, Tommy?"

"When I can't sleep anywhere else."

They went up the front street, which, like the usual thoroughfares in small towns, led to the market-place.

It was market-day, and the little square was crowded, although some of the salesmen were still roaring the unsold portion of their wares.

The first thing that attracted Joe's attention when he had given some longing looks at the various piles of eatables was a man with a peep-show.

He could not see the individual, but the voice seemed familiar, so Joe came to a standstill, and listened.

"Here you are," said the voice; "the same exhibition as was shown to the Prince o' Wales on the werry day he got married to the Princess o' Wales and all the Royal Family. Now, one penny is the charge, and I only wants one more to begin."

"Dang it," said a red-faced lad, working his way through the crowd, "if I don't ha' a penn'orth, 'taint often I be's so rich as I be now."

"Now the first picture I shall show you," said the man, loosening a string and allowing the picture to fall, "is the battle of Sebastopol. There on the right you see the Prince of Cambridge riding on a white horse, and in front of him his big guns; but them you can't see for the smoke. The little black dots—leastways they should look like black dots—is the guards a going up the Alma. Look to the left and you will see a lot of spikes; the spikes is the Rooshans. You can't see any more of 'em because of the smoke, for of course in a great battle like that there was plenty of smoke."

"Now the next scene is——. Look here, little girl with the big baby, I wish you'd go away, for the cries of a hinfant with lungs like that one makes me feel so narvous that I can't go on with the performance; so go away, little girl with the big baby, unless you are waiting to have a look. You ain't? Well go away. I thought——"

"B'aint 'ee going on with——"

"Yes, sir; you've paid your penny, and are entitled to see the whole of the performance; the same performance, ladies and gentlemen, girls and boys, the identical performance as was shown to the Prince of Wales the morning he came to his birthday——"

"I thought 'ee said it was the day he got married."

"So I did, so I did; and I repeat it. He has seen it times, not like the gentlemen of some towns, who stand with their mouths wide open listening to all I have to say, and then not so much as to have a pennyworth of——"

"Look here, maister, ain't you going on with the per——"

"The Prince, gentlemen," said the showman, elevating his voice, "says it's the purtiest sight ever he saw in his life, and——"

"What darned lies you be——"

"The next scene is the grand panoramic views from the thrilling tragedy of 'The Forlorn Milkman; or, the Haunted Mangle,' scene the fifth, act the fourth, as performed before her Majesty the Queen of England, Ireland, Scotland, Wales, Australia, India, and lots more places. This scene represents the forlorn milkman a cleaning his cans. Look to the left, and you will see him. Look a little to the right, and you will see his milk cans. Now, then, you two lads, don't be pushing, or you will have the whole of the machinery over, and the boiler will bust and blow you up. Haven't I told you the scenes are worked by a steam engine? What—what do you say?"

"I can't see the cans."

"Can't you? I pity you then. Bring a pair of spectacles, and put 'em on next time you come. The next thing I must bring to your notice is the mangle. Look to the right and you will see the mangle. Well, while the milkman was cleaning his cans, he hears the mangle begin to work of itself, and looking over his right shoulder he sees the ghost of his sweetheart, Sarah Jane Brown, rising up in a cloud of smoke.

"The next picture shows the milkman's sweetheart a coming up through the smoke——"

"Darn me if I can see the ghost: there's a lot of smoke, that be all."

"Ghosts are not visible in daylight; so you can't expect to see it. Come to-night when the show is lighted up with the great electrical light, and then you'd see all——Well, I'm blessed, if it ain't Charity. What cheer, Charity? Who'd a thought of seeing you here? Wait a minute, old son, and I'll speak to you."

"The next and last scene is a grand representation of Chinese fireworks; you see, when I turn this handle and sets this steam-engine a-going, you see the juveniles a-dancing and kicking up their heels like mad; it was this werry same that the Prince of Wales, when he saw it, says to me, 'You deserve to be made city showman to the Royal Family;' 'but no,' says I, 'I wants to let the people of England see this extraordinary performance; thank you all the same, Prince of Wales, and all the Royal Family!' That's all, gentlemen, so down goes the curtain."

The audience went away, more or less satisfied with the sight, then the showman came forward and shook Joe's hand.

"What, and Toby, too!" he said; "well, this is what I calls an unexpected meeting of friends; "what cheer, Charity?"

Joe told the showman all that had taken place since he left the Borough.

"Come on," said the proprietor of the exhibition; "I was just thinking of knocking off; now I've met you I will, and we'll go and have some half-and-half and a crust of bread and cheese."

A modest little alehouse, called the "Three Jolly Ploughmen," seemed the most suitable, so in the party went, and Joe began the conversation by saying:

"Well, Bill, the last time I saw you it was when you were doing the mute business for Coffin, the undertaker."

"So it was, Joe, so it was, and I've had some ups and downs since then I can tell you."

"Drink, Bill, you must be dry after all that pattering."

"Well, I do feel a little that way, so here's luck to us all, and to your friend."

"Thank you," said Tommy.

"Yes, some queer dodges I've tried, Charity, to earn a crust, before I took to lugging this beastly thing all over the country, but it pays sometimes."

"That's a comfort," said Joe; "So did doing the mute, didn't it?"

"Well, it might for them as could stand it, but I couldn't, Joe; I never could keep still long enough, and the consequence was I used to leave my stick as was covered with black, while I ran round the corner and had a penn'orth of Old Tom; somehow one day I had too many penn'orths—a very cold day it was, too—and when I came back I leant up against the door, and jest as the sorrowing relatives came out, in I goes slap, and couldn't get up again."

"You were so-so then, Bill."

"Well, perhaps I might have been; anyhow I got the sack, and through being a mute so long I'd got a face about as long as your arm, and of course no one would have anything to do with me—pitch into the bread and cheese."

The lads were hungry, therefore no second invitation was necessary, to pitch in.

"So after this," Bill the Showman continued, "I went in for eight articles for a penny, but the patter was worse than the show business;

besides, the bobbies used to hunt me up so that I found it didn't pay, so turned it up."

"The old patter, I suppose," Joe said, "gold wedding ring and keeper, Chinese puzzle, and all that sort of thing."

"Yes, that was it, Joe; it was too old to pay, let alone the cost of the candles, and they used to flare away awful on windy nights."

"But didn't you use brown paper round 'em, Bill?"

"Of course I did, but somehow they was gone long before I'd sold enough to buy two new 'uns."

"What did you do after the eight articles for a penny had failed?"

"I was a sandwich then," the showman said. "Eighteenpence a-day and my board, and a precious high one it was, stuck on a pole; you know, Joe."

"I know what you mean."

"Well, one day," the showman continued, "I was standing at the corner of a street, and a cab-horse ran away, and came so close to me that I bolted on to the pavement; and before I knew what I'd done, my foot slipped on a piece of orange peel, and away went the beastly board right through a large plate-glass window."

"My eye," said Tommy, "it would have taken a lot of your eighteenpences to have paid for the glass."

"I didn't wait to inquire how much the damage was," said Bill, "but hooked it, and left the board sticking there."

The boys laughed at the droll manner in which the showman spoke.

"After that," he said, "I was a broker's man for a little time, but as I didn't like selling other people's sticks, and, besides, one man where I went pitched me out of the window, I gave it up. Is the pot empty?"

"It is," said Joe, "and all the bread and cheese gone."

"We'll have some more," said the showman, "and as I can do a little bit of grub myself, I'll tell you some more of my ups and downs afterwards."

CHAPTER XII.

THE SHOWMAN CONTINUES THE NARRATIVE OF HIS ADVENTURES—A COMMITTEE OF WAYS AND MEANS —THE RESULT, AND HOW IT INFLUENCED CHARITY JOE AND HIS DOG TOBY.

THE second supply of bread and cheese and half-and-half having been paid for, and Bill Adkins prevailed upon by Joe to peck a bit, the showman wiped his lips with the cuff of his coat, and while filling a very dirty and very short pipe, remarked:

"I often thinks this must be a queer world, a very queer world, for no sooner does a man get down than everything seems to go agin him."

"That's true, Bill," said Charity, "quite true."

"There's some queer people in the world," continued Bill Adler. "I don't believe you'd find queerer anywhere."

"I should say not," said Tommy, drily, "What do you think, Joe?"

"That's my opinion," said Joe, "to a T."

"I soon began to find that I was not cut out for a merchant," Bill went on, "nor yet for a sandwich, and as standing still wouldn't keep me, nohow, I looks round for something else; but I must tell you I left my little crib in the Borough, and took another in Walworth Common. You know Walworth, Joe?"

"Should say I do; a dirty-looking lot of little streets." They are what is near Lock's-fields."

"They are; but I takes a little crib, a back room, you know, Joe, and does all my moving without a spring van."

"You had a tidy lot of things, Bill, when I used to come and see you in your old place."

"I had, but somehow the landlord made out he had more right to 'em than me, so I let him have his way, and with an old chair without any bottom to it, and a sack to hold some straw, I goes to my new crib, but bless you, Walworth wasn't a bit better than St. George's Market, for the odd jobs I got didn't run to paying my rent."

"So you sloped, I suppose?"

"Wait a minnit, Charity," the showman said, "you shall hear about it. No, I didn't slope, because I didn't care when the landlord said he'd have a broker in. I used to laugh when he told me, which was every morning——"

"But didn't he know you'd only a chair and a sack of straw?"

The showman tilted his chair back, and laughed as though the question was highly amusing.

"That's the best of it," he said. "I'll tell you, Joe. No, he didn't know nothing about what was in the room, for, don't you see, when I came first it was dark, and I kept going up and down stairs, carrying the chair up, then down again, and every time I went up I banged the old chair about, and made it sound as if I had lots of furniture; and as I always kept the door locked when I went out, of course they didn't know anything about it."

"I understand," said Joe. "Good dodge too; go on, Bill."

"Close to my crib there was a broker—not a

shop full of dirty traps, but a broker without a shop—a regular wretch, he was. There, Joe, if I'd a been a young man, I'd a waited at the corner of that street and given that slimy broker something, or he should have given it me, for he was one of those hatchet-faced, sneaky sort of men—always had good clothes on, too, Joe, but how did he get 'em—how did he get 'em?"

The showman became warm with the question, and struck the table with his clenched fist as though expecting the stained and defaced top to enlighten him upon the subject.

"Bought 'em, I suppose," Tommy Nimble-jaws said, "or stole 'em."

"Yes, he'd stole 'em. Worse than that; the smooth-tongued thief! Many's the time he's turned a poor family out in the cold, wet, cold streets—the little ones crying, and the poor baby looking so pitiful. There, my boys, if I had a been the man belonging to the poor women and children as were turned out like that, I'd have done——"

Honest Bill Adler again thumped the table in his just indignation at the merciless cruelties the licensed brokers are *allowed by law* to commit in the land of freedom, where "Britons never shall," &c.

"Them clothes," he said, "that gold chain as he wears round his neck—it's a rope I'd give him and the whole of his tribe—has been wrung out of poor people's goods; for the slimy, thin-faced 'spectable broker knows how to value the things to pay himself, no matter who goes short."

"They are a lot of wretches," said Joe. "There was one as old Siv used to employ when he collected the rents, but we served him out once for seizing a lot of things. My eyes, but him and his men had to run, or we should have broken their heads, for we'd thrown all the dirty things we could find in the gutters, and had just begun with stones when the broker took his hook and left the traps and truck in the road."

"That's the way they ought always to be served," said Bill Adler. "Here, lad, drink after that, for it does my heart good to hear of such things."

So Joe drank, and the showman resumed:—

"Well, at last this 'spectable broker comes in to seize my traps. I hears a knock at my door, and somebody says, "Open this door at once."

"'You're nearest the handle,' says I, "so perhaps you'd open it yourself."

"In walks the 'spectable broker, and licensed all sorts of things, which, I forgets, but he has it stuck up all over his place.

"'Your name is Adler,' says he, looking

.....und, and pulling a face at the sight of the property. 'You owes four weeks' rent, which I am instructed to collect.'

"'Are you?' says I, 'well, you better begin and seize the goods.' He, he, he! of course, there was nothing to seize, so as he went downstairs, as he said, to fetch a policeman, I calls out

"'You won't get a new coat out of this job, you sneaking, hatchet-faced thief. Who turned the poor woman out into the street, and killed the poor baby as was only two days old? Go home, wretch.'"

"Bravo," said Joe, "that was the way to give it him."

"I wish I could have given him more," the showman said. "I should have liked to have broken the old chair over his sanctified face; but I didn't. When he had gone away I left the crib without so much as wishing my landlord good-bye."

"Had you nowhere to go, Bill?"

"Not a blessed place in the world. I can tell you it wasn't nice to walk down the streets, and feel that in lots of the houses you passed they had plenty of spare rooms, and not one of the people would give you a night's lodging."

"It must have seemed hard, Bill."

"It was, lad, very hard; but I trudged on, glad to get away from Walworth, and 'spectable brokers, and when I got to the park I made a pitch on one of the seats, and stayed there till morning. It wasn't so bad after all, for I had lots of company. There were men, women, and children, all gathered under the trees, and some of 'em told me they would sooner sleep there than go in the casual wards, and I believe 'em, too, after I heard the stories they told about the casual wards, and the hard-hearted workhouse people."

"They're a lot of wretches," said Joe. "I know 'em well, and they ought to be put along with your Walworth broker, and pitched head foremost into the river."

"They ought, Joe," said the showman. "Well, then, next day I trudged about the large streets at the West-end, and, as luck would have it, I got a job or two to hold horses. I got three bob before night, but I only spent fourpence— half a loaf, a saveloy, and a half-pint of porter— and when I'd had this, I went to my seat in the park, and had another sleep till morning; then I .....ted it to Oxford-street, for one of the chaps, ...y, hulking fellow, as wouldn't work if he got ..... came to my seat and told me he'd been offered a job at a cheesemonger's to give away bills.

"I'm not going," he says, "to stand all day giving away bills for two bob a day. I'd sooner cadge."

"I wouldn't," Bill Adler continued. "I never cadged or stole anything, so I went to the cheesemonger's, and he kept me three days, and as I paid no lodging, and it only cost me fourpence, or at most sixpence a day for grub, I soon had a few shillings by me, for I was saving up for something, and I got it, too."

Bill pointed to the show as he spoke.

"Yes," he continued, "I thought about that when I was giving the bills away. I'll have a show, says I; so when the job was over at the cheesemonger's, I asked him what he'd let me have a few egg chests for.

"He looks at me, and——"

Here two men entered the tap-room, and took a seat near the showman and his companions.

"He looked at me," continued Bill, lowering his voice, "and asked me what I wanted them for. I told him to make a show. The cheesemonger was a good sort, for he said, 'Take as many as you want, you'll find a stock of them in the warehouse below; and as you have no home, you can build your theatre in the warehouse.' Now, wasn't he a good sort?"

"He was," said Joe, "a stunner; did you build it there?"

"I did; and when it was all ready for painting, the cheesemonger says, 'There's some men coming to-morrow to paint my house, so leave your frame, and I will get one of them to give it a rub over. I'll make it all right;' he was a stunner that cheesemonger, wasn't he, Charity?"

"No mistake," said Joe; "he was an out-an-outer."

"I went next day to the baths and wash-houses," Bill resumed, "for I hadn't had my clothes off for more than a week, so I had a good wash, and only paid twopence for it; but they ought to have found a towel, for I had to wipe myself on my——"

"I say, it's novelty we want, sir," said one of the new-comers, divining Bill Adler's trade; "novelty, sir, the public are right down tired of your fat women, your learned pigs, your giants; we want something new."

"That's just it," his companion answered, taking the mouth-piece of a trombone from his lips; "that's just it."

The last speaker again placed the mouth-piece in its former position, and, much to the amusement of Tommy, and the disgust of Toby, began to quickly "tootle, tootle" through a very noisy instrument.

"After I'd had my wash," Bill continued, eyeing the strangers out of the corners of his eyes, "I went up to Shoreditch; for I knew I should be sure to find a chap there with a umbrella full of pictures. Of course my show was no good without pictures."

"Of course not," said Joe, and the tall, thin individual "tootled" so loud through the mouthpiece of the trombone, that Toby gave a sharp bark. "Be quiet, Toby, and learn to behave yourself in company."

"This chap," said Bill Adler, "had lots of pictures, and very cheap, too; so I buys four of 'em—the same as is in the show now. Of course I coloured 'em a bit before I could put 'em in the frames—for the boys likes 'em coloured. Well, after I'd got the pictures I buys the bull's-eye glasses at a shop in Hounsditch; then I was set up——"

"Tootle—tootle—tootle!" went the gentleman with the trombone mouthpiece.

"I don't much care for music at the best of times," said Bill, in a whisper; "had too much of it where the 'spectable broker came to seize; my landlord's boy used to grind away upon a concertina all day long, and night, too, sometimes. Well, as the chap in the *Penny Diversity* says, to continue. I puts the traps together and starts off, and so I've been ever since now nigh upon a year, and if I ain't made a fortune I've got a shilling or two to spend with a friend, and maybe a pound to help him if he wants it."

"Bravo Bill, said Charity; "let's have a look at your show, will you?"

"You wouldn't care about it, Joe, it's the patter that takes it off. Lor, bless you, sometimes I jaws away till I forget all about the pictures, and I call 'em sometimes the Battle of Waterloo, sometimes other battles, and all sorts of things, but it don't matter much, as far as that goes, for they are as much like one battle as another, and not much like any that has been fought in our time or anybody else's."

The boys laughed, and the gentleman with the mouthpiece "tootled" so loud, that his companion asked—

"What are you making that horrible noise about?"

"Noise!" said Trombone Mouthpiece; "I'm getting my embouchure. You know very well I'm to take the trombone now, since the fellow who played it bolted away with our Circassian ponies, as came from somewhere out Finsbury way."

"It's a pity you can't get your what-you-call it when you're asleep, not make that noise here."

"Ah!" said Trombone, "so it is. Well, I'll try it, I'll tie my mouthpiece to my mouth when I go to bed to-night."

"Brother professionals," said Bill Adler, "I'll be sworn."

"Yes," said Joe, "especially him with the mouthpiece, he's setting his cap at us."

"Very likely," Bill said. "You lads, what are you going to be up to?"

"Don't know," said Joe, "thought of going to London, but the journey is rather long, and we are without coin."

"Well," the showman said, "I don't know that you'd do much good if you were to go there. Why not join me in the show line?"

"I should like to," said Joe; "but I don't see how I can be of any use. Besides, if I could there's Tommy and Toby, for of course we wouldn't part, as we have come on our own hook together."

"Of course not," Bill Adler said, "I'm not the man to ask you. Come, can't we think of something that will make all our fortunes in no time."

"I'm afraid not," Joe said. "Coin isn't made very easy now-a-days, unless like old Siv, we could keep a loan office, or like old Nip keep a school to starve the poor chaps that have no mothers or fathers."

"I was thinking," Bill Adler said; "but that fellow with his tootle-tootle—why don't he leave off?—I was thinking that we might do a little business together like this. Now, you and Tommy there, when I made a pitch with my show, could come up and have a look, and when there was a mob round me, go among 'em, say it was the splendidest sight you ever set your eyes on."

"Yes," Joe said, "that would do for a time; but if we stayed too long in one place the yokels would soon be up to the dodge."

"That's right enough, worse luck, but as we have met like we have I don't mean for us to part if there's anything to be done. Now, I'm tired of lumping that show about the country, but half a loaf is better than none, so I sticks to it till something else turns up; now, can't you both think of something so as we can all join in, Toby and all——"

"Tootle, tootle, tu, tu, tuk ka, tuk ka ka tuk!" went the thin gentleman through the mouthpiece of the trombone.

"I wish that lean chap," said Bill Adler, "would swallow his blessed mouthpiece, I do."

"It would'nt hurt him," Joe said, "if it didn't stick in his throat; well, now, something that we can all join in—come, Tommy, let's hear what you have to say."

"I wish Toby was a wolf," said Nimblejaws; "then we might do something."

"A wolf!" exclaimed Joe; "a wolf!"

"A wolf!" said Bill Adler; "a wolf!"

"Yes," said Tommy, "a wolf."

A SCENE NOT INCLUDED IN THE PERFORMANCE.

"What for?" Joe asked.

"What for?" Bill Adler said, "what for?"

"Well, I'll tell you," answered Nimblejaws; "because we could have a performance with him, we then might come out as the great wolf-hunters of the dark mountains, or the frozen ocean of the South Pole."

"Did you hear that?" whispered the stout man, companion to the thin man with the mouth-piece; "there's something new for us."

"Yes," whispered the man with the mouth-piece; "tootle, tootle, tu tu, ku ku!"

"Rust that mouthpiece!" said Bill Adler, "but look here," he added, jumping from his seat and sitting down again; "you've hit it, Tommy, you have—you have, my boy—Toby shall be a wolf, and we'll be the frozen hunters of the West Pole."

"South Pole," said Tommy, "of the dark mountains: I think that will take; but how are you going to make Toby a wolf?"

"Easy enough," said Bill Adler, "easy enough; but wait till we get the title pro-perly—ah! I have it, listen to this," and in

excitement of the moment Bill Adler then
.d—

ONGA, THE PERFORMING WOLF, AND THE HUNTERS
OF THE FROZEN MOUNTAINS."

"Bravo!" shouted the stout man, companion
to the thin man with the mouthpiece, "bravo!
I'll engage the lot."

"Tootle, tootlo, tu tu, tut tu, ku ku!" cho-
russed in the thin man with the mouthpiece;
"just the thing—beats the fat woman into fits."

The two were astounded at the sudden offer
made by the stout man, who at once left his seat
and came with extended hand towards Bill
Adler, and the latter took refuge behind the
empty measure in which had frothed the inviting
half-and-half.

CHAPTER XIII.

MR. BANKS ENGAGES THE HUNTERS OF THE FROZEN
MOUNTAINS AND THE JUMPING WOLF, JUNGA;
THEN STANDS A BANQUET OF STEAKS AND ONIONS.

"EXCUSE me," the stout gentleman said, as Bill
Adler took the extended hand, "for making so
free, but I am, like yourselves, in the profession."

"You are very kind," said Bill, "very kind,
I'm sure."

"Don't mention it," said the stout gentleman;
"my name is Banks—Josiah Banks, at your
service."

"I'm very much obliged, I'm sure," said Bill,
"my name's Adler, Bill Adler, and that's my
show."

"Most happy to make your acquaintance,
Mr. Adler," said Mr. Josiah Banks, "and I have
no doubt we shall find our friendship of great
advantage."

"I hope so," said the showman, "but I wish
you'd make him with the mouthpiece hold his
noise."

"Shut up, Trombone," said Mr. Banks to his
thin companion; then, by way of an explanation,
he added, "this gent belongs to my orchestra.
Now let me have the pleasure of standing a little
something, then we will go into business. What
do you and the young gentlemen take?"

"Half-and-half," said Joe, "we like it because it's nice and thick, none of your thin
swipes here."

Mr. Banks rung the bell, ordered and paid for
a pot of half-and-half, then filling a long clay
from a box of tobacco that opened when a halfpenny was dropped through a hole in the lid,
then threw himself back in his chair and said—

"The hirings comes off here in a few days,
but as I have been here every hirings for the last
few years, and with the same company, I wants
a little something new."

"Of course," said Bill Adler, dropping a
copper through the slit in the tobacco-box cover,
while Joe leant forward and read the following
couplet, which was engraved upon a brass plate
on the front of the box—

When you wish your pipe to fill,
Drop a copper in the till.

"Fat woman," continued Mr. Banks; "sheep
with two heads and four tails, red Indians, and
play-acting, for we do Shakespeare sometimes in
my booth."

"No doubt," Joe thought.

"But it all gets flat with the audience; I've
tried everything, sir," continued Mr. Banks;
I've had a giant ten feet high in his socks, I've
had a living skeleton, I've had boa-constrictors,
dogs and monkeys, and industrious fleas, but
they all get stale, and, as I said to Trombone
this morning as we came in here, if we don't get
something fresh, I shall have to sell the booth
for old rags, and he will have to go 'buskin'
with his instrument."

"Yes," said Bill Adler, "things do get flat,
now, there's my show, if I wasn't to call it by
all sorts of battles, the pictures I mean, I
shouldn't get enough out of it to buy soles for
my boots."

"The show business," said Mr. Banks, "is
almost done for now, but the other idea of yours
will bring money into our pockets, sir, if it is
properly worked; and although I say it, as
shouldn't, perhaps, but if there's one man can
work up new ideas, that man is Jonas Banks,
your most humble servant before you."

"Yes," said Bill Adler; "very likely you
can; but although I have thought of the title,
and got everything ready for the business, I've
not made up my mind how to carry it out."

"Leave that to me," said Mr. Banks; "I'll
do all that if we come to business, which I hope
we shall now. As I was saying before, when
Trombone and I came in here, we were wondering how we should get up something new, and
while wondering, I heard you say those blessed
words—words, sir, that will yet be written in
black letters two feet long, and placed right across
the front of the Theatre-Royal, and general exhibition: yes, sir, 'Junga, the Wolf, or the Wild
Hunters of the Frozen Mountain'—the words
are good, sir."

"They don't sound bad," said Bill modestly;
"not half so bad; but what will they look when
they are written in black letters?"

"Look, sir," said Mr. Banks; "they will look
good, terrifically good, and must draw. Now to
business."

"To business," said the showman; "that's the
thing."

Charity and Nimblejaws drew their chairs closer to the table, the momentous moment having arrived, and Toby, as though he understood there was something going forward out of the usual order of things, pricked up his ears and listened to the voluble tongue possessed by Mr. Josiah Banks, proprietor of the Theatre-Royal and General Exhibition.

"Now," said Mr. Banks, "fair is fair, and wrong is no man's right, is my motto, and one I always sticks to, and mean to do as long as I am in the profession. Am I right?"

"True as gospel," said the attenuated machine, "True every word."

"Acting up to this," continued Mr. Banks, "I always do my best for the company as well as for myself; and this is how I does it. Whatever the house holds, I just take one half; which isn't much when you come to consider that I have to find everything; the other half I gives to the company to divide equal amongst them."

"How many is in the company now?" Bill Adler asked. "I ain't particular, you know, Mr. Banks, but I should like to know whether it will pay better than the shares, which it ought."

"Ought, sir," said Mr. Banks; "ought, it will, ten times better. Now let me see, there's six actors, two ladies. We had three, but one of them bolted with the young chap as used to blow the trombone, that's eight; then there's two trotting brothers of the sandy desert, that's ten. Then there's the money-taker and the bill-poster, and the man that looks after the horse; that's thirteen. Then there's the orchestra—trombone, fife, key-bugle, and drum, that's seventeen. Then comes the scene-shifters, two of 'em —that make's nineteen; and if the wild hunters of the frozen mountains join us there will be just two-and-twenty."

"Twenty-two," said Bill Adler, reflectively, "how much does the house hold?"

"As many as we can get in," said Mr. Banks, "the walls are canvas, so they stretches, but when there's a good house we reckon on seven or eight pounds."

"That's four pounds for you," said Joe, "and four for the nineteen, that don't seem much, does it, Adler?"

"Stop, stop," said Mr. Banks, "you forget that we give performances every half hour or so, therefore you see there's no knowing how much it may come to in one day; why, sometimes I've known every one of the company to clear above a pound after all expenses for the day were paid—of course there's a few little expenses, but they don't come to much not all

lumped together, and when there's so many to pay them, why you may say it's nothing."

"Over a pound," Bill Adler thought; "well, that's more than the show brings in for a whole week's tramping sometimes; I don't think we can do better than close, for I haven't coin enough to buy a theatre, and the performing half isn't much good without one."

"Now what do you say?" Mr. Banks asked, "the offer is a good one, I can tell you, an out-and-out one—everything fair and square, and the money every night; if you say yes I'll stand a little supper of steak and onions and everything will be arranged."

CHAPTER XIV.

THE THEATRE-ROYAL AND GENERAL EXHIBITION.—
FIRST APPEARANCE OF THE PERFORMING WOLF,
AND THE HUNTERS OF THE FROZEN MOUNTAINS.

"WHAT do you say, Charity?" Bill Adler asked, "I'm agreeable if both you lads are."

"I'm all there," said Joe, "and so is Tommy; as for Toby, he's up to anything that's going."

"It's all settled then," said Mr. Banks; "now we will order the steak and onions, and shake hands all round."

The steak and onions were ordered, then Mr. Banks shook hands all round.

"I shouldn't like to give up the old show," Bill Adler said, "for there's no knowing what may happen."

"Give it up, certainly not," said Mr Banks; "what made you think of such a thing?"

"Well," said the showman, "the fact is I have no place to keep——"

"Keep, nonsense—isn't there the portico of my theatre that is set aside for a general exhibition? you shall put it there, Mr. Adler, it will be quite safe, and no doubt will be kept in working order by the people who care more for the exhibition department than they do for the performance of Shakespeare and other plays, let alone the vaulting brothers of the Sandy Desert, and the performance of the splendid band of my establishment."

"I'm much obliged, I'm sure," said Bill Adler, "and if the show is any use while I am in the the company, you're quite welcome to it."

At the conclusion of the banquet, Mr. Banks ordered a few drops of cold gin-and-water all round, and when the glasses appeared the gentleman with the mouthpiece put the small instrument into his pocket and rubbed his hands gleefully.

"It's his favourite," said Mr. Banks. "Trombone likes it better than all the foreign wines and such like stuff."

"It ain't bad," said Bill Adler: "I like a little cold at times."

"Now," said Mr. Banks, "gentlemen all, I beg to propose the health of the Hunters of the Frozen Mountains, and success to the performing wolf, Junga!"

The toast was drunk with a proper amount of enthusiasm, then Mr. Banks said:

"Now, gentlemen, as we've nothing particular to do, I propose we go and have a look how the theatre is going on, for I told them to have it up as soon as possible, for although there's a day or two yet before the hirings come off, it's as well to have the place ready, for the public soon get to know what spirited proprietors like a certain Josiah Banks have for their amusement."

The party left; Mr. Banks, Bill Adler, and Trombone walking in advance, Joe, Nimblejaws, and Toby bringing up the rear.

"Well, Tommy," Joe said; what do you think of our luck?"

"Fine," said Tommy; "much better than being a highwayman or pirate. I like the idea of being an actor, don't you, Joe?"

"Yes," replied Charity; "I've only been to the theatre once, and that wos the Vic; it was an out-and-out performance; one sailor with a cutlass in each hand and two more between his teeth, came in and beat about twenty pirates. I thought then I should like to be an actor when I grew up; and didn't I cry out 'bravo!' when the sailor beat all the pirates, and I stood up on my seat to see the sailor finish off the last half-dozen of 'em! but I nearly got chucked over, I did."

"Chucked over!" Tommy asked; "what was that for?"

"Why, you see," continued Joe; "there was a fellow before me, and he said I got right before his gal, and she couldn't see, so I sat down, but when the performance was over, I met my gentleman out side, and we had a turn-up."

"Which of you won, Joe?"

"Well, neither of us; for I tripped him up, and he fell against a stall of whelks and mussels, and over went the lot, so I made a bolt, and left 'em to have it out."

"This is the theatre, I suppose," said Tommy; "what a large place."

About a dozen men were busy renovating the circular theatre when the party arrived, and Mr. Banks, to show his authority before his new acquaintances, bustled about finding fault wherever he could.

"Come, Simmins," he said, "drive this post farther in. That pole is not straight, Jones. Why don't you mind what you are about? Keep those planks outside until the canvas is up. I never knew such a parcel of fools in all my life."

So on until he had abused every man who

seemed doing his best to erect the Theatre Royal and Grand Exhibition.

"Brown," said Mr. Banks to a man clothed in a canvas suit bespattered with as many colours as there were patches on Joseph's coat, "Get up a long strip to go across the front of the theatre, and print on it 'The Performing Wolf Junga and the Hunters of the Frozen Mountains.'"

"The Performing Wolf Junga and the Hunters of the Frozen Mountains. Yes, sir," said Brown." "Anything else?"

"Well, you may as well say the only exhibition of the kind in Europe, and about all the crowned heads as usual."

"Yes, sir."

And the scene-shifter, sign-painter, sometimes actor, disappeared inside one of the caravans in rear of the theatre.

"I think," said Mr. Banks to the showman, "you had better make the most of the time and get well up in your rehearsals. To-morrow morning I will send you down the dresses for the Wolf and yourselves."

"Very well," said Bill. "We shall be at the same place, for I daresay they can spare us a couple of beds."

"No doubt, no doubt," said Mr. Banks; "Buddleton-cum-Peters is not over full yet, good-night, I'll drop in myself in the morning and see how you get on."

The proprietor shook hands all round, and Trombone tootled good-night to the Wild Hunters of the Frozen Mountains.

The tricks Joe had taught Toby were very useful now; and Mr. William Adler was so delighted with the rehearsal that he clapped his hands, and cried out bravo several times.

The rehearsal took place after breakfast next morning; the landlord of the "Two Ploughs," when he found out the quality of his guests, graciously offered them the use of the parlour.

"Now, we'll have it over again," said Bill Adler; "and when Toby jumps over your back, Tommy, you must strike an attitude to represent a hunter suddenly startled from his sleep by the wolf, and——"

"Good morning all," said Mr. Banks, entering the room; "how do you get on? Come in, Simmons, put the properties on the table."

"Good morning, sir," said Bill Adler; "glad you've come, for the dog beats everything I have yet seen in all my life."

"Glad to hear it—very glad; and the young gentlemen, how do they seem to take to their parts?"

"They are all there," said the showman. "You sit down, and we'll go over it again.

TOBY MAKES FRIENDS IN THE KITCHEN.

That, sir, is also Joe's and mine; we invented it last night before we went to sleep.

"Just so," Mr. Banks said, rubbing his hands, "just so. A very good time for study, a very good time, indeed, are the quiet hours of night."

"They is," Bill Adler answered, "but somehow I always falls asleep when I'm trying to think over anything when I goes to bed. But Joe——"

Bill Adler paused, and his honest face gleamed with admiration as he looked at Joe.

"That lad, sir, will make anybody's fortune; mark my words, sir, mark my words."

"Certainly," Mr. Banks said, "certainly, Mr Adler.

"A great fortune too," the showman continued, "for he's got brains, sir, plenty of brains; and so you would have said if you had seen him and heard him last night as he sat up in bed and invented all the performance."

"Very clever indeed," said Mr. Banks. "I'm sure it's clever, although I have not seen it."

"You shall, Mr. Banks. Now, Joe, begin,

and you, Tommy, mind that you keep still until I say Chubbery Chow. That's suppose to mean where's the wolf?"

"All right," Nimblejaws answered; "I shouldn't have moved just now if Joe hadn't pricked me."

The performance began by Joe and Nimblejaw's spreading an old blanket upon the floor, then they laid full length, and seemed to be asleep.

Joe then called Toby, who ran across the room and began sniffing around his master, but, at a word from Joe, the animal walked away.

Interval of two seconds and a half, then William Adler, in a frantic state, rushes upon the scene, and demands, in his loudest tone :—

"Chubbery Chow."

The sleepers start up. Bill Adler gesticulates wildly, and keeps up in his frantic state until the three are about to leave the supposed stage in search of the wolf.

Toby, observing a signal from his master, again appears. Tableaux : Toby stands erect on his hind legs, the hunters level their spears. (Pieces of firewood in this instance, but to be replaced by real stage weapon when the performances came off.)

Joe hurles his spear at Toby. Toby takes it between his teeth, and is about to run off, Joe dashes forward and seizes the dog by the throat, at the same time whispering :—

"Seize it, boy, seize it."

The article to be seized is a piece of thin cord Joe has fastened to the collar of his jacket. Tremendous struggles between the wolf and the young hunter. Joe at last appears exhausted, and falls ; Toby, still holding the cord between his teeth, is uppermost.

Now is the moment for the other hunters to interfere.

"Lie down," Joe whispers when Bill Adler and Nimblejaws attack the wolf with their spears—and, of course, conquer the furious animal. Tableaux : The dead wolf carried across the stage on a litter made by the crossed spears of the Hunters of the Frozen Mountains.

"What do you think of it?" said Bill to Mr. Banks when the performance ended. "Isn't it the thing?"

"Think of it?" Mr. Banks answered. "Think of it? It beats all I've seen. Gentlemen, I am proud to have the honour of bringing you before the British public."

"Much obliged, I'm sure," Bill Adler answered, "and hopes we shall all make a good hit."

"We shall, we shall. Good-bye for the present. Eh, by the bye, how's the dresses? Get them ready, for we open to-morrow. Ta, ta."

Mr. Banks left, his mind filled with the most pleasant anticipations respecting the future.

CHAPTER XV.

IMMENSE SUCCESS OF THE WILD HUNTERS OF THE FROZEN MOUNTAINS. — MR. BANKS EXHIBITS STRANGE MANIFESTATIONS OF JOY, AND TROMBONE PLAYS A SOLO IN HONOUR OF THE PERFORMING WOLF.

MR. WILLIAM ADLER added tailoring to the many qualifications he possessed, and it was lucky, very lucky, that he knew so much of the art of "Repairs neatly done," for the dresses left by Mr. Banks for the use of the hunters were anything but good fits.

For Bill Adler there was a suit made from the skins of rabbits, but so discoloured with dust and wear that a naturalist would have been sorely puzzled to have described the species of quadruped to which they had belonged.

Joe's and Tommy's dresses were of sheepskin, and much too large for the young hunters, they having been used by tall men in a splendid drama called "The Frozen Wanderer; or, the Frost bitten Mariners."

Toby's costume was likewise of sheepskin, and had been worn by a boy who had personated a cat in one of Mr. Banks' pantomimes.

The hunters of the Frozen Mountains had a busy night in fitting, repairing, and otherwise making the costumes presentable to the enlightened agricultural audience who were expected to fill the Theatre Royal to overflowing.

"Walk up," said the man outside the theatre royal, "walk up and see the greatest performance that was ever brought before the ladies and gentlemen of Buddleton-cum-Peters. Play up, music !"

Trombone, side-drum, and fife, struck up a tune, but as each instrument endeavoured to play the solo, the effect upon the ear was not, perhaps, all that could have been desired by a musical assembly; the Buddleton-cum-Petersonians were not very particular upon this point, so the performance of the band passed of very creditably.

"The Grand Exhibition," the loud-voiced individual continued, when Trombone and Fife had exhausted their breath, and Side-drum had made his arm ache, "is now open free; there you may behold the first cannon ball that was fired at the battle of Waterloo—the skin of the lion what used to be in the Tower of London—a stuffed monkey from Gibraltar—a tooth of the whale where Jonah lived inside—and the wonderful panoramic views of all the great battles of England. Remember—hi, hi ! all this is free !—Go on, music."

Music went on, and the loud-voiced man rested his lungs for a few minutes; the panoramic views, by the way, were poor old Bill Adler's pictures in the show made from egg chests.

Side-drum in the said performance succeeded in drowning the notes emitted by Trombone; this gentleman endured the insult a long time, but at last his fortitude gave way, and turning suddenly when the back of Side-drum's head was towards him, he shot out the slide of his instrument, and raised such a bump upon the skull of the noisy performer, that greatly impeded his use of the drumsticks, for whereas he had used both hands before, he had but one to use after the encounter, for the rapidly rising bump required the entire use of the other hand.

The tune came to an end, and the stout-lunged individual began afresh.

"The first part of the performance," he said, "will be the grand spectacular drama of 'Timour, the Magician, the Fairy Princess, and the Invisible Godmother;' the great and powerful drama will be followed by a farce entitled, "Who's got your boots?" After this, Professor Smiffiani will appear on the tight rope; then will appear the Arab Brothers of the Bounding Desert; and to wind up such a performance as you never saw in all your lives, will appear the Wild Hunters of the Frozen Mountains, and the Performing Wolf, Junga. Remember, the Wild Hunters and the Performing Wolf are worth three times the money. Walk up! Walk up! Tuppence in the pit; fourpence in the front seats, and sixpence in the reserved seats. Go on, music."

With such a host of attractions, the Theatre Royal soon filled, and Mr. Banks' rosy face was the picture of genial good humour.

"The wolf, sir," he said to Trombone, as that gentleman left the exterior of the theatre to take his place in the internal orchestra, "the wolf, sir, they could not stand that?"

Trombone was as usual giving out idiotic sounds through his mouthpiece, an occupation he only desisted from to reply to the manager, proprietor, and tragedian, by saying:—

"The wolf? Yes, that's it. To-to-tuk-ker-tu-tu."

The drama was well received, the farce seemed to please better, for there was something so intellectual in the plot—a man—funny man, of course—stops at an inn, puts his boots outside the door of his room, awakes in the morning, minus his boots.

Nobody knew anything about them, except that a foreign gentleman slept in a room opposite.

Foreign gentleman not here, the young man starts in pursuit of foreign gentleman.

Delight of the audience when funny man limps across the stage without boots.

(N.B. He is supposed to be walking over a roadway strewn with flint stones.)

Great delight of audience when funny man stops passers-by and asks them if they have seen his boots, and so on for some time, when the funny man returns to the inn, and makes the discovery that his boots have been found under his pillow, and his pocket handkerchief outside the door, &c.

The tight rope business was received very mildly, the Petersonians had seen that before; the Arab Brothers of the Bounding Desert caused but little sensation; but when the appearance of the Wild Hunters was announced, the audience settled themselves in their seats, and the ruddy-cheeked maidens drew closer to Giles or John, or whatever patronymic the gentleman in remarkble waistcoats and quite as remarkable neckcloths bore.

The overture performed by the trio of musicians was supposed to still the nerves of the audience to the appearance of the wolf, for the trombone emitted sundry unearthly noises, supposed to be the roaring of the wind among the peaks of the frozen mountains.

The side-drum beat a long tattoo, depicting the pattering of the wolf's feet across the frozen ground; a fife blew out the echoes of the distinct screams of women and children who were being pursued by droves of wolves.

This delectable performance over, Mr. Banks, in full evening costume—he looked very much like a seedy waiter—appeared before the curtain, and bowing until the bald shining crown of his head became visible to the very furthermost of those who sat in the back seats, thus addressed the audience:—

"Ladies and gentlemen—Year after year I have had the happiness of meeting the refined, ladylike, and gentlemanly inhabitants of this town and the surrounding villages——"

"Bravo! that be right, that is," said one of the gentlemen, in a voice dulcet enough to scare away a flight of crows, "bain't he, Bet?"

"He be," answered one of the ladylike; "and a nice man he be, too, like all Lunnoners."

"Each year," Mr. Banks continued, "I have endeavoured to bring something new, something novel, and something worthy of the just and appreciative audience now before me."

Mr. Banks here showed the ladies and gentlemen his bald crown, and there was a little enthusiasm manifested—caused, no doubt, by the sight of the well-known crown

"Why should I not do so?" continued Mr. Banks; "have I not always been well received? I have, better than I deserved—much——"

"That be roight," shouted a ploughman from the back seats; "don't he recollect th' lady wi' whiskers all round her face? That wor a sham, for beard fell off when she wor on the stage, I——"

"Turn him out!" shouted one of the company, who had been judiciously placed among the audience to applaud whenever there was an opportunity; "pitch him out!"

"No, no, my friends," Mr. Banks said; "do not, in your excitement, lay hands upon that gentleman who labours under a mistake—do not, I say, give expression to the indignation that burns in your breasts as free-born and enlightened Englishmen, by doing violence to that gentleman's person—do not take him by the collar, and pitch him through the doorway, do not, I beg——"

Mr. Banks uplifted his hands as the gentleman's person was taken by the collar and pitched head-foremost down the steps.

The commotion having subsided, Mr. Banks placed his hands meekly upon his breast, and said—

"I would not for the wealth of the world have my friends here before me entertain the least suspicion of my honesty—no;"—attitude struck—"not for the wealth of twenty worlds."

"Hooray! bravo!"

"Therefore," continued Mr. Banks, "I feel it my duty to explain the cause of the lady's beard falling off."

"Don't mind that fellow; we've chucked him out!"

"I do not mind that person; but,"—here Mr. Banks placed his right hand impressively upon the left side of his waistcoat—"but I do mind my name and reputation as an honest man —a man who would not attempt to impose upon the free and enlightened inhabitants of this town and the surrounding villages by bringing anything before them unless it was the real and genuine article; for I am well aware that a sensible audience like this would soon discern the cheat, and my name would be branded with a felon's stigmatick."

The last word not being understood by Mr. Banks or the audience, caused great applause and sundry waggings of heads from Giles to to John and John to Giles, as they looked at each other, and said—

"Should think we should soon find him out if he tried any dodge on wi' us."

"Such being the state of my heart," Mr. Banks resumed, when the applause had subsided, "I feel it necessary to explain the cause of the lady's beard falling off; it happened thus—the lady was about to quit my company to be married to a gentleman of fortune—a fate, I hope, may happen to all the ladies I see now before me— bless your pretty faces!"

The ruddy-cheeked maidens tried to look confused, and their swains, not quite relishing the idea of the rustic Venuses being wedded to gentlemen of fortune, began to look indignant, until Mr. Banks healed their wounded sensibilities by adding:—

"And gentlemen of fortune are the free-born gentlemen I see before me—the honest, strong, and mighty men who have made England what it is."

Thunders of applause and stamping of hob-nailed boots.

"Well, ladies and gentlemen, the bearded lady being, as I said before, about to leave my company, called in the assistance of a professor of the tonsorial art to shave off her beard; but unfortunately she did this two days before this theatre left the welcome spot it now occupies. Now, I ask you what could I do? The lady was advertised as part of the exhibition, and I would not for a thousand pounds disappoint my friends here before me."

"Thee art a good 'un!"

"But what was to be done? I was nearly mad On my knees I begged her to stay the other two days, and at last, by offering her a heavy bribe, she consented. But a new difficulty then occurred: there was the lady, but the beard was gone. I could not tell what to do until the lady assisted me out of my difficulty. Send one of your men upon one of your fleetest horses, she said: Let him ride to London, and have a beard made. It will be ready before the theatre opens to-morrow. This was done, ladies and gentlemen, but the artist had not made the fastenings properly, for the beard fell off as the gentleman stated; but I, your obedient servant, look upon the falling off of that beard as an additional proof of my fair dealing. For had the lady been in the habit of wearing a false beard, she would have looked after the fastenings better."

"Bravo! that be right. Well done!"

"Now," continued Mr. Banks, "having cleared myself from the charge the person you so kindly expelled from the theatre would have brought against me, I will return to the subject of the Wild Hunters and the Jumping Wolf."

"It be almost time," growled an old farmer; "for thy jaw has been going like an old hen over her first brood of chicks."

"Following the example of the lessees and managers of the leading London theatres," said Mr. Banks, "for, like your humble servant, they have to make their living by pleasing the public —I travel every year when the theatre is closed for the season, and while the lessees and managers of the places I have mentioned seek all over the Continent to find women who can squall louder than any in the last season's company— my flight takes a wider range, for I know a free British audience like would not care for a squalling singer ; therefore I seek the boundless desert—there I found the Arab Brothers, whose performance you have not long since seen."

Mr. Banks paused, and beckoned one of the scene-shifters to bring a glass of cool water (and gin).

"Farther than the boundless desert," he continued, after this refresher, " I travelled since I last saw you, far away, to where the mighty Andes raise their snow-crowned heads, and there, among the frozen mountains, chance brought me in contact with three wolf-hunters, a father and two sons ; a thought struck me——"

"Pity it didn't knock thee head off," said the old farmer to his fat wife.

" When I saw the wolf-hunters had a tamed wolf which they used to decoy other wolves, here, I thought, is a chance of taking home a novelty for my friends of Buddleton-cum-Peters, and if money shall do it, it shall be done. Ladies and gentlemen, I have nothing more to say ; the performance I hope will speak for itself, and perhaps your kind approbation will reward me for my dreary travel among the wild wolves of the frozen mountains. One word more, the hunters having but just arrived in this country, are quite ignorant of our free language ; therefore, it will be necessary for me to stand against the wing and explain the scenes as they occur in reality among the frozen mountains.

CHAPTER XVI.

IS A CONTINUATION OF THE LAST CHAPTER, AND PLACED HERE TO GIVE THE READER AN OPPORTUNITY TO RECOVER HIMSELF AFTER READING THE GUILELESS WORDS SPOKEN BY MR. JOSIAH BANNS WHEN ADDRESSING THE AUDIENCE AT THE THEATRE ROYAL AND GENERAL EXHIBITION.

MR. BANKS lowered himself out of sight, and meeting the wild hunters, who were standing against the wings ready to come on, he said :—

"There, my boys, there's a bit of gag for you ; now go in and create a sensation."

The orchestra having played a short prelude and several false notes, the bell rang, and the curtain slowly rose.

The scene did the Theatre Royal great credit, considering the materials the scene painters used in the get-up.

The back-ground represented huge sugar-loaves : these were the Frozen Mountains. The artist had painted them with a pail of whitewash, and a large brush ; the wings were also touched up with the whitewash brush, and the appearance of the trees was refreshingly cool.

Having given the audience time to admire the wild and rugged realities of the frozen mountains, Mr. Banks took up a position at the side of the stage, and to convince the free and enlightened gentlemen he understood the language spoken in the vicinity of the rocky mountains, he waved his hand majestically and said—

" Jumpaka bu."

At this mysterious command Charity and Nimblejaws, dressed in their proper costume, and armed with spears, came upon the stage, and as Mr. Banks explained their movements to the audience, the reader will be as much enlightened by his words as by a repetition of the rehearsal.

" The young hunters, you will observe, ladies and gentlemen," said Mr. Banks, " are examining the ground for to discover the great wolf of the mountains, who has just left the villiage after eating up all the old women and children."

" Failing to discover the wolf tracks, you now observe the manner in which the wolf hunters retire for the rest of the night."

" There you see them rolled in the skins of the animals they have slain ; now they sleep, but still they grasp their weapons, for they know not the moment when the treacherous wolf may pounce upon them—HA !"

Toby now appeared, looking very uncomfortable in his borrowed skins.

" Here comes the——"

There took place many manifestations of alarm among the rustic Venuses when Toby began to walk stealthily across the stage, in obedience to Joe's low whistle.

"Don't be alarmed," Mr. Banks continued, much delighted at the fear Toby had occasioned ; " for the once fierce animal is now as tame as a pet dog ; besides this, we have, in case his ferocious instincts should return, a couple of men placed ready with guns, pistols, and swords to kill the animal if he makes one step towards the front of the stage."

This was reassuring, and had the desired effect.

" You will observe now," Mr. Banks continued, " the wolf scents the hunters. You see he moves around them, and endeavours to get his nose under the blanket, but the hunters are too well trained in the ways of the savage beast to leave an opening for him to touch their flesh ; for if they were to do so, they would be at once torn to pieces."

Toby was certainly trying to find an opening in the folds of the blanket, for he was wishing to uncover his master's face.

It was lucky Joe drew the covering over their heads, for he was nearly suffocated with laughter; and, out of pure mischief, he tickled Tommy's ribs, and caused that youth the most trying torments to keep from jumping to his feet.

"Hush," said Mr. Banks. "See, the wolf hears a footstep in the distance. He knows that none but the hunter, armed with the deadly spear, frequents his lair among the frozen mountains. He shows signs of fear. Now he leaves the sleepers, and darts into the hidden thickets of the surrounding scenery."

Toby trotted off to the wing, where a man stood holding out a piece of meat.

"See," Mr. Banks continued as Bill Adler rushed upon the stage and stood over the sleeping pair, "the father's joy when he finds his sons still asleep. Now you will observe his joy changes to anger when he finds the wolf has crossed their path while they sleep. See, he strikes them with the shaft of his spear, and demands——"

"Chubbery Chow," yelled Bill Adler. "Chow, choe——o——mi——ney."

"Why they have slept while the night wolf is abroad, who has lately eaten up all the blessed children and the old ladies of the village."

"I wishes we had a wolf here," whispered a rustic youth to his companion, "to eat up all 't'old women in our village, and stop their croaking tongues. "Don't 'ee, gal?"

The fair one did not answer, she was too much engrossed with the performance to trouble herself about the village gossips.

"You observe now," Mr. Banks continued, "how the young hunters spring to their feet and look down on the ground for the marks of the wolf's feet. You see they find them, and are about to start in pursuit, when the wolf again appears, showing his teeth."

Toby certainly looked very fierce from the distance, for the scene painter had ornamented the wolf's mouth by the addition of half a dozen white strokes drawn perpendicularly to represent teeth.

"You observe the splendid attitude the hunters assume; see their levelled weapons—the wolf knows his danger—for he rises up and walks on his hind legs. Ha! a spear is thrown at him by——"

Charity Joe, Mr. Banks was about to say.

"O-li-ki-lo-io, the young and brave—the spear has missed him, but the brave O-li-ko-lo-i, eager for the fight, rushes forward, just as the wolf takes the spear in his mouth, and is about to grind the handle to powder with his fangs."

"Seize it, Toby!" said Joe, turning his back to the audience and showing the piece of cord he had around his neck, "seize it, boy!"

"Now you will observe one of the deadly struggles so frequent in the life of the wolf-hunters," Mr. Banks went on; "the hardy mountaineer begins to lose his strength, and gradually sinks to——"

Two of the rustic beauties gave a scream, and one old lady fainted; but she came to instantly, in consequence of a close and sturdy application of her husband's boot-toe against her shins.

"There's no danger, I assure you," said Mr. Banks, "not the least danger, for this once fierce animal is now so tame that he sleeps at the foot of the young hunters' bed at night."

"He wouldn't sleep at the foot of mine," said one of the audience to his neighbour; "eh, bo?"

"Not a bit o'nt, lad; dogs is all werry well; but them strange animals from furrin parts might go wild again in one night."

"Thee be'est roight there, bo."

"You will observe now," Mr. Banks said, "the young hunter is falling a prey to the wolf; see, he is about to tear him to pieces when the father and brother rush forward to the rescue; behold, now the wolf is slain; see he lies quivering at the feet of the hunters; see, he attempts to rise again, but is held down by the young and brave——" mentally—"hang it, what name did I give, Joe?" then aloud—"hunter who first sought the combat."

Mr. Banks was compelled to add, "See, he attempts to rise," for Toby, when he obeyed Joe's whisper to lie down, espied a little dog belonging to one of the people engaged at the theatre standing near the wings.

"Now you will observe the mode of conveying the wolf home," resumed Mr. Banks. "You see with what ingenuity the hunters construct a litter with the handles of their spears, and return to the village, the admiration of the maidens, and the envy of the men."

Mr. Banks made a low bow and retired slowly, while the audience clapped their hands and stamped their thick-shod feet with a vigour that told how well they liked the novelty which Mr. Banks had brought all the way from the Frozen Mountains for their benefit.

Three performances were given after this. Each time the house was filled. The last house follow the cry of the former houses, for the fame of the Wild Hunters and the Jumping Wolf began to spread far beyond the outskirts of Buddleton-cum-Peters.

Mr. Banks, Trombone, and the Wild Hunters, went into the little parlour of the country inn, when the last performance was over, and so delighted was the manager that he danced and skipped about the room like an escaped lunatic.

"Tum, tum, too-ral-loo," laughed the manager, as he tumbled round the table like a gigantic teetotum, "fol-de-rol, tol-de-rol. One season of such houses as this, and I will take the biggest theatre in London."

"Tut-tu-ku-tu," repeated the tall gentleman through his mouthpiece, "the biggest theatre in London."

"Well, we have done pretty fair," Bill Adler said, "all things considering."

"We did it to rights," said Joe, "and no mistake."

"But I nearly spoilt it," said Tommy, "for Joe began pricking and tickling me, until I nearly yelled out mealy murder."

"Gentlemen," said Mr. Banks, suddenly pausing in his wild career around the table, "we'll have a supper—a supper such as you have not seen for many a day. Eh, Trombone? A supper in honour of the great and wonderful success of the Wild Hunters and the Performing Wolf."

"Tut-tu-kut-tu!" Trombone answered; "a supper? Yes, likes leg o' mutton and trimmings myself."

"If I had my choice," Bill Adler said, "I should say stewed tripe and onions."

"We will have both," said Mr. Banks. "I will go and speak to the landlord, and while I am gone, Trombone, play us a majestic solo in honour of this happy event."

Nothing loth, Trombone took his instrument from its case, and much to the horror of the wild hunters he inflicted upon them for ten minutes a solo of his own composing; but long before it was over Bill Adler had fallen asleep with his head upon the table, and Joe was busy decorating Bill's hat with all the twisted paper pipe-lights he could find in the room.

CHAPTER XVII.

THE UNPRECEDENTED SUCCESS OF THE PERFORMING WOLF AND THE WILD HUNTERS OF THE FROZEN MOUNTAINS CAUSES MR. DUBBS TO ENTERTAIN MOST UNCHRISTIAN-LIKE FEELINGS TOWARDS THE POPULAR PERFORMERS—MR. DUBBS CONCOCTS A MOST DIABOLICAL PLOT.

THE rumours of the great performance to be seen at the Theatre Royal and General Exhibition spread far beyond the town of Buddleton-cum-Peters.

The extreme docility of the savage animal from the Frozen Mountains, and the heroic courage portrayed by the wild hunters from the same cold spot, were the theme of general conversation; and those who had not yet seen the extraordinary spectacle were urged to do so by Mr. Banks.

To make hay while the sun was propitious was one of the proprietor's maxims, and while the orb of success still shone undiminished, Mr. J. Banks caused Buddleton-cum-Peters and the adjacent villages to be plentifully supplied with large posters, which informed the nobility, gentry, and others that, in consequent of an engagement contracted with the Emperor of France, the Theatre and General Exhibition would positively close in two days.

Four performances were given each day, and always to a crowded house. Certainly two or three gentlemen (?) had been bold enough to state that Junga, the performing wolf, was no wolf at all; but Mr. Banks coming forward and asking the sceptics to come behind the scenes and examine the furious wolf in his cage, had stopped such slander at once.

"Sir," said Mr. Banks, when he visited the parlour of the "Three Jolly Ploughmen," "sir, a great and splendid professional career is open before us."

"I hope so, I'm sure," said Bill Adler; "don't you, Joe?"

"Of course I do," said Joe. "Doing the wild hunters is much better than being at old Nip's school, eh, Tommy?"

"Beats it into fits," was the elegant answer.

"Yes, gentlemen," said Mr. Banks," "we will give up the Theatre Royal and General Exhibition, and take one of the vacant houses for the winter season."

"What! a real stage?" Tommy Nimblejaws asked, "gas-lights and everything?"

"A real stage, young gentleman," replied Mr. Banks. "Yes, a legitimate house, and I will see about it as soon as we have closed the season here. Now, let me see, we are to keep open here for two days longer."

"Yes," said Bill, "that will be eight more performances."

"Eight more, Mr. Adler," assented Mr. Banks, "and when the last performance is over, I propose we make the money settlement of accounts for this season; and, if you, gentlemen, have no objection to sign an agreement to stay with me for twelve months certain I shall like it all the better. By-the-bye, do you require any loose cash?"

Bill Adler was rising in the world, therefore he said he should not require any cash until the settling day, although, truth to tell, the hunters were running up a score at "The Three Jolly Ploughmen" for board and lodging.

"I've no objection," Bill said, "to sign any-thing, have you, Joe, or you, Tommy?"

Joe knew by this time that the unusual popu-larity of the Theatre Royal was due entirely to the Frozen Hunters and the Jumping Wolf, and, being a sharp lad, he understood the motives that prompted Mr. Banks to wish to enter into a twelvemonths' agreement.

"Flats," Joe thought, "are pretty good things in their way, but they don't come from the Borough; so if Mr. Banks don't raise the salary he won't get Charity Joe or Toby to sign anything."

"Have you, Joe?" Bill Adler repeated; "be-cause ff you haven't we might as well do it at once, for there's no knowing what may happen, as the chap used to say what preached at the corner of the market in the Borough."

Prophetic William Adler!

"I don't mind going in for business," said Joe; "but I thinks Mr. Banks ought, after the great success of the performance, to give us a little more than the share in half the takings, for we have brought more coin to the theatre than all the rest put together."

"We shall not fall out about terms," said Mr. Banks, "for I was about to propose an extra allowance to you, my friends, for Josiah Banks knows how to be liberal when he has a great success."

Mr. Banks uttered these words in rather a loud voice—so loud that they were heard by an in-dividual who was seated near the door of the parlour.

This individual, whose histrionic name was Percy Fitz Algernon, but in the parish register was written John Dubbs, was the leading tragedian at the Theatre Royal and General Exhibition.

Percy Fitz heard the propitious words, and a scowl passed over his face as he put on his hat and quietly left the "Three Jolly Ploughmen."

"I'll put a stop to their career," muttered Percy Fitz, as he strode up the street, "a parcel of low mountebanks to usurp the drama; it's not to be borne any longer."

"That's all right, then," said Joe, replying to Mr. Banks; "so we'll sign the agreement when you like."

"When we make the arrangements for the new season," Mr. Banks said, "will be ample time to do this. Now I must say good night, gentlemen all. I wish you pleasant slumbers after the labours of the day."

The manager shook hands all round, and went to the theatre to see that all was right before he retired to his lodgings.

The leading tragedian, the walking gentleman, heavy ditto, and the comic man, "put up," during their stay at Buddleton-cum-Peters, at the "Pipe and Pitcher," the leading inn, barring two or three.

Mr. Percy Fitz Algernon strode into the "Pipe and Pitcher;" his air was terrific, solemn, revengeful, and not unlike the appearance he presented when performing in the great drama of the "Black Baron of the Border."

"Gentlemen," exclaimed Mr. Fitz Algernon, folding his arms, "the drama, the legitimate drama is gone to bl——I beg pardon, for, under the excitement of the moment, I nearly used a low word, unbecoming any person connected with the drama, which, as I before said, has gone to bl——I beg pardon, again, is fallen from the high position in which it stood in the time when Pylades wrote the 'Loves of Mars and Venus.'"

"Not so very high, Mr. Dubbs," said the walking gentleman, who hated the tragedian: "not so very high in those days, for the public players were liable to be tied to a pillar and whipped."

"If they deserved it," retorted the tragedian. "Would the same laws were now in force. Perhaps, sir, you will contradict me, when I say that Pylades once rebuked the Roman Emperor Augustus, so that Nero often took part in the quarrels of the players, and upon one occasion broke the praetor's head with a footstool."

"Not having either time or inclination to bother my head about these matters," answered the perambulating gentleman, "I am not in a position to argue upon the matter; if I were—"

"If you were, sir," repeated the tragedian, "if you were——"

"I should not do so with one who has so deeply studied the history of the drama, from its com-mencement to the present time."

The Black Baron of the Border was mollified; more so, when the comic man said:—

"We all know our friend well, and I think from the high position he has so long occupied in our company, there ought not to be any doubts as to his ability to carry out anything he wishes to bring forward to support his argument."

"I am," said the heavy gentleman and cruel uncle, solemnly, "of your opinion, Mr. Clarence, therefore, am anxious that you should make known to us the disturbing element that caused those remarks respecting the drama's decline."

The heavy gentleman delivered these words with an air befitting the elevated walk he strode in the profession.

Thus invoked, Tragedy seated himself opposite Comedy (as represented at the T. R. and G. E.), ordered two of cold gin, loosened the top buttons of his coat, and spoke thus:—

BEHIND THE SCENES.

"Gentlemen," said Mr. Dubbs, glancing at the small quantity of spirit and the large supply of water the red-cheeked waitress placed before him, "we must, for a time at least, forget all little envious dissensions that may exist amongst us, as members of a profession that has from time immemorial been celebrated for —for—little petty jealousies amongst its members hem!"

"From the time," muttered the walking gentleman, "that Pylades broke Nero's skull with the jawbone of an ass."

"I beg pardon," said Tragedy, turning to the walking gentleman, fiercely, "did you apply that remark to me?"

"Remark, sir!"

"Remark, sir! I repeat it, remark!"

"No, sir," said the walking gentleman; "I did not, that I most emphatically declare."

"'Tis well, sir," said Mr. Dubbs: "I accept the explanation."

"Thank you," said Mr. Fadlada. "I beg to say that I have not the slightest wish to disturb the friendly feelings which ought to be more general."

"A proper sentiment," said Mr. Clarence—"a very proper sentiment, sir."

"In which I most heartily concur, I do assure you," said the heavy man, solemnly; "pray proceed, Mr. Percy Fitz Algernon."

"As I said before," Mr. Dubbs resumed, "we must forget all jealousies and unite for the complete overthrow of the common enemy."

"Hear, hear," said the comic man, "to overthrow the common enemy."

"Yes," Tragedy continued, "the common enemy, for I can use no other term to express the party of interlopers who have torn the glory of the drama from us, its impersonators."

The heavy gentleman rapped the table with his knuckles.

"I ask you all," said Tragedy, in continuation, "whether we shall suffer the degradation that has fallen to our lot for the last few days?"

"No! No! NO!"

"Upon this point we are all agreed," said Mr. Dubbs, triumphantly. "I am glad it is so, for a band composed of such—such—hem—clear-headed, talented gentlemen are quite able to carry out the plan I shall have to propose."

"Quite able," said the comic man, "to overthrow the prospects of the theatre if we like."

"Quite so," said Mr. Dubbs, "quite so, therefore let us trample under foot—of course I speak metaphorically, the cause of the coldness with which all our efforts to please have been received by the audience for the last week."

"There has been a marked change in their behaviour," remarked the heavy gentleman—"a very marked change indeed."

"There has," and Mr. Dubbs thumped the table to give force to his words; "and why has this change occurred, I will tell you—yes, mine shall be the lips to acknowledge—to make known the humiliating cause."

A dead silence, the heavy man refilled his pipe, the comic man pensively contemplated the threadbare sleeve of his coat, and the walking gentleman tried hard to repress the sneer that rose to his lips.

"In vain have you, sir," to the comic man, "tried to create a laugh by your famous hat business: no, sir, you might smash the best hat in the world over your eyes now and declare yourself lost, before a grin—yes, sir, even a grin—could be expected from one of the thick-headed audience.

"That's true," said the comic man, "for not only has the hat business failed, but even when I tried the effect of the ragged pocket handkerchief that was as little noticed."

"You, sir," to the heavy gentleman, "have also felt the soul-chilling effects of an audience who wished our performance to end in order that they might see something more congenial to their stupid tastes; in vain have you in the dungeon scene uttered those memorable words:—

"'Convey him to the ramparts and s-t-r-i-ke off his head.' There has been no applause, no sensation, when the daring lover who came to carry off your daughter has been led forth to execution."

"A fact, sir," replied the heavy man, "that speaks for itself, and shows how sadly deficient the audience must be in those ennobling feelings which were, once upon a time, so general among those who frequent theatres."

"Again," Mr. Dubbs said, addressing the walking gentleman, bold lover, wronged heir, &c., "what has been the reception you have met with when you, as the wronged heir, and the hunted prince, meet four bandits in the forest, and engage them single-handed in mortal combat? I ask you, sir, has there been one shout of bravo as you vanquished the host of robbers? Not one, sir."

"No, Mr. Algernon," replied the ill-used heir, "not one encouraging voice has sounded upon my ears. I have leant upon my sword, panting and breathless, not allowed, like the soldier, to wipe away a tear; although the tears of exertion stood thickly upon my brow, and I dared not wipe them off, because, as an injured prince of the middle ages, I was not supposed to carry a pocket-handkerchief."

"Where, I ask, continued Tragedy, "Where has all the enthusiasm gone; the clapping of hands, the shouts of bravo that used to greet me when I entered as the Black Baron of the Border, and exclaimed, 'By my halidom, and the good steel I wear at my hip, I will crush out the power of those who dare to come within bow-shot of the stronghold of Bluster-Dee. Beware the Black Baron of the Border!' No sound has words that were wont to shake the very walls of our theatre. Need I ask you the cause of all all this? I leave it in your hands. Yet, bad as it is to be thus humilated in consequence of the engagement of these low fellows and their dog, there is worse yet to be told."

Chorus: "Worse!"

"Aye," said Mr. Dubbs, "infinitely worse. The—the—my weary tongue refuses to make known the perfidy of the man who has for so long commanded our respect. Yet the truth must be told. He has, gentlemen—he has—and in my presence, offered the low fellows an increase of salary, beyond their share in the half-takings, if they will sign an agreement to stay in our company for one year certain. Shall this be allowed to take place, is all I ask?"

"No," said the comic man.

"Certainly not," said the heavy gentleman.

"By all means let us combine," said the walking gentleman, "and at once crush this four-headed serpent."

So they drew closer round the table and plotted the downfall of the Wild Hunters of the Frozen Mountains and the Jumping Wolf Junga.

CHAPTER XVIII.

THE RESULT OF THE PLOT.—A SCENE NOT INCLUDED IN THE PERFORMANCE.—RETIREMENT OF THE WILD HUNTERS AND THE PERFORMING WOLF FROM THE THEATRE-ROYAL AND GENERAL EXHIBITION.

"THEN we are all agreed," said the tragedian: "all bound to an inviolable bond of secrecy in this matter."

"We are all agreed, and bound to secrecy."

"And you are certain the fellow with the dog will assist us, Mr. Clarence"

"Quite sure, Mr. Percy Fitz Algernon, for he has already expressed a wish for his dog to have a turn-up, as he expresses it, with the wolf."

"By this time to-morrow," said Tragedy, "I hope to see the interlopers disgraced and the legitimate drama restored to its proper position; to carry out this I will do all in my power, even to the cutting of the fastenings of the skin that envelopes the false wolf."

Next day the appearance of the two young hunters was hailed by the audience with the most boisterous applause, and Tragedy, Comedy, walking gentleman, and heavy man smiled grimly at each other, for the moment was approaching when their diabolical plot would be put into execution.

Charity Joe and Nimblejaws rolled the blanket around them; it was not a very sound blanket, for Joe and his companion were in the habit of looking at the faces of the audience through the slits in their coverings.

Toby appeared, and there was much clapping of hard, rustic palms; and when this greeting had subsided, Joe heard one of the audience, who sat in the front seat next the orchestra, say to a companion—

"Tell 'ee what, mate, I'd back Towzer here to beat that animal they calls a wolf in no time."

"You'll see, sur-ree; for d'rectly the wolf comes this way I'll set Towzer at he."

"Towzer can foight," answered the other, "but I don't think he'd do much with a hanimal like that 'ere."

Joe, from his point of observation, "took stock" of the speakers, and saw the owner of Towzer was an awkwardly-built country fellow, about twenty years old. Joe also saw Towzer—a large colley dog, much larger than Toby, but not so well and strongly shaped.

"Hear that," he whispered to Tommy; "he means to set his tyke on Toby."

"Let him," said Tommy; "Toby's able to take the polish off three such mongrels as that."

"Very likely," Joe said; "but if the wolf jumps down among the people there'll be a row and no mistake."

"Don't much matter, I should think," Nimblejaws answered; "for we leave here to-morrow, and the wolf, breaking loose and demolishing that tyke will bring more people to see us—look out, Joe!"

The warning came too late, for as Joe jumped to his feet, Toby sprang forward, cleared the intervening space, and seized Towzer by the neck.

Unfortunately for the veracity of Mr. Josiah Banks, the wolf broke the fastenings of his extra skin, and revealed his true species to those who were near the canine battle.

Quite regardless of the exalted position to which he had been raised was Toby when Towzer sat on the seat beside his master, and, roused by the latter's "Watch him, boy; look at him, good dawg," gave a growl of defiance.

Toby stopped suddenly, and looked at his challenger; the note of defiance was repeated, Toby walked nimbly to the foot-lights, Towzer gave an angry bark—Toby replied with a growl, then made the unfortunate spring that displaced the wolf's covering.

Now a scene took place. Women screamed and fainted, men yelled:

"The wolf was loose!"

"The wolf be eating up folks!"

"Get thee out, Giles. Darn it! don't 'ee stop for door, cut a hole in canvas."

Jack-knives were soon at work making long slits in the canvas to give egress to those who were too far off to escape by the door.

At this aperture a crowd of women, men, and boys were tearing, scratching, and fighting to get out, and the cry of "Wolf! wolf!" was heard above the loud-tongued oaths of the rustics and the screams of the women.

To add to the din, those who were in the pit seats stood up and shouted—

"It bain't a wolf; it be only a dawg; we seed his skin."

"Don't 'ee go there; let us pull down old rattle trap of theatre, and serve out the smooth-faced old cheat who told the lies about the wolf."

Mr. Banks rushed on the stage frantically, and his appearance was greeted with such a storm of yells and hisses that he felt it would not be prudent for him to remain there too long.

Yet there might be a chance of propitiating those who had discovered the cheat; as for those who had passed outside, Mr. Banks cared but little. There was no re-admission at the Theatre Royal and General Exhibition.

"Ladies and gentlemen," Josiah began, "it is with the most profound re——"

"Get thee off, old thing! get thee off, thou liar and cheat, get thee off!"

"Fettle his head," one of the audience suggested; "fettle him well."

This gentleman tore up one of the seats, and his example was soon followed with a vigour not pleasant to the properties.

"Take that, thee lying old rascal."

A board, about three feet in length, whizzed past Mr. Banks's head. The hint was sufficient, the manager retired, and left the Hunters of the Frozen Mountains to fight it out with the audience, two or three of whom began to scramble over the orchestra, much to the dismay of Trombone, who, with his brother musicians sought safety by retiring behind the scenes.

"Hold him, Toby," Joe shouted, forgetting all about his inability to speak English; "shake him, boy, that's it."

"Hunters, be thee, of Frozen Mountains?" said the fellow who had been instigated to create the disturbance. "Come down here, and I'll frozen thee hide for thee."

There never was a challenge so readily accepted.

"Keep them off the stage," said Joe to his companions; "use the handles of your spears; the game's up, so I might as well just punch the fellow who caused it."

Joe jumped from the stage to the orchestra, then clearing the partition, he stood in front of his challenger.

"Here I am, my pippin," he said, "and quite ready for the freezing. Take that to begin with."

Joe's right hand and the lout's nose met; the concussion was not pleasant to the latter, and before he could take the water from his eye, he received a blow in the mouth that caused his teeth to rattle.

"I'll choke thee," growled the lout, "that's what I'll do."

"Exactly so," said Joe, touching the countryman's right eye with his left hand, "but you'll have to be quick about it, or you'll want a pair of spectacles."

So the lout discovered; for the street boy's hands were not idle for a moment, and always dropped upon a place the countryman the least expected.

During the time Joe was thrashing his adversary, Bill Adler, Tommy Nimblejaws, the scene-shifters, and others connected with the theatre, were busy repelling the assault upon the stage.

Twice the mob had gained a footing, each time they were driven back—much the worse for the repulse, for the defenders were armed with sticks, property swords, spears, and hatchets.

The matter was becoming serious, for the assailants ripped up the seats, and thus armed, made another rush to drive back the defenders of the stage.

They partly succeeded—not for the want of pluck on the defenders' part, but in consequence of the "weight" of numbers.

"Hooray," shouted the foremost yokel, "pull down t' theatre; come on."

The cry was taken up. The defenders were forced still farther back. Another moment and the properties would have been destroyed; but, as the mob were about to tear down the scenes, a voice in the rear said, loud enough for Bill Adler and his companions to hear—

"Stand clear! Make your escape by the wings!"

They did so, for it was the voice of Mr. Banks that had spoken; and no sooner were the defenders clear of the centre of the stage, than the distant view of the Rocky Mountains parted, and revealed Mr. Banks, armed with the hose of a small fire-engine.

"Pump away!" shouted the manager. "Go it, my lads."

Cluk, cluk, fizz, fizz, spirted the water through the jet, and the foremost of the assailants were drenched to the skin; and those who were yet safe from the unwelcome bath beat a hasty retreat.

In less than two minutes the stage was cleared, and the boldest of the enemy was seen slinking away, his "Sunday-going" suit a sad and wet sight.

Mr. Banks followed up the advantage by coming forward and playing upon Joe and his antagonist, who were locked in a very close if not loving embrace.

The continuous stream soon separated the pugilists—aye, even Toby relinquished his grip of Towzer, who, by the way, had received quite sufficient punishment, and was glad to limp after his master, who made the best of his way to the door, his watery foe pursuing him until he became wedged in amongst the crowd who were scrambling through the place of exit.

"Pump away," roared Mr. Banks, "pump away, my lads."

The lads did pump, and until the last of his patrons had dispersed, Mr. Banks kept the stream of water playing around their heads and down the backs of their necks.

When the theatre was clear the proprietor resigned his weapon and said—

ANOTHER ROUND OF LIFE'S LADDER.

Dismayed and disappointed as the manager felt at the unfortunate turn which affairs had taken, and the overthrow of his prospects of making plenty of money out of the promising speculation, he could scarcely help laughing at the helter skelter caused by his lucky idea of bringing the fire-engine to his assistance in dispersing the uproarious and combative audience. At last, considering he had sufficiently damped their ardour, he remarked to the assembled company—

"That will shrink the cloth they wear, I know. Now, gentlemen, the theatre will close; look sharp, men, and take it down in case our friends outside may save us the trouble—here, Trombone, take charge of the jet, and be ready to defend any threatened point."

Bill Adler, Charity Joe, Tommy Nimblejaws, and Toby, formed a group, L.H., Mr. Banks, R.H. —a sad looking group they seemed, for the sudden tumble they had sustained from the very pinnacle of success to the abyss of detection was keenly felt and sorrowfully expressed

Meanwhile the arch-conspirators, who were the instigators of the catastrophe, Mr. Percy Fitz Algernon, the neglected and shelved tragedian, the walking gentleman, the comic man, and the other representatives and impersonators of the "legitimate" drama, were inwardly chuckling at the success of their plot to disgrace the Wild Hunters, not reflecting that the event which brought failure and exposure for Mr. Banks must ultimately recoil upon themselves, so that their triumph would be of very temporary duration. Tragedy only was heard to murmur something about having had his "r-revenge."

"This is very unfortunate," said Bill Adler— he felt he ought to say something under the circumstances, "very unfortunate, sir."

Mr. Banks faced the group, he took three pinches of snuff, rapped the box, replaced it in his pocket, folded his hands behind his back, and answered—

"Unfortunate, Mr. Adler! it's more than unfortunate, sir—it's ruin—humiliation—disgrace— Whitecross-street—debtors' prison—transportation—loss of character—my character, sir, what do you think of that sir, eh!"

Mr. Banks stamped his right foot upon the stage, and took more snuff.

"It's very bad," said Bill; "but it was no fault of ours; the dog that fellow had ought not to have been let in."

"Very likely, sir—very likely!" said Mr. Banks, trying to speak calmly; "I shall not argue the point, Mr. Adler, for arguing the point will not repay the cost of the thousands of bills I have had posted all over Buddleton-cum-Peters and the neighbourhood."

"It's very unfortunate——"

"Be kind enough to hold your tongue, sir, until I have finished speaking upon the matter——"

"Look here," Joe said; "it's all very well for you to put all the blame upon us and turn round like this; that dog ought not to have been allowed inside the place."

"No more he oughter," Tommy Nimblejaws said; "so it's him as took the money at the door as ought to be blamed."

"As I said before, I shall not argue the point," replied Mr. Banks; "for arguing the point will not repay the cost of that mutilated canvas, the ruined seats, the utter impossibility for me to bring my company to this town again; no, nothing can repay all this; now, Mr. Adler, I have done; all I have to say is that the Theatre Royal and General Exhibition can dispense with the services of the Hunters of the Frozen Mountains and their confounded dog—or wolf; therefore, the sooner we part the better I shall like it. Jones!"

"Yes, sir," answered a voice from the pit.

"You will have the goodness to bring the peep-show from the entrance-hall."

"The show's all broken up to bits by the people," answered a man from the other side of the theatre, "and they've carried off every morsel of it to make their kettles boil."

"Very well," said Mr. Banks. Then, turning to the hunters, he continued, "As this is the case, there is nothing more to detain you when you have returned the properties you are now wearing to the property man."

Poor old Bill Adler, crest-fallen and dejected, was about to walk away and tamely surrender his hunter's costume and again don his shabby habiliments, when Joe, who had more spirit in him than the broken-down showman, said :—

"Look here, Bill, what about the share in the takings that we are entitled to?"

"Yes," said Tommy; "let's have our money before you give us the sack."

Banks smiled most pleasantly as he re-

"Your share. Can you ask me such a thing after the evil you have done me?"

"Can I?" Joe said. "I should think I can, too, so fork over, or ther'll be another row; and if Trombone interferes I'll smack him over his long nose."

"Oh lord!" muttered mouthpiece, drawing the back of his hand across his nasal organ. "What have I done?"

"I again repeat," said Mr. Banks, "can your share of the last few days' proceeds repay me for the damage I have sustained through that ill-governed brute of a dog of yours?"

"That's nothing to do with us," said Joe. "We want the coin, so hand it over, and then we'll go away directly. If not——"

"Well, if not, what then?"

"Why," Joe answered, squaring up before the manager, "I'll do my best to take it out of you."

"You are quite at liberty to do so," said Mr. Banks, "for I do not intend to give one of you a penny piece, miserable swindlers that you are."

"All right," Joe said, throwing off his wild hunter's jerkin; "here's at you."

"Help, help!" shouted Mr. Banks, holding up his hands, "help, help!"

Tragedy, comedy, the heavy gentleman, and the walking gentleman, advanced from the wings upon hearing this cry, and stood before Mr. Banks.

"You are too many for me," said Joe, stepping back, "but mark my words, you daylight robber, we'll be even with you yet."

"You hear this, gentlemen," Mr. Banks asked, appealing to his supporters, "nice language, is it not, from one of the gang of swindlers who have brought my theatre into disrepute?"

"Swindlers," said Joe, "what do you mean?"

"Exactly what I say; did you not tell me that animal was a wolf? deny that if you can, before these gentlemen."

A wave of the hand indicated the four gentlemen.

"You're a nice one, you are," said Joe. "I see your game now—as for them fellows they would swear anything you wished them too; never mind, as I told you before, we shall be even with you, take my word for it—I can't fight the lot of you," Joe added, "but I can give you a piece of my mind."

Joe did so, a huge piece too, and the words he used were so mixed with the choice flowers of abuse his youthful mind had cultivated in the regions of St. George's market that we cannot enter into more details of the delivery of the speech.

Joe felt refreshed, so he told Tommy when

they were casting off the hunter's skins; after he had done this, and when the little party left the theatre, crest-fallen by the sudden reverse of fortune, Joe was the happiest of the three.

"Something will turn up," he said, hopefully. "What's the use of being down upon it?"

Poor old Bill would not be consoled, he knew how hard the somethings were to turn up, and now that his show had been destroyed, the future was very dreary and hopeless for him.

CHAPTER XIX.

TROUBLES INCREASE WITH UNPLEASANT SWIFTNESS—THE LATE HUNTERS BECOME OBJECTS OF UNWISHED-FOR ATTENTION—THE BEGINNING OF A GREAT BATTLE.

THAT the possession of money has much to do with our comfort, no one in their senses will deny. That the possession of a little of the "filthy lucre" also controls the behaviour of those worldly beings with whom one may be brought in contact is such an established fact, that no more need be said in these pages upon the subject, except as far as it concerns the individuals now on their way from the Theatre Royal to the "Three Jolly Ploughmen."

The tongue of rumour carried in the mouth of a red-headed boy had conveyed the news of the strange scene at the theatre to the host of the "Three Jolly Ploughmen," so when the discomfited trio returned and seated themselves in the parlour, the landlord entered the room holding between the first and second fingers of the right hand a piece of folded paper.

"The bill!" mentally observed Joe, "and not a blessed copper amongst us."

"The bill!" thought Nimblejaws. "What fools we were not to slope instead of coming back here."

"Glad to see you back, gentlemen," said the host; "thought perhaps you might have got hurt by our lads. They be rare high-spirited chaps."

"The bill, I suppose," said Old Bill Adler, mildly.

The subject was not pleasant, so he tried to change the current of the landlord's thoughts.

"Yes, sir," answered mine host, "I thought you and the young gentlemen would perhaps be in a hurry to leave, as the theatre is packing up. You'll find it right, sir."

The landlord's face when he entered the room expressed a little disquiet, but when the ex-showman referred to the bill, mine host's face brightened up, and the oily civility flowed as smoothly as ever from his tongue.

"One pun, seven and tuppence," sighed old Bill; "thank goodness, I'm able to pay it, but there won't be much left out of my little savings."

Old Bill dived his fingers into his waistcoat pocket, and took therefrom a small roll of dirty linen; and during the time he was unwinding the covering of his little store, the landlord rubbed his hands, and mentally observed—

"Well, they are honest, after all, whatever may be said about the wolf business. Hallo!"

The host's exclamation was caused by the sudden collapse of the showman, who had fallen back in his chair, his face expressing astonishment, horror, and fear, while at arm's length he held the contents of the small roll of dirty linen.

The host, Joe, and Tommy Nimblejaws ran up to the old man, who groaned:—

"Robbed—robbed! My savings of a whole year gone. Three half sovs.—bright gold half sovs., have been taken out of this, and three farthings put in. Oh, Lord—oh, Lord!"

"Come, come," the landlord began, "none of your play-acting tricks with me."

"As true as I sit here," said old Bill, "I thought I had the three half sovs. in my pocket. Oh, dear—oh, dear! when could this have happened?"

"Now, look here," said the landlord, "this game won't do. I want my money, and mean to have it; so out with it, or to the lock up you go."

"Wait a minute," Joe said, "don't be so fast about the lock-up, perhaps Mr. Adler has the money in another pocket."

"That alters the case," the host said. "I hope he has. If he has, of course I shall be sorry for what I've said."

"You ought to be," said Joe, "because if we had wanted to have cheated you, we shouldn't have come back."

"Which," said Tommy, "is true—make no mistake about it."

Bill Adler felt in all his pockets, the lining of his coat, even looked in his boots, but there was no second dirty roll of linen.

"I knowed it was no good," said Mr. Adler, "and I might have knowed it was gone, for I've dreamt of a black cat for these three nights running, and——"

"You can't find it, then?" exclaimed the landlord. "Of course you can't, you——"

"No," said old Bill, "I can't; I wish I could, and I wish I knowed the thief what has taken it, and I wish I knowed how they found out it was there."

The publican looked, first at old Bill, then at Joe and Tommy, then his red, angry face was turned towards the showman, and from his lips there came a confused sound as he attempted to utter words which his anger rendered unintelligible.

At last his articulation returned, and shaking his fist within an inch of his unlucky debtor's head, he spluttered—

"You thieving, dirty-minded old play-acting vagabond! so you think to palm this tale off upon me, do you?"

"It's true, every blessed word——"

"Hold your jaw, you old thief, or I'll break it for you; and Dan Smith has broken many a man's jaw—better men than such a grey-headed old thief as you are."

There seemed every probability of the publican's fist and old Bill's face being very closely acquainted, so Joe, who was always ready to fight while he had a leg to stand upon, turned up his cuffs, and, ranging alongside his friend, placed himself in the attitude Ben Smasher, ex-champion of the light weights, had taught him.

"Hands off, old son," said Joe, "or mayhap there will be something like a row in this crib before long—look after the poker, Tommy, make it red hot in case any of the louts should come in."

Dan Smith, the landlord of "The Three Jolly Ploughmen," was not a hero, in fact there was not a man on the face of the sea-girt isle who had less inclination to become a hero than Dan Smith.

Yet he was looked upon as a bit of a bruiser, for more than once he had turned a disorderly rustic out of the tap—disorderly rustic at the same time being much the worse for cold fourpenny.

Dan Smith felt himself ——— ——— task of thrashing poor old ———, ——— ——— ——— saw the attitude of the sturd——— ——— ——— in his fearless eyes a dete——— ——— ——— by his aged companion, Dan ——— ——— ——— lings considerably abated, low——— ——— ———

"So you would squa——— ——— ——— would you, my cock sparrow; wi——— ——— ——— neck."

"That's very likely," re——— ——— ——— should be there when you ——— ——— ——— Tommy wouldn't be far off ——— ——— ——— poker—blow the fire, Tommy——— ——— ——— would keep his teeth clean by tryi——— ——— ness of your calves, so I think un——— ——— cumstances you had better not try t——— ——— Bill's jaw."

"I shall not give you the chance ——— ——— away without paying me," said Dan ——— ——— "for you would have a chance if I were ——— ——— you all a good thrashing, all round, and I coul——— do it as easily as I could kiss my hand."

"Kissing your hand would be easier," Joe suggested.

"No," continued Mr. Smith, "you shall not have the opportunity of charging me with an assault; but I will fetch the constable and have you all locked up for rogues, thieves, and play-acting vagabonds——there!"

The last word was uttered triumphantly, as Mr. Smith suddenly opened the door, then closed it with a bang, and the ex-hunters heard the bolt thrust into its socket.

"Giles, Giles!" shouted Mr. Smith, as he stood close to the door; "be quick, you bandy-legged fool."

"Here I be, measter," a voice answered from the rear of the premises; "wait a minnit till—"

"Come at once," yelled Mr. Smith; "bring your hay-fork with you—there's three robbers locked up in the parlour."

"All roight."

The gentle sounds of a pair of hob-nailed boots followed, then Mr. Smith said:—

"Stand in front of the window, Giles, and prick 'em with the fork if they try to get out."

"Won't I, measter, that's all; be they the play-akters? Thought they be a bad lot; but I'll prick 'em!"

So Giles came to the window, and while his master went in search of the only policeman the town could boast, Giles occupied himself, much to Joe's disgust and annoyance, by making faces through the window.

"I wonder who could have done it?" groaned poor old Bill, resting his head upon the table; "I meant to pay him, I did. Oh Lord! Oh Lord! we shall all be taken to prison."

"It looks like it," said Joe; "but I think we ought to try and get away. Is the poker hot, Tommy?"

"Red hot, Joe."

"Right. I should like to cram it down that fellow's throat, the carroty-headed, bandy-legged son of a——"

"Yah! yah! play-akters be nabbed this toime!" said the sentinel, flattening his nose against the window. "Wouldn't 'ee like to come out. Wouldn't I loike to catch 'ee at it, I'd ——ck 'ee up wi' fork."

"Joe," said Tommy, "as the fellow in the ——y play says, there is but one more between ——— ——— d sweet liberty. You are not afraid of ——— your fingers, are you?"

"——— ——— ut 'em off to get out of this," answered ——— ——— ——— t why do you ask?"

"——— ———," answered Tommy, "I know you ——— ——— like to give that sweet youth with ——— ——— th a dab on the nose, and, if you ——— ——— he glass, why there's a good ———

——— ——— Tommy, but he has left the

window. Most likely he sees the bobby coming. Keep the poker hot, my——"

"Don't do anything," said old Bill, "to make matters worse. Sit down, you lads, and let us be taken before the Justice, I'm sure he will believe our story."

"Not he," said Joe; "he'll side with the publican, and lock us up for cheating. No, Bill, it's no use to think of getting off that way, for if we goes before the beak, we are in for seven days apiece, at the very least; so we'd better get away before the bluebottle comes, if we can."

"You lads know best," said the old man, "only don't do anything rash."

"No," said Tommy, "but flesh and blood can't stand that. Look at him, Joe."

Joe looked, and saw the sentry's nose flattened against the glass, and the large mouth grinning from here to next week.

Keeping as cool as possible under the circumstances, Charity walked to the window, and the rustic, as though mistrusting his prisoner, drew back.

"How do 'ee feel?" the youth asked; "thee be foine play-akters, beant 'ee, mighty foine."

"Sweet youth," said Joe, "how much would I give to pull that flat nose!"

"Thee pull my nose! I loike that. Why, darn thee, if I had thee outside I'd tackle 'ee up wi' fork."

"Come back, Joe," said Tommy, "then he may perhaps flatten his nose against the window-pane; if he does, let him have it."

"Right, old son; perhaps this will draw him on."

So Joe, as he stepped backward, placed the thumb of his right hand to his nose, and joining the thumb of his left hand to the little finger of the right, he made a succession of "Chinese fans"—taking a sight, used to be the term, but Chinese fans is more elegant, and in keeping with the refinement of the present day.

The fans did not please Giles, for he came back to the window, and after making faces at Joe, he yelled:—

"Play-akter folks, what couldn't pay for thee eating and drinking, thee be a foine lot."

"Now," said Tommy, "at him, Joe, I'll follow with the poker."

Joe went very cautiously forward; he feared he should frighten the golden-haired Giles if he made a sudden dash, so he kept up the manufacture of the fans until he came within striking distance, then the right hand was shot suddenly out.

There was a crash of broken glass, a yell from Giles, who dropped his fork with the two prongs, and placing both hands over his nose, he danced

about as wildly and quite as gracefully as a bear upon a hot gridiron.

"Follow me," said Joe, as he threw the window up, "and be quick about it."

Bill Adler forgot his resolution to appeal to the Justice when he saw the window open, in fact he scrambled through before the more active Tommy, and when the trio reached the street, Giles stooped yelling and howling, and set up a cry of—

"Help, help! Play-akter folks be going away."

"Touch him up, Tommy," said Joe, "then after us like a shot."

Tommy had been once to a theatre at Christmas time, and the tricks of the clown with the red-hot poker had greatly amused his youthful mind; he had longed to imitate "Patchy," but up to the present time he had not been successful in obtaining any one to perform the part of pantaloon, for Tommy insisted upon the poker being red hot.

Now the chance presented itself, he held a red hot poker, and the youth who was shouting lustily for help had his back towards the amateur clown.

It was done; there was a strong smell of scorched moleskin, a scorched line across the seat of Giles's lower garments, a howl of pain and terror from Giles's delicate mouth, then the scorched youth applied one hand to the lower part, the other to his nose, and in this interesting position he fled to the interior of the house, yelling—

"Murder, murder! Play-akter devils burnt I and made I's nose bleed!"

"Bolt," said Joe, when the deed was done, and the poker lay fizzing and sputtering beside the fork with two prongs. "This way; we shall soon be clear of the town."

Neither looking to the right nor left, and Toby trotting at their heels, the Wild Hunters of the Frozen Mountains fled from the scene of their brief glory, and paused not in their wild career until they reached the quiet country road. Here they would fain have rested, but, ere they could do so, there came a shout upon the wind that carried terror into their panting hearts. And again they went forward, liberty and nothing to eat before them; in the rear, a lock-up and skilly for their meals.

Buddleton-cum-Peters was one of the quietest of quiet towns, and the streets were never thronged, not even when there was a fair, or "statutes."

Perhaps less at these times than when the Petersonians were leading their every-day life, for, when the revels were going forward, the populace flocked to the sights and shows, and thus the streets were left to take care of themselves—a task they were quite able to fulfil, for, up to the present time not one of them had been known to stray away from this place.

It was owing to this state of matters that our adventurers, to use an original (?) term, were able to carry out their daring plan of escape, and to so signally discomfort the superlative Giles.

This youth, when the "akters" had reached the end of the street, emerged from his place of concealment to go in search of his master and the constable, for he had made the agreeable discovery that he was more frightened than hurt. True, his nose bled rather freely, but that would do him good. As for the hot poker, that had only scorched his moleskins, so, under the circumstances, he felt himself equal to the task of aiding in the re-capture of the foe.

When he reached the street, he was equally surprised to meet about a dozen boys and gawky young men running towards the "Three Jolly Ploughmen;" they had come to his assistance in consequence of the news of the outrage having been brought to them by a small boy, who had seen the whole transaction from one of the windows opposite.

"Where be they gone to?" asked several of the band; "Where be the play-akters?"

"Up street," said an old female, who had been nearly upset by the retreating hunters; "I see play-akting fellows; they run agin' I."

Up street went the pursuers, Giles armed with the fork, another of the party took the poker.

When they reached the end of the street, they caught sight of the fugitives as they slackened their pace to regain their breath.

It was the shouts of Giles and his companions that caused Joe and his companions to turn ward again, and well they might have had nearly a mile, then the poor old fellow was obliged to give in, for his strength was all gone.

"Leave me, you lads," he said, "and go on with them."

Joe's reply was the hasty gathering of the loose stones that lay near, and Tommy followed his example, and Toby, the late wolf, as though he knew something was to be feared from the advancing rustics, crouched down and showed his fangs.

"Coom back!" said Giles, when the party came within fifty yards of the trio; "coom back thee cheats, to measter!"

Two stones, flung with that accuracy of aim so peculiar to the London street-boys, caused the pursuers to halt; one got struck on the

shoulder, another hopped about holding his right leg.

This gentleman's shins had been touched by the missiles flung by Charity Joe.

CHAPTER XX.

THE RETREAT OF THE PURSUERS—OLD BILL FALLS BY THE ROAD-SIDE—A FRIEND IN NEED—COMFORTABLE QUARTERS—AN UNEXPECTED ARRIVAL, AND AN UNEXPECTED CHANGE OF CIRCUMSTANCES.

THE bold stand made by the unlucky trio was sufficient to bring the rustics to a halt, and the two wounded heroes, as usual in warlike encounters, fell to the rear, and urged their companions forward.

"Go on, Giles; thee hast fork—prod play-akters wi' it."

"Thee may have fork," said the obliging Giles, "if 'ee likes to do it theeself."

"Come on," said another, "we be stronger than they; let us run in upon them."

This seemed the best plan, so the boldest advanced, and Toby, urged on by Joe, ran barking towards them at the same time as the late hunters sent in a shower of stones.

Toby's savage aspect did more than the stones, for they could dodge those missiles; but as it was uncertain which of the rustic legs the dog might fancy, those in the rear prudently retired, one remarking—

"Thee all stand here, while I go for constable; he be best."

Toby selected Giles. Possibly the weapon carried by the red-haired youth caused the dog to attack his shins.

Giles valiantly repelled the assault; but Toby was much too careful to get within reach of the fork-handle.

"Help I," shouted Giles. "Beat dog off, some of thee."

His voice was unheeded, for his companions had gone to fetch the constable.

Joe whistled for Toby, and the dog released his grip of the moleskin.

"Now," shouted Joe, "let's burke him."

Giles did not care about being burked, so as Joe, Tommy, and the dog advanced, the rustic beat a hasty retreat.

"Dang it!" he said, "if one goes to fetch constable they shouldn't ha' gone and left I here."

"The enemy having retired," said Joe, "we will follow their example, but in another direction."

"Yes," said Tommy, "we will. Come along, Joe."

Discretion, as we knew, was much the better part of valour, so they trudged on until the spire of the only church in Buddleton-cum-Peters was no longer visible.

"Now," Joe said, "I think we are a safe distance from that unpleasant place. Let us have a chat about things in general."

So they sat down by the roadside, the old man passively obeying his young companions without a murmur.

"Now, Bill," said Charity, "what's the next move, you are the oldest, and know more about these things than I do?"

Old Bill made no reply; he sat with his knees drawn up to his chin, and his face covered by his hands.

"Cheer up," said Tommy, patting the showman on the shoulder; "it's no use to give in like this, something is sure to turn up."

"When I was your age," said the old man, raising his head, "I always thought something would turn up, no matter how much I was down on my luck, but now I know the difference. There is nothing for us but the workus."

"Which," said Joe, "is a crib where they don't catch Charity; he had enough of it when he was a youngster."

"There is nothing else for us, boy, nothing else for us except starvation."

"We shan't starve," said Tommy; "there's lots of vegetables in the fields, and when we are tired of that sort of living we must beg; somebody will be sure to give us something before we get to London."

"London!" repeated the old man; "what do we want to go to London for?"

"Oh," Tommy answered, "there's plenty to be got there, isn't there, Joe?"

"Well, I don't know about plenty, but I think we could manage better there—especially if I found out the old gent as took me to Boots the shoemaker. I wonder," Joe added, thoughtfully, "who I am?"

"Charity Joe, of course."

"That's not it, Tommy; but I must be something, or an old gent wouldn't take me from the workus. What do you think, Bill?"

The showman unheeded the boy's question; he had resumed his old position, and was rocking himself to and fro as he mused over the loss of his little savings and the destruction of his show.

"I wish," said Tommy, "we had never seen you, Bill, because if we hadn't you would not have been in this mess."

"No," said Joe; "it's all our fault; but never mind, Bill, we will tramp to London. I know a chap there as will give us a few old skins, and we will do the wolf business in the streets."

"Bravo," said Tommy, "so we will; if it took so well in the theatre, it will take just the same in the streets, and we shall go home every night with a capful of coppers."

"Yes," said Joe, "a capful of coppers; think of that, Bill—think of counting over a capful of coppers!"

Old Bill looked up, the cheery young voices for a moment dispelled his gloom."

"That might come true," he said, "but I shall never get to London, Joe."

"Never get to London! What nonsense—but you do look ill, Bill, what's the matter?"

"I don't know, lad, I've felt it coming on for the last two days, but don't mind me—leave me here; you lads make your way on, I shall get better; if not, why I may as well die in——"

Joe rapped out a choice expletive, one of the flowers of language spoken in the regions of St. George's Market, S.E.

"What, leave you to die like a mongrel by the roadside?" continued Joe. "May I be rammed, jammed, and pounded up for sausage meat if I stir a peg without you—look here, Bill, Tommy and I have brought all this on you, we have—don't speak—as for you, Toby, I could choke you, I could——"

"But, my boys," began the old man, feebly.

"Look here, Bill," said Joe, interrupting him, "we mean to stick by you, and I hope we shall pay you back for all you have done—lend a hand, Tommy, he's gone off."

They stooped over their old companion, who laid himself down by the footway; he was ill, very ill, the long months he had tumbled about the country with his show, sometimes in the rain and often faint and hungry, had done its work upon his frame.

He spoke the truth when he told the boys he had felt it coming on, but he had battled with his ailment to perform his part upon the boards of the theatre; the mind had triumphed over the body, but now the mind was prostrate the body had yielded, and he seemed like one who was about to sink into that state of forgetfulness from which only the last trump could awaken him.

"What shall we do?" said Joe, wringing his hands. "What shall we do?"

"Don't give way, old son," said Tommy. "Keep up—keep old Bill's head up, I mean, while I climp up that tree and look for a house, and——"

The sound of wheels rolling over the stony road arrested Tommy's words, and the boys, looking in the direction of the coming equipage, simultaneously gave utterance to a joyful cry.

It was a carriage drawn by a pair of horses, a stout, red-faced coachman, and a tall footman were on the box. The occupants were a lady and an elderly gentleman.

The lady was the first to catch sight of the group, and her exclamation caused the old gentleman to look out of the carriage window, and when he saw the sad scene, he gave the check-string such a jerk that it nearly pulled the coachman from his seat.

The horses drew up in an instant, and the gentleman alighted, stepped over to the old man, and asked—

"What is the matter, my man?"

"Please, sir," said Tommy, taking off his cap, "poor old Bill's taken very bad, and we don't know what to do."

"Dear me—dear me! "What are you, pray; Travellers, I presume?"

"No, sir; we was wild hunters; but we got the sack, and somebody eased poor old Bill of his money, and—"

"Not so fast, my man. Dear me, dear me, you can tell me when I have seen—ah——"

The showman raised his head, the sound of a strange voice had aroused him, he feared the landlord of the "Three Jolly Ploughmen" had brought the constable, but when they saw the kind and benevolent face that looked into his, Bill Adler "felt better."

Joe, usually so loquacious, lost his tongue when the gentleman left the carriage, for the boy's eyes had rested upon the lady.

She was very handsome, but it was not this that caused Joe's fixed gaze; she was beautifully dressed, but her gay plumage had nothing to do with the eager, half-frightened expression in Joe's eyes.

There was a something—an indescribable mystic feeling—came over him when he saw her. It was Nature's instinct, but he knew it not, nor thought that handsome lady was his MOTHER.

The maternal instinct was not called into existence within her breast, for she coldly glanced at the ragged boy, then turned her eyes away to follow the movements of her companion. The proud, icy woman knew not that the pale, pinched face before her was the same she had so often kissed and fondled; so often gazed upon with a young mother's pride and tenderness, and looked tenderly to the time when the rosy babe would have grown, and the little tongue would have lisped out the tiny word she so longed to hear.

Those were bright days—sorrow had not fallen so heavily upon her then, as to change her nature from an ingenuous, tender-hearted girl to a cold, selfish friend and ambitious woman of the world.

"Never felt so queer before," Joe thought, as he buttoned his scanty jacket over his breast; "and I don't want to feel so again, so I won't look at her."

So Joe resolved, but no sooner were the words formed upon his lips than he found himself watching the fond, handsome face before him, and wondering whether he had seen it before.

He saw the old gentleman opposite the carriage, and heard him say :—

"Very strange indeed, my dear, the poor fellow being ill, don't know what to do, I'm sure. Think I had better put him in the carriage, and send him on to the Hall. Can't leave him to die, you know."

Joe saw the expression of disgust that came upon the lady's face, and heard her say :—

"You can do as you please when I am out of the carriage. I think your benevolence——"

"But, my dear," said the old gentleman, mildly ; "the poor man is very ill—ahem—quite unfit, I can assure you, to walk——"

"Very well, Sir Charles," said the lady, passionately ; "I will leave the carriage, and walk, and——"

"Not for worlds, my dear. No, no. But you —that is, you are so—so——"

"Ill-tempered. sir. Pray speak out."

"No, no, my dear—no, not that. I was merely about to remark that you are so apt to misconstrue my words. I was about to ask you to go on with the carriage, and send one of the carts from the farm. Will you do so, my dear?"

The lady gave her head a disdainful toss, as she said :—

"If you wish it, I will ; but really I think you might find other employment than making the Hall a receptacle for every beggar you meet on the road-side. Home, James," she added to the coachman, and the carriage rolled away.

The old gentleman took a pinch of snuff, as he looked after the carriage, and, tapping on the lid of the silver box with the forefinger of his right hand, he soliloquised—

"Hem! Lady Helen is a fine woman—and handsome ; but she has no sympathy with my efforts to relieve the poor and homeless ; well, well, there's no accounting for taste—none!"

He walked towards the group, and, seating himself upon a heap of broken stones, said to old Bill—

"Feel better, now, my man—feel better?"

"Yes, sir," answered the old man ; "I feels almost able to walk now ; it was a sort of cold shiver like that came all over me."

"Ah, ague, no doubt; hem, glad you feel better ; now I want you to tell me something about yourself ; this lad here began, but really I could not understand him."

MASTER JOSEPH SAT FUMBLING WITH HIS HAT.

" I've been a showman, sir," said Bill Adler, " for nigh upon thirteen months, and managed to get a crust and a bed out of it; but misfortunes came, sir—regular bad luck—and I ain't got a penny piece, nor a hole to put my head in."

" Dear me, how very unpleasant, to be sure ! And where is your show, my man ? I suppose you do not carry it in your pocket, eh !"

The old gentleman chuckled at the little joke, and Bill Adler replied—

" No, sir ; it warn't very big, but it was too big for that—much too big ; no, sir, it's all broke up—smashed up to little bits, and the pictures all torn up to ribbons !"

" Bless me ! ah ! how did this happen, pray ?"

" It's a long story, sir," said Bill Adler ; " but I will tell you if you like, sir."

" The very thing I should like, my man. Mind you do not omit the slightest particular, for I am writing a book—a book, my man, that will yet make the country shake ; a book relating to the poorer classes, so mind you give me all the information you can."

" Yes, sir."

So old Bill told the story of his meeting with Charity Joe and Tommy, and their adventures up to the present hour, and his listener sat with pencil and note-book in hand, jotting down such portions of the recital as were of use for the great book he had in preparation.

"Now," said Sir Charles, "I shall be glad if you will tell me a little of your life previous to your meeting with these lads?"

"It's very kind of you, I'm sure, sir," old Bill said; "very kind of you to listen to my ups and downs; of course, I'll tell you as much as I can."

So the showman related that portion of his career already known to the reader, and Sir Charles took copious notes.

During the time this was going forward Charity and Tommy Nimblejaws sat apart from the narrator and his listener, Joe moody and thoughtful, Tommy keeping up the name he bore by rattling away as quickly as possible.

"I say, Joe, we've dropped in with a good sort. Don't you think so? I do. We shall have no end of a good feed when we get down to the old swell's house; heard him tell the lady to send a cart down for us. Didn't you? I did. I say, what will you have if they ask you what you like? I know what I'll have. I say, what's the matter with you, found a penny and lost a lucky sixpence? You look like it. What's up, Joe?"

"Nothing."

"Oh, nothing. Well, nothing makes people look as though there was something the matter. I say, ain't there?"

"Ain't there! What?"

"Something the matter."

"No."

"What makes you look so glumpy, then?"

"Well, I don't know that we have much to make us look anything else."

"What a crammer! Ain't we going to this old swell's house? I say, I hope he'll ask us the same as he has asked Bill."

"What has he asked Bill?"

"To tell him all about his ups and downs. I say, if he asks us, won't we show old Nip up? I wonder how he gets on, and all of 'em at Baream. It ought to be Barebone."

"I don't know," said Joe, "that it would do us much good to say anything about old Nip."

"It won't do us much harm," said Tommy. "But this I know, there is something the matter with you, or you would not be so jolly disagreeable. Now, isn't there?"

"Well, there is," Charity replied, "and a sort of something I never felt before. You saw that lady, Tommy."

"Should say I did, too."

"Come nearer. I don't want to shout. Did you ever have a dream?"

"Dream?" Nimblejaws repeated. "I should say I have, and a good many of them, too."

"Did you ever dream anything that you remembered a long time afterwards, and when you thought of it made you feel queer all over?"

Tommy fingered the last button that remained upon his jacket, and when he had succeeded in twisting it off, he exclaimed—

"Yes, that I have. I dreamt once, when I was at home, that my mother-in-law's husband was giving me a tanning, and when I woke up my dream was right, for he was laying on to me with a bed-rail. Yes, I remember that, for I got every whack with the stick just as I had dreamt it, only a jolly sight harder. And I dreamt another time, when we were at old Nip's. Of course I had gone to bed awfully hungry, and while I was snoring I dreamt I was at a table feeding upon beef-sausages and nice new bread, and a mug of beer to wash it down. Yes, I remember that dream, too, for it was skilly day at old Nip's."

"That's not the sort of dream I mean," Joe said, "for I don't seem to know when I had the dream. Perhaps I should not have thought of it at all had I not seen the lady's face; and when I saw it, I felt quite queer. I can't tell you how I felt, though it was such a curious feeling. My heart beat ever so fast, and there seemed to be something saying to me, 'Go and speak to her.'"

"If you had," said Tommy, "wouldn't that flunkey have given you a topper, that's all?"

"He could not have stopped me," said Joe. "It was her voice when she spoke that made me feel quite giddy, for I'm sure I've heard it before, and seen her face before; either in a dream, but I can't remember, or—yes, it must have been a dream I had long before I was taken from the workhouse."

No, Joe, it was a reality; but you were too young at the time to remember the home wherein your childhood was spent, too young to remember a handsome bearded man who taught you to lisp a few words, too young to remember the mother who wept so often over the little fatherless prattler. Better that you should think it all a dream, for the awaking to the truth would be a heavy sorrow for one so young to bear.

"Dreams," said Tommy, "doesn't ought to be remembered, for when I——"

The appearance of a light spring cart put a stop to Tommy's reminiscences, and, much to the delight of the younger members of the party, they were soon seated in the vehicle, and the three-quarter-bred bay "spanking out" towards the residence of the benevolent gentleman and his proud, cold lady.

The appearance of the unlucky hunters did not excite the least surprise among the servants, one of whom took them to the servants' hall, and on the way showed more airs than his master would had he conducted the party below stairs.

"Ah!" said the powdered gentleman, "this way. Now, do not keep too close to me. Ah, that's it, and mind you don't put your fingers on the paint, for we have just had it cleaned."

The gorgeous had only time to reach the head of the stairs when a carriage drove up to the door, and a practised hand performed a solo on the knocker.

"Wait here," said the magnificent. "I will return directly."

It was but natural that Joe and his companion should look towards the door, and when it was opened, Joe said—

"That's the ole gent as took me from the workus."

CHAPTER XXI.

TOBY MAKES FRIENDS AMONG THE LADIES AND GENTLEMEN OF THE SERVANTS' HALL—JOHN JAMES EXPRESSES HIMSELF UPON BENEVOLENCE AND OTHER MATTERS—JOE GLEANS A FEW PARTICULARS ABOUT THE GENTLEMAN WHO CAME IN THE CARRIAGE.

ELTHORNE HALL, the country seat of Sir Charles and Lady Elthorne, was one of the few remaining structures that had not been rendered ugly by the addition of new wings and other modern improvements, that seem to have but one effect upon the noble piles which were erected by our ancestors, as much for defence as for comfort.

Sir Charles had too much veneration for the home of his race to have it modernised; so the old oaken stairs, the long corridors, the small, diamond-shaped windows, the banqueting-hall, and the massive gateway, remained much in the same condition as they were in the days when one Sir Charles Elthorne, a staunch loyalist, withstood three days' siege by Cromwell's psalm-singing Puritans.

Tommy Nimblejaws had but little veneration for the antique, for he whispered to Joe, as they stood humbly awaiting the return of the gorgeous footman :—

"It's a queer place, ain't it?"

"Hush," said Charity, "that's him."

"You said so before; why don't you go and speak to him, then?"

"I will," Joe said, and was about to run forward, when the plushy gentleman returned.

"This way," he said, and Joe obeyed, for the tall, military gentleman had gone up the stairs "this way; and mind what I told you about the paint."

Charity reflected as he went down the stairs, and the result was that he abandoned his intention of pursuing the military-looking gentleman until he had gleaned a little information about him, and the people whose house he was in.

Joe, who, like the generality of London boys, had but little respect for the magnificent being who condescended to wear the Elthorne livery, and accept Sir Charles's quarterly allowance for so doing, somewhat startled that august person by bluntly asking—

"Who's that old gentleman that has just come?"

The footman glanced down at his white clad calves, adjusted his cravat, pulled down his waistcoat, then gave vent to his surprise by uttering the single word—

"Ah!"

"Look here, John," Charity said, "you might tell us what's his name."

"Young man," said the flunkey, severely, "we are not in the habit of being thus questioned, but if you must know that person's name, it is General Dixon."

"Thankee," Joe said, "I think I shall speak to him when he comes down. Let us know, will you?"

The footman surveyed Joe; and the undue familiarity with which that youth treated one who was in the habit of being sir'd by all the tradespeople, so offended his dignity that he spoke not until the party reached the hall.

Here the greater portion of the servants were assembled, and John James Rupert said :—

"We have brought some more Samaritans for you to feed, cook."

"Samaritans," said the butler, "you have made a mistake, Mr. John. Sir Charles is the Samaritan; these are the publicans and sinners."

"Very likely," said the gentleman in livery; "at any rate here they are, and I——Oh, murder!"

A growl from Toby, a yell from a member of the feline tribe, followed John James Rupert's exclamation, and the company, looking in the direction of the sound, beheld an appalling sight.

A large black cat had sprung upon Toby as that well-behaved animal followed Joe; and the sharp claws of this unexpected foe not being pleasant, Toby rolled over, and dislodged his enemy; and, as the cat stood with raised back and bristling hair, evidently for another spring, Toby made a sudden flank movement, in the hope of catching his foe in the middle of the back.

In this he was foiled, but he succeeded in getting the end of Tommy's tail between his teeth; and Tommy, in an agony of rage and fear, fastened on tooth and claw to the object nearest to him.

This object, alas! was the right leg of the magnificent creature, John James. There the cat clung, clung madly, teeth and talons, to the silk-clad calf of his right leg, and John James spun round upon his left foot, the cat's grip being firmer every time he moved; and Toby, with bared fangs, snapping and growling as he showed the silken supports of the column of plush.

Such was the scene that met the eyes of the gents and gentesses of the servants' hall, and pained am I to be compelled to make known the inhumanity of the ladies and gents, who, in place of at once flying to arms and annihilating the animals, gave vent to a roar of laughter; and Joe put the climax upon this unfeeling action by calling out—

"Go it, Johnny, keep it up! My eyes! what a fine teetotum you'd make."

Now I ask the reader—if the reader can ever aspire to become one of those fashionable gentlemen, whose duty it is to lead pet lap dogs, and carry old ladies' books to church, put coals on the fire, and adorn their heads by the aid of the flour dredger—one of these pillars of fashion, who look so princely and so noble in their splendid parti-coloured suits — graceful, yet haughty beings who should be called a gentleman retainer, but who, alas! is termed by the very lowest and most ragged of street boys, a FLUNKEY.

Now, I again ask the reader, if he were one of these gentlemanly retainers, if he were dressed in silk stockings, brilliant shoes, glittering buckles, red bre—ahem—lower garments, a yellow waistcoat, green coat, dazzling with plated buttons, large whiskers, and well floured hair, what would be his feelings if he were called Johnny by a ragged boy, and likened to a teetotum?

What would he feel if, in addition to this splendour of outward garb, and that feeling of proud confidence so general with the class, he had had a savage cat clinging tooth and nail to his flesh, and a large ugly dog barking and snapping as he performed a wild dance to shake off his attacking foe, and howled with pain?

The man would, I have no doubt, have armed himself with the rolling-pin, nay, with a stewpan, and at once inflicted a terrible chastisement upon the innocent ragged boy, perhaps broke his skull, in order that a proper amount of respect should

have found its way to the interior of the ragged boy's skull.

But John James, with that lofty dignity so well in keeping with his haughty mind, did nothing of this; no, he continued to spin round, and at last, when the pain caused by the cat's teeth and talons became too much for his stoicism to bear, he yelled out—

"'Enry, Chawles, Mr. Bung! dwive hoff these 'orrid creechaws, or I shall be marked for life!"

'Enry Chawles, the page, and Mr Bung, the butler, flew to arms; 'Enry Chawles seized a broom, Mr. Bung a toasting-fork, and rushed to the rescue.

"Come here, Toby," said Joe, and Toby left the silken clad calf and the savage cat, and lay at his master's feet.

From information I have received, I am of opinion that 'Enry Chawles, the page, had a secret dislike to John James, the gentleman retainer.

He felt envious of that majestic creature, his whiskers were a source of continual torment to the mind of the juvenile specimen of "flunkeyhood."

John James's calves and his silk stockings, too, were sources of continual discomfort to 'Enry Chawles, and his envy at last reached its culminating point when he saw her ladyship, in dismounting from her horse, or alighting from her carriage, assist her descent by leaning upon the ready arm of the superlative John James.

Such being the state of the youthful gentleman retainer's mind, it is a matter of but little doubt that, when he rushed to the rescue with the long broom, the seemingly accidental blows that fell upon the shins of the unfortunate John James were wilfully administered in place of upon the cat's back.

"'Enry Chawles," said the martyr, "you are a-hitting my legs instead of this most dreadful creature."

Mr. Bung, who had joined the rescue, now came up, and valiantly attacked pussy with the prongs of the toasting-fork until that monster released the well-developed, but now sadly-marked calf; and 'Enry Chawles completed the victory by charging the terrible creature as it fled from the hall.

Quiet being restored, and John James having retired to examine his wounds, the cook spread a substantial, if not a sumptuous repast, before the hungry trio.

"This is what I call first-rate," whispered Tommy to Joe. "It puts me in mind of a feed I once had when I went to see my Uncle Ben. He was an uncle, I can tell you; such a fat old chap. And when he saw me coming up to the

"FOOLISH BOY, YOU DO NOT KNOW WHAT YOU HAVE LOST!"

house—it was in the country he lived, you know——"

"Yes. Hand over the mustard, will you?"

"What! mustard again? That's three times," said Tommy. "Well, he runs out when he sees me coming, and catching hold of both my hands, gave them a squeeze that made me hallo. And my cousin—she was a stunner, Joe."

"Was she?"

"Yes. When I halloed, she laughed, and says 'that's father's way, he likes to give everybody a warm reception.' Barring my fingers all being squeezed up to thumbs, it was a stunning place to go to."

"Why don't you go there now?" Joe asked; "it would be better than knocking about like this. I wish I had somewhere to go."

"So do I. Can't go there, you know, because the old chap has gone to America."

"Would your dog like a bone?" the stout, red-cheeked cook said to Joe. "If he would I have one for him."

"Thankee," said Joe, "I know he would, for it's not much he's had to-day. Stand up, Toby, and ask for a bone."

Toby stood upon his hind legs and barked, much to the amusement of the gentlemanly servitors, and the lady-like "servitresses."

"Say thankee," said Joe, when Toby had received the bone. "Come, sir!"

Toby dropped his prize, and after two or three failures succeeded in balancing himself upon his head, and returned thanks in the "doggie" language.

This feat pleased even more than the one preceding it, and while the company were laughing heartily, John James entered the hall.

"I hope you are not hurt," said Joe. "You look all right."

"I am not severely hurt, certainly," said the powdered being, serenely stroking his wellgreased whiskers, "yet that animal's claws have marked me more than ever I was marked before."

"Sorry to hear that," said Joe, kicking at Tommy's leg but hitting old Bill's shin instead. "Now what's the matter, Bill?"

"Nothing," said the old man, "only something hit me on the shin."

"Oh," said Joe, "that's not much to pull such a face about, is it, Tommy?"

Tommy made no reply, but was busily engaged talking to Mr. Bung, telling that very stout and superlatively gentlemanly gentleman, how they met Sir Charles Elthorne.

"He's a kind gentleman," said Mr. Bung, "and goodness! how many poor people he brings to the Hall to feed. "Sometimes," added Mr. Bung, "I finds he is too benevolent, for he does not stop to inquire whether the persons he brings or sends up to the Hall are poor persons or rascally tramps. I believe I am correct when I say this, am I not, Mr. John James?"

The magnificent ceased the severe manipulation of his whiskers, placed his hands under the tails of his coat, and answered—

"Well, Mr. Bung, as you appeal to me, who ought to know about these matters, I must say we are not so particular at all times as we ought to be."

"No," said the butler, "not by no manner of means."

"Of course," continued Mr. John James, "benevolence is a fine thing—a very fine thing, Mr. Bung."

"Yes, Mr. John James, it is."

"Such being the case, I think benevolence ought to be used for one purpose only: that purpose, Mr. Bung, ought to be to give to such gentlemen as you and I all the spare cash the gentleman we condescend to serve may have in his pocket."

"Them," said Mr. Bung, "is my sentiments, Mr. John James, to a T."

"And mine," said the housemaind.

"And what I thinks, too," said the cook.

"Mr. John is quite korreck," said the pretty chambermaid; "but it ain't often benevolence goes that way except the General; he does sometimes give me a chuck under the chin and half-a-crown."

"The General is a strict man," said Mr. John James; "although he is her ladyship's father, he is a troublesame man to have in the house."

"Her ladyship's father," thought Joe. "Keep your ears open, Charity."

"Yes, said Mr. Bung, "he is a very troublesome person; he thinks nothing of making a gentleman run up and down stairs for nothing. I believe I am correct, Mr. John James?"

"I well know it," said the effulgent. "I know one thing, I should not like to be this person's gentleman, for when we were in town, her ladyship druv to his house in Eaton-square, and I heard him a cursing his gentleman up hill and down dale."

"Eaton-square," Joe mentally repeated.

"I've heard say," said Mr. Bung, "that the old General made her ladyship, that now is, marry our Sir Charles, or she wouldn't have had him, if every hair of his head was stuck with diamonds. I believe I am correct, Mr. John James?"

"Well—ah, yes, Mr. Bung. I have heard something like this, but you know as we are a very rich baronet, people will scandalise us."

"Well," said the chambermaid, "if I was a lady, Sir Charles is just the husband I should like, for he lets her do just what she chooses, and never says a word."

"Well, well," said Mr. John James, surveying his plush and stockinged legs, tenderly smoothing his whiskers; "you know, Susan, there's no accounting for tastes. Now, if I were a lady, I should prefer to marry a gentleman of face and figure, no matter what his station might be—no, not even if he was a gentleman in livery."

This speech so tickled Tommy and Joe that they made a kick at each other's legs under the table, and, both boot-toes missing their object, the shins of poor old Bill Adler suffered.

"Oh, Lord!" he gasped, and the tears came to his eyes; "oh, Lord! what's that for?"

"I was going to kick Toby," said Joe; "hope you ain't hurt, Bill."

"You know, Mr. John," said the housemaid, "it ain't every gentleman, no, not even if he was a dook, has such a face, such a pair of whiskers, and such a figure as some gentleman as I could name; and, perhaps, you know, Mr. John, the lady didn't see the gentleman as I could name, or she would have made love to Lim, and left Sir Charles in the lurch—give him regular turnips!"

"Mary," said Mr. John James, "those sentiments does you——confound the bell! I wonder who it can be?"

The haughty being ran quickly upstairs, and the paces detracted from his dignity, but it went far to prove how affable he was that night, or he would not have cared how long any "person" remained at the door.

Visitors were not plentiful at Elthorne; and there was much speculation going forward among the ladies and gentlemen, barring the three ex-hunters, as to the quality and condition of the visitors.

Presently Mr. John James returned, his face and deportment plainly showing there was something of importance to communicate.

"Who is it, Mr. John James?" asked Mr. Bung, the butler, "The ladies will have it it's the paper-hanger come to see the drawing-room, but I say it's the carrier from London. Am I correct, Mr. John James?"

"You are all as far out as Robinson Crusoe was when he climbed up to the North Pole to look for a cold leg of mutton. No, ladies and gentlemen; the persons who are now talking to Sir Charles is the—"

"What? WHAT? WHAT?" different voices cried.

"The constable from Buddleton-cum-Peters, and ever so many people at his back."

"The constable from Buddleton?"

"That is the very identical person," John James said. "The constable from Buddleton-cum-Peters."

CHAPTER XXII.

BILL ADLER, JOE, AND TOMMY NIMBLEJAWS PERFORM BEFORE THE PUBLIC IN A MANNER NOT QUITE AGREEABLE TO THEIR FEELINGS.

WERE the dome of St. Paul's suddenly to take wing and soar upwards, before the city gentlemen whose custom it is to set their watches by the clock every day at 12 noon, they would not be more astonished than our heroes (I believe that is the correct mode of expression) were when John James gave utterance to that sentence which closed the preceding chapter.

"The constable from Buddleton-cum-Peters, and ever so many people at his back!"

Old Bill Adler's arm fell to his sides, and, as he upturned his eyes he gasped, in a melancholy manner:—

"Oh, Lord, oh Lord! we shall be all transported!"

Charity was taken aback for a few moments, and Tommy looked up the wide chimney, as though calculating the chances of escape by that sooty aperture.

Mr. Bung, John James, and 'Enry Chawles looked profoundly wise, and the ladies quitted their seats and collected in a group as far as possible away from the late Hunters of the Frozen Mountains.

"Haw, really," said Mr. Bung, pulling down his vest; "really, quite an event here—a officers of the law! I believe I am correct, Mr. John James?"

"Quite correct, Mr. Bung," the magnificent responded, as he tenderly manipulated his glossy whiskers; "in fact, I may say it is superlatively correct; but it is nothing more than we have expected, Mr. Bung."

"Nothing more, Mr. John James, nothing more."

"No, Mr. Bung; if we do bring persons of a certain description to our Hall, all I have to say is that we ought to expect this sort of thing. What are you laughing at, 'Enry Chawles?"

"Nothing," answered the page; "I wasn't laughing at nothing."

"He means," said Joe, who soon recovered from his confusion, "that you are nothing, Johnny."

"How dare you, sir," said John James fiercely, his face the colour of his plush; "how dare you address yourself to me? Do you think that I am to put up with the owdacious remarks of a person whom the law is about to claim; for understand I know the cause of the officer's appearance here."

"Do you?" was Joe's saucy answer; "it's wonderful you are so clever. I should hav thought the lot of flour you have put on your hair would have got into your head and made a pudding of your brains, that is if you ever had any."

John James's frame trembled with indignation. He looked at Mr. Bung as though expecting that gentleman would at once rush upon Joe and annihilate him.

He looked at 'Enry Chawles as though expecting that youth, instead of grinning, would assist at the annihilation.

But Mr. Bung only twisted his watch-chain and said—

"Really—ahem—quite out of the usual manner in which gentlemen are addressed."

"'Enry Chawles tried to look as though he did not enjoy John James's discomfiture, and to add to that gentleman's misery the page said—

"I wouldn't stand that, Mr. John."

The ladies were present, and John James felt bound to appear valiant, so after ascertaining that he could not count upon any assistance from his fellow-gentlemen in retainership, he assumed the lofty and majestic tone of a hero who too much despises his foe to inflict a chastisement upon him commensurate with the offence he had committed.

"Fellah," said John James, "low, ragged, ill-bred fellah, were it not for the high position I stand in, and the credit of our name, I would inflict upon you such a thrashing as you would remember to the last day of your life!"

"High position," said Joe; "you lick-plate-powdered, mean, conceited flunkey. I would sooner be a crossing sweeper than such a kitchen-fed, lap-dog-cleaning, run-of-errand, mean-spirited-cur. You are not a man or you would not wear those clothes."

Whatever else Joe would have added,—and there is no doubt his speech would have wound up with a challenge to single combat—was cut short by the dining-room bell ringing and a sudden disappearance of the exalted John James up the dingy flight of stairs that led to the entrance hall.

"You took the shine out of that flunkey, Joe," said Tommy. "My eye, how savage he looked. I thought he meant to pitch into you once."

"Wish he had," Joe said; "I'd have taken the flour off his head and the gilt off his buttons."

"Hem! really," muttered Mr. Bung, "a wis-cious poor person. I hate poor persons, especially wiscious poor persons."

'Enry Chawles gave pantomimic signs of the delight he felt, by going behind the respectable Mr. Bung and winking at Joe; then he indulged in a performance of having a person's head in chancery, and kept it up until Mr. Bung chanced to turn and detect the aspirant to plush and stockings.

"Impertinent young wretch!" exclaimed Mr. Bung, "take that."

"And 'Enry Chawles did so, and fled, holding one hand to his right ear, which looked very much inflamed.

"I should like to be a young flunkey, I should," said Master Thomas Nimblejaws; "shouldn't you, Joe?"

"Sooner be a mudlark," said Charity, "any minute."

"You boys, you boys," said old Bill in a low, frightened voice, "how can you keep your spirits up?"

"What's the use of being down over it?" Joe said. "It won't make things any better; besides, we haven't done anything very wrong. It wasn't our fault; we couldn't pay."

"No," groaned the old man, "but the law won't say so."

Joe said something about the law, not polite enough to be here rendered; and John James entered the hall.

"This way," he said. "You persons are wanted in the hall."

He kept well in advance of the persons, and Joe and Tommy kept up a series of remarks about John James's calves not pleasant to that gentleman's feelings.

The Buddleton-cum-Peteronians were drawn up in a body in the hall. Foremost was the constable and the landlord of the "Three Jolly Ploughmen;" and the former, when he saw the late hunters, said—

"Them's the people."

"I'd swear to that," said the landlord; "the hang-dog looking rogues."

"That's the chap as burn't I with poker," said Giles, pointing to Tommy, "and that be t'other as hit I on the nose."

"That's sufficient," said the constable, drawing his staff. "I arrest you all in the name of the law."

"Who's he?" said Joe "and what's he got to do with us?"

"Silence!" said the official. "Remember, you are my prisoners, and it is my duty to warn you that all you may say will be used in evidence against you."

"That's a nice nose of yours," Tommy remarked. "Wouldn't it make the water fiz if you were to fall in the river."

The constable felt this allusion to his red nose, and bitterly regrotted it was not in his power to put a gag upon his prisoners."

"Hold your tongue, you vagabones, or it will be the worse for you."

"Will it?" said Joe. "I say bobby, is there much rabbit-pie about your beat?"

The constable made a forward movement to pull Joe's ears, but the master of Elthorne Hall making his appearance from the dining-room, caused the official to remember the dignity of his cloth.

"Hem! Bless me," said the philanthropist, "so young, yet so inured to crime, and one so old to lead these youths from the paths of innocence and virtue."

"No, he didn't," said Joe. "Old Bill is a good sort, and whoever says he isn't, is a—"

"Hush—s-s-h-h," said the master of Elthorne, "Can you be ignorant of the nature of the crimes of which you are charged?"

"We aint done nothing to be ashamed of." Joe said, "We didn't intend to cheat the landlord; we meant to pay, but as we were turned away from the theatre without any money, we could'nt pay any."

"Dear, dear," said the old gentleman, "I see it is as you have said, Mr.——"

"Dan Smith, sir."

"Never heard that name before," interrupted Joe. "Did you, Tommy."

"Yes, Mr. Smith," continued the master of Elthorne, "they are bad persons, very bad. Constable, I'm afraid you must do your duty."

The official, like his town brethren, was quite equal to the task; he flourished his staff, called upon the half-dozen rustics who had accompanied Dan Smith and Giles to Elthorne, to assist in the Queen's name, and the party were marched off, much to the delight of John James, but to his confusion when Joe turned his head and called out—

"I say, Johnny, don't you be making of sheep's eyes at the housemaid. I saw you, and if I was your master I'd soon put a stop to——"

The footman closed the hall door, and looking very red in the face he crept past the dining-room, fearing every moment his master would emerge from thence and charge him with the remarkable liberty of being partial to one of his fellow servants, such things being expressly forbidden under pain of instant dismissal.

Thus was Joe taken from his mother's house, and the proud woman, from one of the windows, watched the group pass down the avenue, and wondered how it was possible her husband could have his mansion polluted by suffering such ill-dressed people to cross the threshold.

The lock-up at Buddleton-cum-Peters only consisted of one spare receptacle for the evil-doers and law-breakers, when the party reached that old-fashioned structure. There were more chambers, but owing to the fair and the statutes they were all filled.

Old Bill sank upon a stool, and hid his face in his hands. It was the first time he had been imprisoned, and the poor fellow felt the humiliation keenly.

Not so his companions. They looked upon their incarceration as a rare piece of fun, and put their juvenile wits to work to pass the time away pleasantly.

They sang snatches of all the songs then popular in London, made Toby perform all sorts of antics, and when tired of this Joe espied a bell fixed in the wall just over the bed.

"Hallo, Tommy, here's a bell. I suppose it's put there for us to ring."

"Of course it is; so here goes."

They gave such a peal that the attendant, thinking one of his captives had committed suicide, ran to the door, and pushing back the slide, looked through the grating and inquired —

"What's the matter in No. 4?"

"Does your mother know you're out, old cockalorum?" said Joe.

"All right," answered the gaoler. "I'll get you something for this."

"You're a beauty, you are," said Tommy. "Wouldn't your face do for an old knocker, that's all?"

The gaoler closed the slide and went away, much enraged by the above conversation.

"The young varmints," he growled; "I'd like to tie 'em to a cart's tail, and give 'em a good whipping—that's what I should like to do."

The next morning, after a sumptuous repast of skilly, the trio were taken before one of the great unpaid, and his justiceship having heard the evidence of Dan Smith and Giles, thus summed up and sentenced the aggressors:—

"The country," he said, "is overrun with gangs of tramps; but a more daring set I never had before me. You go to a respectable man's house; you eat and drink of the best, then have no money to pay. Of course not. You think your old tricks will do here, but I'll let you see that we have justice in this town; and I will take care that you are made a warning to others; therefore I sentence you all to be placed in the stocks for two hours; then, if you do not pay Mr. Smith for the food and lodgings you have tried to cheat him out of, you shall all go to prison for seven days. Take them away, constable."

Old Bill sobbed like a child; he would have implored for mercy, but his heart was too full for him to speak.

As for those young gentlemen, Master Joseph and Tommy, they were so astonished at their sentence that they could not chaff the red-nosed policeman.

That relic of a bygone time—that terror to the evil-doer—the stocks—was a favourite mode of punishment at Buddleton, and the hapless prisoners were here at all times a source of much amusement to the juvenile population.

The news soon spread that three "akters" were to be imprisoned in the wooden machine, and long before they reached the place of punishment, there was an expectant, if not an admiring crowd.

The stocks were made to hold four, and when the upper half was raised to admit the legs of culprits, Toby, with his usual curiosity, put his head in one of the unoccupied holes, and the constable closing the machine at the moment, Master Toby was made prisoner with his master.

The spectators laughed at the unusual scene, and this merriment aroused the ire of Tommy and Joe; poor old Bill was too much broken down to care whether he were a subject for the rustics' merriment. Fate had done its worst, and he wished himself in the quiet grave.

The most active among the tormentors was Giles; that youth dancing with joy and clapping his hands, brought the quartette more prominently before the public by shouting:—

"Lookee, that be old hunter, they be young uns, and that be wolf. Hoy, hoy! bean't they a foine lot?"

Joe wriggled and twisted with rage, as he endeavoured to get free; he would at that moment have given ten years of his life to have had a fair up and downer with Giles.

His hands and legs being thus fettered, he had but his tongue, and the volley of choice expressions he hurled at Giles and the crowd would, had they taken effect, have caused a great decrease in the population of Buddleton.

He culled the rarest flowers of language from the bouquet before mentioned in this history, and they lost none of their fragrance by the manner in which they were distributed.

Joe had to pause to regain his breath, then Tommy took up the cudgels, and his speech was quite as effective as Joe's.

"Eh, swear away, thee plap-akters," said Giles; "that's all thee can do—hah, hah, hah!"

"You turnip-headed, hobnailed, clod-hobbing chaw-bacon!" roared Joe; "I'll mark you for this, if it's seven years to come."

"Ee'll do lots after thee gets seven days' skilly, won't thee? I'll tell 'ee what, if constables were not here I'd pull thee nose for thee!"

"You—you!" yelled Joe; "I'll—"

Joe's utterance became indistinct, and so did Tommy's, who joined his friend's challenge to fight the whole of the male population of Buddleton-Cum-Peters.

Never in this sublunary sphere were two youths so thoroughly roasted with the chaff of a delighted audience as were our friends, and their rage became so great that they fairly howled at their inability to get at their tormentors.

As for Toby, he looked up every now and then at his master in a wistful manner, as though seeking for an explanation of the peculiar situation his canineship had so suddenly and unexpectedly found himself.

Matters had reached this stage when the swift approach of a carriage caused the crowd to separate, and Joe, looking up, saw the lady and gentleman from Elthorne seated in the vehicle."

The lady was calling the master of Elthorne's attention to the culprits, and Joe saw them both smile at the droll sight.

The proud lady little knew that the object of her scornful words was her only child, little imagined the face she declared bore the impress of vice and crime was the same face she had so often kissed and watched with a young mother's care and pride.

There was John James, too, on the box, and he laughed as he pointed the criminals out to the fat coachman.

Joe saw this, and his rage increased, and at the top of his lungs yelled out—

"Lick-plate flunkey, sneak, hound, kitchen sneak."

And Tommy shouted in chorus—

"Johnny, bring up the coals. Flunkey, wash the dog, and take him out for a walk."

All this was very vulgar; but it made John James's very whiskers tremble with anger and mortification, for the rustics, whom the lordly John James looked upon as quite an inferior class of beings to his exalted self, took up the cry, and used epithets not pleasing to his refined ears.

"If," said John James to the coachman, when they were out of hearing of the crowd, "I was a king, I'd have all them sort of persons hanged."

The coachman nodded a ready assent, and after an effort said—

"So would I, Mr. John. I hates them wulgar pussons."

Soon after the carriage passed, a slim, genteel-looking youth of about seventeen summers, autumns, winters, and springs, wended his way towards the market-place.

He was a traveller. That was told by the dust upon his boots and the small carpet-bag he carried.

The stranger forced his way through the crowd, and looking for a moment or so at the faces of the captives, exclaimed—

"Well, I'm blessed!"

CHAPTER XXIII.

GENTLEMAN BOB, A FRIEND IN NEED—ANOTHER FRIEND—SOME PARTICULARS OF THE CAUSE OF GENTLEMAN BOB'S VISIT TO BUDDLETON-CUM-PETERS—AND SOME NEWS ABOUT BAREAM-IN-THE WILLOWS.

THE slim young gentleman with the carpet-bag and the dusty boots would have gone closer to the instrument of punishment had he not been told to keep back by the constable with the red nose.

"Charity and Tom Nimblejaws! Well, I never thought to have seen them here," thought the slim young gentleman. "I must ask what they had been up to before I speak."

Before the genteel youth could make the necessary inquiries he was recognised by Joe, and that youth gave a shout of joy, and called out—

"Why, Bob, who'd have thought of seeing you here?"

"How do, Charity? how do, Tommy? what, and Toby too? well, this is a sight for free-born Britons, who never shall be slaves. What have you been up to?"

"I'll tell you eight days hence," said Joe, "if I see you. But, Bob, I want you to do me a favour; will you?"

"Anything, my boy, that I can, except lend you a crown; that is impossible."

"I don't want that," Joe said; "but if you will oblige me by giving that red-headed thief there, him to your left, a—something—good hiding I shall never forget your kindness."

"With pleasure," said Gentleman Bob. "You can consider it done."

The slim young gentleman began to "peel," but before he had taken both arms from his jacket Giles retired in a very undignified manner, as he said to milk the cows, but mayhap the slim young gentleman had something to do with it.

"Our friend," said Gentleman Bob, "has retired from the scene. Now, my boy, is there anything else?"

"I know my duty," said the constable, "so you keep back. There's no talking allowed with these 'ere prisoners."

"My friend," said Gentleman Bob, "believe me, I have the most profound respect for your knowledge. Why did you not tell me this before?"

"You ought to have knowed, I should say."

"Quite true, my friend, quite true. I ought to have done so. Still—eh?"

The query was addressed to a person who came up at that moment; a person whose outward garb might have led to the supposition that the wearer was a journeyman tailor out of employ, or a shoemaker keeping Saint Monday; for his habiliments were, at least they were once, blue-black, but age and wear had deprived them not only of the gloss, but of their colour.

"I begs pardon," said the mysterious personage; "but are you a friend of those poor fellows?"

"A sincere friend," Gentleman Bob said, "a bosom friend."

"That's all right, then," said the mysterious stranger; perhaps you will give the old chap this when he gets out of limbo."

"Certainly," Gentleman Bob began, as he held out his hand to take a small roll of dirty linen. "Certainly, with——"

"My savings!" shouted old Bill, when he caught sight of the little roll; "my savings. That's the scene-shifter of the theatre."

"I am the scene-shifter," said the mysterious individual, "and this little parcel is Mr. Adler's, and I should not have known it was his if I had not been to the court this morning, and heard him say he had lost his money at the theatre."

"Precisely so," said Gentleman Bob, who didn't understand the meaning of these explanations, but by his ready tact made it appear he was thoroughly in the late wild hunter's confidenc. "Yes, I perfectly understand."

"I thought it was gone," said old Bill; "I thought it was gone. Thank God, it hasn't; we can pay now, and shan't have to go to prison for seven days. Hooray!"

Old Bill's hooray was but a feeble attempt at that lusty mode of expressing joy, but it did him good.

"Why don't you held your jaw?" said the constable to old Bill. "Havn't I told you I knows my duty? Now open your mouths again, any of you, and I'll bring you before the justice, and he'll give you another hour in the stocks."

The threat had its weight, the time of punishment had nearly expired, so even Joe thought it better to keep his mouth closed for ten minutes than to have another hour's punishment.

"Keep back, all of you," the constable said to the audience; "if I catches one of you near the prisoners I'll take any of you up."

The constable's nose was redder than ever when he uttered this awful threat, and the rustic crowd, awed by the great man, retired, and left the culprits to pass the remainder of their sentence in peace.

The genteel young gentleman with the carpet-bag and the scene-shifter retired beyond the group of idlers, and the latter in a mysterious whisper, said—

"I am glad you are a friend of those poor fellows, sir."

"Most happy to hear the knowledge of our friendship gives you pleasure," said Gentleman Bob; "most happy."

"You see, sir," the scene-shifter said, "I was almost afraid to bring this money back, for I thought it very likely I should get into a little scrape over it."

"For bringing money to those not overburdened with that article!" Bob said. "My dear fellow, such an extraordinary occurrence was never yet placed upon the records of even the most primitive countries."

"Wasn't it, sir?" the mystified scene-shifter said; "perhaps not, but, of course, you know best about that, but why I was afraid I will tell you, if you like, sir."

"Shall be delighted to hear it, I assure you."

Gentleman Bob arranged the ends of a very seedy necktie, and prepared to listen to the scene-shifter's revelation.

"You see, sir," the scene-shifter said, "us chaps at the theatre used to get up to all sorts of larks, and one day we found Mr. Adler's clothes after he had dressed for his part, and of course we looks in the pockets, and found three half sovs. tied up in a little piece of rag."

"Precisely so; but with no intention of keeping the money, yon took it away."

"Yes, sir; and put three farthings in its place. Well, we thought it would be a lark for the old chap to find the farthings, and the next day we were to put the three half sovs. back, and when he found them of course he would be in a queer state. We should have done this but the theatre was packed up all of a sudden and there was no time; but I have come back from the place where we are now performing to give Mr. Adler the money, and I shall be glad, sir, if you will tell him I am very sorry he has got into trouble all through us. They are going to let 'em loose, so I will cut, sir, for I don't want Mr. Adler to see me."

The scene-shifter walked quickly away, and turned sharply down the first side street.

Gentleman Bob went to his friends, and would have shaken hands, but the red-nosed policeman would not allow such a departure from the duty about which he professed to know so much.

"No, young man," he said, "you can do all that sort of thing when they have finished their seven days, for they will have to grind wind upon the mill unless they stumps up one pound seven and tuppence to pay the landlord of the 'Three Jolly Ploughmen.'"

"Release your captives, base minion of the law," Gentleman Bob said, grandly; "here is the money."

The constable looked at the three gold pieces, bit them, weighed them, and finally jingled each coin upon the kerb; he devoutly hoped that one at least would turn out bad, for he had looked forward to Joe's punishment as a salve for the wounds his dignity had received.

"They are all right, worse luck," he said, "so come this way, and mind you, sir," to Joe, who was turning up the cuffs of his jacket, "if you commits any 'sault upon anybody, I'll lock you up, sharp."

Joe was compelled to forego the pleasure of chastising a few of the audience, but he solaced himself with the reflection that it's a very long lane that has no turning.

The appearance of the constable and his companions at the open portals of the trio of Jolly Ploughmen, gave the golden-haired Giles quite a turn.

He caught sight of Joe and Toby, but luckily for the preservation of the peace, Joe did not discover his tormentors."

"Mr. Giles, the red-headed," said Joe to Tommy, "I wonder whether we shall meet; look out for him, Tommy."

Mr. Giles had by this time made his escape across a fence at the back of the house, and in a dry ditch sat trembling and fearful every moment he should see the muzzle of Toby appear above the low fence.

Gentleman Bob conducted the arrangements; he would not allow the late hunters to enter the house, for he had heard sufficient from Joe and Tommy as the party came from the scene of punishment, to put him on his guard.

"Now, liveried slave," he said, coming to the door, and showing the constable the receipt. "You can depart, and get that nose of thine back to its proper colour. Go — away — avaunt!"

"Play-acting fool," said the constable, "I wish I had thee in the stocks."

"Quit my sight," Gentleman Bob said, "or I will have thee cast into a dungeon, and thy tongue blistered with living coals."

"Should like to catch you at it," remarked the fiery-nosed policeman, as he walked away, "I would soon have you up before the justice."

"Now, my friends," Gentleman Bob said, "let's have a little toothful, and then bid a fond adieu to this hospitable town."

They had a toothful at a pub. on the outskirts of Buddleton. It was paid for out of the balance of poor old Bill's money.

Walking down the quiet, country road, Joe told the genteel youth with the small carpet-bag how ill the fickle dame had behaved since he had left the joys of Baream.

Gentleman Bob laughed heartily at the whole business, and patted Toby on the head, and called him a good dog.

"Now," he said, "it's my turn for a yarn. I suppose you were both surprised to see me?"

Tommy and Joe admitted this.

"I can tell you I was surprised to see you both such objects of popular regard," Gentleman Bob said, "for I made sure you would both have made your way to London."

"We should have done so," said Joe, "had we not taken the wrong road and met with Bill Adler."

Perhaps it's as well you did not," said Bob, "for soon after you cut away from Baream the man who brought you down there came to take you back, and when he heard you had bolted, there was a row between old Nip and him."

"Was there?" said Joe; "well, I'm glad I was not there, for I had quite enough of old Siv I can tell you. How is it you have left, Bob? Did you cut?"

"No, my brother sent for me; you've heard me speak of him. He was a strolling actor, and I did not know what part of the country he was in until he sent me a letter. Goodness knows how he found me out."

"He's an actor still, I suppose," said Joe, "isn't he?"

"No," Gentleman Bob answered; "he's got a theatre now, and he wants me to join him; you know I always had a taste that way, Joe."

"I know you had, for you were writing a play when we were together at Baream."

"That play," Bob said, holding up the carpet-bag, "is here; I have finished it, Joe."

"Have you, though? how clever you must be, Bob."

"No; it was born in me, I suppose, for my father was an actor—not a bad one, either."

Gentleman Bob's father trod the London stage for many years, and after his death Bob's mother married again; the eldest boy not liking his father-in-law, left home to fight his battles with the world, and the youngest one was sent to a cheap school, afterwards to the cheaper one conducted by Mr. Samuel Dothem.

"What about Baream?" Joe asked; "does old Nip go on the same as ever?"

"Much about the same," Gentleman Bob answered; "but he was not so bad for a few days after you left; but his youngest daughter, Deb, bolted with that carpenter who lived at Baream township, and it made old Nip so savage that he used to whop the little chaps every day."

"The old brute!"

"We had a rare game two days after you left," Bob said; a Government Inspector of schools came down, but old Nip was ready for him; we were all called in to dinner—such a dinner it was, like a Lord Mayor's feast."

"Shouldn't I have liked to have been there," Tommy said; "I like feasts."

"Old Nip," Gentleman Bob continued, "only had the spread to deceive the inspector; he did not think we should ask for any of the extra joints, but he was taken in, for when he asked us one by one what we would have, we asked for the different things, until every joint and dish was cut into."

"Old mother Nip liked that, I should say."

"She did; you should have seen her face; but she dare not say anything then, except to call us her dear boys. It was dear James, dear Bob, and dear Tom, instead of the old way of talking to us."

"I'll warrant she made up for it afterwards."

"She did, Joe; about half the school were docked of their dinners every day; but the dodge of the big feed got over the inspector, and he went away quite satisfied."

Much more of this sort of conversation was kept up, until the party reached the pleasant little town of Stormouth.

Here Gentleman Bob intended to take the train, but having found his old schoolfellows without any visible or invisible means of support, he proposed that they should all go to Winkletop, a seaside town, where his brother's theatre was situate.

"We don't open for a week yet," he said, "and I don't suppose the company is quite made up; therefore, if you like to chance it and come with me, I will do all I can. Of course you can say you have been on the stage."

"I'm very much obliged, I'm sure," old Bill said; "but I don't think I can be of any use. I——"

"We don't go without you," said Joe, "so shut up."

"Yes," said Tommy, "we stands by you, Bill, no matter what turns up."

"It's all settled then," Gentleman Bob said; "now it only remains to see how the exchequer stands, then we can act accordingly."

Bob, with the usual free and easy manner in which he managed everything, had appointed himself the keeper of old Bill's pence.

He added the small remnant of the three half-sovs to the few shillings he had in his pocket, and the grand total assured him they could venture upon the luxury of a supper, bed, and breakfast at Stormouth.

"Then," said Gentleman Bob, "we will stump it to Winkletop, and see what's to be done there besides picking up cockles on the beach."

CHAPTER XXIV.

THE THEATRE ROYAL, WINKLETOP—THE COMPANY— THE HEAVY MAN WITH A PARTIALITY FOR BITTER ALE—AND OTHER MATTERS RELATING TO GENTLE-MAN BOB'S FRIENDS.

WINKLETOP was not a large town, neither was it dissipated as regards pleasure, not even in the very height of the season.

It was the height of the season when Gentleman Bob and his friends arrived; and Bob, after he had surveyed the deserted streets, remarked—

"Well, if the Theatre does not fill better than

the streets, I am afraid we have performed our long voyage upon the marrow-bone stage for nothing.

"Bob," said Joe, "don't give us the blues already. It will be time enough when we find out all our misfortunes."

"Misfortunes!" Tommy said; "don't talk of 'em, Joe. Here I am, with my ten toes looking out for daylight. I wish I was Toby; he never wants new boots."

"I think," old Bill said, "I have been here before; at least, I know I have; but I didn't think it was a place as had a Theatre."

"Oh, yes," Bob said, "there is one somewhere, although candour makes me confess that it is more used for tea meetings and treats in place of the legitimate drama—as my poor father used to term the performances."

"Teas and treats," Joe said, "don't speak for the tastes of the people; for, when these sort of things are much believed in, it's a pretty certain go that theatres don't get much custom."

"You are not far out, Joe," Bob said, "but never mind, let's be jogging; for, while we stand here, the unpleasant look of affairs will not become pleasanter. Hallo! here comes a real live Winkletoponian. I'll ask him if he knows where the theatre is situate."

Bob asked, and the inhabitant—evidently a fisherman—became buried in the most profound thought.

"There be a theatre," he answered at last, "but it's so long since any play-acting folks has been there, I had well nigh forgot we had one. Keep straight on; you are sure to see it. Looks like a big shed, only it's white."

"Thanks, trusty friend," said Bob. "I would reward thee, but having nothing but bank notes in my pocket, I cannot do so. Farewell until we meet again. But stay; what is thy name?"

"John Brown."

"Thanks. Although I never heard it before, I shall not forget it. Adieu."

Bob waved his hand as the party moved forward; and the astonished fisherman looked after them, great wonderment upon his weather-beaten face.

"Queer lot," was the honest man's mental remark. "Wonder what they be? T'owd chap looks like one of them thumpers as come down here and tells us we be all going to the wrong place. But t'others beats me holler. I wish the missus was here; she'd reckon 'em up in no time."

Bless the ladies! how clever they are in that branch of arithmetic, especially in reckoning each other up!

The travellers, after following their noses,

and passing right through the little town, came in view of the Theatre Royal, and all confessed it was not a prosperous-looking concern.

But for the fact of several yellow posters announced the appearance of a splendid company from the leading London theatres, the place looked as unlike a house of entertainment about to open for the season as it is possible to conceive.

During the time the party were surveying the exterior of the Royal, a door opened, and a greasy-looking individual, with a short black pipe in his mouth emerged.

He glanced at the group, whose faces did not express the most frantic delight at the appearance of the Theatre Royal, Winkletop, and would have passed on, had not Gentleman Bob politely accosted him by saying:—

"Can you tell me where I shall be likely to find Mr. Moore?"

"Inside the crib," replied the greasy one with the pipe, "and going on like anything."

"Indeed," Bob said, fancying his informant was of a combative turn, "I am sorry to hear that."

"It is enough to make him go on," the gentleman with the pipe said, "for more than half the company he engaged to come down here has turned it up."

"Ah!" Bob said, not feeling quite sure what had been turned up by more than half the company; "very disagreeable, no doubt."

"Should say it is when we can't open—so short-handed as we are."

"I see," Bob said, "the company is short-handed, in consequence of some of those engaged not fulfilling their engagements?"

"That's it; and if something doesn't turn up, we shall have to put off the opening until it does."

"I see by the bills," Gentleman Bob said, "that you intend to open with 'Hamlet.'"

"We did; but as those who were cast for Hamlet, the Ghost, Laertes, and Polonius, hasn't turned np, why, it can't be done."

"Don't despair, my friend," said Bob, "for you see before you gentlemen of the sock and buskin, who, having heard of the predicament in which your manager, the very respectable Mr. Frederick Moore, has been placed, have thrown up lucrative engagements to come to the rescue of the Theatre Royal Winkletop."

"No; you don't mean it. You are, then, brother actors?"

"We are—that is to say, these gentlemen are; I am but a humble author, although," Bob added, modestly, "not unknown to fame."

The greasy gentleman seemed about to embrace the whole party, but he changed his mind and said—

"I shall yet make Winkletop ring, for I can now play my favourite character of Claudius, the King of Denmark. But come, this is dry work; let's adjourn and partake of a glass of bitter"

The gentleman, who was the heavy man as well as being a gentleman, jingled two penny pieces and a key to impart the idea to his new acquaintances that he was possessed of boundless wealth, and was about to move off in the direction of the place where his much-loved bitter was to be obtained, when Bob excused himself from accompanying the party.

"I will join you soon," he said; "meanwhile carouse and quaff bumpers of the sparkling bitter. Adieu!"

"Clever young gentleman, I should say," remarked the heavy man who was cast for Claudius. "What's his name?"

"Bob Moore," said Joe; "he's brother to the manager."

"Ah, indeed, have heard the governor speak of him; but here we are."

They entered a small public-house, and the heavy gentleman wished the buxom landlady good morning and begged to introduce the party as stars of the first water, who had just arrived from London, &c., &c.

The hostess did not seem much awed by the presence of so much greatness, and something very much like a smile passed over her ruddy face when she saw Tommy Nimblejaws trying to hide the ventilating processes of his boots.

The hostess, with ready hand placed upon one of the handles of the beer-engine, awaited her customers' commands, but none were given, although the heavy gentleman jingled his penny pieces together and his key.

The tall hunters looked at each other; they had seen enough of the strolling portion of the theatrical profession to understand the cause of the heavy gentleman's reluctance to give an order for the sparkling bitter.

The fact was, the heavy gentleman had not the wherewithal to do it, and the same cause affected the rest of the company.

At last the inviter spoke.

"Dear me," he said, "how very forgetful I am. I changed my clothes to attend rehearsal this morning—for you see the theatre is undergoing a complete renovation, and one does not like to spoil good clothes by coming in contact with dust and paint, and all that sort of thing—and coming out in a hurry, I quite overlooked the fact that my money was in the breast-pocket of my frock-coat; perhaps one of you gentlemen

will oblige by doing the needful. I will return it immediately we return to the theatre."

"How unfortunate," said Joe readily, "we should be in the same predicament, for we have, for the purpose of economy, travelled in our old clothes, and for fear we should meet any desperate footpads, we placed our purses in our leather portmanteaus, and they will not be here until to-morrow, for the weight of our luggage has broken down two light carts, and the waggon will take some time to trail from the town where we last performed."

"What a bore!" said the heavy man; "well, but I suppose it does matter. I daresay the landlady will oblige us——"

"Very sorry, sir," said the landlady, pointing to a notice which was suspended behind the bar; "but that is our rule, and we never break it."

"Ah!" the heavy man said; "I see—'No Trust.' Well, it does not matter. Come, gentlemen, accompany me to my apartments, and I will open a bottle of wine."

The disappointed and thirsty Thespians emerged from the inhospitable hostelry, and despite the air of nonchalance they tried to assume, one and all felt by no means dignified while they remained within the scope of the landlady's vision.

"What a bore!" the heavy man said; "now I remember. I have left the key of my apartments at the theatre; so we are done out of our wine as well as our beer."

"It's of no consequence," said Joe; "we are not thirsty."

Which was not true, Joe, for none of the party had breakfasted that day.

"I know where the key of the wine is," Tommy whispered to old Bill; "it is on the same bunch as the keys of our luggage."

"If that's the case," said Bill Adler, "it won't open many locks, so we shan't be taken up for housebreakers."

To the intense relief of the whole party, a gentleman was seen approaching, and without his carpet-bag.

"Come on," he exclaimed; "it's all right— you are all engaged. Before we celebrate the auspicious event, you had better see my brother."

"Shall see you by-and-by," the heavy man said; "when you have arranged business and so on. I should advise you," he added aside to Joe, "to make a draw, in case your portmanteau does not soon arrive."

"All right," Joe replied; "shall I bring the key of your wine-cellar, as I'm going to the theatre?"

"No, thank you," the heavy man answered;

" you would not know where to look for it ; ta, ta ! see you soon."

" Ta, ta !" said Joe ; " if you should see the waggon with our luggage, send it on."

The heavy man jerked his thumb over his left shoulder and went on his way, and Joe hastened to overtake his companions.

The interior of the theatre was not particularly bright ; the rain had trickled through the roof, and from thence down the walls, leaving dirty streaks, and in some places patches of blue mildew.

These signs of a long-shut-up house were being removed by a man armed with a plentiful supply of whitewash and a large brush.

The scenes and wings looked mouldy in the daylight, but they were being renovated by the scenic artists, whose tastes ran upon large brushes and bright dabs of colour.

Under the seats of the pit there was a collection of empty ginger-beer bottles, a few broken pipes, and a plentiful display of dried pieces of orange-peel.

The place smelt of stale orange-peel and damp, yet to Joe and his companions it was a palace, for they were " engaged ;" and that engagement to perform in the musty theatre was the only barrier that stood between them and starvation.

Gentleman Bob, after several stumbles up the dark staircase, piloted his friends to the stage, and introduced them to his brother.

" Most happy to make your acquaintance," the manager said ; " most happy ; for your opportune arrival has relieved me from a most unpleasant predicament."

Joe and Tommy made suitable replies, and old Bill took off his hat, and answered with his usual—

" Very much obliged, I'm sure, sir."

" You have all been on the boards, so Bob informs me," the manager said, " therefore we have nothing to settle except the salary ; will you oblige by coming this way ?"

Of course they would, and the manager led them to a musty chamber, called by courtesy the green-room, where the financial arrangements were completed.

Bill Adler was to receive £1 1s. a week, Joe 15s., Tommy, 12s., the salaries to commence on the opening night.

It was Tuesday, and the theatre would not open until the Monday following, then a week would elapse before the current coin of the realm would touch their itching palms.

Such was the substance of the thoughts that came to the minds of the trio, and gloomy enough they felt, for they were well aware their appearance was not calculated to inspire any lodging-house keeper with sufficient confidence to give them nearly a fortnight's board and lodging before " seeing the colour" of their money.

The manager broke in upon their thoughts by saying to old Bill—

" You will perform Polonius ; you, Mr. Cholmondeley, Hamlet ; and your friend will have rather a light part as the Ghost. To-morrow, Bob will give you your parts—good day."

Gentleman Bob again became pilot, and when the party reached the open air, Joe said—

" Here's a go, Bob, what are we to do until the first week's coin is due, providing we ever earn as much ?"

" Ever earn as much ? Why not ?"

" Well," said Joe, " there's just a chance that we may be hissed off the stage the first night."

" No fear of that," Gentleman Bob said. " The clowns here don't know much about Shapespeare."

" I'm glad to hear that," said Joe, " but even then the case remains the same as far as we are concerned. You know we can't live upon air for so long——"

" I have thought of that," Gentleman Bob said, " and borrowed half a sov. for you. My brother is not rich, or he would have advanced more."

" That's oceans," Joe said. " Give it to me, Bob. I'll soon work the oracle."

Joe's first move towards working the oracle was to get the bright coin changed. They had a pint of half-and-half between them, and Charity took especial care to make it known to the landlady (the same who had referred the heavy man to the notice suspended inside the bar) that there was plenty more where that came from.

" I suppose," Joe asked, jingling the change, " you could not tell us where we could obtain a respectable lodging ?"

" Well," the lady said, " there are plenty of rooms to let in the town, but wouldn't it be better if you had one nearer the theatre ?"

" Much better," Joe said, " but there's no house in the town except yours."

" I know that," the hostess said ; " therefore I was about to propose something to you."

" By all means let us hear it."

" Well, you see, I have a room empty. It has two beds in it, although it's rather small. I think you would like it."

" We are not particular," Joe said, " as long as the place is clean, and all that sort of thing ; which of course it is in a house like this, and with such a mistress."

Joe rose in the lady's estimation after this politic and gallant speech.

A WARM WELCOME.

"Perhaps you would like to see the—"

"No," said Joe; "you shall not have the trouble of going upstairs, so we will consider the room taken; now about the board?"

"I don't, as a rule," the lady said, "find my lodgers in food."

"Very well," Joe said, "I shall starve, then, for there is no place in this town that I could fancy anything in except here."

"I was about to say," interrupted the landlady, "that I would not mind doing my best for you, but you—"

"Anything will do for us," Joe said; "how about the terms?"

"Suppose we say 10s. 6d. a week each, and 6d. for the dog."

"That will do," Joe said; "and to seal the bargain I will give you a few sovereigns—hang it! I forgot, our luggage has not arrived. Well, here's two half-crowns—that will do for a deposit."

Having thus settled a rather difficult matter, Joe proposed a walk to look at the town during the time dinner was being prepared.

The landlady had not bargained for this; but before she could make any objections, Joe adroitly drew his companion from the house, and left the hostess no choice but to comply with their request.

CHAPTER XXV.

MISS LOUISA GUSHERTON—JOE'S GALLANTRY—A REHEARSAL—THE OPENING NIGHT—THE GHOST SCENE—ONE TOO MANY ON THE STAGE—A TABLEAU.

UNDER Gentleman Bob's tuition, Joe made very fair progress in his part. True, his personification of the great poet's wondrous conception was not perfect, yet it was better than Bob had expected.

There was one person in the company who thought Joe's 'Hamlet' perfect. This was a certain Miss Louisa Gusherton, the lady who did all the love-sick business.

Joe had a good voice and a retentive memory.

He was tall for his age, and his well-knit figure looked to advantage in Hamlet's sable close-fitting garments.

With these advantages, Gentleman Bob's corrections in elocution, and Miss Gusherton's kind offer to teach him how to make love, and his own self-possession, Joe made rapid strides.

There was a dress rehearsal ordered the day previous to the opening night.

Scene—The Green Room.

PRESENT.

HAMLET	...	...	Charity Joe.
LAERTES	...	...	Gentleman Bob.
POLONIUS	...	...	Bill Adler.
OPHELIA	...	...	Miss Gusherton.
GHOST	...	...	Tommy Nimblejaws.

Tommy Nimblejaws—in a hollow voice, for the helmet and suit of armour were much too big for him—"I say, Joe, I can't move my legs; the joints of this suit won't work."

Hamlet :—"Grease them, then."

Polonius (half-audibly reciting his part):—"He hath, my lord." A pause. "Wrung from my—Ah, me; my slow brain—by laboursome partition, and—and—and—— Oh, dear—oh, dear !"

Polonius refers to book of words.

Laertes :—"My dread lord, your leave and favour to return to France; from whence, though willingly, I came to—I say, Joe."

"Well."

"What have you got for dinner to-day?"

"Boiled mutton."

"Good. To show my duty in your——I say, Joe."

"Don't bother so. I have nearly forgotten my part already."

"All right. Yet now I must linger; that duty done—mumble, mumble, mumble."

Ghost :—"Look here, Bob, you must tell them

to do something to my suit. I can't move nor yet see."

"You'll be all right when you get warm."

Bob answers and continues :—"My mariners are embarked. Farewell," &c., &c.

Miss Gusherton to Joe :—"I never saw anything become anyone so well as that dress becomes you, Mr. Cholmondeley."

Joe :—"Thank you, Miss Gusherton."

Miss G. :—"I have played Ophelia many times, and with some good performers ! but I must say I never saw——"

Bell rings; Miss Gusherton arranges her dress, and tries to look killing.

The fair Louisa belonged to that class termed old-young ladies. She had performed tender heroines for the last fifteen years, and her first performance was given when she was twenty years of age ; but strange to say she had stopped the hour-glass of time when she became twenty-three ; and although she had seen five-and-thirty winters, and as many summers, she was but three-and-twenty years old.

To carry out this belief, she had recourse to all the known devices practised by old-young ladies to hide the marks of time ; and Joe, upon whom she had made a dead set, used to smile when he saw the lines and crow's feet under the thick coating of powder with which she veiled her face.

Scene—The Stage.

(The manager standing in the centre.)

Scene supposed to be a platform before the Castle of Elsinore ; it bore a strong likeness to a terrace-scene used in the preceding farce.

Francisco pacing to and fro on sentry.

Enter Bernardo.

Dialogue.

Enter Horatio and Marcellus.

More dialogue.

Marcellus :—"Peace—break thee off. Look where it comes again."

Cue for the Ghost to enter; but no Ghost making his appearance, the manager stamps his foot and repeats :—

"Look where it comes again."

Still no Ghost.

Faint and hollow voice in the distance :—

"It's no use, I can't move. I tell you the joints won't work."

Another voice (Joe's) :—"Go on; don't be a fool."

"I tell you, Joe, I can't move; I can't bend my knees ; so how can I walk ?"

Manager, looking very red in the face, rushes off, returns presently with the Ghost, who walks as stiff as though he had his legs encased in iron shafts.

After a little delay, the Ghost is made to walk on and off the stage in obedience to the proper cues. End of the first scene.

The King (Bob's brother):—"Have you your father's leave? What says Polonius?"

Polonius (old Bill), he knew every word of his part before he came on; now his mind is a perfect blank.

"What says Polonius?" the manager repeats.

"He—wrung—no—hath wrung my—leave—no—from me—"

"Come, Mr. Adler" (the manager's voice is rather stern, and frightens the old man), "this will never do."

"I'm very sorry, I'm sure," old Bill began; but he was cut short by the manager saying—

"Come, come, your part. Now, prompter."

"He hath, my lord," says the prompter.

"Yes, that's it," exclaimed Polonious. "He hath, my lord, wrung from me my slow leave, ect., etc.

Joe's delivery of Hamlet's reply to the King was a little nervous at first. By-the-bye, the heavy man should have been present to rehearse his part of Claudius; but "sparkling bitter" had led him from the path of duty, thus the manager had to do the best he could under the circumstances.

Joe's nervousness wore off by the time he had passed on to the soliloquy which begins—

"O that this too solid flesh would melt."

Scene the 4th.

Enter Hamlet, Horatio, and Marcellus.

Dialogue until Joe comes to the cue for the Ghost to enter.

Hamlet—"Doth all the noble substance often out, to his own scandal?"

Horatio—"Look, my lord, it comes."

Hamlet—"Angels and ministers—"

Manager, in a passion—"Stop, stop; where the deuce is the Ghost?" At the top his voice, "To his own scandal."

Voice at the side (Tommy under the Ghost's helmet)—I hear, but I can't find my way; this beastly helmet's so big that it has settled down on my shoulders, and I can't see."

Crash! then a howl from Tommy. He had run against the wings, and flattened the pasteboard visor upon his nose.

"Mr. Dillon!" roars the manager, "Mr. Dillon!"

Enter the property-man, looking very red and uncomfortable.

"Here, sir."

"For goodness sake do something to that confounded Ghost's dress, or we shall be in a pretty mess to-morrow night."

Ghost: "Yes, sir." Moves off and captures Tommy, and adds:—"Of course; couldn't expect anything else; no business to put boys in men's clothes."

Joe and Miss Gusherton laughed at Tommy's mishaps; the stage manager fiercely talks at them, but addresses himself to the call-boy.

"Do you think a rehearsal is got up for your amusement, sir? Take that—I'll teach you to laugh, sir."

Kicks call-boy off the stage, then waves his hand and says:—

"Now, please, scene the fifth."

Hamlet: "Whither wilt thou lead me? Speak! I'll go no further."

Ghost: "Mark me."

Hamlet: "I will."

Tommy appearing at side: the property-man has drilled two holes in his visor: "All right now. Mark me."

Hamlet: "I will."

Ghost: "My hour is almost come, when I to brimstone—"

"Sulphurous" roar the manager and prompter in one breath.

"Sulphurous and e— tormenting flames must render up myself."

Hamlet: "Alas, poor Ghost."

Ghost: "You may well say that—no I mean, pity me not," &c., &c.

So the rehearsal goes on, and about half-past four in the afternoon the company break up, thoroughly tired and worn out.

The young old Miss Gusherton sticks to Joe, and he has to see her home.

Poor old Bill plods to the inn, and mentally wonders whether it will ever be more natural to him to begin his part when he comes on the stage instead of feeling inclined to say—

"Very sorry, I'm sure, but oh, I remember; I ought to say, 'What is it, Ophelia?'" Dear me! I don't think I shall make an actor. That lad will; that lad will; he is a genius; but I am not. The show would suit me better."

The opening night comes. The posters have done their work.

Hamlet to be performed by the youngest living actor. People came from all the outlying villages, and the Theatre Royal Winkletop is full.

The performance goes on without a hitch. Even Tommy manages to feel comfortable in his particular suit; and the heavy man had abstained from bitter the whole day; and old Bill does not require prompting more than at every second line.

Scene the 4th closes; scene the 5th must be given as it occurred. The reader will please to understand that Toby had taken a bitter dislike to the Ghost, and when the light was thrown upon the figure, to add to the supernatural effect, Toby fairly howled with fright.

This had occurred at the rehearsal, therefore Joe left his canine friend at home on the opening night.

The interview between the Ghost and Hamlet goes on very smoothly until Tommy in his speech says—

"I could a tale unfold, whose lightest word would harrow up thy soul; freeze thy young blood:

"Make thy two eyes, like stars, start from their *sockets*.

"Thy knotted and *combed* locks to part, and each particular hair to stand *bolt upright*.

"Like *frightful* quills upon the *ugly* porcupine.

"But this eternal blazon must not be.

"To ears of flesh and blood. List, list, O, list!"

"If thou did'st ever thy dear father love."

Hamlet: "Oh, Heaven."

Ghost: "Revenge this foul and most unnatural murder."

Toby suddenly rushes upon the stage, and begins to bark furiously at the ghost.

Hamlet: Murder!"

Toby: "Bow—wow—wow!"

Ghost: "Murder most foul——"

Toby: "Bow—wow—wow!"

Hamlet (aside): "You, Tommy, here's a go."

Ghost: "As in the best it is. But this most foul, strange, and unnatural (aside) Give Toby a kick."

Hamlet (aside): My shoes are so thin they won't stand it. Curse the dog! the audience are laughing at us." Continuing his part: "Haste me to know it, that I with wings so slight as meditation or the thoughts of love, may sweep to my revenge. (Aside.) Hang the dog! the house is an uproar."

Toby: "Bow—wow—wow! Growl—growl."

Hamlet (Shakespeare slightly altered): "What ho, my guards! remove this fierce and untamed animal."

Toby is removed by the Danish soldiers, some of them dressed in brigand costume, and the audience shout—

"Bravo, bravo!" and clap their hands at Joe's ready wit.

Joe saved the credit of the house by the utterance of those few words, for the manager, appalled by the way in which Tommy had rendered Shakespeare, had already begun to look upon his prospects as ruined, when Toby's unwished-for performance put the culminating point to his agony.

CHAPTER XXVI.

GENTLEMAN BOB'S PLAY—A FAC-SIMILE OF THE ANNOUNCEMENT—AN ADDITION TO THE COMPANY, AND JOE'S PLANS OF REVENGE FOR THE CONSPIRACY AGAINST THE WILD HUNTERS OF THE FROZEN MOUNTAINS.

IT was lucky for the manager and his company that the inhabitants of Winkletop knew as much about Shakespeare as they did about the individual who designed the Great Pyramids.

Had they been familiar with the merits of the great poet's works, the first performance would have been sufficient.

At the second representation, when the Ghost scene was taking place, the "gods" manifested some impatience, and when the Ghost bids Hamlet adieu, a number of the intelligent (?) audience in the gallery yelled out:—

"Come back, t'owd chap; the dog ain't been on—you mun wait for he!"

Hamlet with a dog not being quite the text, the Ghost made his exit, and Joe began his soliloquy:—

"Oh, all you host of——"

"The dawg—where be the dawg? Hold thee jaw, and fetch the dawg!"

Cat-calls, shrill whistles, and stamping of feet gave emphasis to the demand, and Joe said to the prompter:—

"Send for the manager; he must explain the matter to these fools."

The manager, alarmed by the uproar in the gallery, made his appearance before the footlights; but when he attempted to speak, the clamour increased threefold.

"Give th' chap a chance to speak," roared a lusty young fellow in a blue Guernsey; "give him a chance."

The noise abated a little, and the manager, placing his hand upon his left breast, and bowing very low, looked towards the gallery and said:—

"Ladies and gentlemen, the appearance of the dog last night was a mistake, for Shakespeare never intended a dog to perform in the——"

"Let him alter th' play, then; we like a dawg in th' piece."

"But, ladies and gentlemen, who ever heard of Hamlet and a dog——"

Cat-call, yells, and whistles followed, and drowned the manager's voice for a time.

"You shall have a dog," he said; "we have a splendid melo-drama in preparation, and——"

A piece of orange-peel struck the manager on the mouth, and he retired, his speech as he passed the wings not being complimentary to the enlightened audience.

The retreat of the manager seemed to put the gods in good humour again, for they told Joe "To get on wi' his jaw."

And Joe went on, and the play was gone through in tolerable quietude.

And after the curtain had fallen, and the audience were leaving the house, the manager assembled the company upon the stage.

"Had I not," he said, "embarked every penny I have in this speculation, I would turn the business up; but as it is, I must stay here until we are in a position to seek a fresh field. Now the best thing we can do is to get up something that will suit these thick-headed fools; therefore, I shall be happy to see you all here at ten to-morrow morning sharp, to rehearse the new piece.

Next evening the walls of the theatre were smothered with posters, announcing, in gigantic letters, the appearance of the new drama.

THEATRE ROYAL, WINKLETOP.*

On Wednesday Night will be performed, for the first time, the great drama of
THE SILVER BUTTON!!!
Or, The Bandit's Son! The Smuggler's Daughter!! and Kosmos, the Dog-Avenger!!!
Immense Attraction!!!!
Be in Time!!!!!

Remember, never before seen upon any stage.

VINCENTO (a young officer, in love with the Smuggler's daughter).....Mr. J. Cholmondeley.

BERNARDO (the Bandit's son, a deep-dyed villain, also in love with Nina)........Mr. Roberts.

DAGGERANDE (Bernardo's companion, a ruthless ruffian, ready at any time to commit the blackest crime)..................Mr. Thomas Nimbleton.

KARL (a poor but honest peasant)
Mr. William Adler.

BOB MIZENROYAL (a true-blue son of the ocean, ready and willing at all times to shiver any land-lubber's timbers and throw the main deck overboard)..............................Mr. Fitzmore.

GOMEZ, the bandit (father to Bernardo, a cruel and merciless man)....................Mr. Topham.

WILL SHEAVEHOLE, the smuggler (a man whose life has been rendered miserable by the persecution of his enemies, but whose heart is yet the dwelling place of virtue and love)
Mr. William Rabits.

NINA, his daughter (a fair flower of the most perfect loveliness, wasting her sweetness upon the sea coast air, in love with Vincento, and persecuted by the villain Bernardo)
Miss Flora Gusherton.

* This is a fac-simile of a poster that appeared on the walls of a theatre at a small seaport town not more than three years ago. The names, for obvious reasons, are slightly altered, as many of the little company have since risen in the profession, and hold a good position on the London boards. The author, Gentleman Bob, is now a clever dramatist.

LEONIE, a village maiden (friend of Nina's beloved by Bob Mizenroyal, persecuted by Gomez)
Miss Loveday.

KOSMOS, THE DOG-AVENGER.
Peasants, bandits, smugglers, sailors, maidens, by the Company.

ACT I.
Scene 1.—The brow of the cliff with the dull roar of the breakers in the distance—Nina's peril—Mine! mine! ha! ha!—A true-blue to the rescue—Bernardo is hurled into the midst of the foaming billows—Leonie's jealousy—Bob's despair—appearance of Vincento and his dog.

Scene 2.—Alive yet—Ha! ha! she shall yet be mine; "at him good dog"—faithless weapon; accursed be the hand that forged thee!

The glitter of the bandit's stiletto is seen—the waves close over the noble dog and the black-hearted villain. Tableau of misery, despair, and revenge.

Scene 3.—The bandits' cave—the band—the noble dog a prisoner—Karl, a poor but honest peasant, joins the band.

HE OVERHEARS THE DIABOLICAL PLOT.

ACT II.
Scene 1.—The smuggler's lugger—the moon rises—a view from the sea—quick! quick! a rope.

"False villain! I denounce thee!"

The bandit's son confronted by the gallant blue-jacket.

"Fools, fools! one step and I cast thy vessel to the winds—behold! Tableau.

Scene 2.—A lonely wood—immense and wild flowers—the wolf appears—help! help! save me! save me! from these men.

"Hark! it is the bay of the noble dog; unhand me, you villains; come Vincento, come."

"I am here—at them, good dog!"

Terrific combat—virtue triumphant.

Scene 3.—The gallant officer and his dog on their way to the battle-field—the dog pauses and refuses to go further.

Scene 4.—A wood—the ambush—"Ah!" I have lost my bullets! quick, a button from thy jacket, Daggerande."

Painful sensation.

The shot—the cry of pain—flight of the assassins—a woman's voice of agony startles the stilly night.

The Dog-Avenger upon the assassin's track—a British tar's resolve.

ACT III.
Scene 1.—The bandits' cavern by the sea—Mina and Leoni in the bandits' lair—the villains rejoice—the maidens despair.

Scene 2.—The deck of the smuggler's lugger

—an old man's grief—a sailor's consolation—Ha!—A small skiff is seen upon the waters.

Scene 3.—The bandits' carousal—drink to the Bandit Queen—sudden appearance of the Dog-Avenger—the cup torn from the bandit's grasp—the ready knife—the boom of a gun stays the deadly blow—to arms! to arms!—the cave is battered in by the smuggler's guns—the attack—a foul deed prevented by a timely shot—the silver button avenges the bandit's treachery.

The dead alive—the embrace—innocence and bravery rewarded.

TERRIFIC TABLEAU!!!

The intellectual treat (?) promised by the foregoing announcement had its due effect upon the inhabitants of Winkletop, especially the rising generation, who forthwith began to "save up" to see the play.

Even Shakspeare with a dog stood no chance with "The Silver Button, or the Bandit's Son," and until the opening night came there was always to be seen a goodly assemblage in front of the bills, every reader dilating upon the events so temptingly set forth.

The manager was in ecstacies, and the company worked hard to learn their part; and at night, poor Shakespeare was more mercilessly mangled than before, by the performers mixing extracts from the new play with the text of "Hamlet."

Upon the strength of the anticipated success, the manager was tempted to make an addition to his company, for he had no one available to perform the not over arduous part of Gomez, the bandit.

The new arrival announced himself by letter as Mr. Topham, but when he arrived in the flesh, Joe and Tommy Nimblejaws saw in the person of Mr. Francis Topham, the walking gentleman of Mr. Banks's company.

Mr. Topham and the heavy man, who liked bitter ale, seemed to be old acquaintances, for when they met in the street there was much handshaking and wagging of tongues between them.

Joe and Tommy watched this performance from the window of the inn, and retired as the pair advanced towards the door.

"I thought so," Tommy remarked, "old Fitzmore is about to celebrate the meeting in his usual manner."

"Which," Joe said, "means that F. Topham, Esq., will have to pay; but I say, Tommy."

"Well, old boy."

"If I don't make a mistake, this Topham is one of the fellows who rounded upon us at Buddleton."

"No mistake about it, Joe."

"Under these circumstances," Joe said, "it will not be my fault if we are not even with him before he has been long here."

Tommy struck an attitude, and exclaimed—

"Revenge! ha—ha!"

"Yes," said Joe, "revenge! Here they are, draw back from the doorway, Tommy."

Mr. Fitzmore and his friend came to the bar and Mr. F. called for a foaming tankard and kindly allowed his friend to pay for it.

"*En persong*," said Mr. Topham, "what sort of a company have you down here, Fitzey?"

Mr. Fitzey did not misquote French, he was not up to that, but he made amends for this by pulling up his limp collar, and striking an attitude, supposed to convey an impression of the most sovereign contempt for the company at large.

"Well," he said, "you ask me as a friend, and as a friend I will answer: they are not the sort we have been used to. No, my boy, but, like yourself, I just came down here for a week or two to breathe the country air, for one does get tired of London, no matter how great a favourite he may be with the audience."

Neither of the talented gentlemen had appeared on the London boards, but they did their best to make each other believe so, and of course succeeded?

"The screw's all right, I suppose?" Mr. Topham asked, "for though one does come down here for a little relaxation it does not pay to let these country managers have the whole benefit of our talents."

"Certainly not," responded Mr. Fitzmore, "certainly not; therefore, my boy, be at rest about the screw, it is small but always forthcoming."

"Glad to hear that, one can put up with having to associate with a third-class company under those circumstances; by the way, what sort of women have you?"

"Very dickey," said Mr. Fitzmore, ungallantly, "the youngest is nearer forty than nineteen, and like all young old girls she is spoons upon the youngest gentleman of the company."

"Just the way with them," said Mr. Topham; "well, I suppose a fellow must put up with the nuisance of having to perform with venerable girlhood. By the way, Fitzey, what sort of a fellow is this Cholmondeley, I see he is down in the bill for a good part?"

"Quiet lad enough," answered Mr. Fitzmore, "and will make an actor some day if he has luck."

"H'm. Well, I suppose I must endure him for a time, for of course there will be an alteration in the caste in future, that is, you and I must have all the good parts."

"I don't know about that," Mr. Fitzmore said. "I thought my talent would have had a better field for display, but these fellows are friends of the manager or his brother, therefore you know the rest."

"Yes, sir; fellows, what do you mean by that?"

"Fill the tankard again, please—why there are three of them and a dog."

"A what?"

"A dog."

"An old one and two young ones."

"What, dogs?"

"No, fellows."

"An old one and two young ones."

"Then it must be the same."

"Eh!" inquired Mr. Fitzmore, "what's the same?"

"These fellows and the dog, the same gang that I helped to run out of old Banks's."

"Ah!" Mr. Fitzmore said, "something good, by your laughter."

"Good, Fitzey, magnificent! You shall hear it if you like."

Mr. Fitzmore did like, so his friend related the plot against the Wild Hunters of the Frozen Mountains, and the performing Wolf, Junga, and the result of the plot caused both gentlemen to laugh long and heartily.

There were two gentlemen sitting in the parlour who did not laugh; they had overheard every word, and one of them, Charity Joe, had to be held by his companion, J. Nimblejaws, Esq., or he would have rushed upon Mr. Topham and "spifflicated" him on the spot.

Such was the inelegant but forcible term used by Joseph Cholmondeley, Esq., and hard work Tommy found it prevent the spifflication taking place.

"Be quiet, Joe; don't be a fool," said Tommy, "we can pay him out another way—let's plan a revenge."

"Let me go, Tommy, or I shall hit you."

"Can't help it, old fellow; you must hit if you like, but I shall stick to you tight."

"Let me alone, Tommy."

"Not if I know it, Joey; let's plan a fine revenge."

Joe was entirely pacified, and consented to sit quietly and plan an ample measure of vengeance.

CHAPTER XXVII.

SOME ACCOUNT OF THE PERFORMANCE OF GENTLEMAN BOB'S PLAY—GUSHERTON MAKES LOVE IN EARNEST—THE HERO OF THE PLAY IN A FIX—HOW TOBY AVENGED THE WRONGS DONE TO THE WILD HUNTERS OF THE FROZEN MOUNTAINS.

THE night came for the first representation of the terrific melo-drama, and young Winkletop mustered in force at the gallery door, middle-aged Winkletop crowded the pit entrance, and respectable Winkletop had secured boxes for themselves and families.

There was much noise and strange words outside the house, when the first-comers were put to the test of the full amount of pressure the human frame can endure before the human frame becomes flattened out as thin as a sheet of paper.

There was much grumbling by the middle-aged Winkletoponians because the pit doors were not opened three hours before the performance.

Here the grumblings were steady, and not enlivened by the sweet sounds and many scuffles that took place at the gallery entrance, for here every youthful representative of the ancient and fishy town desired a front seat, and did their best to fulfil their desires.

Four youths, who had taken an early position against the door, found some difficulty in holding their post, for other and envious youths took the caps from the heads of the early birds, and threw them among the crowd, but capless they stood, and held out the most enticing promises to their companions in the rear, if the latter would take care of their lost head-coverings.

"Billy Jones," said capless No 1, "I'll save you a front seat if you bring me my cap."

Nos. 2, 3, and 4 held out a similar promise. They were in turn promised if they tried to keep a seat for the capholders, there would be black eyes and broken noses before the curtain rose.

They were further told that being knocked into the middle of next week would be nothing to what they would get if they were even caught trying to save a seat.

Inside the house all was joy; the manager nearly dislocated his brother's arm, as he kept shaking hands with Gentleman Bob, and saying—

"You will make our fortune, Bob; I always knew you would."

Bob felt much refreshed at this, yet he inwardly wondered why his brother had never told him so before.

Miss Gusherton, for a wonder, was pleased with her part, and to show her approval she wore shorter skirts than ever, and used so much powder to her face that Joe trembled for the fate of his new cotton velvet doublet, and wondered what the audience would think of the black sleeves, impressed by a life-size impression of Miss Gusherton's face; for in one scene she would have to rest her head upon Joe's shoulder, doing a terrific combat with three furious bandits.

We will pass over the overture, many of the

audience would have liked to have done so too, for the music was enough to harrow up the feelings of even unsophisticated Winkletop.

Behold the curtain raised; or as a youth in the gallery poetically remarked—

"The rag is up."

Enter, to pathetic music, Nina ; she gazes upon the boundless ocean (about two square yards of white and blue canvas), and listens to the roar of the breakers (a broom handle performing a solo on an old tea tray.)

She speaks—she weeps, for her lover, the gallant Vincento, is about to leave her to face the dangers of the painted canvas—no, the raging main.

Music, more pathetic, as she comes forward and sings—

"Why will my lover leave me,
Why will my lover leave me,
Why——"

The remainder of the song is inaudible in consequence of the orchestra choosing to fall out about time, and will insist upon playing the symphony instead of the pathetic air.

The groaning of the instruments and the squeaking of Miss Gusherton's voice subside, then the plaintive lady informs the audience that it relieves her bursting heart to sing.

Sing is the cue for the orchestra, they perform a hurried bar of music (?) and the youths in the gallery know this is the prelude to the entrance of the villain of the piece.

Enter Bernardo (Gentleman Bob) in a pair of whiskers much too large for him.

"I have thee now!" he exclaims. "Thou art mine for ever! for thy lover has——"

"Never! villain, will I be thine," Nina answers warmly. "Sooner will I throw myself in the bosom of the boundless ocean than, than——"

"Ha ! ha !"

She goes to throw herself in the bosom of the boundless deep ; but, upon the verge of the giddy precipice (three feet high) the villain seizes her wrist.

Terrific struggle, during which she seizes the dagger in his sash (a table knife in a red worsted comforter).

Imposing Tableaux !

"Advance one step further, and this glittering blade shall drink thy life ! (A novelty, blades to have mouths. Perhaps it was one of the thirsty blades we hear about).

The villain pauses, but—"ha, ha!" draws a pistol from his sash, fires, and knocks the dagger from Nina's hand.

Sensation, especially in the gallery.

Again they struggle. This time the villain is triumphant, drags virtue from the brow of the cliff, and is about to carry her off. (Qy., why did she not take the leap into the bosom of the boundless deep when the kni—dagger—was knocked from her grasp?)

Another struggle close to the footlights.

"Ha, ha ! she is mine."

Voice in the distance: "No, you long-shore land-lubber, you pirate," and many more seafaring terms (not) used by seamen. Then enters Bob Mizenroyal, the true-blue son of the ocean.

"What !" he exclaims, "a petticoat in distress ! Why, you pirate, dash my top-masts, take that."

Takes quid from his mouth, *knocks villain down with it.*

"You will protect me, sir ?"

"Protect you, my frigate under sky-scrapers ! Ask Bob Mizenroyal to do that when he's a true-blue salt of the briny ocean ? Ha !"

Villain draws another pistol, and fiercely exclaims, as he pulls the trigger—

"Take that for your pains, meddling fool."

Pistol misses fire, of course—villain and true-blue struggle desperately—true-blue victorious—then, to slow and dreadful music, hurls Bernardo over the cliff.

All Winkletop, at least all that are present at the theatre, show their appreciation of this feat by shaking the very walls with their applause.

"Now, my sweet craft, take in your signals, eh?"

Rushes forward in time to catch Nina in his arms, and as he chafes her forehead with the cuff of his jacket, Leoni enters.

"Faithless wretch !" she cries, "is it thus—"

She prepares to scratch her rival's face, but the son of the ocean waves her off, and says—

"What, my clipper beauty, would you have a man stand by when——"

Flourish of music, enter Vincento (Joe) and Kosmos, the Dog-Avenger (Toby).

Tableaux—Supposed to represent Leoni and Vincento's feelings at beholding the baseness of their sweethearts.

Drop scene, and more applause.

Sepulchrous music announces the next scene, and, as much in the way of scenery is left to the imagination of the audience, Bernardo floundering about the stage with a few yards of green gauze about his body, is supposed to be in the bosom of the boundless sea, and the villain swimming.

A few feet behind the swimmer the giddy rocks are seen (about three feet high), and when the villain loudly announces the fact of his existence, and informs the audience Nina shall yet be his, Vincento appears upon the verge of the mighty precipice.

He sees the villain, for all has been explained,

and, pointing a pistol, tells him to "Die, miscreant!" but the piece does not go off, and Vincento, like all stage heroes, utterly regardless of the cost of his fire-arms, hurls the faithless weapon into the sea.

This is the cue for Toby, who jumps down after the pistol, but Joe exclaims, "At him, good dog," and the audience are frantic with delight at Kosmos' sagacity.

A piece of meat in the villain's hand aids the deception, for while Toby is trying to get it away from Bernardo, a very good idea of a deadly struggle between the noble dog and the villain is given.

Despair of Vincento, who sees his dog stabbed by the villain; but the latter must be wounded by the dog's fangs, for the green gauze—no, the boundless waves close over them as they sink through the trap.

This scene is termed a carpenters' scene, it gives them time to prepare scene the 3rd, the Bandits' Cave.

Unearthly music, as the scene opens, and discovers the bandits asleep, except one solitary watcher, Toby, his neck bandaged, is seen tied to the leg of a table.

N.B.—The whole strength of the company, save of course those who have to speak in the scene is used for the bandits' band, even the Misses Gusherton and Loveday have large cloaks and slouched hats, and recline in one corner of the cave.

Vincento is also a fine bandit, as far as the hat and cloak are concerned.

More unearthly music, then Gomez the bandit chief yawns, rises from his rocky bed, and says—

"Still they sleep."

A remark surely unnecessary considering the stillness around.

"What—ho! sentinel, is all well?"

"All's well," Daggerande (Tommy) answers, "and the moon is rising."

A yellow object about the size of a cheese plate appears at the opening of the cave, and substantiates Daggerande's words.

The bandit chief strides to and fro the stage in deep thought, and to convey an idea of his cruel and merciless disposition (as per account on posters) he kicks all the sleeping bandits who lie in his path, and they groan most dismally. The sound seems pleasant, for the chieftain amiably remarks, "Groan, dogs, what else are ye fit for but to be spurned by my foot?"

So he kicks them all round again, and they groan with pain as he passes on, the last recipient of a kick starts to his feet, stiletto in hand.

"Hah! Bernardo," exclaims the delighted chief; "I see thy father's spirit animates thy breast, but come hither, lad, I would speak with thee."

They go hither—close to the foot-lights—and are about to speak, when a low whistle was heard without.

"Ha! a stranger," and the bandit father and son grip the handles of their knives.

"Who goes there?" demands the sentinel; a voice answers, "Friend."

Slow torture—more music. Enter Bill Adler, the poor but honest peasant, he cowers beneath the fierce looks of the chief and his son, and the former asks—

"Well, slave, what has brought thee here to the bandits' lair?"

The poor but honest peasant expresses a desire to join the band, and he is told his wish will be granted if he has the nerve to go through the customary rites.

"To-morrow," says the chief; "thou and ten of my trusty band will go forth, and the first man, woman, or child you meet must die by your hand—thus."

The gesture accompanying the last word implies that the hapless man, woman, or child must be killed by Karl's hand drawing a knife across the victim's throat.

The poor, but honest peasant retires to the wings, wringing his hands and giving other tokens of his dislike to the interesting rite.

Now the father and son converse; the father admits his love for Leonie, the son for Nina.

Poor, but honest peasant listens attentively, and wrings his hands all the more.

Before another moon rises the "gurls" are to brought to the cave, and the elder bandit, who does not explain his reason, expresses the most violent hatred against Nina's father.

Declares he would like to make mincemeat of Bill Sheavehole, the amiable smuggler, who has been made miserable by his enemies, but whose heart is the dwelling-place of virtue and love.

The son experiences much about the same kindly feelings for Bob Mizenroyal.

"Ha, ha! the lugger returns to-morrow at eleven; you are a good surmiser—re—ve—nge is ours!"

Now the plot is unfolded; Bernardo disguised is to be taken on board the smuggler's vessel.

He will then drill a hole in the bottom and—

"Ha, ha!" so perish those who stand in the way of Gomez, the bandit chief!"

Poor, but honest peasant nearly wrings his hands off during this interesting conversation—at least he is unable to listen any more, so creeps away home through the opening at the back of the stage. Sentry suddenly espies him leaping from rock to rock and fires.

CHAPTER XXVIII.

A CONTINUATION OF THE LAST CHAPTER.

" HAVE you hit the fool?"

"I have, dreaded chieftain. I saw his body fall from rock to rock, and it now lies three hundred feet below."

"What a lie," remarks a youth in the gallery. "Why it ain't no distance under the stage, I was under it turning the wheel for the man who gave a lecture, and said he had found out perpetual motion; so he did, as long as I turned the—"

"Order, order, turn him out, chuck him over!"

Act the first closes, and there is a demand for ginger-beer, apples, oranges, and nuts.

ACT II.

Scene I.—Depicts the deck of the smuggler's lugger, the smuggler chieftain paces the deck with folded arms and a moody brow.

A yellow object about the size of a cheese plate appears, and Will Sheavehole attentively watches its erratic course.

"'Twas such a moon," he soliloquises, "when I first left the paths of honesty and became a smuggler, it was—but I talk like a fool."

"That be right, t'owd chap," one of the gods remarked. "Who made your boots, they're a plaguey sight too large?"

Not heeding this remark, the smuggler continues.

"Persecuted by those who once were my friends, such has been my fate, yet my heart is not turned from the world—no, still there is room left for virtue to dwell therein. Ha! what is that?"

"Save me—save me!" says a faint voice.

Then Bernardo is seen buffeting wildly with the yard and half of green gauze.

"Quick," Will Sheavehole cries out. "What ho, a rope, here is a fellow creature alone in the midst of the ocean."

One of the smugglers brings a rope, then Bernardo is dragged on board.

He is supported by two smugglers, and led to the centre of the stage, and during the time Will Sheavehole bends over him, Bob Mizenroyal suddenly appears from below.

The author of the piece does not in any way account for the true blue son of the ocean's appearance at such a moment or on board the lugger, which by Will Sheavehole's soliloquy had only just returned from a long voyage.

Perhaps, Gentleman Bob thought only of the situation, and did not trouble about the appearance of the sailor in such an unexpected manner.

"Ah!" True Blue exclaims, "what have we here, a wreck stranded upon a lee shore?"

"Ay, ay, Bob," the smuggler chieftain replies;

"it is like the shoals of life where the quicksands are—"

"No—what—yes!" Bob Mizenroyal cries as he recognises the face of the supposed castaway; "yes, it is; why look here, Smuggler Bill, this is a pirate in disguise, a longshore landshark."

Bernardo, seeing further disguise is useless, jumps to his feet, and True Blue exclaims:—

"False villain, I denounce thee! (vide play bill), I denounce thee as the son of that land pirate Gomez!"

"Ha!" exclaims the smuggler, snatching up a hatchet; "this is the son of the enemy who has persecuted me, and although my heart is yet the dwelling-place of virtue, I must slay thee with this——"

"Back, fools!" Bernardo shouts; "advance but one step and I blow thy vessel into the air!"

He points a pistol down the hold. True Blue, Will Sheavehole, and smugglers, fall back in dismay. Bernardo shouts—

"Ha! ha! ha! ha! ha!" as the scene changes and closes on the tableau.

Query.—Was the smugglers' hold supposed to be filled with loose powder, and would the pistol have gone off after the length of time it had been under water?

Scene 2.—A lonely wood—moonlight—Nina appears, and begins to gather wild flowers.

Enter Bernardo, Daggerande, and the ruffian Gomez.

They point to Nina significantly, then Gomez and Daggerande retire to the back of the stage.

"Good night, fair maiden," Bernardo says, ironically. "What is a more fitting place for lovers to meet than under the shade of these mighty trees?"

Nina throws the bunch of wild flowers from her, and putting out her hands, recoils with horror.

"Ha! ha! What, afraid of me, pretty one?"

"Leave me, monster, leave me, before I raise a cry that shall bring me——"

"Phew! listen to me, girl. I have sworn you shall be mine, and now to keep my vow, so come away to the bandits' lair."

Terrific struggle—Nina throws villain off, and is about to escape, when Daggerande and Gomez rush forward and seize her arms.

"Help, help! save me from these men! help! help!"

"Gag her!" suggests the amiable Gomez, "or I'll draw my knife across her throat!"

"Bow, wow, wow!" (Toby in the distance.)

"Hark!" Nina cries; "it is the bay of the noble dog! unhand me, villains!"

Daggerande and Gomez during this speech try

to gag the persecuted girl. She again tears the bandage from her mouth, and screams—

"Vincente, save me! Vincente—Vincente—come!"

"I AM HERE!"

Wild flourish of music, tremendous cheering and stamping of feet by the audience, as Joe bounds upon the stage, sword in hand.

The situation was telling.

"What now, villains!" he exclaims, when the applause had subsided, "unhand the maiden, or my good sword shall cut her from thy grasp!"

Preparations for terrific combat. Joe points to Gomez, and cries—

"At him, good dog!"

Then hurls Daggerande aside and tears Nina from his grasp.

For some time Joe had but one foe to battle with, for Toby seized on Mr. Topham, not by the clothes, but by the flesh, and that gentleman had quite enough to do to battle with Toby.

Joe must have done this on purpose, for while he was battling with Tommy he whispered—

"He's got him, Tommy."

"Yes," said the hopeful, "dash it, Joe, yes, Toby has him by the flesh, and the wild hunters are avenged."

Bernardo and Daggerande are disarmed by Joe, and Gomez begs for mercy, and as the poster announced,

VIRTUE IS TRIUMPHANT!!!

Scene 3.—Another part of the wood—slow music as Daggerande enters and conceals himself (but quite visible to the audience).

Martial music announces the coming of the young officer—enter Joe and Toby.

Joe tells the audience about his devoted love for Nina, etc., and winds up by saying—

"Now, good dog, let us seek the red field of battle."

Walks half-way across the stage on his way to the red field, then Toby refuses to go any further.

"What, ho! good dog. Come, let not thy heart sink at the thought of danger."

But Toby is deaf to entreaties, he would not move, so Joe draws his sword, then seizes the dog by the neck, and exit.

Unearthly music as Daggerande and Bernardo follow him.

Scene 4. Another part of the wood.

Enter Daggerande and Bernardo again; they are in search of their victim.

Dreadful music when Daggerande points to the wings and says—

"He comes."

The villains hide. Enter Joe and Toby.

Bernado loads his pistol, but having lost his bullets, gives way to an exhibition of frantic rage.

Suddenly he espies the buttons on his companion's jacket, and exclaims—

"Quick, a button from thy jacket, Daggerande."

Receives the button and puts it in his gun.

Painful sensation among the audience.

The assassin fires; Joe shrieks out with pain, and falls; Nina shrieks, and rushes in L H and the assassin flees R H.

Enter True Blue, son of the ocean, shivering everybody's timbers, and talking about signal guns, sees Nina bending over Joe.

N.B.—Visible on the left shoulder of Joe's black doublet is a white patch left by Nina' powered face, where she reclined upon Joe during the terrific combat.

"What, my girl," Bob Mizenroyd said, "have the long-shore lubbers sent him to Davy Jones."

"He is dead, dead, dead."

"Dead!" says Bob; "may my toplights be shivered, and the forecastle be thrown over the masthead, if I rest until I fall foul of the rascally pirates."

This is the British tar's resolve, which he no sooner makes than Toby runs off the stage.

"See," the True Blue exclaims; "see my lass—there goes the Dog Avenger upon the assassin's track! I will follow!"

ACT III.

Scene 1: The Bandits' Cave.

Nina and Leonie in the brigand's power, the carousal, and the maiden's despair.

Scene 2: The deck of the smuggler again.

Will Sheavehole is struck down by grief through the news Bob Mizenroyal brings him.

"The sun has no light now for me, Bob."

"Cheer up, old man; she may yet escape. Don't forget, there's a little cherub that sits up aloft to look after—"

"Ha!" the smuggler exclaims: "here comes a small skiff."

Small skiff is seen only by the smuggler and Bob; but soon the rowers enter, in the person of Karl, the poor, but honest peasant, and Vincente with his head bandaged.

Affecting meeting.

"Will you aid me to recover your daughter?"

"I will, Vincente."

"Unfurl your sails, double-shot your guns, and we will to the pirates' haunt. My noble dog is on their track, and will point out their hiding place."

(How this was possible does not seem very clear, but it must have been understood by the audience, for they clapped their hands as the scenes closed upon Vincente. True Blue and the smugglers standing with their right arms above their heads.)

Scene the 3rd, and the last (quite time too, thinks the reader).

The Bandits' Cave again.

Drinks to the bandit queen. Gomez is about to drink from the goblet, when Toby rushes in and knocks it from his hand.

" Ha ! ha !" he exclaims, and draws his knife to intimidate the noble dog; but, before the blow could be struck, the report of a cannon caused the bandits to fly to arms.

The cave is battered in, but Bernardo will be "avenged, ha ! ha !"

He draws his knife, seizes Nina, and is about to slay the fair flower of the most perfect loveliness, when a shot is fired from without.

Bernardo falls, and, *plucking the bullet from his heart* holds up the silver button he fired at Vincente.

Enter Will Sheavehole, True Blue, Vincente, Karl, and smugglers.

Nina embraces her lover, Leonie embraces Bob, and Will Sheavehole is seen blessing them after the approved manner of stage fathers.

There is innocence and bravery rewarded, and then comes

THE CURTAIN.

The " Silver Button " had a long run at Winkletop, but thin houses at last warned the lessee it was time to depart.*

Gentleman Bob's brother made sufficient money to take a theatre in one of the manufacturing towns, but before he left Winkletop he politely told Joe and Tommy they were too young to perform before an audience who were used to so good company.

Old Bill he said was too old, but if they liked to stay as " supers," and await the time of——

But here Joe cut the manager short and told him they had seen quite sufficient of the stage, and as they had saved a little money, they would go to London, &c., &c.

It was very ungrateful on the manager's part to cast aside those who had done so much to increase his riches.

But it is the world's way, and ever will be, I am afraid ; therefore, the best plan is to look out for No. 1 at all times, and in all cases.

CHAPTER XXIX.

HOW JOE AND TOMMY'S ROMANCE ABOUT A SAILOR'S LIFE WAS DISPELLED, AND THE TRIO RESOLVE TO GO TO LONDON, SET UP IN BUSINESS, AND JOE'S FIRST STEP TOWARDS BEING LORD MAYOR OF LONDON.

AT the house where Joe and his companions lodged, an old gentleman was wont to come in at evening time and smoke a quiet pipe over a single glass of grog.

Joe had heard from the landlady that the quiet old gentleman had in his young days served under Lord Nelson, and our hero, like most youths, had a great liking for the sea (as he pictured it), not as a sailor's life is in reality. On the night of the departure of the company from Winkletop, our friends were talking over their future, and Joe said—

" Well, if I had my wish, I should go to sea."

The old gentleman placed his pipe on the table, and, looking at Joe, said—

" Just the way with all lads of spirit; but they soon find out their mistake."

This was the first time the old fellow had been so communicative, so Joe and Tommy drew closer to him.

" I soon found it out," he continued; " shall I tell you, lads, why I left the service—why I became disgusted with it?"

The lads expressed a wish to hear the cause of the old gentleman's disgust.

" I am getting an old man, now," he said; " just past fourscore, my lads, and my mind is not as clear as it used to be ; so don't interrupt me when I'm speaking, or I shall forget all about the thread of my story."

The expectant pair promised to be as quiet as mice.

" I was a middy when I served in the ' Erebus,'" the old man began, " and while in that ship I witnessed one of those murderous transactions, a flogging round the fleet. I call them murderous, because I know that in many instances death has been the speedy result, and I believed that it is always hastened by them.

" This most barbarous custom was one of those things of which people heard occasionally, but of which those who have not been eye-witnesses have no more perfect idea that the people of China may form of a railway or Thames Tunnel. If it is still in existence, it is evidence that all we hear of the boots and other instruments of torture, the horrors of the Inquisition, &c., is not mere fiction. I shall endeavour to give you an idea of the horrible transaction which, in my seventeenth year, made such a lasting impression on my youthful mind, that it can never be obliterated on this side the grave.

" The perpetual flogging on board the ship had brought the men into such a state of despair, I

---

*Apology to the author of the " Silver Button."—The jesting manner in which I have given a sketch of the play is not intended to depreciate a really good drama—considering the author's youth and inexperience. Further, I beg to add, that a drama now being performed nightly in one of our London theatres, is not more connected in its details than the crude composition of a lad fresh from school.

JOHN JEAMES BRINGS LOW "PUSSON" A LETTER.

may call it, that they were continually getting drunk to escape from the reflection of their miserable state. On one occasion, a half-idiot Welshman had been drinking beyond all the bounds of prudence; he was three parts intoxicated, or what sailors would term "three sheets in the wind."

"In this state he was reprimanded by a very violent, bullying master's mate, for helping himself to water without permission.

"Some degree of insolence marked the tone in which Evan Evans replied; and the officer (who, by the by, was afterwards turned out of the service) gave him some hearty cuffs, which

so excited the angry feelings of the Welshman. that he instantly took out his knife and stabbed the master's mate.

"The man was secured, put in irons, and as soon as convenient brought before a court-martial.

"Everybody knows that in a civil court the previous provocation by blows would have been taken into consideration, and a much lighter punishment inflicted for the stabbing than if it had been done in cold blood.

"The court-martial heard evidence of the facts, and they also took the provocation into consideration, and pronounced a less severe sentence than death, which they might have legally visited upon the offender. They sentenced him to receive *five hundred lashes round the fleet*, and afterwards to undergo two years' imprisonment.

"The unhappy man was taken down to the gunroom of the ship, and again placed with both feet in irons, so that he could take no exercise; and what with this confinement, which from the time of his offence to that of punishment endured, three weeks, and the excitement of fear of death, in the first place, and subsequently fear of the dreadful punishment which awaited him, he was wan and worn, and seemed when he came on deck on the (to him) fatal morning, more fit for the hospital than the torture.

"It was at a few minutes before 8 o'clock in the morning, when the first lieutenant of the ship ordered me to take charge of the launch, and see the punishment carried into effect.

"Had he given me orders to mount the sides of an enemy's frigate, at the head of a launch's crew, it would not have distressed me half so much; as I might have considered that my good luck might bring me a broken head or a lieutenant's commission; but here was a service devoid of honour and full of painful consequences, from which, however, there was no chance of escape.

"I must needs obey; and the heaviest, bitterest hour of my life was when I stepped into the boat to superintend the infliction of five hundred lashes on the back of poor Evans.

"It was on a dull, misty, gloomy morning towards the end of October, and there were ten line-of-battle ships and frigates lying in the Downs, alongside of each of which he was to receive fifty lashes with the cat-o'-nine-tails, or 4,500 strokes in all.

"The launch of a line-of-battle ship is a large wide boat, which may contain easily from thirty to forty men.

"On this occasion it was to be taken in tow by other boats, and, therefore, there were no rowers in the boat.

"Its crew consisted of the steersman, four active seamen to superintend the holding on the boat when alongside the different ships, and to attend to the fastenings which were to be passed round the knees and elbows of the prisoner; also two others (his own messmates), to place or remove blankets around him as occasion might require, give him water, &c.; also the drummer, who was placed in the bow to beat the rogue's march while passing from ship to ship.

"The surgeon, to watch the pulse; the master-at-arms, to count the lashes; four marines with fixed bayonets; and, lastly, myself to command the boat.

"The boats from the fleet, one from each ship, with an officer and six or eight seamen, and two or more marines in each, were now assembled round the ship by signal; and exactly at half-past eight o'clock the prisoner, in charge of the master-at-arms, came down the side and stepped into the boat, in which I had already taken my station.

"The seats of the boat were covered with gratings, and above them was erected a stage, consisting of two triangles, one at each end of the boat, between which were lashed two strong and long poles.

"To these poles the knees and arms of the prisoner were fastened with small cords, and, he being stripped all but his trousers, was then covered with a blanket tied round his waist and another thrown over his shoulders.

"The men on board were next ordered up to the rigging, so that every person on board might see the whole operation.

"The captain, taking off his hat, which was followed by all on board and in the boats, which were lying on their oars within ear-shot, then proceeded to read the sentence of the court-martial.

"This effected, the boatswain of the ship himself stepped into the launch; the blanket was removed from the culprit's shoulders, and he (the boatswain) inflicted the first twelve lashes.

"The poor fellow screamed and groaned and struggled; but all this, like the struggles of a dying sheep under the knife of the butcher, passed unheeded.

"The boatswain returned on board, and two boatswain's mates came down and completed the number of fifty lashes. The blanket was immediately thrown over his shoulders, and the people were piped down out of the rigging.

"I gave the word of command to shove off, and the boats which took the launch in tow began to row towards the Admiral's ship, the drummer striking up the Rogue's March. The origin of this idea of having music in the boat was no doubt to drown the groans of the sufferer, lest the ordinary feelings of humanity should revolt against the barbarous practice of so mutilating the body of a fellow-creature.

"A quarter of an hour elapsed, during which the poor Welshman's groans mixed with the vile sounds of the drum, and we were again alongside of a large two-decked ship, the men of which exhibited themselves in the rigging on our approach.

"The towing boats lay on their oars; we hooked on to the ship, and three stout fellows jumped into the launch, with each a new cat-o'-nine-tails ready in his hand, prepared to expend his strength on the back of the sufferer.

"The first lieutenant of the ship came to the gangway. I handed him a copy of the sentence, which he read aloud to the crew, and the boatswain's mates removed their jackets ready for the infliction.

"The cats, as I have just observed, were new; their lashes or tails were made of strong white cord, just the thickness of a common quill; and the glue or size which is worked into the cord had not been removed by soaking in water: they curled up, and were literally almost as stiff as wires.

"As officer of the boat, I objected to their being used, for the first time, on the poor man; and others were procured, which had been well worn, and told many a tale of suffering. He looked at me gratefully, and said in a weak voice:—

"'Thank ye, sir.'

"The blanket was removed, and I observed the poor fellow shudder as the cold air struck the bleeding sore on his flesh.

"The next moment, a heavy lash fell on it, and his screams were agonising. He received a dozen lashes, and then began to cry out for water. The punishment was stopped till he had taken some.

"He afterwards told me, that at this period, the thirst he felt became intense; and that each lash caused a violent burning pain at his heart, and seemed to fall like the blows of a large stick on his body; but that the flesh was too dead to feel that stinging smart he felt at first, and when the flogging was renewed.

"The same scene was repeated alongside two other ships, with the like interval of misery to the sufferer, and of disgust and vexation to myself. My reflections, indeed, were painful enough, for I utterly condemned myself for ever becoming one of the many unfeeling wretches, who were so seriously occupied in torturing this poor wretch.

"Perhaps many others felt as disgusted as I did. Two hundred lashes had now been inflicted with a cat-o'-nine tails, or eighteen hundred strokes with a cord of the thickness of a quill. The flesh, from the nape of the neck to below the shoulder-blades, was one deep purple mass, from which the blood oozed slowly.

"At every stroke a low groan escaped, and the flesh quivered with a sort of convulsive twitch; the eyes were closed, and the poor man began to faint. Water was administered, and pungent salts applied to his nostrils, which presently revived him in a slight degree.

"At this period I gave the doctor a hint by asking the master-at-arms, in a loud tone, how many lashes the prisoner had received.

"'Two hundred lashes exactly, sir,' was the reply. I knew this very well, but it answered the purpose, for I saw the doctor look at me, and then order him to be taken down. This was instantly done, and I ordered a fast boat in the vicinity to take him on board.

"The poor fellow was laid on some blankets in the stern-sheets, the sail hoisted, and in a quarter of an hour he was in his hammock in the sick berth, and the doctors were engaged dressing his wounds.

"Five weeks after this I was again compelled to superintend a further mutilation on the back of poor Evans. This time he looked more miserable than ever, his frame was shrunken and his cheeks fallen, and when his shirt was removed I observed that the wounds were barely healed over, and that all about the sides of them there were dark discolorations, which indicated a state of disease. I was surprised that the medical men allowed him to be again taken out for punishment.

"The first six lashes, given by the arm of a Herculean Irishman, brought the blood out from the old wounds, and then almost every blow brought away pieces of skin and flesh.

"It would be disgusting you to detail again the minutiæ of this second flogging. Suffice it to say that the poor fellow fainted when he had received another 150 lashes; but the surgeon, deeming him still capable of a little more punishment, another thirty-three were inflicted.

"A second faint and a convulsive action of the eyes put an end to his torture; he was removed to the guard-ship, and, having taken 383 lashes, the remaining 117 were remitted by order of the Admiral.

"The ship sailed for a cruize in the North Sea; and some months after we heard that poor Evans had been sent to prison, where he went into a consumption and ended his days.

"This was just what I had expected; for it was clear that the first flogging had given the death-blow to the unfortunate Welshman.

"This, my lads, was the cause of my quitting the service before I was eighteen years of age. I don't know whether such things are done now, but I know they still flog men; so I say to you lads, don't think of the sea."

"After that," Joe said, his face scarlet with indignation at the old man's story; "I think we had better do as Bill Adler wishes; go to London and set up in the greengrocery line."

"Ay," said the old man; greengrocery's better than going to sea."

CHAPTER XXX.

MESSRS. ADLER AND CO. IN THE GREENGROCERY
LINE.—THE LADY WHO FED THE POOR OF THE
NEIGHBOURHOOD WITH TRACTS.—JOHN RECOGNISES
THE "PUSSONS" AND THEIR DOG.

THE whole of the funds in the possession of the
trio when they reached London did not amount
to more than five pounds sterling.

But it proved amply sufficient for the object in
view.

A small shop and parlour were obtained at a
very low rental, and the first conspicuous article
purchased was a large card, bearing this inscription :—

NO TRUST.

"It's a good neighbourhood for business,"
Joe said, "but a bad one for tick, so it won't do
to give any.

Next morning before daylight, Joe trudged off
to Covent-garden, trundling a barrow before
him, and Tommy went to Billingsgate to procure
a supply of fish.

The lads were pretty keen hands at making a
bargain, thus when they returned laden with a
multitude of purchases, old Bill lifted his hands
in astonishment.

"And not spent all the money!" he said.
"Well, I hope we shall sell all these things, if
we does, we shall soon make a fortin?"

You would have supposed had you seen Joe
retailing his wares that he had been used to the
business all his life.

They had been fortunate in their choice of the
situation of the shop, for the place, although
inhabited by a very poor class, was very populous,
and as the stock was composed only of the cheap-
est and most needed articles of daily consumption, there was no lack of customers up to dinner
time.

"What's the price of these herrings, young
man?" an old woman would ask—"they seem
very small for the time o' year."

"Small, mum, small, they were the biggest in
the market or I should not have bought them."

"How do you sell them?"

"Sell them, I don't sell them, mum, I almost
give them away; now look," taking up a fish,
"at this one's back, isn't it plump, don't it make
your mouth water, isn't it a prince of a herring?
ah, here's another one to match, and you shall
have the two for three halfpence, I won't be
hard on you."

"Three halfpence—a penny you mean."

"A penny, no, mum, they cost me more than
that in the market."

"If you please," said a little girl with a big
baby in her arms, "mother wants to know when
you're going to send the fourteen pounds o'
coal I hordered ever so long ago."

"What," says Joe, "haint they been sent?
Here, Tommy, go with this little girl and take
the coals; tell your mother, my dear, we are
very sorry, but we have been so busy."

That was not true of Joe; but he thought it
looked well to appear overburdened with business.

"Now, mum," said Joe, "what do you say,
have them or leave them; I know you will not
match them in all London at the price."

"Look here, young man, I will give you tuppence for three."

"Very well, I don't like to lose a customer;
but upon my word I shan't turn my money in
again; here, Bill, clean these turbots for a lady,
and wrap them up nicely in a cabbage leaf."

"How much are the cabbages?"—to a pale
but pretty young girl who came up at this moment
—"well, they are awfully dear in the market
just now, but you shall have one for a penny."

The young girl held open the basket she
carried, and as Joe placed the cabbage inside he
saw the forefinger and thumb of her left hand
were worn by the constant use of the needle.

"Thank you," she said, tendering Joe a six-
penny piece; if you give me a penny that will
be right, for I want you to send us over a quarter
of a hundred of coals."

"Yes, miss, where to?"

"No. 2—just round the corner. Knock
twice."

"All right, miss. Book the order, Bill
quarter of coals at No. 2."

"If you could send them soon," the pale young
girl timidly said, "we should be much obliged."

"I will bring them myself," Joe said, "if you
want them at once."

"Thank you"—turning to leave, but pausing
as she caught sight of a pile of rosy-cheeked
apples—"what lovely apples."

"Yes," Joe said, "they are stunners; only a
penny a pound."

The girl looked at the apples, then at the
penny-piece she held between her fingers. The
temptation was strong, but she resisted; for,
poor child, there were a dozen ways for every
penny her little fingers earned.

"Not to-day," she said with a sigh; "perhaps the next time I come."

Joe had a feeling heart. He understood the
cause of the young girl's hesitation, and, without a second's thought, he went to the heap of
tempting fruit, selected three of the largest, and,
running after his customer, said—

"Here, miss, take 'em. I ain't rich, but I can
afford to give you these."

He placed them on the basket, and turned towards the shop, as the girl, with tearful eyes, said—

"Oh, thank you. My poor little brother is so fond of apples, and——"

"Scrumpings about!" yelled a gawky ragged boy in her ear, and, before she could prevent the theft, the apples were taken away.

Unfortunately for the juvenile highwayman, Joe saw the performance, and before the thief had gone a dozen yards our sturdy hero had him by the collar.

"Now, then, who are you a-touching of?"

"Put those apples back," Joe said, digging his knuckles in the youth's neck, "and I will tell you more about it."

"Leave off, will you? Hi, Jemmy Dennis, come here and prop this cove."

Joe whistled for Toby, and the astonished Jemmy Dennis paused in his run, for the dog showed a set of fangs that caused a shiver to run all over Master Jemmy's frame.

"Put those apples back," Joe repeated, "or you'll be sorry for it."

He well nigh throttled his captive, as he pushed him towards the pale-faced girl.

"Here's your apples," the light-fingered youth said. "I only did it out of a lark! so you let me go, Mr. Fast."

Joe did so; but he added a lusty kick, that sent the young thief sprawling in the middle of the road.

"Now," Joe said, "if you want any more you can have it."

But the youth appeared quite satisfied with what he had received; and muttering some vague threat about when he caught Joe down his street, he shuffled off.

"Wait a minute," Joe said to the young girl, "here's Tommy coming back, so I can take the coals home along with you; I would have done so at first," he added, "but we can't leave the shop to old Bill, for the boys about here are such thieves that they would clear the front in no time if old Bill was alone. I've had my eye on 'em all the morning. Tommy," he added, "weigh a quarter of the best black diamonds."

"Where are they for?"

"I'll take them, Tommy, that will give you a rest."

Tommy looked at Joe, then at the young girl, and mentally exclaimed—

"Well, here's a go!"

Joe took the coals home; it was not far, but it was a pleasant walk, for the little maiden was not in the least proud; she chatted to her companion, and he in turn made her laugh with his quaint sayings.

She led the way upstairs, told him to be careful of a broken stair, and when they reached the second floor she opened the door very wide, and when her mother wanted to know who it was, she said—

"Only the coals, mother;" then to Joe, "this way, please, in this cupboard."

So Joe shot the quarter of a hundred in the bottom of the cupboard, just underneath the larder.

"Ah!" exclaimed Tommy when his partner returned, "you know who to take the coals home for."

"What's up, Tommy?"

"Nothing; only I don't mean to take the coals home for all the old women, and you take them home for the young 'uns."

"You shall take all the coal orders home except to the second floor at number 2 round the corner."

"Ah, ah, ah!"

"What are you sniggering at, you little wretch?"

"Ha, ha! ain't he going to stick up to the girl what orders a quarter——"

"Shut up, Tommy, and I'll tell you something."

"What is it?"

"Why, I don't want you to chaff me about that girl, that's all."

"Chick-or-um," yelled Tommy, "here's a case of stick up. I say, Joe, who's going to starch your collar when you go out on Sundays?"

"There's a half-hundred," old Bill said, "to go to No. 5 up the court, they've been ordered ever so long, and two bundles of wood as well."

"That's my luck," said Tommy, placing an empty sack on the scale, "to hump that lot."

"Look after the shop," said old Bill to Joe, "there's a party a-feeling the herrings."

During the time an old woman was bargaining for a couple of fresh herrings, and just as Tommy was about to quit the shop with his burden, an elegantly dressed lady passed the shop, and to the unbounded astonishment of Joe, Bill Adler, and Tommy they beheld the effulgent John James following the lady.

His aristocratic face bore evidence of the inward disgust he felt at being compelled to pass down such a common street, laden with a thick parcel of books.

"My eye!" said Tommy, "there goes the flunkey what don't like common persons."

"I say, calves," said Joe, "how much for your hose? Here, Toby, look after him."

And Toby, like an ill-bred dog, barked at lordly John James until Joe gave the whistle of recall.

Who can picture the feelings of the lordly
John James? "To have to escort her leddyship
was bad enough, to carry a bundle of tracks," as
he said to the housemaid, when he rushed home,
was "badder," "but, Susan Ann," here he struck
an attitude, "to be set upon by a low common
dog was worser."

"And, Susan Ann," he said in conclusion, "if
me and her leddyship will leave our carriage to
go down the streets, all I has to say is that her
leddyship must find some other gentleman, for I
won't come in contack with the wulgar and
common 'pussons' as her leddyship does; it may
suit her, Susan Ann, but her feelings isn't near
so refined as mine. Draw me a glass of beer,
Susan Ann, before I expire at the recollection of
the insults I have to put up with, all through
chiverality in escorting her leddyship!"

"That's a fine lady!" remarked the old woman,
who was cheapening Joe's herrings; "she has her
name down as something or the other to some
institution, and comes round a-giving us tracts."

"Good things in their way," said Joe; "but
to my mind a four-pound loaf would be better."

"You are right, young man—quite right, and
so I says to Mrs. Jones; and she says, 'Mum,' she
says, 'them's my sentiments to a T, and—' what
did you say, young man?"

"How many herrings did you choose?"

"Three; here's the money."

And the old lady went homeward, repeating to
herself her opinions of tracts and tract distri-
butors in general.

"Bill," said Joe, "that was Lady Elthorne."

"Yes."

"I will find out where she lives."

"What for, Joe?"

"I want to see the old gent the flunkey called
the general, and see him I must, and—"

"Ah, Joe, my dear boy, how do you do?"

Joe looked up and beheld Mr. Sivins—Mr.
James Sivins—standing with outstretched hand
and a smiling face.

CHAPTER XXXI.

THE READER IS LET INTO THE SECRET OF JOE'S
BIRTH AND PARENTAGE, AND WHY MR SIVINS
MAKES SUCH A GUSHING PROPOSAL TO JOE.

MR. JAMES SIVINS could, with truth, have added
to his greeting—

"Joe, my boy, I am glad to see you." For
he was very glad; he had been months trying to
ferret out Joe's whereabouts, and chance had
realised that which he had expended time and
money to obtain.

Mr. Sivins had visited the second floor at No.
2 round the corner for the purpose of ascertaining from the poor widow why she had not kept
her loan paid up.

He had been told the reason, Kitty had been
ill and unable to work, but now all would be
right again, and the fines would be paid up
within a week.

"Mind they are," said Mr. Sivins, sternly,
"or I shall put the brokers in."

Ah, Mr. Sivins, when you made that speech,
you were blissfully ignorant that the poor widow
and Kitty had a friend in Charity Joe.

Now to disclose the secret, if the reader has
not already found it out. If not, he will be
much interested in the following account of the
manner in which Mr. James Sivins found out all
about it.

When Joe so unceremoniously quitted the
hospitable establishment known as Baream Hall,
Mr. Dothem wrote to his friend, Mr. Sivins, and
told him of Joe's ungrateful behaviour.

So Mr. Sivins came down to the Hall, and, as
Gentleman Bob said, there was a row between the
two rascals about the disappearance of our friend
Joe.

Mr. James Sivins returned to London rather
perturbed in spirit, for the old gentleman,
known to the reader as the General, had allowed
Mr. Sivins eighty pounds per annum for Joe's
maintenance, but he gave the General's agent to
understand that if anything happened to the
youth the money would cease.

Being a very prudent man, Mr. Sivins looked
upon the loss of the eighty pounds per annum
as a misfortune hard to be borne, but in the
midst of his despair there came a gleam of hope.

He would find out the cause of the General's
patronage, he would discover what the stern old
officer had to do with the "workhouse." But
how?

There was the General's gentleman—an old
soldier, who had been with his master many
years—he would possibly know the connection
that existed between them.

The old soldier and Mr. Sivins were pretty
good friends, for the servant had been in the
habit of bringing the quarterly allowance to the
house, situate in that narrow street leading from
St. George's-road, S.; and upon these occasions
the men had celebrated their meetings by sundry glasses at the adjacent pub., where Mr.
Sivins took the chair, and presided over the con-
vivial meetings of the "Sons of Melody."

So the next time the servant came with the
cheque, Mr. Sivins was most polite. He asked
his visitor to take a seat, then he brought forth
a bottle of whisky, two glasses, a lemon, and
some sugar, and mixed two glasses—one much
stiffer than the other.

"Been with the General some time, Mr. Moore, I think I've heard you say?"

"Yes, just over twenty years."

"Then you were in the service together?"

"Yes," said the servant, "that's how the General is so fond of me. I saved his life in India; so, when he left, he brought me with him."

"Let me mix you another glass."

"Thank you."

They chatted away upon insignificant subjects for some time, and soon after the General's confidential man had taken his fourth glass, Mr. James Sivins returned to the original subject by saying—

The General must be a good master."

"That he is; there's not a better in all London, although he is at times as hot as Cayenne."

"I should think him a good-hearted man," Mr. Sivins said, "from what little I have seen of him."

"Yes, he is, Mr. Sivens, a very good-hearted man when he likes."

A pause—another mixing process.

"It is not often, remarked Mr. Sivins, slowly stirring his whisky and water, "that we find a gentleman taking such an interest in a poor boy as he takes in Joe."

The servant screwed up his face, placed his finger against his nose, and then sipped his grog and winked at Mr. Sivins.

"No," said the latter; "you don't mean to say so."

"Say what?"

"Why, that Joe is his son."

"No! I don't mean to say so, but he is his grandson though."

"You don't drink, Mr. Moore; isn't it to your liking?"

"Capital! first-rate! To prove how well I like it, I'll have another."

He had another, and it deprived him of his caution.

"His grandson, eh!" Mr. Sivins said with assumed indifference. "Have a cigar, Mr. Moore?"

"I don't mind."

"Mild or full flavoured?"

"Full flavoured, please."

Mr. Sivins gave him one of the strongest he had, and the narcotic, mixing with the fumes of the liquor, soon brought the man in a condition that gave Mr. Sivins cause for much sweet rejoicing.

"So Joe is the General's grandson; well he will do the old gentleman credit, for I heard he placed him in a first-class academy."

"I don't think he cares much about what you do with the lad," the servant said; "as long as he is kept out of his mother's way."

"Oh, then, his mother is alive."

"Yes; and I don't believe she troubles much about him now, although she did at first."

"What strange doings you people of the world become acquainted with," Mr. Sivins said; "and this I should think is one of the strangest cases."

"Very strange, Mr. Sivins—very strange, where do you get these cigars; they are very good?"

"I will get you a box," Mr. Sivins said, "as you like them so well."

"I will be much obliged."

Another pause; then Mr. Sivins said:—

"There are some strange goings on in the fashionable world, Mr. Moore."

"Very."

"And this one, as I before remarked, is one of them."

"It is, but there is nobody knows anything about it, except the General, her ladyship, and myself; would you like to hear it, Mr. Sivins?"

"Well, as a matter of curiosity, yes."

"Of course, I speak to you as a friend."

"I quite understand all you would say; you can rely upon my silence, no matter what you may please to tell me."

"Well, sir, this way," the General's confidential servant said, "the boy's mother married very young; in fact, she bolted with a young officer of ours, while her father was up the country, and when he came back he found they had been to Calcutta and got married."

"He did not like the match, then?"

"No, not likely; he was poor enough himself, so he did not want a poor husband for his daughter."

"I understand."

"But the young fellow didn't trouble him long; he was knocked over by a matchlock ball at the storming of Ghuznee, and precious glad the old fellow was."

"And the lady?"

"She went on like mad; but by the time we came to England the governor had talked her over to say nothing about her marriage, and she consented, for there was no one in this country likely to split upon her."

"Was the boy alive then?"

"Alive? yes, and kicking. Why, he was over four years old, and a nice little fellow too; I've nursed him many a time; but nice as he was, the governor took a mortal dislike to him, and when he talked his daughter over to his way of managing the business the boy was taken away."

"And sent to the workhouse?"

"Not by the governor; no, he was given to some person to take care of; and I've heard since that they put the poor little chap in the house and stuck to the allowance the governor made 'em."

"That was not right."

"No, not exactly. Well, soon after he comes to England, the General gets acquainted with Sir Charles Elthorne, and he takes a fancy to my mistress: and I don't wonder at it, for she was uncommon pretty, and as she held her tongue about her husband that was killed at Ghuznee, they were married, and a grand catch it was for her, I can tell you."

"After this, I suppose, she did not trouble about the boy?"

"Not much. She seemed to get colder and prouder than she was before she became Lady Elthorne; but for all that she made a bargain with the General, that if ever she found out that her boy had not been well looked after, she would up and tell her husband all about the Indian marriage; and she would keep her word, too."

"This is the reason," Mr. Sivins said, "the General gave me such particular orders about the lad."

"No doubt of it, for although she does not, of course, wish to see her son, it is but natural she should wish him to be all right."

"Precisely so."

"Do you know," the confidential servant said, "I often think the General drove his daughter into this marriage; but he's awfully afraid of her; and no wonder, for his money does not go far, and he could not do as he does unless she gave him a trifle now and then."

Mr. Sivins reflected over this intelligence after his visitor went away, and he came to the conclusion that he could not do better than make his own terms with the General.

"I have it," he thought, "I will tell him I received my information from a soldier who belonged to his regiment, but who has since died. Yes, that's it, the best and safest plan; and unless he does the handsome, I shall visit her ladyship, who will, I daresay, pay me for holding my tongue."

Mr. Sivins sought and obtained an interview with the general, and the old fellow was very wrath when he heard the cause of the smiling gentleman's visit.

"Quick march! you rascal. Quick march! Out of my sight!"

"Very well, general," said Mr. Sivins. "But if I march from here, I shall beat up the quarters of Sir Charles and Lady Elthorne."

The general paced to and fro the room, and after indulging in a volley of strong language against Mr. Sivins's meddling, he faced suddenly round, and asked the name of the person who had enlightened his visitor's mind.

"With pleasure, general," replied the urbane Mr. Sivins. "My informant formerly served in India, and thus became acquainted with the——"

"Did he? did he?" exclaimed the old officer, savagely. "Where is the rascal now?"

"He died a month since, general."

"Glad to hear it, glad to hear it. One tongue stopped, at all events. Now, what do you require to stop yours?"

"General," Mr. Sivins said, assuming a virtuous tone, that was extremely refreshing, "I did not come here to extort money."

"What, the——"

"One moment, if you please, General. I loved that boy, but I am a poor man—a very poor man or I would not have humbled myself to ask you to assist me in finding him."

"Finding him?"

"Yes, general. The poor boy has run away from the school—driven away, I should say, by the harshness of his master. He is a noble, high-spirited boy, general."

"Hum! so was his father. Well, what do you require?"

"A little money to help my search for him, for I cannot rest until I have found him; I cannot, indeed, general."

Mr. Sivins used his yellow silk handkerchief in the most effective manner at this avowment.

"If this was all you required," the general said, "why did you come here with the whole story of the boy's birth upon your lips?"

"I don't know, general, unless it was that my feelings overcame me at the stern manner of my reception I—I—I——"

"Go on."

"And I thought, if you would not assist me, his mother, her ladyship, would."

"Harkee," the old officer said, "her ladyship does not want to hear anything about the boy, but I do. I want to know where he is—you understand—I want to know. Now, how much do you require?"

Mr. Sivins named a modest sum—he was afraid to go too far for the first time; and the general gave him a cheque.

"Now," thought Mr. Sivins, as he left the general's house, "the ice is broken, and the game is mine. The lady has made it a condition of her marrying this Sir Charles that the boy is well looked after. I must find him—give him a lift with the general's money, then go to her ladyship, and tell of my goodness. I think that will work."

Mr. Sivins sought after Joe for many weeks, and it was not until he went to visit the poor widow about the loan that he found him.

"How are you, Joe?" he continued; "so glad to see you; hope you have a good situation here?"

"Situation!" Joe said, proudly. "I'm a partner in the business; there's three of us."

"Ah! Toby too. Come here, Toby, poor fellow! give me your paw."

Toby got behind Joe, and growled at the soft-speaking gentleman.

"He forgets me, Joe. Don't you think so?"

"No," Joe said bluntly; "he knows you, Mr. Sivins, and as he never liked you it isn't likely he will now."

"What a funny chap you are, Joe. Well, I'm glad to see you doing so well, and if I can do anything for you I will."

"What, a loan?"

"Yes, my boy, why not? But it wouldn't be a loan the same as to other people. No, Joe, I will lend you £10 to improve your business, and you can pay me when you like."

"No, thankee," Joe said; "I daresay I shall manage to get on all right."

"Well, well, I'll drop in again. Good-bye, Joe, good-bye."

So Mr. Sivins strolled off, and two days afterwards John Jeames, the effulgent, came to the shop and handed Joe a letter.

Could a painter have transferred the expression of John's face upon canvas, and exhibited the picture in the Royal Academy under the title of "The Disgusted Footman," that painter's fortune would have been made.

Not only did John's face express the most intense disgust and wounded self-respect, but his waistcoat seemed to blush a deeper colour, and the very cockade—"smokejack" that vulgar youth Tommy termed it—bristled with indignation at the martyrdom of its wearer.

Joe was seated at dinner when the "harristocrat" arrived, and Toby was begging for pieces. Tommy was exercising his lungs, and yelling out—

"All Ware, four pound tuppence! here's your fine broccoli sprouts and cabbage plants! apples a penny a pound!"

Old Bill was busy serving a customer with two pun' of all the Wares.

Such was the scene that met John Jeames's eyes, such were the sounds that saluted his refined ears when he came to deliver that letter to the common "pusson."

"Hallo, Johnny," Joe said; "is that for me?"

John Jeames turned his back on the low "pusson," and replied—

"It is for you, and—"

"All Wares," yelled Tommy, "here's another guy, pull the string, boys, and—"

"You shut up," Joe said, "don't you see there's a gentleman in the shop."

Tommy, thus reproved, was silent.

"Who's it from?" Joe said to the bearer of the letter, "speak up, Johnny, don't be afraid."

The footman majestically waved his hand as he said—

"Young man, I've done wiolence to my feelings and the exalted position I occupy in the station of life that is between us in bringing you that epistolatory communication, therefore it is not in keeping with my dignified character to answer any questions you may put—I've to wait for an answer, so give it me, for the smell of these obnox-i-ous vegetables affects my olfactory system to a degree that is quite offensive."

No wonder the smell was offensive, for Tommy had cut a large onion in two, and as the majestic John Jeames kept his face averted from the "pusson," Tommy rubbed the juice of the onion upon the ends of the superb being's swallow-tailed livery coat.

"Oh, very well," Joe said, not at all abashed by John's elocution, "well, as it is addressed to me, I'll read it."

This is what Joe read—

"You are requested to follow the bearer."

"And I?" said Joe. "Well I won't, so you can take that for an answer, Johnny, and take yourself off at the same time."

CHAPTER XXXII.

JOE DONS HIS SUNDAY CLOTHES AND GOES A-COURTING —HOW KITTY MILLER RECEIVED HIM—AND WHAT MRS. MILLER TOLD HIM ABOUT THE RESPECTABLE MR. SIVINS.

JOHN JAMES was only too glad to take himself off, and while passing up the narrow street, his majestic person was made the subject of the rude remarks of a number of ragged boys who were playing at buttons.

"Ho, no! Ha, ha, ha! My eye, Joe, here's a lark!"

And Joe turned and was much surprised to behold his partner, Tommy, lying on his back in the middle of the shop nearly black in the face with laughter.

"What's the matter, young'un?" Joe asked, "get up, or I'll fetch the fire engine, and——"

"Ha, ha! ho, ho! ha, ha!"

"What's the fool laughing at?"

"The flunkey, Joe—I—I—ho, ho!—smeared his coat with a raw onion—crikey, won't his missus hunt him out of the room, that's all!"

it was now Joe's turn to laugh, and old Bill's to shake his head, and say—

"It is too bad, I'm sure, such a beautiful coat too."

When the younger partners had laughed to their heart's content, Joe handed the letter to Tommy, saying——

"Here's a go, Tommy, read that."

Tommy did so, and asked—

"Why didn't you go?"

"Because," Joe answered, "I knew who sent."

"Do you? Who was it?"

"The lady we often see coming down the street with a bundle of tracts in her hand."

"What could she want of you, Joe?"

"I know well enough. She wants to give me a lecture, because she saw me give a fellow a domino for trying to sneak some pears off the board. Besides, I haint time to go with the flunkey if I'd been inclined, to get a bundle of tracts to wrap up our herrings in."

"Haint time? How's that?"

"Well," Joe said, trying not to look confused, "because I'm going out."

"Are you?"

"Yes."

"Where are you going, Joe?"

"Not far, so I will go and put on my Sunday goings, and——"

"Oh!" Tommy exclaimed, "that's it, is it?"

"What?"

"Sticking up. Oh, no wonder some people likes to take home——"

"Now, look here, Tommy, I don't want any chaff, so leave off."

"Who's chaffing?"

"You are."

"Well, now," Tommy said, grinning, "I didn't say you were going out to tea. I didn't say you were going to dress in your Sunday clothes to see Kitty. I——"

Exit Tommy, laughing, as Joe made a rush forward; and old Bill said—

"She is a nice creature, Joe, and if I was only young again, I——"

Joe made his escape into the back parlour, and when he again appeared, arrayed in his finest suit, Master Tommy, seated on the top of the coals, saluted him with—

> " When I'm dressed all in my best,
> To walk abroad with Kitty."

Joe shook his fist at his tormentor; but Tommy only laughed the louder. He knew Joe would not risk his clothes by scrambling up the heap of coals.

"I say " (Tommy's farewell shot), " you ought to have Toby's tail tied up with pink ribbon."

Joe was soon out of hearing, but ere he could turn the corner of the street, an impudent youth yelled out :—

"Who's your tailor? Should say your togs was made for you to grow to."

"Enough room up the back," remarked another critic, "to take home a bunch o' greens."

Joe could not compromise his dignity by chastising these free-spoken young Britons, so he gave them a look of supreme disdain, and they were so overawed thereat, that they put their thumbs to their noses, and wagged their fingers at him.

When Joe reached the house, he knocked twice, and his heart gave two responsive thumps against his side; for Joe, in spite of his assumed bravery, felt very nervous—so much so, that he walked quickly away before the door could be opened, and took refuge in a toy shop.

Joe had lost no time in improving his acquaintance with the pretty Kitty and her mother, and the elder lady, when she heard from Kitty the story of the apples, invited Mr. Joseph to tea.

The reader has seen how Joe's courage failed when he knocked at the door.

"I'll buy something for the little boy," Joe thought, when he hid himself in the toy shop; "it will look the thing to be kind to the little one."

So Joe invested sixpence in the purchase of a peculiar looking wooden animal, whose skin, if the artist who designed the model was worthy of belief, was covered with bright red spots.

"It might be a zebra," Joe thought, as he surveyed the interesting animal; "it might be a rhinocerus, but a horse it certainly is not; however, it will do."

Joe wrapped the spotted quadruped in his pocket-handkerchief smiling, and with a beating heart he repeated the double summons at the door.

Mrs. Miller admitted him, and said—

"Come upstairs, Mr. Joseph, please."

Joe followed the widow, and so great was his trepidation that he forgot the broken stair and stumbled.

"You are not hurt, Mr. Joseph, are you?"

"No, ma'am."

Kitty was industriously sewing when Joe entered the room, and she looked up for a moment and said—

"How do you do, Mr. Joseph?"

"Nicely, thank you, Miss Kitty; how are you?"

"Pretty well, Mr. Joseph, thank you. Won't you sit down?'

There was a chair standing close to Joe, so he seated himself upon the extreme edge, and, unfolding the corner of the spotted animal, he displayed its beauties to the admiring eyes of little Bobby, who was seated on the hearthrug.

"Look, Bobby," his sister said, " there's a nice horse Mr. Joseph has brought."

" For me, Mr. Josef ?"

" Yes, Bobby."

" Tank you, Mr. Josef."

Bobby took the present, and retired to his position on the hearthrug, and Joe's excuse for talking having passed away, he felt as bashful as before, and began to fumble his hat.

Mrs. Miller was busy making the tea, and Kitty kept her eyes upon the shirt she was making.

Joe fumbled his hat with greater perseverance than ever, and began to feel very uncomfortable until Kitty raised her eyes and slyly glanced at his face.

Joe dropped his eyes immediately, and a smile came over Kitty's face, and Joe happening to look up, saw the smile, and felt a little more courageous.

"What a fool I am," he thought. " I can't say a single word to her, now I have come, but I will though."

Again the brim of his hat underwent the fumbling process, and the operation, combined with the smile from Kitty, gave him courage to blurt out—

"Things are very dear in the market, miss."

" Yes, Mr. Joseph, very dear."

" Especially potatoes."

"I am sorry to hear that," Mrs. Miller said; "for poor people like ourselves require a great many potatoes."

"Yes, ma'am."

Another long pause; then Joe addressed Kitty.

"Don't you get tired," he asked, " of sewing so much?"

"Well, I do sometimes," she said, " but it's no use being tired before the work is done."

"Poor Kitty!" Mrs. Miller said, sadly; " it is killing work, shirtmaking. I never thought my daughter would come to that, Mr. Joseph."

" No, ma'am !"

"No, we were not always as we are now. When my poor dear husband was alive we were better off, and never thought we should be so poor."

"They don't pay as much as they ought," Joe said, " for that work, do they, ma'am?"

" No, Mr. Joseph; it is only next door to starvation; but what are we to do ?"

"Never mind, mother," Kitty said, " it's better than nothing, and I don't mind it as long as I have my health."

" 'That's Kitty all over," the mother said, fondly. " She says just the same when she sits up working until she is almost blind."

" Mother !"

"It's true, Mr. Joseph, every word, but she won't give in to it."

"It's a shame," Joe said, " that poor people should be made to work for so little money ! but never mind, Mrs. Miller, I hope some day Kitty will meet with a—a—somebody who will keep her without doing any work."

"That," said the widow, " is my hope, Mr. Joseph; but I'm afraid it will be a long time before Kitty will meet with a good, sensible, and kind husband; but there's plenty of time——"

"Mother, don't talk such nonsense; I shall never want to leave you."

"If you do not get a chance, Kitty. I used to say the same when I was a girl—but there; come to tea. Draw up to the table, Mr. Joseph."

Mr. Joseph did so, and Kitty laid aside her work, and as Joe watched her cut the bread and butter, he wondered if, when he grew old enough, whether Kitty would have him.

In after years Joe sat at many grand feasts, but there was not one of them he so much enjoyed as that simple tea at Mrs. Miller's.

"Do you take sugar and milk, Mr. Joseph?"

" Yes, miss."

Joe inwardly wondered whether there could be people in the world so foolish as to refuse sugar and milk.

"For shame, Bobby," Mrs. Miller suddenly exclaimed, " keep your greasy fingers off the gentleman's trousers."

Joe looked down, and a thrill passed through him when he beheld Master Bobby rubbing his bread and butter on the knees of his new trousers.

"It doesn't matter," Joe said, patting Bobby's curls, " it will all rub off again."

Although Joe took the matter so easily, he was far from feeling assured it would all rub off, and he cast a rueful glance every now and then at the grease spots which were rapidly increasing in circumference.

"Is your tea sweet enough, Mr. Joseph?"

" Yes, ma'am, thank you."

"Do put down your work, Kitty," Mrs. Miller said, as Kitty began to sew, " every slave has time for meals."

"You forget about to-morrow night, mother."

"To-morrow night! What of to-morrow night?"

" Nothing much, only if I don't get these half-dozen shirts done we shan't be able to keep our promise with Mr. Sivins."

Joe almost dropped the cup he was raising to his lips when he heard the familiar name.

"Sivins!" he repeated, " not the Mr. Sivins I know, I hope."

"This one," Mrs. Miller replied, "keeps a loan office near the St. George's-road."

"That's him," said Joe, "he's a bad lot, I know him well. But you haven't—have you, ma'am—you haven't had a loan?"

"I have," said Mrs. Miller, sadly, "and unfortunately we are in arrears in consequence of Kitty having been laid up."

"Have you got much behind, mum?"

"Yes, several weeks."

"And he hasn't summoned you?"

"No, Mr. Joseph; but he came here a few days ago and told us he should be obliged to put the brokers in."

"No, mum," Joe said, "he can't do that, he must go to the County Court—"

"He would have to do so under ordinary circumstances," Mrs. Miller said, " but we owe him four weeks' rent, so you see he could seize our goods for that."

"Whew!" whistled Joe, "so this is one of the houses he is agent for, is it?"

"I don't know," Mrs. Miller said. "I always thought he was the landlord; at any rate he collects the rents, and many poor creatures he has turned out into the streets; that would be dreadful for us, for we have no place to shelter us beyond this room."

"But he don't turn the people out, does he?"

"No," the widow answered, "he employs a broker from somewhere in Walworth, a sneaking Methodist-looking man, who talks as if butter would not melt in his mouth."

"I've heard of him," Joe said, "Bill Adler knows him too; shuuldn't I just like to set Toby at his respectable heels, that's all, and I will too, mum, if you don't mind."

"If they come," Mrs. Miller said, tears coming into her eyes, "we must let them take our little home."

"They shan't," Joe said, adding an expletive that shocked Kitty. "Don't you pay him anything, ma'am, but leave it all to me. Besides," Joe added, "I'm sure that half-dozen shirts won't pay all you owe."

"No," said Kitty, "but we have a little saved up, and—"

"They shan't have a farthing of it," Joe said. Don't you be afraid, ma'am; I can put a stopper on that in no time. When did he say he would put the respectable Walworth broker in?"

"The day after to-morrow."

" And he will keep his word," said Joe. " He's a bad lot, is old Siv—a bad lot to the back-bone But don't you pay him. He shan't touch your things."

"But you will get into trouble, Mr. Joseph if I consent."

"Not a bit of it, ma'am. Say yes, and leave it all to me. I know old Siv, and he knows me."

Joe at last overcame the widow's scruples and she consented to leave the matter in Joe's hands.

Kitty accompanied Joe to the street door when he bade them good evening. She carried a candle, to show Joe the broken stair.

"We'll have some fun," Joe whispered to the young girl, "when old Siv puts the brokers in, such fun as you have never seen before."

Kitty hoped he would not get into trouble, and held out her hand; and Joe, hurried away by the thoughts of the trick he intended to play Mr. Sivins, actually kissed Kitty, and ran off before she had time to say—

"Well I never!"

CHAPTER XXXIII.

HOW MR. SIVINS PUT THE BROKERS IN, AND HOW JOE PUT THEM OUT—MR. SIVINS AND THE RESPECTABLE BROKER COME TO HIGH WORDS— THE RESULT—JOE'S DETERMINATION TO FIND OUT THE REASON THE GENERAL TOOK HIM FROM "THE WORKUS."

BILL ADLER was putting up the shutters, and Tommy stood at the door chaffing a group of boys, when Joe came dancing into the shop.

"Hallo!" Tommy exclaimed, "he is gone of his chump. Look at him, Bill. That's the result of sticking up to a girl."

"Old Bill shook his head, and sagely remarked :—

"He do seem queer."

Joe's demonstrations of joy ended by his foot slipping upon a piece of orange-peel, and the next moment he lay full length among the coals.

"It's all right," he said, jumping to his feet: "such a lark!"

"Where?" Tommy asked, "where? What falling among the coals with you Sunday going on?"

"No, stupid, the day after to-morrow."

"Get out of the way, Toby," Tommy said. "Joe's gone mad. Mind he don't bite you."

"Look here," Joe said, "come in to supper, and I'll tell you all about it. Shut the door, Bill, and tell those fellows outside if I catch them chalking on our shutters they's get a prop."

Joe's orders were obeyed, then the trio retired to the little parlour, and during supper Joe's explanation of the coming lark caused peal after peal of laughter to come from his listener's lips.

THE LORD MAYOR'S SHOW.

Mr. Sivins was true to his word, for on the day succeeding the evening he should have received the promised payments, a smart-looking individual, dressed in black cloth, and wearing the whitest of linen and the longest of watch-chains, knocked at Mrs. Miller's door.

The widow answered the summons, and when the respectable individual and a rough seedy-looking individual entered the room, mother and daughter turned very pale, and little Bobby desisted from sucking the red spots off the six-penny charger Joe had given him.

"Your name," said the respectable partiy, "is Miller, I believe?"

"Yes, sir."

"You owe Mr. Sivins a certain amount of money, I believe?"

"I do, sir."

"Are you prepared to pay the amount and my expenses?"

"I am not, sir."

"Very well, I must leave my man here. Very sorry, of course, but people must be paid; here,

Banks, take possession, and mind there's nothing removed from these premises."

"Werry well, sir; s'pose I'd better take a 'wentory. One fender—ditto poker—one chimbley——"

"You can do that when I am gone, Banks, and——"

"Oh, sir," Mrs. Miller said, "pray do not leave this man here; he is not sober, and this, sir, is the only room we——"

"Very sorry," said the respectable party "but can't help it; people must be paid, and the law must take its course—good morning."

"No, you don't," said a voice behind the respectable party; "as you have come up here we can't let you go without having a little refreshment."

The party with the long watchguard and smooth tongue surveyed the speaker with a proper amount of scorn, and loftily asked—

"Pray, who are you?"

"Joseph Chudleigh Cholmondeley," said Joe, "and this is my partner, Tommy Nimblejaws.

and this is Toby, and rare teeth he has too, so mind you don't feel 'em. This way, ladies, please; watch 'em, Toby, hold on, good dog, if they try to get past you."

Joe was certainly master of the situation, for as Mrs. Miller, Kitty, and little Bob retired, Toby, in obedience to a gesture from his master, stood before the open door and showed his fangs in such an unmistakable manner that he of the respectable exterior kept out of the way.

"What is the meaning of this?" he asked; "how dare you——"

"Hold your tongue," said Joe: "you ought to be ashamed of yourself to speak so cross when two gentlemen asks you to lunch with them."

The broker and his man were mystified.

"I have business to attend to," the former said: "so I can't stay; my man, I dare say——"

"Well, you can go, then."

The party in black cloth made a step towards the door, but he went back two when Toby stood up and gave a low angry growl.

"Call your dog away. What do you mean? I'll give you in charge if——"

"Call the dog away yourself," was Joe's savage answer; "you want to know what I mean. I will tell you; it's just this—the ladies have been kind enough to lend us this room for a short time; for Tommy and me are wegetarians, and we are going to have a roast cabbage for lunch, and for fear anybody should come in, Toby minds the door——"

"I'll fetch a policeman——"

"You'll have to get past Toby first. Then again, if you did, the peeler couldn't touch us. We are going to have our lunch, if you don't like it, why you've no business here."

During this interchange of civilities, Tommy had suspended a large cabbage in front of the fire, and as the leaves became scorched there arose such a stifling effluvium that the respectable one was compelled to plug his nostrlis, and his seedy assistant retreated to the farthest corner from the fire, muttering—

"I'm blest if I can stand this. Sooner turn up the job than stay here."

"Stir up the fire, Tommy, let's have it well done."

Volumes of smoke followed these words, and soon the room became so unbearable that Joe and his assistant were compelled to thrust their heads up the chimney to escape the fumes.

CHAPTER XXXIV.

TOMMY NIMBLEJAWS FINDS A MOTHER-IN-LAW— JOE PAYS A VISIT TO THE GENERAL—SEES HIS MOTHER, AND TELLS HER A LITTLE OF HIS MIND.

"I DON'T believe a word of it," roared the angry Mr. S., "it's a pack of lies; so beware, for I shall seek Sir Charles—will go straight from this door to——"

"Pray do, you will find one of her ladyship's cards in the hall, and there's a cab rank at the end of the street. Good day, Mr. Sivins, I wish you a pleasant journey."

The General rang the bell, and Mr. Sivins, considerably crestfallen, was shown out.

He did not take a cab and proceed to Sir Charles's; there was too much truth in the old officer's manner to admit of the least doubt about his statement.

Certainly, if ever a man encountered a galling and most unexpected turn in a career of rascality, that man was Mr. James Sivins, general agent and money lender.

.   .   .   .   .

"Here you are," shouted Tommy one morning, "there's potatoes, fine young greens, and Brussels' sprouts, and lots of kolliflowers, a penny each."

A stout lady, who was passing at the time, turned suddenly, and gazing at Tommy, exclaimed—

"My dear Tommy!"

And before that youth had any idea of the good lady's presence, he was enfolded in her arms, and a large market basket which she carried nearly drove the breath out of his body.

"Hallo!" Tommy exclaimed. "Here's a go. Don't choke a chap, missus."

"Missus!" said the lady indignantly, releasing Tom, and boxing his ears. "Don't you know who I am?"

"That clout," answered Tommy, rubbing the tingling part, "and that voice, tells me you are my sainted mother-in-law."

"Yes, Tommy, I am. Where have you been all this time?"

"Just looking round the world a bit, mother."

"Bad boy," she said, "to leave school and not let us know where you went to, for we've been inquiring everywhere for you, and Mr. Brown has spent I don't know how much money in advertising for you."

"You took a deal of trouble," said Tommy, "to find me out just to give me a whopping."

"No, Tommy, my dear, said the lady, "we don't want to whop you; oh no, Tommy, you will never be whopped again—no, not if you were to come home now."

"No! What not with the broom handle?"

"Not with nothing, Tommy."

"Whew!" whistled the hopeful, "what's up?"

"You remember your uncle, Tommy, don't you, that dear, kind, good, old uncle that emigrated?"

"Yes, my father's brother you mean."

"Yes, Tommy, well, he's come back, and he's ever so rich, and he wants to see you."

Tommy's face brightened up.

"Where does he live?"

"I can't tell you that, because he didn't tell us; but he comes every week to inquire if we have found you, and when he finds we haven't he says dreadful things, and swears we put you out of the house because we didn't want the expense of keeping you; we didn't do that, did we, Tommy?"

"Can't say, I'm sure, mum; but considering the amount of broomstick I used to have it did seem very much like it."

"You ungrateful little wretch," said the lady; "didn't we send you to a tip-top boarding-school?"

"Yes, ma'am, you did, and Mr. Dothem was the master. But never mind that; when shall I see my uncle? I'm tired of humping coals up and down stairs."

"He'll come this afternoon, Tommy, so you had better go back with me."

Old Bill and Joe were glad to hear of Tommy's change of fortune, although they were a little sorry at the prospect of losing one who had been their companion in their wanderings.

Tommy was soon dressed in his best, and walking beside the stout lady in the plaid shawl.

"You won't say anything to your uncle, Tommy dear," said the lady, as they went home, "about the way that brute of a husband of mine used to go on with you."

Tommy screwed up his face as though trying to swallow a pill that was much too large for him, as he thought of the share the good lady took in the matter; but he remembered her kindness before she married Mr. Brown, and came to the conclusion that he would not mention the matter to his uncle.

"I don't suppose," he said, "it will make much difference to either of you whatever I tell him, will it?"

"Yes, it will, my dear Tommy—my handsome Tommy——"

"Don't lay it on too thick, ma'am."

"Too thick, you little wretch! You shouldn't y that, my boy, when you knew how I always ought you so handsome."

"Yes, ma'am."

"Then you shouldn't say such wulgar things, as 'don't lay it on too thick,' when you know I was only speaking the truth."

"No, ma'am——Hallo, fat Jack in the bone-house!"

"What cheer, coaley?" responded the slim

youth hailed by Tommy; "you're all the way there in your best togs."

"Yes," Tommy said, "and half way back again."

"You must not speak to sich low boys as that, Tommy."

"No, ma'am, not now."

"That's a good boy; now, as I was saying before, you won't, will you?"

"No; what is it?"

"Why, you won't say anything to your uncle about that brute of a husband of mine?"

"No, ma'am, not if you will tell me why it makes any difference to you or Mr. Brown."

"Well, I will tell you, Tommy, my good Tommy; it is just this, your uncle has promised if we find you, and you don't have anything to say against me or Mr. Brown, since your dearly-beloved and much lamented father died, he intends to make us a present of a little money for the trou—the care we have taken of you."

"I won't say anything for your sake," Tommy answered, "for you were once kind to me, but as for that brute, your husband, I'll wait until I get a man, then—then—"

"What, Tommy? What?"

"Why, I'll prop him, that's all!"

Tommy saw his uncle before the day was over, and the old fellow took the lad home, saying in his blunt way—

"Look here, I mean to make a man of you, and if you don't behave yourself, I'll break every bone in your skin."

Tommy did take care of himself; he had seen enough of this world's ups and downs not to value the opportunity thus given to him.

When the busy time was over, Joe, arrayed in his best suit, gave old Bill special directions to keep his eye upon the light-fingered youths who abounded in the vicinity of the "warehouse," and sallied forth to obtain an interview with the old General.

He had kept the address in his mind from the time he had heard it from the superlative cream of flunkeys, the aristocratic John Jeames.

When he reached Cavendish-square, and stood upon the door-step, he surveyed the bell handles, and soliloquised thus:—

"One says 'servants,' t'other 'visitors.' Now, I want a servant to open the door, yet I am a visitor. Now, which ought I to ring? That's a point as old Bill says, requires argification, and as I havn't time to argify it, I will pull both to prevent mistakes."

He pulled both, and with no gentle force; and the fat hall-porter, who was dozing in his leather covered chair, ran to the door, thinking it must be the General's old friend, Field-Marshal Popgun.

Great was the fat one's surprise when he beheld Joe; and, pulling down his red waistcoat serenely, he observed—

"Well, sir!"

"Pretty well, thankee," said Joe, "how are you?"

"I did not mean that, sir, confound your impudence. I meant, what did you pull both bells for?"

"Because," said Joe, "there was two bells to pull."

"I wonder you didn't come with a double knock, I'm sure.

"I should," Joe replied, "if I'd noticed the knocker. You can shut the door if you like, and I'll oblige now, it's not too late."

"Imperent rascal; what do you want?"

"Is General Dixon at home?"

"What!"

"Is your master at home?"

"Suppose he is, what of it?"

"I want to see him."

"You!"

"Yes, Johnny."

The hall porter looked very much inclined to shut the door, and Joe divining his intent, placed his right foot on the mat.

"No, you don't," he said; "I've seen your sort before to-day; now leave off grinning, and tell the General I want to see him."

Joe had got as far as the mat by this time, and the servant seeing he meant to keep his position, said—

"How can I send up your name when I don't know it?"

"Just say, Mr. Joseph Chudleigh Cholmondeley, Esq., dealer in coals, coke, wood, and greens."

Now the General had given orders that he was to be disturbed on no account, but that when he was disengaged he would ring, and so the hall porter, in strict accordance with his orders, walked quietly away, leaving Joe to his own reflections in the cold stone hall.

"Well I'm blowed!" ejaculated our hero. "What a fool I was not to drop him a hot 'un. If this is visiting one's uncle, may I be sugared!"

Truth was, the General had quite forgotten his appointment.

In ransacking his drawers the previous day, in the hope of falling across some old documents that he had stowed away, he discovered a declaration, written on parchment, and which, for the edification of the reader, we will follow word for word.

"Nelson had sailed from Porto Ferrajo with a convoy for Gibraltar, and on reaching that place proceeded to the westward in search of the Admiral, Sir John Jervis. Off the mouth of the Straits he fell in with the Spanish fleet, and before sunset the signal was made to prepare for action, and to keep during the night in close order. Being a favourite of Commodore Nelson's my father was removed with him.

"At daybreak the enemy were in sight. The British force consisted of two ships of one hundred guns, two of ninety-eight, two of ninety, eight of seventy-four, and one sixty-four; fifteen of the line in all, with four frigates; a sloop, and a cutter. The Spaniards had one four-decker of one hundred and thirty-six guns, six three-deckers, of one hundred and twelve, two eighty-fours, eighteen seventy-fours; in all twenty-seven ships of the line, with ten frigates and a brig.

"The Spanish Admiral, Don Josef D. Cordova, had miscalculated the English force, which, although inferior to his own, was not so to the extent he had anticipated. To aid the deception as regarded the numerical strength of our fleet a fog came on and concealed their numbers.

"The British fleet kept compact, and it was well they did so, for on engaging, and before the Spaniards could make any kind of formation, Sir J. Jervis, by carrying a press of sail, passed right through the fleet, then tacked, and thus cut off nine of their ships from the main body. Only one of these ever rejoined, the other eight were put to an ignominious flight.

"Sir John thereupon signalled the fleet to tack in succession, but Nelson, who was stationed in rear of the British line, promptly disobeyed the order on perceiving that the Spaniards were bearing up before the wind, with the evident intention of effecting a junction. He ordered his ships to wear, by which he was brought into action with the 'Santissima Trinidad,' one hundred and thirty-six guns, and six other vessels of an almost equal rate. At this critical juncture Nelson was joined by Troubridge in the 'Culloden,' and between them they sustained for nearly an hour this unequal contest.

"It was a grand sight to witness Nelson's heroism—he was foremost at every point of danger, animating his men, who fought like heroes. Not one of them flinched, and for his sake they cheerfully confronted odds which might well have appalled even stouter hearts than theirs.

"During the engagement, Nelson particularly noticed my father. He was stationed on the poop, in part command of an important gun, which did terrible execution among the enemy.

"'Bravely done, my fine fellow,' he said, as he slapped him on the back, 'only keep the enemy well supplied for a little time longer and they must strike.'

"At this speech hearty cheers rent the air, and although men were dropping right and left under the iron shower, which fell like hail all around, there was not one present who did not take up the cheer, until it swelled into one mighty hurrah, sounding loud above the noisy din of the furious cannonade. The 'Blenheim' came up and gave them a respite. Nelson next brought his vessel into the thick of the fray, and actually sustained the concentrated fire of three first-rates, besides the 'San Nicolas' and a seventy-four at close range.

"It was a wonder that his ship, the 'Captain,' was not blown completely out of the water. Had the Spanish gunners only plied their guns as effectively as did ours, nothing could have saved her from destruction. At this time the 'Blenheim' was ahead, the 'Culloden' crippled and astern, and only the 'Excellent,' commanded by Collingwood, was in a position to render him any assistance.

"The 'Excellent' ranged up with her mainsail hauled up just astern, and passing within ten feet of the 'San Nicolas,' delivered a most tremendous fire, which staggered her, and passed on to the 'Santissima Trinidad.'

"The 'Captain' was now in a most pitiable condition. In fact, she was almost incapable of further service, either in the line or in chase. She had lost her foretopmast, not a sail, shroud, or rope was left, and her wheel was shot away. But, nothing daunted, he took up his station abreast the 'San Nicolas' and 'San Josef,' and close alongside.

"Every person on board the ship now knew what was coming. Nelson ordered Captain Miller to put the helm a-starboard, and then the cheering cry of 'Boarders to the front!' rang out, and was nobly responded to.

"Nelson then led the way, followed by his men, and then ensued a hand-to-hand contest. My father, although quite a stripling, found himself opposed to three tall, brawny-limbed Spaniards. He finished one, and dirked another. But he was completely at the mercy of the remaining one. He saw the fellow's sword raised above his head, saw it gleaming in its descent, when, as if by magic, the hand that wielded it was arrested, and lay still in death.

"Turning to thank his deliverer, he found it was none other than Commodore Nelson himself.

"'I was just in time, you see,' he said to my father. 'You are too brave a youth to lose.'

"He seized his hand passionately, kissed it, and would have poured forth his thanks, had not Nelson interrupted him, saying—

"'Tut, tut, my lad, you will perhaps repay the debt before the day's out. There is more work to be done. This way.'

"And he rushed on to the poop, followed by my father. They found that Captain Berry was already in possession of it, and had hauled down the Spanish ensign. Finding that this part of the ship was in possession, Nelson passed on to the forecastle, where he met three Spanish officers and received their swords.

"The 'San Nicolas' was now a British prize, and all were congratulating themselves upon the cheapness of the victory, when a new danger menaced them. A fire of pistols and musketry opened upon them from the Admiral's stern gallery of the 'San Josef.' But Nelson proved himself equal to the emergency.

"He placed sentries at the different ladders, and ordered Captain Miller to send more men into the prize, then gave directions to board the 'San Josef,' which was obeyed with alacrity. He himself led the way exclaiming—

"'Westminster Abbey or victory.'

"The fight was not a long one, but it lasted long enough to allow my father to perform an act which he was ever afterwards extremely proud of.

"On boarding the Spanish vessel, Nelson, with his usual intrepidity, rushed in the middle of the fray, dealing death around him. My father was following him closely up, when his attention was arrested by a sight which chilled him with terror almost.

"Advancing stealthily behind Nelson was a Spaniard. There was a sardonic grin on his countenance, and evidently he knew who it was that he was intent upon striking down. Nearer and nearer he came, and still my father's arm was as if paralysed. He carried a pistol, certainly, but he dared hardly use it.

"The reason of this was as follows. The advancing Spaniard was in such a position that he was assailable only at a risk of striking Nelson. Apparently no one observed his approach but my father, for no friendly hand was raised to stay his progress. In sheer desperation he raised his arm, and although the obliqueness of the line of fire gave him only a slight hope of hitting his man, and an almost certainty of wounding, if not slaying, Nelson himself, he fired.

"One agonising moment of suspense. 'Thank God he is safe,' he murmured, then sank to the deck in a swoon. When he recovered he found himself in the arms of one of the sailors, who on perceiving his consciousness return, said:

"'That shot o' yourn, sir, was a rare good one. It saved the Commodore's life.'

"'Where is the Commodore, now?'

"' On the quarter-deck, sir.'

"Finding himself strong enough, my father went aft, and witnessed a sight that tended more to restore him than did aught else.

"The Spanish captain was delivering up his sword to Nelson, and in succession every other Spanish officer also delivered up theirs.

"When this business was disposed of, Nelson turned to go, when he caught sight of my father.

"' My brave youth, come here,' he said, and taking his hand he continued, 'You this day saved my life. How can I recompense you?'

"' Aye, you forget, Commodore, that you first saved mine,' he replied.

"' Nonsense, my act was nothing compared to yours. Is there anything I can do for you to show my gratitude?'

"' Give me something, Commodore, as a souvenir, and I will be content.'

"Taking out his gold watch he placed in my father's hands, saying—

"' Wear this for my sake; it is but a small gift, entirely inadequate for the service rendered.'

"For this victory, which was in reality achieved by Nelson, Sir John received the title of Earl St. Vincent. Nelson, who previous to the action being known in England, had been appointed rear-admiral, had the order of the Bath conferred upon him.

"He never lost sight of my father, who, when old enough, was promoted rapidly, and had he not been altogether disabled by wounds, would have risen to high rank in the service. Nelson, when speaking of the affair, used always to refer to it as 'THE MIDSHIPMAN'S SHOT.'

To this there had been a signature, which was erased, but there was a postscript which informed those whom it concerned that the document would some time be of great value and importance.

"Tut, tut!" grumbled the old General. "Whom can this concern? Humbug! Confounded humbug, or I'm—Oh! what the deuce is that?"

This ejaculation was caused by a noise preceeding from below, followed by a sudden rush up the stairs, and Joe, brushing past the servant, went straight up to the old fellow, and said—

"Look here, General; I've been standing at the door, arguing with that over-fed lump of flesh for the last half-hour."

The General stared at the lad. He had no occasion to ask his business, for he saw in Joe's features a counterpart of his dead son-in-law.

"Egad!" he said mentally, "the boy's like his father; and, had he been kept away from his low surroundings, he would have been a pretty fellow." Then aloud—"So you want to see me—eh?"

"Yes, sir," answered Joe, "but you ain't a-going to let that flunkey off, are you?"

"I'll settle with him by-and-by. You come this way."

The servant opened the dining-room door, and Joe followed the General inside.

"So you want to see me, my man?" the old soldier said. "Take a seat—here, near me."

Joe was not the least bashful; the splendid furniture had no effect upon him; so, instead of sitting on the edge of the chair, he threw himself back, crossed his right leg over the left, and answered—

"Yes, sir, I want to see you, or I should not have come here."

"Quite so, my man—of course. Now what may you require?"

"I want to know," Joe said, "who I am."

"Who you are? Egad, don't you know yourself?"

"No," Joe answered, "that I certainly do not."

"Come, that's good—confoundedly good. And how do you expect me to know, eh?"

"Because you took me from the workhouse."

"Suppose I did, could not a gentleman do a charitable action once in his life without knowing the pedigree of——"

"That's all very well, sir," Joe said, "but I'm not quite green enough to believe that you should pick me out by chance from all the work'us kids, and take me away to that brute of a shoemaker. Now, sir, look here, I don't want anything from you or anybody else, but to know whether I have a mother or a father alive, because I don't want fellows like old Siv to live out of me, for I know very well he must have some coin or he would not have kept me a day in his house."

The General tapped the table with his fingers nervously during the boy's speech; for once the old soldier was at a loss to know what to do.

He saw that too much of the street boy yet clung to his grandson for his mother to claim him, and there was an earnestness in the boy's appeal that demanded an answer.

"Egad!" he said, at last, "it is out of my power to tell you anything at present, but I'll do something for you if you like."

"What's that, sir?"

"Well, I'll give you some money every month, enough to keep you without work, if you will promise me something."

"I shall make no promise, sir, that I feel I am likely to break."

"That's right, my man. I don't think you

will break this when I explain everything to you."

"I shall not, sir, if I pledge my word."

"Very well, listen to this; now you must, in the first place, cut all your acquaintances, and remove from your present abode; that done, you must go to school, and work; study hard to become a gentleman; then when you have done this come to me and I will tell you all you want to know. Will you give me your sacred promise to do all this if I supply you with money?"

Joe reflected for some minutes before he spoke.

"From what you have said, sir," he made answer, "it appears to me that I am too ignorant, too vulgar, to be claimed by some person or persons to whom I am related."

"That's it exactly, my man."

"And this person or persons have had no more affection for me—no more feeling, than to put me in the hands of those wretches in the workhouse——"

"My man——"

"Do not interrupt me, sir, if you please; then to transfer me to a drunken shoemaker, and from him to a cunning rascal who placed me in worse hands than even the workhouse people. Now," continued Joe, fiercely, as he rose to his feet, "because I am old enough to wish to learn something of myself, I am told to shake off my low associates; call them so if you like, but they have been kinder to me than my high relations; I am to set my face against them, and learn to be a gentleman before I know to whom I belong."

"Egad! my man," said the General, "you have the power of speech pretty strongly."

"And you think I will do this for the sake of hearing who my relations are, do you?"

"Egad! I know I should if I were like you."

"Perhaps you would, but I shall not, I do not wish to know now who they are if you are a specimen of them——"

"I have told you, sir," the General angrily said, "that I cannot enter upon this matter until you become more presentable to good society than you are at present."

"Good society and you may be jiggered!"

Here we must stop, for Joe distributed such a shower of the flowers of eloquence he had picked up during his sojourn near St. George's Market, that the old General, and he could do a little in that way, was quite appalled.

Joe came to a dead halt when he saw the same beautifully dressed lady standing near the doorway he had seen at Elthorne Hall.

She was very pale now, and seemed scarcely able to stand, even by the aid of the chair, upon the back of which she leant.

Joe felt a little ashamed at first that the lady should have been a listener to the language he had used, but the feeling passed away when he thought of the miseries he had suffered.

"This is the lad," the General said to his daughter, "you so much wished to see. I suppose you have heard and seen enough of him now."

The lady took no notice of her father's words. Her eyes were fixed in a strange, wondering manner upon Joe's face, then an expression of sorrow swept across her face as she said—

"Foolish boy, you know not the evil you have this day brought upon yourself."

"No," said Joe, "neither do I care. I suppose you have heard me swear. Well, I don't care if you have. I daresay it's very bad to your ears."

"Boy!" said the General, sternly, "do you know to whom you are speaking?"

"Yes," Joe replied, "I know this lady. She is a sort of missionary. One of those who creep about poor people's houses with a scented pocket-handkerchief to their nose; one of those who give starving families a bundle of tracts to feed their children with——"

The General jumped from his chair, and snatched up the Malacca cane that lay on the table.

"Don't put yourself to any trouble on my account." Joe coolly said, "I have said all I have to say, now I will rid you of my presence."

So saying, Joe left the room, and a moment afterwards father and daughter heard him say to the hall-porter—

"Open the door, pot-belly, and be something to you."

"Horrible!" said Lady Elthorne, "horrible!"

"What would Sir Charles say to him, my dear?"

There was a heavy fall, and the General ran to his daughter, and bent over her prone form, muttering—

"Confound it—the devil—she's fainted. What am I to do?"

CHAPTER XXXV.

A SHORT ONE, AND THE LAST.

WHEN Joe returned to the shop, he was welcomed by Tommy, whom he found in a high state of glee.

"It's all right, Joey," the hopeful said. "I've squared it for you. Jerusalem! won't we have some larks when we go to the evening-school together?"

"What's the matter with you, Tommy?"

"Nothing, only we are both going to turn up

the tater line. I told uncle all about you, and
he says you are a brick, and he'll make a man of
you if you will come with me."

Joe's eyes glistened as he asked—

"To school?"

Yes," Tommy answered, "I've settled every-
g. We are to leave the business to old Bill.
engaged a strong-backed chap to hump the
ls up-stairs for him, and I told the chap that
u and I would look down here now and then
see how things were going on, and if he didn't
go on all square we'd prop him, just to keep our
hands in."

"And Bill, what does he say?"

"It's very kind of you,' the old man said,
coming forward, "to give me all the business;
why, it's a a regular fortin', I shall soon have lots
of money."

"Hope you will," said Joe; "we shall often
come and see you, and as soon as I get on my
own hook you shall come and see me."

"Very much obliged, I'm sure, that I am."

"Tommy," Joe said to his friend a few days
after this, "I should not have accepted your
uncle's kind offer but for one thing."

"What was that, my flower?"

"I want to show some people in the world
that I can get on without their assistance."

Joe did get on, as he termed it. Early and
late he studied, and his application soon bore
its fruit, for within six months of his interview
with the General, Joe, through the interest of
Tommy's uncle, became clerk to a rich bullion
merchant in the City.

This was his first and only situation, for a few
years after he went there the old man died, and
as he had no relatives except a daughter Joe was
left sole trustee and manager of the business for
the benefit of the young lady, and so well did he
fulfil his trust that he became master of the business, and as the husband of the bullion merchant's
daughter he soon became a man of note in the
City.

"What a shame!" says the reader, "then he
d not marry Kitty after all?"

No, he did not, for Joe was wise, very wise;
e kept true to Kitty until the bullion merchant
died; then his love cooled, and he allowed a
young carpenter to carry off Miss Kitty as his
wife.

Most sensible, too, was this conduct of Joe's,
for he was a rising man, and Kitty had a large
family of very poor relations, therefore, he prudently retired but when she married the young
carpenter, Joe made them a very handsome and
valuable present.

In due time civic dignities fell to the bullion

merchant's share, and at last he became king of
the City for twelve months, and during his
magisterial capacity he had the pleasure of sending Mr. Sivins to prison for fourteen days, for
that estimable gentleman the older he became
the worse he seemed.

Having achieved the highest honour that could
fall to one man's share, for Joe in time was
knighted by his sovereign, and became Sir Joseph
Cholmondeley, he set about clearing up the mystery of his early days; and profound was his
astonishment when he discovered the lady he had
been so rude to some years before, was his
mother.

She was very proud of her son, and her son's
wife, and all the little ones, and Joe was very
fond of them, too, and they were very proud of
an old dog, who was so old he could scarcely see;
but he was a happy dog—the happiest of all dogs
—for there was no muzzle law in those days, and
Toby, dressed in his silver collar, could bask in
the sunshine without any fear of being collared
by a policeman.

Thomas Nimblejaws became a War-office clerk.
He used to say it was a bore to have to attend
four hours a day for his country's benefit.

But as his country gave him a very handsome
salary, and he had nothing much to do, except
stroke his whiskers and draw caricatures on
Government paper and with Government pen
and ink, he managed to get through it until his
uncle died and left him plenty of "tin."

Old Bill Adler did very well in the greengrocery line, and managed to save enough money
to retire; and had he not died of old age it is
very possible Joe, when he became Lord Mayor,
would have conferred upon him the honour of
wearing that fur porringer so conspicuous at the
civic displays.

Mr. Dothem's specious villainy was cut short
very suddenly. One of his pupils died for want
of proper care, and the amiable Mr. D. was tried
by a jury of his fellow-countrymen and transported.

Of Samuel nothing is known, for he bolted
with all the ready money in the house at the
time of his father's apprehension, and the portly
Mrs. Dothem was compelled to go out charring
for eighteenpence a day and her "wittals."

Sylvia the romantic married a cobbler, and
when he had too much bad beer he used to tan
Sylvia with his strap leather."

Ring down the curtain, please, for this is the
end of the story of Charity Joe, who from a
Street Boy became Lord Mayor.

THE END.